LAY DEATH AT HER DOOR

A MYSTERY

ELIZABETH BUHMANN

RED ADEPT PUBLISHING
Unlocking New Worlds

Lay Death at Her Door
A Red Adept Publishing Book

Red Adept Publishing, LLC
104 Bugenfield Court
Garner, NC 27529
http://RedAdeptPublishing.com/

Copyright © 2013 by Elizabeth Buhmann. All rights reserved.

First Print Edition: May 2013
ISBN-13: 978-1-940215-00-6 (Red Adept Publishing)
ISBN-10: 1940215005

Cover and Formatting: Streetlight Graphics

To Craig

CHAPTER ONE

IN 1986, A MAN WAS murdered. I was beaten and raped. The ensuing trial dominated local headlines until my eyewitness testimony sent a man named Jules Jefferson to prison for life.

I lied.

Lately, I'm reliving the crime. It wakes me in the small hours of the morning. My arm is yanked, and my head bangs against the car door before I'm thrown halfway across the road. Stones bite my knees and elbows, and before I can cry out, my mouth is smacked shut. *Pow!* My ears ring.

I sit up in bed so fast I lose my breath. My heart pounds, and my temples throb. Another memory, more recent, reeks of gun powder from a Ruger—and of blood. These crimes, the murders and the perjury, have rotted out the center of my life. They've also, in a more practical sense, ruined me. In the course of one summer, the fundamental fraud of my life has been exposed.

It is the end of August, and although the days are still hot, the early mornings have the chill of an advancing season. I'm wrapped in a warm shawl, sitting at my desk in the attic of this lovely old house deep in the country, ten miles outside of Lynchburg, Virginia. The window in front of me looks out to the mountains, but sunrise is another hour away, so all I see is my face reflected in the lamplight. The only sound is the faint ticking of the keys of my laptop.

The one way I can see to mitigate disaster is to offer up the whole story, told as only I can tell it. I'm sick of other people spinning it and getting it all wrong. I made terrible mistakes when I was very young, hardly more than a child. How could I have imagined consequences that would reach across decades of my life? We can't think that way when we're young and light hearted. We are reckless, think we are invulnerable. We think we can leave mistakes behind us, start over, move on with impunity. We don't know!

Then I lied about what I'd done, and that was another misjudgment. I lied for so long that the lie became truth to me.

I hate to bare myself; it violates my every instinct. I've spent half my life guarding against a slip of the tongue, and reticence is second nature to me. Are there people who can tell their deepest secrets and remain standing? I suppose there must be. I cannot fathom it.

Two months ago, on a Friday afternoon in June, two men from the sheriff's office came to tell me that Jefferson was going to be released from prison. I had just gotten home from Richmond, where I had an apartment and a fledgling landscape design business. It had been storming all day, and it was still raining so hard I got drenched just running from the car to the house. I came in the back and let the screen door bang shut behind me. Pop had already made dinner. That's what I called him. It had come to sound stupid to me. I'm forty-two years old.

He'd made beef bourguignon, one of his many specialties. He was quite the chef, Pop. Everything was perfect, just so, as usual: new potatoes browning on the stove, a crusty loaf on the cutting board. I paused to dry my face with a dish towel, then tore off a piece of bread and wolfed it. I was feeling good, full of energy and hope. I had a new project, and I had a new man in my life for the first time in a long time.

A salad made of greens from the garden was chilling

in the fridge, dressed with vinegar and olive oil, and I ate some with my fingers, catching the sharp taste of fresh oregano. I found an open bottle of my favorite French Chablis, poured a glass, drank it down, and poured another. I knew Pop would be in the study on the far side of the house, but I didn't go to greet him. The two of us had lived together in this house for twenty-five years, and we had our routines.

I went out and sat in the big wicker chair on the screened-in porch in the front corner of the house. Cold, damp air was blowing in, but I liked to sit out there for a while before dinner and read. I wrapped up in an old blue afghan and sat there thinking—about Tony, of course. He was never far from my thoughts. I'd called him on the way home, and his voice, the way he said my name, echoed in my mind.

Then I heard a car on the gravel driveway, followed by car doors slamming. Footsteps. The doorbell. I couldn't think of anyone I'd want to see. I thought, *Let him get it.* I heard Pop opening the door.

"Mr. Cranbrook?" A man's voice.

I craned my neck, but shrubbery obscured my view.

"Miles Cranbrook. Yes."

"Is your daughter here, sir?"

I leaned forward, but I couldn't make out the rest of the exchange.

From where I was sitting, I could see into the living room and hall, and somehow I was not surprised to see two men in county sheriff uniforms. One was tall, beefy, middle-aged, the other too short, too slight, too young to be a sheriff's deputy. They followed Pop through the living room, gawking at the polished furniture and oriental rugs. I stood up when they reached the porch.

Pop said, "Kate, these two officers say they have some information for you."

The tall cop, who seemed to be the leader, introduced himself and his partner. I paid no attention to their names.

3

But I remember everything he said.

He asked if we had ever heard of the Justice Project. Pop hadn't. I thought I'd heard of it, but I wasn't sure what it was. Pop still held the newspaper he'd been reading, and he tapped it impatiently against his leg.

The cop explained that the Justice Project was a nonprofit founded by a well-known defense attorney. "They exonerate criminals who they think have been wrongfully convicted."

That struck me as faintly comical, very much a cop's point of view: exonerating criminals. I said, "I know the one you mean. They've gotten some innocent people out of jail, haven't they? Using DNA."

I was looking at him like, *So what?* But an alarm rang in the back of my head.

The deputies glanced first at each other, then at Pop, before facing me. Pop had rolled up the newspaper, and he was turning it in his hands.

The tall cop said, "That's right. They specialize in old cases that might be weak, where there's evidence to test. When they find a case where a DNA profile might show the guy is innocent, they file an appeal."

I doubled over slightly, swallowed hard, and found my mouth had gone dry.

Pop's voice was muffled in my ears. "What does this have to do with us?" He thrust himself between me and the two men, his shrunken frame drawn up to full height. For a flash, I had a glimpse of the strong, broad-shouldered man he used to be.

The sheriff's man remained expressionless. "Jules Jefferson." He said other words, but I heard only the name.

I was breathing hard, my mind scrambling. I tried to say something, failed, and they all looked at me. I tried again. "They have evidence to test?"

"Yes, ma'am. We preserved all the evidence."

The rape kit. My clothes and shoes—they had never

4

returned them, not that I ever wanted to see them again. And the bullet they dug out of Elliott's dead body.

I folded my arms over my chest. "But it's been more than twenty years."

"Yes, ma'am."

"It can't be any good, can it?"

"They say it is. I'm not sure I believe it, but they say so." He cast his eyes around the room,

The shorter cop piped up for the first time. "Courts accept it. DNA profiling is pretty incredible these days."

Pop made a dry, spitting noise. "That's ridiculous."

The tall cop rocked a couple of times on his feet. "There's nothing we can do about it. As far as we're concerned, the case was closed when the jury found him guilty and put him away."

I couldn't help myself. "You're calling me a liar. You do realize that, don't you?"

Pop touched my arm. "No, Kate...."

But I shook him off. Both deputies looked down, embarrassed.

I said, "It was my testimony that convicted him." Did that mean I'd lied? Couldn't I have been mistaken? I forced myself to slow down and think it through. Of course I could have been mistaken. No one could say I lied. I could say it must have been someone else. But no. I should offer nothing. Hear what they have to say. Find out what they know, what they think.

I said, "So they tested it. The evidence." The word was foul in my mouth. We were referring to the semen they had found on me.

The tall one wagged his big head apologetically. "Yes, ma'am. It's not a match. They say."

Pop scoffed at that. "So now they're saying Jefferson is innocent? They're overturning his conviction?"

"We don't know that yet. It's in the court of appeals. It's a possibility they'll let him out."

I said, "It was him at the Tavern earlier that night. I know that."

"Yes, ma'am."

During a moment of silence, the sound of rain intensified. I sputtered, "But everyone was so sure."

"So I understand, ma'am." But then he cleared his throat and added, "If they set aside the rape, they'll set aside the case for murder, too."

Pop smacked the newspaper in his left hand and made us all jump. "Testing twenty-year-old evidence. Preposterous. If they've got some scientist to say he's innocent, get another one. He'll say the opposite."

The big man rocked on his feet, his expression neutral. "Yes, sir. It's not up to us. You could call the state attorney general. That's who handles it on our side. You could hire an attorney and fight it yourself. I can't say I'd blame you."

It occurred to me that both men were strangers.

Pop must have had the same thought, because he said, "I don't remember you from back then."

The older one said, "I wasn't part of the investigation, but I remember the case."

The short one, who was much too young to know anything, added cheerfully, "Everybody does."

I felt their undisguised curiosity then. Men look at me, I'm used to that, I like it, but their scrutiny was different. It felt like rubbernecking at the scene of a car crash.

Pop growled, "What exactly do you want from us?"

The tall cop cleared his throat. "Nowadays, we tell crime victims they have a right to be informed when their offender is released. You wouldn't have been told about that back then. I thought you might want to know you can be notified if he gets out. You can request that from the DOC. The Department of Corrections."

He took a card from his breast pocket and held it out to me. When I didn't take it, he dropped it on the table and pointed at it. "You can call that number or go to that website there."

Brazen, I thought. He just wanted to see me up close for himself, the crazy local spinster who was raped and didn't leave home for the next twenty years. He wanted to see how I reacted when I heard the news.

Pop was looking bullish, so I cut him off. "Is anyone who was involved in the investigation still around?"

"No, ma'am."

I nodded.

But then he said, "Lieutenant Gabriel still lives in town. She retired last year. She keeps in touch. Matter of fact, she's the one who thought you might want to know."

Elsa Gabriel. The one cop who never did believe my story back then. I turned my back on all of them, because I couldn't trust my own face.

They told us the AG's victim advocate would call, and having nothing more to offer, they showed themselves out. The car crunched away in a fresh downpour.

When they were gone, I slowly sank back into the wicker chair and pulled the afghan up to my chin. My wineglass was empty. Pop hovered nearby, staring out at the soaking trees that hovered over the side of the house, and I glanced at him, weighing his mood. He had a scar where his left eyebrow should have been. You couldn't help looking at it. He had a way of seeming mild and inattentive with his left eye, but it was a lazy eye, nearly blind. Then you'd realize he was watching sharp with the right. It was unnerving.

"They can't blame you," he assured me. "It was dark. You were confused."

I once thought Pop was handsome. Some might have called him handsome for an old man, dapper, I suppose, in his old herringbone jacket, fit and trim for his age. But to me, he was just old, dried up, and scrawny. I was sick of him. I wanted him to go away and leave me alone to think.

"You never said you absolutely knew it was him. You said you knew it was him at the Tavern." Pop had heard every word of testimony, mine and everyone else's.

7

I considered that. "You know who Gabriel is."

"Lieutenant." He made a grunting noise. "She wasn't a lieutenant back then."

"He said she's retired." A flame of old anger licked back into life. "I wish she were dead."

Another grunting noise.

In the end, Pop absorbed the news with his usual sangfroid and went back to his magazines in the study. I sat and stared, seeing nothing.

Jefferson had threatened Elliott and me at the Tavern, no doubt about that. If I said I was confused later on, misidentified my attacker, it would be believable enough. It was dark, true. God knows I was terrified. But was I confused? No, not at all. Of course not. I knew who murdered Elliott Davis... and why. I lied to protect myself. No use wondering if I could have made a different choice. It's what I did. It's what I live with.

I shivered. I heard Pop working in the kitchen, serving dinner as if it were any other night of our lives. I felt a prickling of little hairs on my neck and arms when I thought about a name I had not so much as breathed in all the long years.

I tried it out, speaking very softly. "Carl. Carl Brewer."

I hadn't used the name, even in my thoughts, for so long that it sounded strange and scary to my ears. That thought almost made me laugh.

From where I sit today, writing in the first light of dawn at my desk in the attic, I can see that I could have weathered Jefferson's exoneration if I'd only stayed home and left well enough alone. Instead, I am now cornered. I never should have hired Max or tried to make a go of it with Tony. I want to reach back in time and warn myself, but of course this is impossible, and anyway, it's hindsight. There is no point in this line of thinking.

What I did, being who I am, was plunge forward, just like Pop, pretending I could go my merry way. And I set in motion all the same forces that were my undoing in the first place. What can I say? For everything I did, I had my reasons.

CHAPTER TWO

T HE HOUSE SITS ON A hilltop surrounded by rolling fields and woodlands. It's a beautiful house, spacious and comfortable, with heavy white woodwork and black marble fireplaces in all the major rooms. The windows still have mostly all the original thick, wavy glass panes, and the floors are dark, wide-planked pine. From the veranda that spans the back of the house, I can see the Blue Ridge Mountains.

Incredibly, after all that has happened, I still sit scribbling away at my desk in the attic, looking out at the hills as I've done for so many years. The late summer sun fades to soft gold on the blue horizon, and though I have often chafed at the isolation and sometimes felt confined and even imprisoned here, I love this house and land more than anything in the world. Am I going to be able to stay here? A hundred times a day, I double over with anxiety about this very question: Can I go on living here?

I didn't grow up in this house; we moved here in 1983, when I was seventeen, and I went to college at nearby Sweet Briar. Everybody knows that. What they don't understand is how we got here. The news stories make it sound as though we appeared mysteriously, strangers out of nowhere. Maybe it seemed like that to the locals. We were far from home, and our background was so unusual for these parts that we were not readily accepted. I didn't even grow up in the States, and I don't have an accent anyone could place. In western Virginia, the lack of a regional accent sticks out. Even well-educated people, if they come from here, sound like Virginians. Since I don't, people want to know where I'm from, and when I say Kenya, they go bug-eyed. I was easily the only person anybody here had ever met who came from Africa. Not all of them were even quite sure Kenya was in Africa, so I usually supplied both facts: I was from Kenya, in Africa. I was born there.

Most natives of western Virginia understand church-going Christians, however, and I soon found that they were reassured when I told them my mother's family were missionaries. I didn't tell them I had never met any of my absconding mother's missionary family. I just said my parents were divorced. Actually, they weren't, but they might as well have been, and although divorce is not such a good fit with the concept of a missionary, it explained the absence of a mother. So we were the missionaries from Africa. Pop certainly was no missionary, and we never went to church, but whatever. We lived quietly and kept to ourselves, until the murder blew our lives to bits three years later.

The weekend after the cops came, I sat in my study searching the Internet. From the Justice Project's website, I learned that a four-year letter-writing campaign by Jefferson's family had finally persuaded Project attorneys to review his case. I clutched the collar of my shirt and bit my knuckles when I read that Jefferson's attorney said, "It was just another case where an innocent man went to prison because a white girl pointed at the first familiar black face. She was the only witness to the crime."

Luckily for Jefferson, the evidence from his trial had still been right where it was supposed to be in storage. So they had a DNA profile for the perpetrator of the 1986 Amherst County rape and murder, and that perpetrator was not Jules Jefferson. In my gut, I felt the whole thing opening up again. The crime was unsolved. What's more, it could be solved if they had DNA to compare with the profile. But that was only if they had a suspect, which they didn't.

Saturday evening, as I sat on the porch before dinner, the phone rang. Pop answered.

I heard him say, "May I ask who's calling?"

A pause.

Then, "She has no comment."

A moment later, he came onto the porch. "Reporter wants to know how you feel about putting the wrong man in prison for twenty-two years," but I was already mutely shaking my head in a violent no.

Pop put the phone back up to his ear and said again, "She has no comment." He listened a moment more then hung up without another word.

I watched the phone after that as if it were a live thing, a snake coiled on the table in the entryway.

That night I again scoured the Web, but although I read half a dozen stories, I found little mention of the unnamed eyewitness who had put Jefferson away. Rape victims generally are not identified by the media, but a lot of people where we live knew who I was. My college classmates all knew. It dawned on me that I'd already heard from one of them, my friend Lisa.

"Are you okay? What's going on?" she'd written in an email just the week before.

It spooked me to think I hadn't even known what she meant. She must have seen one of these articles. I read on with fresh eyes, imagining what someone like Lisa, who had known me back then, would think. I couldn't stop myself from reading the comments below the articles. I don't usually look at these. They're anonymous, often angry, and uninformed. They're what people really think, though. I stood up and turned away. Then sat back down and read.

Most of the vitriol was aimed at the cops and prosecutors,

but they didn't altogether overlook me. They took sides. Some said you couldn't blame me, others said I should step up and apologize or even compensate. My silence rankled, as if I should come forward, throw myself to the lions. Words stabbed at me. "Liar." "Racist." Unfair! It crossed my mind that it might be smart to make a statement, but I knew I couldn't do it. I, who had lived a lie for so long that I couldn't remember what it was like to be free of it, couldn't tell another lie: that I'd been honestly mistaken. To be mistaken is forgivable. What I had done was not.

I snapped shut my laptop, another snake coiled on another table, and looked out the window toward the mountains. In my mind, the night sky reached over to the sharper, drier hills of my childhood. Such a beautiful place it was in those days, an Eden of acacia trees and flowering grevillea, fields of maize and sisal. I wanted to return to a time when I was innocent. But I could only see the things that had happened to me, things I had done, that one by one inexorably brought me to this pass.

My father never would have left Africa. He was from Massachusetts, but he dropped out of Dartmouth in his junior year, traveled widely, and wound up in Kenya. In the '50s, he took the kinds of jobs that white men did on plantations for white landowners. He worked as a secretary, foreman, or overseer, that kind of thing. He married my mother hastily and unofficially at home, her father presiding and possibly compelling. Anyway, she really was a missionary's daughter.

I was born in 1965, two years after Kenya's independence, in a time when the old way of life was rapidly disappearing. My friends were the children of colonials. Even then, I lived in two realities: a world of large, quiet rooms with high ceilings, someone sweeping, polishing and serving, cool smooth floors, clean fresh linens, windows giving onto tended prospects. And my home. Small, bare, rudimentary. My mother huddled with a dog-eared black Bible, hissing at me, who did I think I was, when I'd spent the day in a big house and didn't want the dinner she slapped on the table.

"I suppose you think someday you'll be living that way. Think you belong among them?" And, "Pride cometh before a fall."

I was smart in school, and as I grew older, people started saying I was pretty. Always angry and suspicious, my mother called me Jezebel and Delilah. It wasn't my fault that boys, and even men, noticed me. My father drank and called my mother stupid, until when I was fourteen, she left. Maybe she was right about me after all, because unsupervised, I began to run around and flirt and tease and look for trouble.

Then one day my father got a letter from his mother. I have no idea how she even knew where to send it. Her second husband was a used car dealer that my father always called "that fat drunk," and the way I picture it, she married the car dealer for security and money for her son's sake, and her son never spoke to her again. In the letter, she said the fat drunk had died, and she offered everything to her only child, holding out the used-car business as a plea to come home.

That just made my father roar. "Can you see me selling used cars?"

Later I retrieved the plaintive letter, smoothed it out, and read it. "You are the only Cranbrook left," she wrote. "You will have my jewelry for your wife if you should marry." She didn't even know he'd had a wife.

I began to dream of going to the States, but when I asked, my father only bellowed, "Used cars!"

By the nineteen eighties, all but a very few white landowners had sold out, and the kind of work my father did was hard to come by. We'd moved so many times we hardly had anything left. I asked again if we could go to the States.

"She said she'd send you money for the trip if you needed it."

He waved me off, drunk again.

At that time, we first came across the now-infamous Mr. Brewer. That was what I called him then, "*Mister* Brewer."

A laid-off accountant like my father, he took a shine to me the minute he saw me. He wanted me to call him Carl, but I liked to tease him about being much too old for me. When we left the highlands for the capital, he tagged along, and I half-thought it was because of me.

Pop knew about a warehouse in Nairobi, so the two men pooled their money and cooked up some sort of scheme for an export business. My father did a brief stint as the agent for a plantation owner who was pulling out of the country, and he somehow got his hands on an inventory. I had the impression it was all very underhanded, risky, and maybe even illegal, I still don't know. Nobody told me anything, and I didn't care. I was barely sixteen and rebellious. My father paid no attention to me. What kind of father doesn't notice when his teenaged daughter starts to play around with a hard man more than twice her age?

Play with him is what I did. He was swashbuckling and handsome, lean and muscled, always shifting around those endless boxes. I slipped through the stacks in the flimsy little sun-faded dress I wore all the time. Bars of light filtered through the blinds, and dust motes floated in the hot, stuffy air. I laughed when I startled him, then hung around close, got in the way until he reached for me, and then I ran away like the silly girl I was. I didn't think it was all that serious, but I could not have been more wrong.

One day, I made up my mind I'd let him kiss me. I held up soft lips, and he fell on me with an open mouth. I twisted away and wiped my face with the back of my hand. But it was still a game to me.

I said, "Wait. Like this," and lightly touched the tip of my tongue to his.

He lunged at me, knocked his teeth against mine and hurt my lip. I shrieked and slapped at him, and we stood off from each other, breathing hard. No other man has ever looked at me the way he did at that moment. I almost ran away. Instead I crept back up to him, laid the full front of my body up against his, and made us both gasp. Then the situation got out of hand pretty quickly. Next thing I knew, he'd pinned me against the wall. He didn't exactly force me, but when I tried to squirm away, he was just so strong and heavy. A full-grown man. In minutes, he had hiked me up by the backs of my thighs and just about tore me in two before he finished with a ragged groan. I pulled away and doubled over, staring with disbelief at the blood on my shaking fingers. Then he kept saying he was sorry, kept kissing me on my face and neck and shoulders, running rough hands through my hair until finally I wrenched myself free and rasped, "Leave me alone!"

Later that night, he was stiff and formal with my father and wouldn't meet my eyes. I'd been afraid he was going to give me away, but when he acted clumsy and nervous, I realized he thought *I* would tell on *him*. I acted as though nothing had happened, and he looked so relieved it was comical. It was going to be a secret we would both get away with. I stayed away from the back of the warehouse for a while. But before long I started hanging out around him again, at first only when my father was nearby. Then I started going when my father went elsewhere.

He wanted me to run away with him to South Africa, where he was from, and I said I'd go, but only because he pressed me. Oh, I was in love. I couldn't think about anything but the way he smelled and the way he dropped everything when he saw me, as if it made him weak to look at me. I was in love with the way he made me feel when he fumbled under that dress and into my underwear. But for me, it was an adventure and a way to pass the time. I was in love with the idea of getting out of Nairobi and the hole I was in. He loved me like a man who's been around and knows exactly what he wants. I was blind to the depth of it.

He'd grip my shoulders and say, "I love you, Kate," with fire burning in his eyes, and I'd laugh and call him Mister Brewer, because I didn't know how to match that kind of intensity.

I was in way over my head. I told him I wouldn't go anywhere without money, and he said then he'd just have to get some. He was a little scary.

But then my father got another letter. I found it wadded up in a pile of trash. A lawyer had written to inform him that his mother died, leaving everything to him and that he would get the proceeds from the sale of the car dealership, along with her house, its contents, and some cash. I was jubilant. There was no mention of my grandmother's jewels, and that worried me. What if someone stole them? I was feverish to go, but unbelievably, my father still refused.

I said, "It's no good for me here, no good for either of us. What do we have?"

Nothing. Nothing was what we had, and not a free dime, thanks to that hare-brained business venture. Every time they made a little money, they would turn around and pay off a man named Umbuyu. We lived in squalor, got by on the cheapest street foods, and slept with guns. I didn't think South Africa would be much better than Nairobi. I made up my mind I had to get to the States.

The door was wide open, but my father still thought he was going to make a killing with that scheme of his. So I told him, "Carl Brewer's going to run out on you. He's going to take the money and run before you know it." He would have, too. Where else would he get the money? There was no love lost—and no scruple—between those two men.

My father spit and growled. "How do you know?"

"He told me he wants to go back to South Africa." I didn't say he wanted me to go with him.

I don't know what would have become of me if it hadn't been for an unsuccessful coup in 1982. What was reported worldwide as a three-day minor skirmish was, for those of us on the ground, a frightening interlude of utter lawlessness. We heard shouts and gunfire, then glass breaking, and I saw my chance.

The official story, the one I have always gone along with, has Pop gunning his way out of Africa and me clinging to his coattails for dear life, but at the crucial moment, he was strangely ineffective. I took the Ruger from his hands. It was almost too heavy for my wrists when I held the barrel level, but I knew how to use it, knew to hang on when I fired it because it bucked. To all appearances, I was a girl fleeing under the protection of her father, but it was more like the other way around. I was the one who took what there was from the till before we ran. When Pop was stunned and blinded by the blood running from his eyebrow, I led him through the streets, found the car, and drove as fast as I dared through a mob that pounded on the windows and shouted at us.

I talked my way past armed guards at a blockade, told them looters overran the warehouse and we barely got out with our lives. "My father's partner's back there," and I told them where to look. I said they might find Carl Brewer's dead body at that warehouse, if it hadn't already burned down.

While we waited to leave the country, Pop rallied and managed to unload the entire inventory on Umbuyu for a fraction of its value, and that was enough. We arrived thirty-six hours later at the airport in Richmond, Virginia, wearing the same filthy clothes we'd escaped in. I chose our destination. Pop didn't care where we went. We agreed it would be someplace temperate, fertile, and well out of the way. There'd be no trail from Africa; I didn't think we could be found, or that anyone would look.

But it wasn't over, couldn't be. We still had nothing. I told Pop we had to go to Massachusetts. I'd kept the letter from the lawyer. But he'd lost his nerve entirely, acted as though the enormity of what had happened in Nairobi had used him up. He sat on the edge of the bed, drinking cheap wine straight out of the bottle in the cheap room we'd taken while I washed my dress in the bathroom sink. He thought we could get by the way we were, that it was safer.

I was having none of it. "Fine. Stay here. I'll do it all."

He threw the last wad of bills in my direction, and although I was only seventeen, I went north.

I flew into Bradley field with nothing but that same flowered cotton dress and a sweater. It was freezing cold. I took the bus to Northampton and walked all the way from the bus station to the Northampton Inn, where I checked in and called the office of the lawyer who was my grandmother's executor.

His secretary asked, "What is this concerning?"

I told her I needed to see him about my grandmother's estate. When she pushed for more, I told her quite tartly that I would talk to him about that.

Silence. Irritation and suspicion crackled through the line.

Then she said, "One moment," and put me on hold. A few minutes later, she came back and said he would see me late that afternoon.

Pop had given me just about the last of the money we had fled with, and I used it to buy a businesslike suit and a briefcase for the slim file of papers I had brought with me.

The attorney was a slob in an expensive suit. It didn't look to me as though he did much work. His office on the first floor of an old house was nearly bare, and the secretary, who was pointedly cool to me, seemed absolutely idle. The man's name was Wendell or Windmill or Waddle,

19

something like that. His shoulders were narrow and thin, his arms overlong, and his belly wide and ponderous to match his drooping lips. The suit was cut to fit him. While he studied my passport and birth certificate, I tried to picture him in a jacket bought off the rack.

He couldn't seem to get past my age. I had taken the precaution of mailing him a letter, signed by Pop, advising him that I would be coming there to inspect the contents of the house and decide what should be sold and what we would send to Virginia. But when he saw me and realized I was a minor, on top of being a girl, he balked.

Several minutes went by without a word, and I began to worry. I almost felt like giving up and running away, but I shook off my doubts. I had faced much worse than that silly man to get there. "Is there a problem?"

He looked up at me. "There is nothing in the will about a daughter."

My reading of this was that he had no idea what to do. "There is something about a daughter in the letter you received from Miles Cranbrook last week. I want to see the house, to confirm that we will sell it and not keep it. You can see for yourself—" I pulled out a copy and passed it to him "—that he is leaving this up to me. If I want to keep it, we will. If I don't want it, we'll sell it. I need to see it. I also need to go through the contents of the house to decide what, if anything, we'll keep. He's leaving that up to me, too."

He studied the letter.

I twisted in my chair with impatience. "You did receive that letter, didn't you?"

He harrumphed and equivocated without conceding anything.

I pulled out a copy of the letter my father had received while we were still in Kenya. "You did send this one?"

Again, he mumbled as though it pained him to cooperate.

I tried not to sound too annoyed. "In his letter to you,

responding to the letter you sent to him, he informs you that his daughter, Katherine Cranbrook, will dispose of the house and contents. What I have given you is a United States passport with my picture on it and my birth certificate. That should be adequate identification."

He peered for the umpteenth time at the passport and then at my face. Then he studied the birth certificate. From Kenya. Kisumu District. I could read his mind when he looked up to take in yet again my fair skin, blue eyes, and golden hair. He planted a heavy index finger on the blank where the date of my parents' marriage should have been.

I cursed inwardly. Why hadn't I filled in a date for the marriage? I could so easily have done that. I decided to challenge him outright. "Do you doubt that I am what I say I am?"

"What you are," he said, showing a little spine at last, "is a very young lady in possession of two letters and an incomplete birth certificate from a country in Africa."

"And a passport!" My heart pounded in my ears.

"Perhaps it would be better if your father—"

"My father has neither time nor inclination to deal with this matter. He has made his wishes clear." I couldn't resist adding, "What is your problem?" But even as I spoke, I had an idea. "As executor, do you not collect a share of the estate?"

His expression changed at the thought of money coming his way. His office was pretty crappy after all.

I said, "Ten percent? Of the money and the proceeds from the sale of the house?"

Still he hesitated, but I saw him calculate as well. I said through clenched teeth, "Do you have the keys to the house? I know where it is."

He sighed and slapped down the papers I had given him.

I stood up. I wasn't going to waste any more time on him. Crisply, I demanded back my passport and birth certificate. I told him he could keep the copies of the two letters, in case his own file was incomplete. And so in the end, he capitulated. Laziness and the prospect of ready cash won out over his suspicions, whatever they were, and his unwillingness to deal with a seventeen-year-old girl. I left with the keys, went back to the Northampton Inn, and celebrated with an excellent dinner, which I ate alone in the dining room. I even succeeded in ordering a glass of wine.

The house, which was on the outskirts of South Hadley, turned out to be a hideous three-story box-like structure on a small, overgrown lot. Inside, it was musty, dead feeling with the windows all blinded. I tried the lights: no power. Thick oriental rugs absorbed my footsteps as I passed through rooms of handsome and substantial old furniture half-obscured by neglected clutter and a thick coat of dust. I wondered how the house had been shut up when my father's mother died. Had she died at home? Did she lock up and go to the doctor and never come back? Was a friend sitting with her at the end? Waddle would know, but I was not about to ask him. Again, I worried that the jewelry had been stolen.

As if drawn by a lodestone, I climbed the stairs to the second floor and found a very large room, about twenty-five feet square, unmistakably the master bedroom, with a fireplace and windows on two walls. The bed was spookily half made. A brooch sat on the white Italian marble top of a massive, bow-fronted dresser as if someone had just laid it there. I crossed the room, hesitated, then on impulse turned and trotted quickly down the stairs and through the hall to the front door, which I locked. I went back up to the dresser, took a deep breath, and picked up the brooch, a tiny bouquet of yellow, pink, and blue stones in a silver setting. Crystal, I thought. Not precious, but handsome.

Feeling like a pirate looting without a conscience, I began to open drawers. At first I was hesitant, almost flinching as I plucked through sad old-lady underpants and slips, nightgowns and bras. When I started finding boxes, I forgot all my misgivings. They were jewelry boxes, all kinds: stiff cardboard boxes with gold printing, velvet jeweler's boxes, and various ornamental ones of silver, wood and bone china. I stacked them all on top of the dresser. I rubbed my hands together, took a deep breath, and plundered them.

Ah, what a treasure find! One or two were empty, but most contained multiple pieces, some carefully tucked into little slots or stands, some jumbled carelessly together. Some of the larger pins and rings were costume jewelry, but much of what I found looked real. I found a huge amethyst ring with an elaborate setting, a diamond pavé cuff, beads of rose quartz and jet. Some of it was classic: a large diamond solitaire pendant, a sapphire ring and matching drop earrings, an emerald and diamond tennis bracelet, two gold watches, numerous strings of pearls of all sizes and colors.

Last of all, I lifted a soft chamois bag, savoring its weight. Carefully, so as not to spill anything precious, I spread the drawstring and poured the contents of the bag into my hand—and gasped out loud. Heavyset, graduated stones clicked and slid as I handled what appeared to be a diamond necklace. I slipped off my jacket, unbuttoned my blouse and laid the cold jewels against my bare neck and shoulders. I gazed in the silver-clouded mirror, motionless, entranced, for I don't know how long, until my arms were gooseflesh, and I began to shiver. It was freezing in that house.

I found scissors, tape, pen, and paper in a desk and used them to mark every piece of furniture I thought I'd keep, along with the carpets on the floors and the paintings on the walls, which included one large portrait of a priggish-looking man who actually somewhat resembled Pop. I had to laugh. I would take it. From the dining room, I would take twelve place settings of old silver and hand-painted bone china, serving dishes, leaded crystal, damask tablecloths, and napkins monogrammed with Cs for Cranbrook. I would take the very chandelier. Why not?

I returned to Richmond in triumph, like Caesar returning to Rome, my every plan a stunning success. I had gotten us out of Nairobi, made sure we got my grandmother's money, and secured all her finest earthly goods. Pop, at that point, was along for the ride. He would learn soon enough to love the luxury.

In the spring of 1983, with my grandmother's money, Pop bought this three-story brick house built in 1845, on sixty-five acres. When we moved in at the end of April, apple trees were blooming. I hung the portrait of my dour ancestor over the sideboard in the dining room of our new home and never looked back. I was living a dream. I was a beautiful, rich American girl in a big old house, ready for a golden future.

It seemed as if I had reached the safest place on earth, but it was there that I was crushed in one terrifying night, when the dream came up against reality. For Pop, after that night, I suppose life was a matter of building and maintaining protective barricades. As for me, I never thought I'd spend the next twenty years in this house, but before I knew it, I had. I often wondered: Whatever happened to the brave young woman I once was?

CHAPTER THREE

SUNDAY AFTERNOON, THE RAIN STOPPED, and the sky began to clear. Pop had been hovering around me every minute since the cops came, and I knew he wanted me to talk to him about the old case breaking open. My thoughts were a terrifying jumble, and there was no way I was going to get into it with him. So I pulled on high boots and slipped outside to walk the hills around our house, as I often did when I wanted to be alone.

The long, wet grass had the fresh green of early summer, and I picked my way around stands of yellow toadflax and red clover. As always, the sheer beauty of the rolling meadowland soothed me, but I couldn't see my way forward. How could I just go about my business with a giant gavel poised above my head? My testimony all those years ago had been proven wrong, but so what? Witnesses are wrong all the time. They're not punished for it, not if they're just mistaken. My mind bounced off that last part. I felt helpless. There was nothing I could do but wait and see what happened next.

I spun toward the house. Pop was standing outside the back door. He scanned the fields, saw me looking at him, and went back inside. That was my other problem: Pop, every time I turned around, watching me, and not just since the cops came.

This was how we lived. I'd been withering in this isolated place for more than twenty years. I'd soon be as old and dried up and sexless as he was. Oh, I loved my fine old home and gardens, loved the breathtaking mountain views, the wildflowers, and the deep, quiet woods. But I was missing something, too. My life had started out with so much excitement and adventure. Then it collapsed into this tiny world, idyllic to be sure, but lonely. Enervating. Dull.

I hadn't given up, though. I taught botany and horticulture part-time at the local community college, and on top of that, I'd been slowly building up a business designing gardens, starting on my own land with a walled garden. Then I had gone back to school and gotten another degree, one in landscape architecture. I was working out of Richmond, partly because there was not enough business out here in the country, but also because in the city no one knew me. I felt safer there, anonymous and freer. I wanted nothing less than a new life—new people, new contacts, new projects—and the toehold in Richmond was where it would begin.

A puffy breeze dried the ground on the high spots, and between clouds, sunlight flickered bright and warm. My pace quickened as I spun bright plans for the future. Then I hit the wall of Jefferson's exoneration. Clouds shut out the sun, mirroring my mood. What if I got dragged back into that whole dark maelstrom once again—investigations, courtrooms, testimony? What about my plans then? Slowly, I resumed walking, hugged myself.

I said out loud, "Tony."

I wondered what he was doing at that moment, and I wished he was there with me, or I with him, wherever he was. The sun came back out and warmed me. I turned my face up, closed my eyes, and pictured the way he smiled when he saw me. His lips would slowly curl up at the corners where I wanted to kiss him. Then he'd dimple up and grin as if he were making fun of me, but in a nice way, indulging me. Nothing ever seemed to knock him off-balance. He had the kind of sunny, laid-back disposition that is so incomprehensible to nervy Type-A personalities like me, that and smooth brown skin and muscles rippling to the surface every time he moved.

I had my schedule set so all my classes met in the first three days of the week. After that, I could head for the city. And Tony. I'd see him this week. Three more days. Frustration brought me back to my senses. I looked at the house, and there he was again. Pop. I glared at him, and far off as I was, I must have been projecting something, because he backed off and went inside.

Wednesday night at dinner, Pop asked me if I planned to go to Richmond as usual the next day. Then he pretended to be indifferent. He cut a small bite of tenderloin and examined it for doneness, nodding as he tasted it, finishing with red wine. The soft, wrinkled wattle of his neck moved as he swallowed.

Just as casually, I responded, "Why not?"

He lifted his glass in the direction of the window and studied the color of his wine.

I put down my fork. "Please explain to me why Jules Jefferson's possible exoneration should keep me from going to Richmond this week."

He tilted his head and squinted. "It's nothing to do with that. I mean, isn't it a bit soon to go running back there? You just got home."

"I have work to do."

He made a little hand movement like flicking off a crumb and concentrated on his dinner. He had these minimalistic motions he would make at me. The awful thing was that I understood them perfectly. "Just asking. Last week you said you were finishing a job. I thought maybe you'd be home for a while."

"I didn't tell you. The cops came, and I completely forgot to mention it. I have to go to Richmond because I have a new client, a very good one."

I figured that would be the end of it, and it did shut him up for a bit. He poured me another glass of wine, plying me with liquor as he often did. It does loosen me up.

27

I told him a woman had called me after reading an article in *Southern Gardens* magazine. "She has an old Virginia plantation home, and she wants me to restore the grounds to what they would have been in the eighteenth century. It's perfect for my book."

"I thought the book was going to be about the gardens here."

"It is about the gardens here, and the one I did at Longwood, but they've already been featured in the article. I need more. I told them I had more." I'd had faint encouragement from a publisher. "Anyway, I told her I would start work this week."

He asked me if I'd stay in town overnight. I said yes, and at first he didn't reply. But again he couldn't let it go. He hated it when I stayed in town, wanted me to come home every night of my life.

"It isn't safe, staying there alone."

I didn't bother answering; we'd had this argument before. For the longest time after the crime Pop wanted me never out of his sight, and in the early days, I didn't fight it. But eventually, I realized he was going to keep me there forever if he could.

"That neighborhood," he added.

That was nonsense. My apartment was in gentrified Church Hill. From the outside he might have seemed protective; in reality he was possessive.

He buttered the same dinner roll three times over, clattering dishes and silverware right and left. "You know what the crime rate is in Richmond."

We never once called it what it was: I was staking out a separate life, however late in the day. I was the center of his universe, but I was restless, and he knew it.

"First you start driving back and forth every chance you get, then you get an apartment you say you'll use as an office, then you start spending the night, now you live there half the time."

"Half the time? What are you talking about? I'm there two days a week."

A noise. A movement of his fingers.

"What?" I asked sharply.

He winced and held up a hand.

"No, what?" I slapped down my napkin, ready to get up from the table.

Pop said in a low voice, "Don't trifle with me, Kate."

We both let that one hang.

I paid the rent for the apartment with my own money from the teaching job. I had to because Pop didn't like me having my own separate place. He didn't like to pay for anything connected with my business, anything that might smack of independence.

The property and money left by my grandmother all went to Pop, and he controlled it with a vengeance. I had the benefits of money. I lived in a house cleaned by a housekeeper he paid, ate the food she bought with his money, drank the wine he bought by the case from a wine merchant he knew, and ate the vegetables and fruit tended by the gardeners he employed. I left my credit card bills on his desk. He paid them.

He started nattering between bites about investments and his CPA-slash-attorney, Melson. My grandmother's fortune had not been vast by any means, but it was a decent stake for an investor such as Pop turned out to be. He'd never worked a job again, and there was always lots of money. I never knew how much.

I interrupted him. "Is there some sort of spreadsheet that shows it all? The money."

"Yes, of course. It needs to be updated, though."

"You always say that. You keep me in the dark. What if something happened to you?"

He shrugged. "It's always changing. Melson keeps it up to date with my will."

Another document I'd never seen. I pointed that out, and he smiled.

"There's nothing much to know. You, as my darling daughter," he paused for a courtly bow.

I said, "Please."

"You will inherit everything when I die."

Pop liked to tell stories about people who squandered money. He didn't care about anybody other than himself and me, but he was intensely interested in people who came into huge amounts of money and ended up penniless a few years later. Professional athletes, lottery winners, and certain entertainers were special favorites.

I hardly listened as he went off on this familiar rant. "Not everybody is a fool with money. Look at you. Look at what good care you've taken of the money you inherited."

He laughed with genuine good humor. "But most people would be better off with a fixed investment income. It's actually the best situation for a lot of people." Then he started off on annuities and trust funds.

I was about to tune him out again until I realized he was explaining how he could leave his money so I couldn't touch the capital until I was old. I stared at him. I couldn't believe my ears. I was fuming.

When he saw my face he laughed again. "So defensive, Kate. I've left it all to you. But I'd like to think it wouldn't just slip between your fingers. And the way most people lose money is by trying to make it into more."

"My landscaping business does not lose money."

A dismissive move of one finger. "I wasn't talking about that." But he was.

"You wouldn't have any money if it weren't for me. You'd be picking tea leaves in Kericho."

He dabbed his dry, lipless mouth with a napkin and poured the last of the wine.

"I admit I don't make a lot of money yet," I said. "That's why the book is so important."

His fingers fluttered. That meant he didn't think the book, if I could even get it published, would make what he considered real money either.

He said, "I give you everything you want. I always do." But what I wanted was to get away from him.

After dinner, Pop poured cognacs, but I left him downstairs and brought mine up to my study, as I usually did.

I remember pacing the length of the attic, from the window facing the east to the window facing the west. Not just that night. It could have been nearly any night of my life in this house. This was my prison, my bolt-hole, my tower. It still is. I make the rounds of the dormers, looking down on the lawn from the ones in front, and out through the crowns of the tall trees in back.

That night, I had another email from Lisa. She was my best friend in college, though we hadn't had much contact since.

She sent a link with the message: *"Isn't he the guy who attacked you and Elliott???"*

I didn't answer—what could I say but yes—but I did check to see what she'd been reading. It was all the same stuff I'd already seen, nothing new except an item on the small matter of a killer still being on the loose somewhere. What if they reopened the investigation? How could they, after all those years? I got a fright when I recalled what the tall cop had said about Elsa Gabriel: She thought I might like to know that Jefferson was going to be exonerated. *Thought I might like to know.* How courteous. How thoughtful.

I Googled myself and found all the usual links: my website, some articles about my landscape designs. There was still nothing on the Internet to connect my name with the case in the news. I was supposed to be off-limits to the press, but local people might remember that I was the unnamed "under-aged female college student" who had testified at the trial, and I thought again about Lisa and a few other classmates and friends from back then. I worried, because anyone can say anything on the Web.

I pictured people speculating, and the idea made me squirm. Was there anyone who'd call me a liar? Why would they do that? And the answer popped right into my head. Back then, every reference to the "sole witness" in the news hinted at misbehavior or sneakiness, of me being where I never should have been: in a car late at night after drinking in a bar with an older man.

By 1986, sniping at the behavior of a rape victim wasn't considered politically correct. The part about Elliott and me, why were together that night, was swept aside like something it would be better not to look at too closely. I denied that there was anything between us, but no one believed me, and of course it wasn't true. I had loved him.

We were together such a brief time, and so long ago, that I struggle to recapture the feeling. I can barely see his face now—the clean jaw line, a muscle in his cheek that would move as he tried to keep a straight face and not react to me when I flirted with him. But his eyes were so lively, his eyebrows like dark wings. He was the smartest person I have ever met.

I haven't thought about him much in a long time and don't like to be reminded. I was so young, only twenty. He thought I was a virgin, and I played along, pretending to be scared and shy. It was fun. I could see myself as a fresh young girl, would have liked to be that way for real. What was sweet about him was the fact that he was not as self-assured as he let on. It gave him confidence to see me as a helplessly infatuated ingénue. Our brief time together had all the thrill of young romance, and I thought we had a love that could last forever. I really did. He was perfect for me. I was sailing, coming around in front of a breeze. And then my past caught up with me, caught up with both of us. And he was dead.

I knew it would be best to lie low since they were threatening to reopen the murder case. But how could I? For the first time in so many years, for the first time since Elliott, I felt myself coming alive again.

I pulled up a map of the new job site. It was not in Richmond, but outside Petersburg, on the Appomattox River, near its confluence with the James. I'd been there just once. I studied the aerial satellite view, then Googled Anita Blore and found a newspaper article or two, in the *Living* section, and a photograph that didn't do her justice. It showed a double chin and made her look a little heavy, but in person she didn't seem overweight. Plump, maybe. Comfortable and curvy. Pretty for her age, which I estimated at close to sixty. She was a widow, too, and that set me thinking. I figured my next problem was that, since I had made it clear that I was going to Richmond the next morning, Pop would try to tag along. Fine. I had an idea about that.

When I went to Charlottesville for grad school, Pop followed me. He rented a house there during the week, and we came home on the weekends. That was only a couple of years after the murder, and I was still afraid. I should have made a break two years later when I finished my degree. I had an offer of a job halfway across the country, in New Mexico, which I figured ought to be far enough away, and I told Pop I was going to take it.

He said, "Fine, we'll move to New Mexico."

Of course, that wasn't what I meant. I told him I was going to go without him, and we had a bitter quarrel, but the fact was, I didn't want to live in New Mexico. I love it here. I told Pop, "Why don't you move to New Mexico, and I'll stay here." He thought I was joking, so I said, "I wish you were dead." But I stayed.

It was a strange sort of marriage we had settled into: I, who had been knocked to my knees by a terrifying blow, and Pop, who guarded me like a dragon. People on the outside thought the past was past, crime solved, threat removed, and maybe they thought this was all that was left of me. Traumatized crime victim unable to move on. That happens. Maybe Pop thought I had just settled down to make my life quietly with him.

Here is a little-known fact about me, one that never has come out and never will, but since I'm telling all: I actually took a job as a waitress once in a dive off Highway 29. This almost makes me laugh now, except that it's so sad. I wore a wig and strange makeup. I must have looked crazy. I would sneak off and refuse to say where I'd been. I was slumming. I wore sexy little short skirts, picked up men, and had sex in cars in the back parking lot in broad daylight. That was the summer after I started teaching at the college. One day, somebody I knew from the dean's office came in the bar when I was working. I left by the back door, threw my apron in the dumpster, and never went back.

Anyway, I learned one thing: the reality of what you can earn in a job like that is harsh. In those days, I would think, *What kind of life is this? How long am I going to cower?* I kept thinking I could go somewhere far away, a big city like Los Angeles or New York, or to Europe or even Africa. But then when I pictured it, I would think, *Where? Would I make enough money? Anyway, why should I have to move away?* I wanted the house, the land, the money, and the life, all of which I was entitled to, damn it. It was my birthright. I was where I wanted to be, except for Pop.

Pop gave me no space. He was suffocating me. I was like a paid companion, but I didn't get vacation days. Pop liked it when we built our own garden, but he didn't like it when I advertised in the Richmond paper and started getting jobs. He didn't want me to have any life apart from him. Oh, I blame Pop, but I was also prisoner of my own decisions. Pop said he worried about me. Oh, he worried all right. When I first started out in landscape, I worked long days in Richmond and sometimes got home in the middle of the night to find Pop waiting, pacing, in an agony about me being out alone. The truth is, he suspected me of using my "business" (the claw-like quotes were his) as a front for some sort of torrid secret risky sex life. His jealousy could be obscene.

I don't deny that there were men, a few. Most I only saw a time or two. Then the article appeared, and calls started coming in. I started making money—not much, but some—and I had the idea that I could rent an apartment that would be an office and a place to stay in the city. A base camp.

"Don't think that'll be necessary," was what he said, in a tone that brooked no further discussion.

By that time, I had met Tony—another reason I wanted an apartment. I taught at Longwood College, a visiting one-semester job while their main botany professor was on sabbatical, and then I designed a garden for the college, gratis. Tony got the contract to install it. When I told Tony that I wanted to rent an apartment and couldn't because of Pop, he didn't understand.

"Why don't you just do it? Would he really mind that much? And anyway, what if he does?"

He made it sound so sensible: Why not just do it? I had a business that was growing, my gardens were in magazines, and I was hoping for a book contract. So in the end, I rented an apartment. I thought, *I'm on my way at last.*

I went home, dumped my purse, coat, and briefcase in the hall, and said I'd found a place. "It's small. And cheap. But it's convenient, and it's safe." I turned my back on him—but not before I saw the pain and fury in his right eye.

By the time the Jefferson case reopened, I'd had the apartment for almost a year, and I was feeling strong. Pop and I had reached an uneasy détente. He sometimes came to Richmond with me, and I pretended not to mind, just as he pretended he wasn't hanging on to me.

I rose early on Thursday and smelled bacon as I came downstairs. Pop had made french toast, which he'd dusted with powdered sugar and served with chilled grapefruit and oranges slices.

As we sat down for breakfast, Pop asked, "Shall I come with you?"

Pop was the type who became more determined when you opposed him, so I said mildly, with a smile, "No, no need."

And of course, he came back with, "Maybe I should."

"Okay. You can come along and see the new project."

He looked so suspicious I had to laugh.

He asked, "It won't be strange, you showing up with dear old Dad in tow?"

"I don't see why she should mind. Anyway, it's what you want, isn't it? I mean, were you going to take no for an answer?"

CHAPTER FOUR

WE ARRIVED MIDMORNING IN THE picturesque old part of Richmond called Church Hill, after the church where Patrick Henry said, "Give me liberty or give me death."

The streets were lined on both sides with cars, but I found a parking space within two doors of my apartment. The herringbone brick sidewalk where we got out was heaved up by the roots of a half-century-old magnolia just coming into bloom, drenching the cool air with intense perfume.

The morning was beautiful, quiet and sunny. The houses on my street stand close together or conjoined, and close to the street, with tiny well-kept front gardens of clipped English box, dogwood, and Chinese holly. My apartment is the second floor of a small, freestanding brick house shaded by an ancient sycamore tree. We climbed a narrow wooden staircase in an alleyway on the side of the house. Pop barely allowed his fingertips to touch the handrail. He hated my place.

Inside, the floors were bare and creaky. I used the front half of the apartment—a single large room with windows on three sides—as an office, with a printer, plotter and drafting table on one side and a conference table and four ladder-backed chairs on the other. The décor was severely functional except for the walls, which were covered in my own hand-drawn, brightly watercolored sketches and designs of gardens, both those I had created and those I imagined.

The working area and the meeting area were divided by the only piece of upholstered furniture, a five-foot-long canvas-covered loveseat. Pop dropped his overnight bag next to it with a sour face. He considered sitting, rejected this idea, and began wandering about the room while I sat at my desk downloading photographs from my camera. I took my time looking through them and picking out the ones I wanted to print. He picked them up one by one as they came out of the printer, until I got up and took them away from him.

"That's where I was last Friday," I said. "Photographing the gardens at Westover and Berkley in the rain."

I packed up the photos along with a number of sketches and books on historic gardens and native plants of Virginia. I would be showing Anita what kind of garden she wanted and how it could fit into the natural setting.

Pop said, "I could be your foreman, you know. Get you into the installation end of things. There's more money in that."

I thought I might as well prepare him. "No, she already has a crew. Remember Tony Reyes?"

"What about him?" The right eye raked back in my direction.

"He's doing the work. He recommended me. That's why she hired me."

A heavy double door separated the front room from my living quarters. The bedroom was barely large enough for a single bed, a bedside table, and a wardrobe with mirrors on the front. I studied myself carefully. I wore slim dark blue jeans, low lace-up boots, and a lightweight linen shirt with a faded, Japanesy print of red peonies on a sky blue background that I hoped would pick up the color of my eyes. I had dressed for Tony. I tucked the shirt into my jeans, then turned and twisted around to check out how I looked from the back. What I saw in the mirror was Pop in the doorway.

I glared at him, and he backed up. I could hear him griping as he snooped in the kitchenette.

I called out, "What?"

"I thought it was the magazine article. Why she hired you."

"It was both. Tony already works for her. His crew does her yard work. He texted me and told me he'd given her my name. She'd seen the magazine, but I don't think she'd really thought about calling me. So it just came together like that."

I could hear him muttering behind me as we headed out. He'd hated Tony from the moment he first saw him. Pop had come along to see the site at Longwood College when I started work on the garden there. Tony introduced himself to both of us and said some nice things about the plan I'd drawn and that he was looking forward to working with me. Ironically, I wouldn't have especially noticed Tony that day if it hadn't been for Pop. The immediate hostility was palpable, not on Tony's side, just Pop's.

Afterward, Pop referred to Tony as a tomcat. When I asked him what he meant, he claimed Tony couldn't take his eyes off me. So I looked again and realized how handsome he was. He was younger than I was, muscular, with smooth dark skin, dark hair, and a touch of honey-gold in his brown eyes. In jeans and a white T-shirt, he could have been a model in a magazine. But a tomcat? I hadn't thought so. Then my eyes caught on his. He gave me a slow smile, and I got a little warm buzz going inside.

I met Tony for the second time the next week when the Longwood project got underway. We walked across the grassy middle of the campus in the early morning heat, talking plants and trees and soil. I unfurled my drawing, and he held one side while I held the other. We considered how exactly we would fit the garden into the open space, while I tuned into the nearness of his body. I let my arm and shoulder brush against his as I leaned in to point out where the pathways were supposed to be. By midday, we had painted in all the lines, and sweat tracked down the sides of our faces.

Tony's crew broke up the turf at the surface, and I followed them around, picking at the edges, straightening the lines. At one point, I tried to tell them they were getting way off, and Tony came up behind me. I felt his hands on my shoulders, gently moving me aside. I was bemused by his touch. He redirected them exactly as I wanted. The damp cotton of his T-shirt hugged the muscles of his back. By the end of the first week, we could see the whole design laid out in the freshly broken ground.

At home, I unwisely repeated things Tony said and described things he did, mainly because he was always on my mind, but also because I wanted Pop to think that Tony wasn't bad, that he was just a friend, and that we all had common interests, but of course, it only made things worse. Pop ragged on him incessantly, suggesting that I wasn't safe around him, calling him my Puerto Rican gardener in a denigrating tone.

I told Pop, "Tony's Cuban, not Puerto Rican, and a damn good gardener."

Pop said, "Defending him now, are you?"

Pop followed me to work half the time. He made excuses, saying he liked it there. He said he liked to sit on the bench and read the paper in the open air. He insisted he particularly liked a restaurant in Farmville for lunch, and there was a coffee shop nearby where he loved the biscuits. When he saw Tony, he was rude, embarrassingly so. It was almost funny: here was this insanely jealous little old man radiating hatred and contempt, and there was Tony, totally oblivious: "Nice to see you, Mr. Cranbrook, sir." It was the same old story, Pop ever on the lookout that I might get a life that would take me away from him.

When we started prepping beds in earnest, I ditched Pop at the biscuit place in the morning and just about crashed my car getting back to Tony. He had a crew digging out roots and rocks, turning up sweet-smelling dirt. It was hard work, and Tony labored right alongside his crew. I got out my own spade and pitched in until I was just as sweaty and begrimed as he was.

He said, "You don't have to do that."

I smiled at him. "I want to."

He winked. "I like a girl who's not afraid to get dirty." I had just about concluded that this was supposed to be suggestive when he added, "You're a real gardener. A lot people have ideas, but they don't know enough about plants. I have to figure out how to tell them their ideas won't work. But you really know what you're doing."

His approval made me more light-hearted than it should have. And I started thinking I might like to get down in the dirt with Tony. As the days passed, I looked for every chance of incidental contact, and it seemed as though he touched me back or brushed up against me more often than he had to. We were always surrounded by the other guys, but we had our own private thing going on right under their noses.

One day he showed me a truckload of garden soil he'd hauled in. "What do you think?"

I looked at the bed of his truck and all that soft new dirt, and all I could think was how much I wanted to roll around in it with him. I started laughing.

He asked, "What?" But then I think he read my mind, because he gave me that slow smile. "What are you thinking, Miss Katie?"

I was laughing so hard, I had to wave my hands and turn away. When I turned back to him, I was thinking it was going to be the moment we'd been building up to. And it would have been. Our eyes met, we both drew breath to speak at the same time, and then we both smiled. I was so dazzled by that tawny color in his eyes that I didn't hear the guys behind me. I just saw Tony's smile change from intimate to casual and friendly.

"Hey, Tone." That was Mike, Tony's sort-of partner, a real blue collar type of guy with straight, dark blond hair. He was always there, always in the way, acting as if he thought I was going to bite him. Tony didn't seem to mind. In fact, he dropped me cold every time Mike came around, which seemed like every time I was making some kind of headway. That was the day it first struck me as a pattern: flirt all day, build me up, then sit around with Mike and the guys and talk about PVC pipes.

All I could say was, "See you tomorrow."

The flirting went on while the irrigation pipes got laid, and the paths got laid, all the plants got planted, and a fountain with a wood nymph got erected in the center of the garden. By the time I sat down for dinner every night, I was frustrated half out of my mind. Pop kept asking me what was the matter, and I kept saying, "Nothing."

Or he would say, "What are you upset about?"

To which I'd lash out, "I am not upset!"

But I couldn't be mad at Tony. First thing at work every day, he waved and smiled and called me Katie, which nobody else had ever done. We laughed and joked, about work mostly. We were warm and easy with each other. He had a Poe T-shirt, red with a black raven on it, so I asked him if he liked Edgar Allen Poe.

He said, "What? Oh yeah, 'Quoth the raven.'" That was apparently all he knew.

But it didn't matter. He couldn't do anything wrong. I fantasized about him all the time. Mostly I imagined what it would be like to taste the sweat and grit on his body or to tangle with him in the dirt. But I also thought a lot about what it would be like to be with him for real. I pictured showing him the walled garden at the house. Pictured both of us taking care of it. I hadn't felt like that since Elliott. I would think, *This can't be.* Then I thought, *Or can it?*

I thought of ways to call his hand. "Hey, Tony, want to

go into town and get a drink after work?" Anything to get him alone and away from those guys. But I didn't want to have to ask for it. I wanted him to want me. I wanted to be courted, or at least I wanted him to make the first move.

Men aren't usually indifferent when I play up to them the way I played up to Tony. I'm beautiful to men; I know I am.

I couldn't figure out what was going on. Doubt crept in. Was I getting old? Had I lost it? I didn't think I had changed that much, but I never did get Tony in the dirt that summer. When the Longwood job was over, I thought I might never see him again. I convinced myself he was afraid I'd turn him down, so the last day, I gave him my card and told him to call me sometime. He gave me that smile, but he didn't call. He dropped out of sight.

After a while, unable to stand it, I called him. I lured him out to my apartment on the pretext that I was going to give him the name of a woman who needed a good yard crew. I really did have a name for him, but I could have told him on the phone. I pretended I'd forgotten. But when he showed up at my apartment, damned if he didn't have Mike with him. I couldn't believe it. Tony gave me a smile that made my knees weak for my trouble. That and a thank you, and there it stood, until he texted me about Anita. I called him.

"Hey, Miss Katie." I could hear the smile. He told me what Anita wanted and said, "I told her I got a girlfriend who's real good at that."

Girlfriend? I should have asked him what the hell he meant by that, but I just kind of woozed out. Right before we hung up, I couldn't stop myself from saying, "You'll be there?" Breathless.

"I'll be there."

And there I was with Pop in tow again. I wondered at the wisdom of it, not that I had much choice, but it was part of a plan. I thought I knew what I was doing. I'd met Anita Blore the week before, and it had been growing on me how perfect she would be for Pop. I thought, *Why not? Why shouldn't he meet a woman near his own age?* She was a soft, sweet woman, ten or fifteen years younger than Pop. Apparently, she had money. I wouldn't want to set him up with a gold digger, so Anita was perfect.

It's a wonder I hadn't tried it before. I'd seen women chase Pop—not often, because we got out so rarely, but it happened. He came off gentlemanly, well to do, reserved. Respectable and unattached. But they were usually older women, lonely, looking for a man, and he was always critical. I would think, *Who does he think he is?* Did he really think that he, an old man, deserved a perfect, beautiful young woman? I knew for a fact that he hadn't had sex in ten years.

Can a man live that way? I barely can, and I'm a woman. Some Greek philosopher said that he was glad to be old because he didn't care about sex anymore. Maybe you don't miss it when you don't have the desire, but I was panicky about losing the desire. What went on in Pop's head? I wasn't going to ask him. I didn't want to know. But I did wish he would go for it. I was feeling magnanimous, because disappointing though it was so far, I was in love, and I was hopeful. I had this fantasy that Pop would get together with Anita Blore, and I would have my own life with Tony. How amazingly normal would that be. How civilized. How wonderful.

We arrived at Anita's house shortly after noon. The plantation, at the edge of a small town called Sedgewick, originally had a thousand acres, but it now sat on six. Even so, it was an impressive holding, considering its nearness to the heart of Virginia plantation country and its waterfront, several hundred feet at least, on the Appomattox River. I turned to see Pop's expression when we pulled off the road and emerged from a line of tall trees onto the open lawn. He allowed the barest flicker, but I caught it.

"You can help," I told him as I parked the car. The drive on the street side of the house circled an enormous black walnut tree that must have been two hundred years old. "You can occupy her. Keep her out of my hair. Charm her. Find out how much money she has. Talk to her about how this could be a bigger job. Make sure she's going to go through with it. Talk to her about our house and gardens. You could help, you know, if you tried. Be an asset for a change."

He gave me sharp look that I pointedly ignored.

The house was made of very old dark red brick. Like many authentic plantation homes along the James and Appomattox Rivers, Anita's had its riverside styled as its front, with a two-story colonnaded gallery and wide steps descending to a terrace by the water. I was leading Pop around the house when Anita Blore emerged from the front door.

I was nervous, both for having brought Pop with me to the job and because of what I was trying to do with him. I tried to see Anita through Pop's eyes. She had a small waist but a slightly rolling gait, as if one leg was too short. She was a little heavy in the hips, and where I could see the shape of her body through the fabric of her pants, there was a panty line and a dimpled bulge on the outside of her thigh. I felt as though Pop was seeing right through me, and although I was pretty sure the scorn on his face was visible only to me, I could see it there, all right. I know my face got red. I was thinking, *What, are you comparing her to me? How dare you?* He should look at himself, a crabbed old man.

She was in great shape for her age. She was elegantly dressed in a white silk blouse and pleated beige slacks. She wore a single strand of large and lustrous pearls. She smiled at me, then she saw Pop. She froze. I held my breath. Her face changed colors, from pink to white and back again. She had been very diffident and sweet the first time I met her. Now she seemed confused and awkward. Pop's face was a calculating mask.

Hating the moment, I opened my arms to both of them and put on a bright face. "Pop, this is Mrs. Blore. Mrs. Blore, this is..." I trailed off.

Pop's eyes lasered right through her, toward me, and what I saw was rage. I thought, *If he screws up this job, I'll kill him.* I felt the silence stretching out.

Then Anita said, "Here's Tony."

I looked behind me and realized what Pop had seen: Tony's truck in the driveway.

Anita was oblivious. She held out her hand to Pop for what seemed a very long time. I gritted my teeth and screamed inwardly at him: *Take her hand, for God's sake, you craven old fool!*

And then you could have knocked me over. With a flourish that should not have worked but did, Pop took Anita's hand, bowed, and said, "Wonderful site for a garden."

Pop turned to contemplate the fine expanse of sparkling river, and she turned with him, her face near his shoulder. And they began to talk. I think I actually broke a sweat.

Pop could make a wonderful impression when he wanted to. I don't know where he learned his manners, but with strangers, he could be quite gallant. His scar, far from disfiguring his face, gave him a rakish air. His hair, though shot with gray, was still thick. In fact, I think she was stunned. And suddenly she was pretty. Her smile was very sweet, her eyes soft. Unbelievable.

We began to walk and chatter then, Anita and I, like happy little birds, Pop trailing us and murmuring benignly. She pointed out traces of an old flight of stone steps and the remnants of a maze of ancient English box, hastening to defer to me with every mention of a plant.

She wanted to know where we lived, and we talked about the James River and the mountains. Moving on to the garden site, we talked about sunlight and the riverbank.

"Full sun all the way up to the house," I pointed out, "in spite of how tall the trees are on both sides."

As she relaxed, she was all silky charm. I was almost giddy. And for his part, Pop questioned her in detail about the plan for the garden, the site, and the possibilities of the project. As we circled back around to the far side of the house, I hung back to allow the two of them to drift ahead. And I set off after Tony. I was almost skipping at that point.

Three men were working at the wood margin with chain and bow saws, rakes, and loppers. Tony had his back to me. I fetched a handheld GPS from my car and started clicking off coordinates, working my way around until I stood next to him, watching with him. I wanted to slide my hand across his shoulder, stroke his arm, and run my fingertips up under the sleeve of his T-shirt. He was so absorbed in what his crew was doing that he didn't know I was there until I spoke, and then when he turned around and smiled at me, I fell right back under his spell. He called me Miss Katie, as friendly as ever, but then he turned back to what he was doing.

So I asked him, "Isn't it a bit early in the season to be pruning dogwoods?"

He told me he had talked to an arborist. "May is early, but anytime in the summer is okay, starting in June."

We talked about what needed to be cut down, headed back, limbed up. We talked about restorative pruning on some huge old rhododendrons, and about the bridal wreath that lined the drive. He let his eyes linger over me enough to keep me in thrall, but he freely interrupted both himself and me to say, "Cut this," or "Don't cut that," never quite disengaging from the job. He asked about the GPS, and I told him I had the property lines from a recent survey. I was mapping in the major features so I could start the scale drawings of the plan. It was all about plants and landscape, exactly the same as when I worked with him at Longwood.

I kicked the dirt and tried not to pout. "Thanks for telling her about me."

"Sure, Kate, you do beautiful work. I would have liked to try my hand at it. I did a garden not far from here, but she wouldn't even go to see it. She's a sweetheart, but she wanted the credentials. I'm just a yard guy."

I looked for signs of resentment, but his face was untroubled. A little rueful maybe. "I'd like to see the garden you did."

"Maybe some time."

"Sometime when I don't have Pop in tow. He gets jealous of you."

Tony glanced at me briefly, seeming perplexed. Then he looked away again. He didn't know much about me. It was crazy that I should be so captivated by him when I hardly knew him, but I was. And I still wasn't getting anywhere with him. So I gave up and went back to the house.

Inside, I found Anita chatting up Pop in a sunroom where they lounged in white wicker chairs with cushions in a blue-and-yellow-toile pattern.

Anita brightened when I came in. "Kate, I was about to say, surely you can both come to my party."

I hadn't told Pop about that. I'd met her only once, and she'd invited me, so I figured she was asking everyone she knew. She said it would be big, on a Friday night in two weeks. She was going all out, apparently.

"I'll have music on the lawn," she added shyly. A suspicious frown passed over Pop's face, and she added quickly, "An ensemble, not a band." His face relaxed. "And lots of food, catered."

I had meant to leave Pop at home, but in view of my new plan for him and Mrs. Blore, I said, "Pop, you really should come." To her, I said ingenuously, "Would it really be all right if I bring him?"

Oh, she insisted on it. There would be so many people he would like to meet. And they would all be so amazed with me and my plans for the old garden. Pop would be so proud of me. He was prim and collected, but he agreed to come. *We*, he said actually. *We* would be there.

"Nice work," I told him in the car when we left a little after five. "See? You've charmed my client."

I had a message on my cell, which had been turned off all afternoon. I dialed and heard, "Kate, Merit," then cut it off to listen to later.

Pop was instantly suspicious. "What was that?"

"Nothing. A vendor. They drive me crazy."

We had dinner at an Italian restaurant within walking distance of the apartment. We sat outside between high stone walls and potted red geraniums. An aria drifted overhead: Mimi's song from *La Boheme*.

A copy of the Richmond *Times-Dispatch* lay on a chair near our table. Pop, who was addicted to newspapers, picked it up, glanced at it, and put it back, facedown.

When I reached for it, he said, "It's nothing."

I looked anyway. Jefferson's exoneration was not the headline, but it was prominent above the fold. I scanned the article. Nothing new. Just one brief mention of the witness testimony in the old trial. The focus was on DNA, the Justice Project, and how many cases had been overturned in recent years. It occurred to me that I was not the only witness being proven wrong. There was nothing in the article that pointed to me. I tossed the paper back, again facedown onto the table.

No one in Richmond would know that I was the victim in the Jefferson case—unless some classmate from back then had moved to town. Not such an unlikely thing, once I thought of it. I bit my lip.

Pop peered at me over his menu. "What are you afraid of?"

"What?" I realized I was hunched over and peering around like a sneak thief. I straightened up and tossed my hair back. "Nothing."

Pop shook out his napkin and snuck a look at me with his beady right eye. "That reporter."

I stiffened. "What reporter?" I resisted the impulse to check behind me.

"The one that called the house."

When? The phone in the hall flashed into mind, and I snatched my hands off the table. "What about him?"

"*Her.* She said she knew you."

My voice came out an octave higher. "I don't know any reporters. Not a single one. And I didn't know any back then." He held up his hands, and I got myself back under control. "She was trying to trick you into putting me on the phone."

"That's what I thought." But his expression was serious.

A sharp-eyed waitress had crept up on us and made me jump. She said, "Oh sorry," with a little nervous giggle. Neither of us smiled at her.

After we ordered, I stretched and shook off the mood with determination. Richmond was my new life, my fresh territory. I sent my doubts and fears packing with a conscious effort to appreciate the summer evening and the soothing murmur of relaxed dinnertable conversation. The soprano moved on to Madame Butterfly: *Un Bel Di.* The muscles in my neck and shoulders slowly let go.

I commented cheerfully on everything and everyone in sight before weaseling my way toward the topic of Anita Blore. "That's quite a house she's got, don't you think? It took me forever to find out anything about it. I was hoping there'd be a description of the original garden somewhere. I never did have any luck with that, but I finally figured out it's listed on the National Register as Mary's Grove. That's the old name for the house and plantation from when it was first built about two hundred years ago. Mary was Mary Carter, related somehow to King Carter. They've been calling it Blore House since Anita's husband's family bought it. Anita was going to call the project Blore House Garden."

I pulled on my sweater. It was getting chilly. "Doesn't that sound awful? Blore House. We'll go back to calling it Mary's Grove. Much better, don't you think? She's the client of my dreams, does everything I tell her to. Don't you think she's nice? She's obviously very taken with you."

"What are you up to, Kate?"

"Nothing! I don't know what you're talking about."

He put on his reading glasses and studied the menu. "You're trying to set me up with her, aren't you?" His voice was deceptively mild.

"What are you talking about? I just said she's a nice client."

"You think I don't see what you're doing?"

"You're the one who's suggesting it, but since you do, why is it such an awful idea? She's nice, and she's rich. She's not old, Pop. She's not even sixty. What are you? Seventy?"

He stared at me mutely.

I pressed my advantage. "You wanted to come. I introduced you to my client, and now you complain. I do think she likes you. I can't help that, can I? Is that my doing? Is that my fault? You think I have an ulterior motive for everything I do. I can't breathe without you clinging and dreaming up suspicions."

His eyes were unreadable behind his glasses. He kept studying the menu, even though he'd already ordered. I snatched it away, shut it, and slapped it down on the table just as the waitress arrived with our bottle of wine. She gave me a funny look. What would be the use of explaining? I got so sick of people thinking he was so pitiful and I was so mean.

I waved her off. "We don't need to taste it. I'm sure it's fine."

Maybe I was cruel to him. If I was, it was because I felt so trapped. He was there with me, wasn't he? I was having dinner with him once again, wasn't I? He wouldn't even think about another woman, would he?

I said, "I'll be there all day tomorrow. We have to go over the plant list in detail. I'm sure she'd be glad if you wanted to come. Of course, I'll have to spend some time with Tony."

He started grousing under his breath about Tony. I asked him what he was mumbling.

"He sells you the plants and profits on the markup."

"He doesn't sell them to me, he sells them to her. He profits off of her, as do I."

"But he collects all the profit from the plant sales, after you pick them out."

"She gives him the money to buy them. He finds them, goes and gets them. It requires a big truck. The wholesale nurseries are all over. It's a lot of driving around. There's not that much in it for him. I'm not in the nursery business, Pop. I make money from my designs, and I hope to make some from my book. I can't be roaming around buying plants and shipping them, let alone preparing beds and laying pathways. And I have no intention of dealing with the workmen he hires, like those tree men. Did you see them?"

Silence.

"Gorillas. I don't want to spend my time buying plants and dealing with gorillas. I want to sit at home like I've always done and write and design gardens. You don't want to be working at this either. You sit at home and do your thing with the money. This way, I'm only away from home two days a week, just the quick run into Richmond and then I'm back in my little study, teaching my classes and cutting my roses."

He mumbled some more.

I said sharply, "What?"

The damned waitress was hovering again.

Pop spoke up. "Just thought I could be useful."

Poor old man! He did that kind of thing on purpose all the time. I told myself, *Why should I care what a waitress thinks?*

That night, I buried myself in catalogs, and we both turned in early. I went to sleep thinking maybe, just maybe, I could get my new life working the way I wanted.

CHAPTER FIVE

THE NEXT MORNING, POP REFUSED to come to Mary's Grove. I stopped with my hand on the doorknob and counted to ten. "What are you talking about? Why not? I thought you enjoyed yourself yesterday."

He was immovable.

I asked him, "What? What are you up to?"

"Nothing. Tired."

"You are not tired."

He made a little cringing movement, and I admit I was shouting at him. It was so exasperating. Difficult. Why did he always have to be so difficult?

In truth, I was of two minds myself. I wanted him to spend more time with Anita, but I wanted another chance to be with Tony, without having to worry about Pop. It wasn't up to me, in any case. Pop's mind was made up. I left him at a coffee shop with a full array of newspapers, magazines, coffee, and pastries.

"Take a nice walk, have a nap." I left him my key and even kissed his cheek, since I was getting rid of him.

In my car, before I set out for Anita's house, I texted Tony: *Pop not with me, can I see your garden?*

The first thing Anita said was, "Oh, didn't your father come?"

She was even better dressed than the previous day. Her blouse was woven with pastels that flattered her fair skin and ash blond hair, and the buttons had been left undone far enough to offer a peek of cleavage. Turquoise and silver called attention to her clear, light blue eyes. She looked wonderful. Too bad it was wasted on me.

I sank into one of the cushiony chairs in her sunroom. "Pop's got his papers and coffee. He can't think about anything but money in the morning. He's like an old lion with the bones of the kill between his paws."

"My husband had investments. He didn't manage them himself, but it fascinated him to no end. I don't understand any of it."

"It bores me to death."

"He's a very distinguished-looking man, your father is. He told me he was retired. What did he do before that?"

"My father had family money, but he never cared about it. He went to Africa as a young man and made his own fortune."

"Africa! How interesting." It never failed.

I said, "You'll have to ask Pop all about it at the party."

"He will come then?"

"He'll come." I would see to that.

"Was his family from Virginia?"

"No, Massachusetts."

He was perfect for her. I could tell she thought so, too. I still thought it would work, given time.

She sighed, then brightened and leaned forward. "A reporter wants to write a story for the *Living* section."

"Really! How did that happen?" That was great news for me.

"The news editor is a friend of mine. He'll be at the party, too. It'll be about the party and the garden. He's going to send somebody out to photograph the site next week. Will it be all cleaned up by then?"

I said I'd ask Tony and excused myself.

I found him nipping at azaleas and asked again if I could see the garden he designed.

"It's just a long border, Kate. I don't do designs like you."

"You said it wasn't far. Can we take a quick look?"

So reluctant. Playing with me? Laughing at me? I was on the brink of telling him to never mind and flouncing off, when he finally responded, "Okay, if you can stand my truck." He opened the passenger door for me and stepped back.

The house was just a few blocks away, unremarkable in front, new with grass and a pair of crepe myrtles. Tony shut off the truck, tried the owner on his cell, and got voice mail. We walked around to the back, which was mostly more grass and trees, except for one deep border that outlined the square lot.

But what a border. Deep blue delphiniums formed a backdrop for searing orange dahlias. In the mid-range, masses of sunny zinnias alternated with blue and white phlox, tiger lilies, and *nicotiana.* I examined every plant up close, then backed up and took in the whole bed one more time from a distance.

All I could say was, "Wow." But he could tell. He was expressionless, but I could tell. We understood each other perfectly. It was amazing.

Then I noticed roses anchoring the whole arrangement. I studied one but didn't recognize it, so I asked him what it was.

"Tara Belle."

"I don't know that one." I asked about another, and he responded with another unfamiliar name. I know roses. Half the time, I can name them when they aren't even in bloom. "Whose are they?"

"Mine."

I looked for a tag and didn't see one. "Is it a new English rose? I don't recognize it."

"No, it's mine. I didn't get a patent on it. I patent all my roses now, but this was one of my first."

"You... what? You bred it?"

"I've done it for years. It's a hobby. It's a crap shoot, but some of them turn out okay."

Okay? They were wonderful, every last one of them. I asked him which ones were his, because I still couldn't believe what I was seeing.

"All of them."

They were all in bloom, large, healthy shrubs, much like old garden roses. The flowers were cabbage-like but modern in color: coral, shocking pink, pure deep gold. Some had excellent myrrh-type fragrance. Unlike a lot of old garden roses, Tony's held up their heads. The stems were not overly long, except those supporting sprays of blooms, but they were strong and thicker than my fingers. I picked my way among the flowers, stepping carefully and bending to inhale sweetness or a spicy smell, trailing soft petals through my hands.

I returned to him and brushed my hair back from my face. "They look like they would make good cut flowers."

"The best."

"But are they tough? What about disease? Black spot, mildew?"

He shook his head. "I don't spray. If they get spots or mildew, I rip 'em out and throw 'em in the trash. No mercy."

"I am blown away. Lucky for me, Anita wouldn't come see this. I'd be out of a job."

"Yeah, well, I'm good with plants, maybe good with color, but I can't do the kind of thing you do. That sketch, the whole mapping thing."

"We'd be great in business together."

Tony had a serious, considering look on his face, but he said, "I don't know."

Why so hard to get? I wanted to grab his collar, kiss his mouth, but I had an awful fear that he would put warm hands on my wrists and smile and push me away. My confidence was at an all-time low. I sighed, and a heaviness settled on my chest. "I gotta go. Pop'll be going crazy."

"Where is he? Where's he staying?"

"At my apartment."

He got a puzzled look on his face. "Where does he sleep?"

"On the couch."

"What couch? That thing in the middle of the room? Are you kidding?"

"I can't have him getting too comfortable. He'll follow me here every time I come. I can't get rid of him. He's on me all the time. Doesn't want to let me out of his sight."

"Maybe he's lonely."

"I have hopes for him and Anita, but it might not be that easy. I'm trying to fix them up, but I have to be careful. It makes him angry."

"What's wrong with fixing him up? She's nice."

"You'd have to know him. He thinks I'm looking for a way to fly away forever."

"Are you?"

"I've told him a million times I'm not. I mean, he doesn't have any reason to believe it. But do I have plans that don't include him in my future? Of course I do." I clasped my hands in front of me. "I'm young, Tony. He's an old man. He's seventy! I've been locked up in a house in the country with him for the last twenty-five years. He won't live forever. He's had a long life. I need a future of my own." I was close to tears. "Tony, why? What is it? Am I too weird, too crazy? You think I'm mean to Pop? Am I too old?"

Tony squinted like he was in pain. "No, Kate, nothing like that. It's not you." He wouldn't meet my eyes. "I just can't."

"You're gay."

He made a little noiseless laugh and shook his head.

"You're seeing someone." *What difference would that make?* I took the plunge. "Drop her. Start seeing me instead."

But he was still shaking his head. "No, Kate. No. It's worse than that. I'm married."

I stared at him. Of all the mundane obstacles, I had

never even thought about that one. "You never mentioned a wife."

"What was I supposed to say about her?"

"You know what I mean. You say 'my wife this' or 'we that' to let me know."

"I'm telling you now. I'm married. I have four kids."

CHAPTER SIX

WHEN POP AND I GOT back from Richmond on Friday afternoon, I sped right past the mailbox on the way to the house.

Pop looked back and said, "The mail."

"I'll get it." I pulled up in front of the house and tossed him the keys without waiting for an argument. Then I headed back down the drive.

The weather had been clear and sunny in Richmond and at Mary's Grove, but at home, mist rolled down from the mountains, and the air smelled like rain. Gravel scraped the soft leather sides of my pale beige shoes. I moved to the grass on the side of the drive and felt my heels sink into the mud. I cursed under my breath. *Yes, Lieutenant Gabriel, I can ruin a new pair of leather shoes walking the length of our coarse gravel driveway.* Why hadn't we ever paved it?

I sifted through the mail and found a letter I'd been expecting along with a few others. I knew it fueled Pop's curiosity when I was secretive about my mail, but I couldn't help it. Back at the house, I held my own letters against my chest and handed Pop his. He took them without a word. I brushed by him, snatching up my overnight bag, purse, and briefcase.

Upstairs, I tumbled my things onto my bed, closed the door, and locked it. I kept a wingback chair with soft down cushions in front of the window that faced the mountains. I liked to sit there to watch the sun set. The beauty of the scene never failed to draw me out into the calming distance.

I'd been dying for a chance to think alone. I replayed in my head everything I'd said to Tony that afternoon and everything he'd said to me.

I'd asked him, "Why didn't you tell me?"

I had my back to him, and my eyes kept going over the mass of blue phlox and the flaming orange of the dahlias as if I could find the answer there, but I wasn't really seeing them.

I turned back to him and waited. I had never seen him so uncomfortable. Gone was the lazy confidence, the casual flirtiness.

He swiveled left and right, avoiding my eyes, and I thought, *How can I just get away? I don't even want to get back in that truck with him.*

Then he said, "I was pretending."

"What?" I shook my head and lifted my hands. I felt my face get hot with anger. Was it some kind of adolescent joke, the way he played with me and led me on?

"I was pretending. I was putting it off. I didn't want to tell you."

I still didn't understand, but the anger washed away, and I began to feel a kindling inside.

Tony cleared his throat. "Maybe I was keeping it alive, even though I know it's hopeless." Our eyes met, and he added, "I can't do it, Kate. I want to, but I can't." He started walking back to his truck.

I had to run a few steps to keep up with him. When we reached the truck, he didn't open the door for me; we each got in from our own side, pulling the doors shut at the same time. Neither of us spoke as he pulled away and began driving slowly back to Mary's Grove.

Then he confided, "I know I led you on. I'm sorry. I led myself on at the same time. That's all I can say." He shook his head and pressed his lips together as though he wasn't sure he should say any more.

61

I waited.

Finally he said, "It was stupid." He gave me a rueful smile. "Oldest trick in the book I fell for. I was just a dumb kid right out of high school. Supposedly, she was being careful, but I guess not." He stole another look at me. "It's been years since we had anything in common. All she's into is kids. I mean, our kids are great. Don't get me wrong. But it's all we ever talk about. Half the time, she talks baby-talk to me." He jabbed a thumb at his chest when he said that.

A picture formed in my mind: a mousy little wife and four small children underfoot. He told me they lived in Virginia Beach, which made me think about how easy it would be for him to travel to wherever we had projects and stay a night or two. He was already doing that. How easy would it be to take the next step?

I whispered, "It doesn't matter." Then in a normal voice, facing front but watching him in the corner of my eye, I repeated, "We'd be great in business together."

He pulled into the drive at Mary's Grove and let the truck idle. "I don't know, Kate." He smiled again, seeming more like himself. "Miss Katie." He studied me, every facet of my face, my hair, my eyes. "I don't know if I could handle it."

He meant that I would be too much of a temptation. I could feel it plainly. He made me feel exactly the way I wanted to feel.

He shut off the truck and got out. I got out, too, more slowly.

He said across the body of the truck, "I'm not free, Kate."

"I know." I began walking toward my own car.

This time, he was the one who ran a few steps to catch up with me. "You have your freedom," he said gloomily. "A great career, beautiful home."

He hadn't seen our house, but he'd seen the pictures in the magazine. I had to wonder how squalid his own home was, with all those kids and a wife, who I didn't like the sound of.

When I got to my car, I took out my keys and turned to say good-bye.

He looked around almost as though he thought somebody might be watching. "Aren't you seeing anybody?" It sounded like, How could I not be?

I struck a tragic pose, folding my arms on the roof of my car and gazing up into the tops of the trees. "Something happened to me." I leaned my back against the car. I told him I was locked into isolation at the point in my life when I might naturally have moved from girlhood to womanhood, and next thing I knew, everyone had paired off, and I was alone.

I took a huge breath, sighed, and looked away again. "Everyone was taken. I was left at home, missed the boat entirely. Life has passed me by. There is no one for me."

I wasn't putting on an act. I really did feel that way, but I was enjoying how the whole thing affected him. It was better than shooting my way out of Africa. I was a tragic heroine. And he was spellbound.

"I live my whole life shut away in the country." I hugged myself.

I could almost have worked up some tears, because it was true. Where was I ever going to meet a likely man? All of Lynchburg was out, all of Amherst County. It was too close to home, and anyway, all the men were either too old or too young and redneck besides.

But it makes me laugh to think about Tony's face that day, feeling so sorry for me and wanting so badly to be the man who made it all better. I wasn't laughing at the time, though, and I wasn't laughing later that afternoon, reliving it upstairs in my room at home. I kept thinking, *What would it be like, if I could have a man like that?* I got up and wandered around the room. I stopped in front of my grandmother's bow-fronted dresser and looked in the cloudy silvered mirror. What did I want? Him. I wanted him.

You could say nothing happened that day. He didn't touch me. He didn't say anything would happen. On the contrary, he told me that nothing could happen. But I didn't believe it; neither of us did. A deep shift had taken place. I felt a surge of power. I was exultant, totally in love. I'd been more than a little bit in love with him before that afternoon, as much as a woman could be in love with a man she hadn't even kissed, which of course could be quite a lot. But before, it all took place entirely in the realm of fantasy. Though no less powerful for that, it was painful and lonely, whereas after what had passed between us that day, I had hope. More than hope, I had confidence. Something was going to happen; I was sure of it. A feeling of great calm washed over me, a physical sensation of well-being.

I heard Pop calling me. That meant he was opening a bottle of champagne, and I should go downstairs. Great. He'd left me alone for what, fifteen minutes?

I was still holding the letter I'd been waiting for: an invitation to speak in Portland, Oregon. It was the follow-up to a phone call, and I had already accepted unofficially. I tore open the envelope and read quickly to make sure. They would buy my ticket. Perfect. I locked the letter in my briefcase. I would tell Pop about it at the last minute, with just the right tone of casual indifference. No way was he coming with me. It would be a chance to get away from him for a while. Then I was struck dumb by a truly brilliant idea. I was supposed to talk about designing rose gardens, and Tony had developed a new line of roses. Oh, those roses! And how he'd used them! I lost myself for a bit remembering the colors and the fragrances of his garden.

So when I accepted the invitation, I would suggest that they ask Tony, too. I went spinning off on a tangent: Tony's and my business, publishing an article about his roses in my gardens.

A guilty feeling spread over me like a tonic. In a funny way, I felt reconciled. For the time being, I would go right on living with Pop, spending two to three, maybe even four nights a week in Richmond, maybe in a bigger apartment. Pop wouldn't have to know where. And then, who knew?

I changed into a soft pullover and a long, slim skirt and trotted downstairs, my mood entirely repaired. I found Pop in the kitchen. "Smells great."

"Don't look."

That meant he was cooking with anchovies. It would be delicious, but I never wanted to know, since I didn't like anchovies by themselves. He handed me a glass of champagne.

"Still so wet," I said, peering out toward the garden. It was too dark outside to see anything from the well-lit kitchen. I drained my glass and turned back for another.

I saw Pop's mild disapproval mixed with relief that my mood had changed, and everything was all right again. I took my second glass and wandered through the house. Pop had set the table in the dining room and left a California merlot breathing on the sideboard. I doubled back to the kitchen, grabbed the bottle of champagne, and went out to the screened-in porch. I sat in my wicker chair with the old blue afghan on my lap and poured a third glass of champagne.

Taking Pop to Anita's party integrated him into my life in Richmond beyond what I had ever contemplated. It transformed her into a spy. I resolved that if she was going to be a conduit of information to Pop, she must not suspect anything about Tony and me. Still, I was convinced that pairing them off was an inspired move. He needed to have his own life. I needed mine. Why could we not grow apart and go our separate ways?

I tackled him over dinner. "Gorgeous old house, Mary's Grove. Don't you think?"

He made an irritated flicking movement with his fingers while savoring the taste of his veal.

"Oh, come on, Pop. It'll be fun. We haven't been to a party in forever. I can't remember the last time we went out anywhere. She's an important client, and she wants to hear all about your adventures in Africa. I told her you turned your back on the Cranbrook estate to make your own fortune in Kenya. She's got a lot of old family money herself. She's willing to be charmed."

"What am I, some kind of flimflam man swindling gullible widows with a pack of lies? Still trying to fob me off on her, Kate?"

"Fine, maybe you would prefer to stay here while I go to the party alone. That would be okay with me. In fact, I'd prefer it. She'll be disappointed, but there's no point in leading her on if you can't even be friends with her."

"I'll come."

Hopeless. It was like a mad chess game in a nightmare where we played the same moves over and over.

Pop cleared his throat. "You had two messages. A woman named Suzanne, from victim services, I think it was, Attorney General's Office. Wants to come by on Monday."

"What for? Did she say?"

"Not really. Said she was 'following up' on the Jefferson case."

I put down my fork. Jefferson's exoneration came screaming back to mind. It took me a while to find my voice. "What does she mean, 'following up'?"

"She didn't say. Seemed to think you might be upset about him getting out."

"Oh. She's looking in on the traumatized rape victim. You know what I hate about this place? I hate who I am in everybody's eyes. It's like I'll never be anybody but the weird girl from Africa who got raped, witnessed a murder, and never went anywhere again. I go shopping at a store where they know me, I run into an old classmate, and I see myself through that person's eyes, and I hate what I see."

"You place entirely too much stock in the way other people see you."

"They think I'm an old maid living out her life with her father, frozen in time."

"How do you think they see me? An old man living out my life with my grown daughter. Do I complain?"

"I hate it here."

Pop's right eye glittered. "We could move away."

I shot him a dirty look. "An old maid. I get tired of that role." I stirred my food, appetite gone. "Or worse, they see me as the lying white girl who sent an innocent man to jail."

Pop said nothing. "They" were the Jeffersons, who still lived in Cooper's Hollow, a large extended family that included Jules Jefferson's mother, his one-time fiancée, and his two children. None of them had ever believed me. The police had believed me, all but one, and she didn't count. The judge and jury had believed me. But no one who knew Jules Jefferson ever had. The world would soon find out that "they" were right all along. I always got a cold, sick feeling when I thought about the Jeffersons.

Pop rose and took our plates. "There was also a message from a woman in Portland. Oregon. Wants you to give a talk about designing gardens with roses. Might be nice to get away for a while. Never been to the west coast. Been a long time since we took a trip anywhere."

Later, up in my room, I stripped and studied myself in the full-length mirror in my dressing room. I searched for changes in my body, signs that I was no longer young. My body was no longer girlish, but my skin still felt soft and smooth. Tony's wife was younger by almost fifteen years. I wanted someone to appreciate the beauty I still had before it faded. The idea that no one ever would again made a panic rise in me like a newborn terror.

I had one more thing going: the voicemail from Merit Chenobo. He was from a life long gone, almost a dream. It gave me a chill. We had been so utterly cut off from Africa for more than twenty-five years. Out of the blue, I had gotten an e-mail forwarded by *Southern Gardens*. Merit was African and my childhood friend. He was older than I was, big and calm and strong, patient when I tagged after him. He knew me before I had ever left the valley for Nairobi, even from before my mother left. He knew me before I ever did anything wrong, before anything bad happened to me, before I made any bad decisions. He knew a long-lost innocent me. Merit had been involved in politics, too, maybe even dangerously so. All things considered, I was eager to see Merit, but without question, I would keep him separate from Pop, who would have no desire to encounter anyone from those days.

Merit, I learned from his e-mail, was teaching African Studies in Southern California, which was no big surprise. He was brilliant. He had received an offer to lecture at Virginia Commonwealth for a term and been about to turn it down when he found out I lived near there. I encouraged him to call me on my cell if and when he arrived.

I listened to his message while I pulled my laptop from my briefcase. The sound of his voice made me smile and think of deep golden grass and vast distances. I sent him an e-mail saying I'd missed his message while in Richmond but that I'd call him in the coming week when I would be there again.

I examined my newly scuffed and muddied shoes. Presumably, the shoes I had worn on the night of the murder were still in evidence. Everyone was so excited about my clothes at the time, especially the red lace thong they found on the floor of the car—how titillating for them—that the shoes had slipped right by, except for... what was she then? *Detective* Gabriel. How could I forget? Short, stout, swaggering, and with a definite chip on her shoulder, she threw around her title at every opportunity. She was a detective recently promoted, as it turned out. It was her first homicide, I heard someone say.

She kept harping on my shoes. "Brand new. Not a scratch," she said, running a stubby finger over the soft kid.

She had no credibility, luckily for me. They ignored her. They thought she was just commenting on my shoes, but I got her point. I looked her in the eye and saw no pity whatsoever.

One of the other cops asked, "Do you want to talk to a woman?"

I answered, right in front of her, "Maybe, just as long as it's not her."

She didn't like that.

The other cops disliked her, too. She was shunted to the sidelines not long afterward, but throughout the investigation, every time I thought about the shoes, I felt her animal breath on my neck. Nothing came of it back then. Again I wondered if they would they reopen the investigation.

Gingerly, I checked for more news about the case and found an article about Elliott's surviving family. His wife, I learned, had remarried. I knew she'd moved away. She refused to comment. His sister was a lawyer. I hadn't known that. She was younger, and I didn't think she was a lawyer back then. We would have heard about her if she had been. She was reserving judgment for the outcome of the appeal. They mentioned me briefly, not by name but as the victim whose testimony would be set aside. I decided there was no insinuation in the reference to me. The article was not sensational and not a big item in the news. The emphasis was on a justice system flawed and full of prejudice, subjective testimony, tragic error.

The article concluded with a few random updates. Elliott's father was dead, his mother in assisted living. The Jeffersons had appealed the conviction twice before with no success, once alleging incompetent defense, once objecting to the trial judge's refusal to hear evidence about Elliott's and my alleged relationship. Very few people questioned Jules Jefferson's guilt in 1986. Elliott's family shunned me at the trial, but they did it quietly, their enmity reserved for Jefferson. My involvement was a shock to Elliott's wife and parents, and they didn't want to know too much about me. He was a professor, I a young college student and surviving victim in the crime. They looked away whenever I had to be near them. None of them ever spoke to me. Not once.

I shut the laptop down, turned off the lights in my room, and crept barefoot up the stairs to my third-floor study. Glass-fronted bookcases held all my text books on biology, botany, and soil chemistry. Stacked on the steamer trunk were huge picture books of famous gardens and reference books of plants: trees, flowering shrubs, ornamental grasses, annuals, and of course, roses. My desk was strewn with ideas I'd sketched for Longwood and Mary's Grove.

On the back wall of the study, I opened the door to the unfinished side of the attic. The space was empty of furniture, and the floor had been sanded smooth and heavily varnished. Mirrors and a brass barre ran the length of one wall, and posters of Degas ballerinas decorated the others. Through my twenties, I had danced alone up there for hours.

I crossed the room through the slanting moonlight. I lifted my arms and tried a rusty chaîné turn, but I felt the wine in my head and lost my balance. I started violently at the sound of Pop laughing softly behind me. I whirled.

His face was dark and inscrutable in the shadowy stairway. I hadn't locked the door.

"Still up?" He raised a snifter in a toast and took a sip of brandy.

"Get out of here. Leave me alone."

CHAPTER SEVEN

AFTER THE CRIME, I DROPPED out of college until the trial was over, missing most of what should have been my senior year. My friends, including Lisa, graduated without me. Still numb and self-conscious about being the girl who was raped, the one who was with the professor when he was shot, I made no friends in my new class before we all went our separate ways. The other girls went back to where they came from or went off with the husbands they had found while in college. I went home. I never reestablished contact with anyone from back then. Lisa called now and then, or wrote or sent a card. More recently, she'd email on occasion. But I was unresponsive. She got married, then divorced, then moved to California. She had a life, in other words, unlike me.

The victim services people offered me counseling after the crime, practically forced me into it. I did one session. I found it frightening, the way it suckered you into betraying your innermost thoughts and secrets. I refused to have anything further to do with it, and of course, Pop backed me on that.

To this day, I have no close friends. Back in June, I had no one to share the good news about Tony, no one who could understand about Pop. I certainly couldn't talk to Pop, seeing as he was the main problem. When I need to talk, I go for long walks in the hills and end up talking to myself. Rather, I talk to imaginary friends. I picture someone wise who loves me and wants to understand me.

Sometimes it's a man, sometimes a woman, sometimes a person I've actually met, but it's always someone totally trustworthy, on my side, and tirelessly interested in listening to me. Sometimes I spend time conjuring up a whole story about who my confidant is and how we've met. I don't talk out loud. I move my lips. Sometimes I whisper, and sometimes I get pretty emotional. I suppose I look insane. I've been caught at it once or twice. I'm sure that over the years it has fed the image of the crazy local spinster who got raped and lived forever after with her father.

On the Saturday after Pop and I went to Richmond, I was walking and thinking in circles about Pop and Anita Blore and Tony. The sun came out as I climbed the hills and tramped through the low, squashy seams between our land and the vineyard next to us.

By the time I returned from my walk, the late afternoon sun lay in long golden lines across the grass. Pop was talking to a woman who stood in front of a small, dust-colored car. She was rail thin, with soft, curly brown hair. Pop had his back to me and didn't hear my approach.

The woman, who was a bit younger than I was, spotted me over Pop's shoulder. "Are you Kate?" Her voice was soft, sweet, and breathless. She moved around Pop with a little dip that was almost like a curtsey. "My name is Suzanne. I am the victim liaison for the Attorney General's Office."

I shook her hand. It was thin almost to the point of nonexistence, and it trembled slightly, but the grip was warm. She had gray-blue, frightened-looking eyes, but they were comprehending eyes, and I felt an immediate connection.

Pop said, "I thought you were supposed to come tomorrow."

Suzanne's eyes held mine as she answered him. "I was in the area. I can come back if it's not a good time."

It was on the tip of my tongue to say there would never

be a good time for me to talk to anyone from the Attorney General's Office. I felt the old nerves rising up, but I smiled. "Oh no, now is fine. Thank you. Please, come in and sit down."

"I'm not a peace officer," she said as if she sensed my anxiety. "I'm just here to keep you informed."

We settled on the screened-in porch, I in my wicker reading chair and Suzanne across from me. Pop settled up against the doorjamb out of her line of sight where he could watch both of us and listen. He never said a word.

She quickly summarized what I already knew and asked me if I had any questions. I couldn't think of a single one except the one I was afraid to ask: Had anyone suggested that I might have deliberately lied?

She cocked her head, and I saw nothing but compassion in her eyes.

"How are you doing? Are you okay? I know this has to be a shock."

I stirred uneasily. "So there's no doubt about it? They won't fight it?"

"Probably not. Does that make you angry?"

I couldn't meet her eyes. "He's innocent. Isn't that what they're saying?"

"I don't know if I could accept that in your place. Do you believe it? That he could be innocent?"

"I..."

"Don't blame yourself, Kate. I know it must be so difficult. If he really is innocent, I mean. It's almost too awful to contemplate. I can't imagine how I'd feel if I had done that to someone, even knowing I was honestly mistaken. I don't know if I could forgive myself—" She broke off, bit her lip. "I understand, I do. But you mustn't think that way."

I blinked and reached for my refrain: "It was dark. He'd threatened us—"

She said, "No, no. No one can blame you. You were an

innocent victim."

I was hardly that. I got up and paced. "All I can say is, I don't want to have to testify again. It was too horrible. It was the worst part."

"I know how you feel."

I looked up then, and my skepticism must have shown, because she added, "I don't know exactly what it was like for you, of course. But I was a crime victim, too. I had a... similar experience."

The corners of her mouth twitched in a fleeting smile. "A lot of crime victims go into advocacy. We cope by reaching out to others." She hesitated, then continued. Her voice was soft and low. "I was twenty when it happened. I know that's how old you were."

"It was the worst experience of my life." From the corner of my eye, I saw Pop frown and lower his eyes.

She said, "It's beyond that. What is the worst experience of a twenty-year-old's life? Breaking up with a boyfriend? Flunking a test? My life wasn't perfect, but this was all out of proportion."

"What...?"

She smiled again, understanding the question I couldn't finish. "I was raped repeatedly and held prisoner for four hours. Then he got high and got on the phone and started talking to somebody. He was laughing and smoking cigarettes. Claimed he was 'hanging out with some bitch.'"

Pop looked up at the word, and she said, "I'm sorry. His word. That's what he thought he was doing: hanging out with me. I escaped and ran down the street naked. I banged on doors until somebody let me in. He didn't even realize I was gone. They caught him right there in my house." She told her story calmly. I was the one who flinched.

I asked, "So there was no doubt who did it?"

"None at all. I knew him slightly. He broke into my apartment and attacked me in broad daylight."

"Was he arrested and convicted?"

"Oh, yes. My waking nightmare was that some day they would let him out."

"And did they?"

"After only five years. He disappeared for two years after that, ran out on his parole. Then he was arrested in Wisconsin. He's back inside now."

"You keep track?"

"Oh, yes. So I'm only imagining how you must feel, knowing that Jules Jefferson could be released."

I pulled my sleeves down over my hands and looked out the window while Suzanne described how terrible it was at the trial, to be in the same room with the man who raped her.

But she had drawn strength from the confrontation. "I pointed to him and said, 'Him, that's him. That's who did it.' It was so difficult, but a part of me was exulting. I accused him. I told the world he was the one who did it and that it was wrong. He didn't think so, you know. He thought I liked it."

I fell silent, remembering my own trial, the questions. Over and over: Was I sure? It was dark. Did I really see his face? I would have wavered, but beyond the defense attorney, I could see Pop, every day in the courtroom, front and center, his eyes never leaving me, propping me up, making me sure of what I had to do. My voice would become steady when I met Pop's eyes. I could see Jefferson's face, earlier that awful night at the Tavern, and hear him telling Elliott, "I'll kill you," and I focused on the moment when Jefferson turned burning eyes full of hate on me. And that was when I found it in myself to say, "I'm sure."

Suzanne sat quietly while all that passed through my mind. Pop left the room.

"I could never do it again," I said. "I could never do it now. With me, the thing is that I thought it was closed, done with. Now it's not. I want to be free of the past."

Suzanne cocked her head. "Free, yes. I can understand that. But for me, that means I have to own my past and reclaim my life."

"I want the whole thing out of my life. It's like I'm being followed. Hunted."

"At least there's truth. I wanted truth. Don't you? Doesn't truth mean something?"

"No, I want the door shut. Not truth, freedom."

Safe, was all we could agree on. For Suzanne, it was about the loss of innocence.

"I will never be entirely carefree again," she said. "I felt guilty, dirty, and ashamed. I know you must feel that. It's natural. Most rape victims feel that way, but it's not right that you should."

She had long bony fingers and long bare nails. Pop brought us a pot of tea and teacups, and we sat quietly on the porch, drinking our tea. Suzanne's cup and saucer clattered softly, thanks to that peculiar tremor in her hands.

"When Pop and I first came to live in this house, when I started college, I thought this was the sanest, cleanest, safest place on earth, and it should have been." I shifted in my chair and glanced at Pop, who had sat down again. "That lasted three years."

Silence stretched between us, until Suzanne stood up to say she had to go.

I stood also. "I'll walk you out."

Pop seemed lost in his own thoughts. Suzanne nodded at him, and he lifted a finger.

When we were outside, Suzanne said, "My life is divided into before and after."

"I thought I could run away from the violence. It followed me like a wolf, tracked me down."

"It's not about you."

But of course it was. "You don't understand," I said.

That wasn't fair. She is a supremely empathetic person, but she couldn't know what I meant. I tried to explain, only because I had been thinking about it all day. "I'm trapped here." I jerked my head toward the house. "He's utterly dependent on me. I can't get away. I want to move on, put it all behind me. I—"

She touched my arm with faintly quaking fingers. "I know how hard it is to move on. It is for all of us. Look, here's what I can do. I feel reasonably sure that you won't have to be involved in any of the court proceedings to exonerate Jules Jefferson. I can check on that, but I'm pretty sure. That needn't worry you. What I don't know is if there will be a new investigation to find out who did murder Elliott Davis, and whether you might need to be questioned again in connection with that. I'll find out. The man who headed up the original investigation all those years ago is dead. But one of the detectives still lives here in town. She's retired, but she'll know what's going on, or she can find out. I can talk to her."

"You mean Elsa Gabriel. No. Suzanne, please don't bother. I don't want you to. I can't tell them anything now, twenty-two years later, that I didn't tell them then. Leave it alone."

She nodded, but I wasn't sure she would let it go.

"Really, Suzanne. Thank you. But it isn't necessary. If they want to talk to me, I'll tell them what I've told you. I don't know anything. Leave it."

She bowed her head, then touched my arm and left. I stood looking after her for the longest time, feeling edgy, until Pop called me in for dinner.

CHAPTER EIGHT

L ATER THAT NIGHT, I WAS browsing news and blogs in the attic when my phone hummed. I read the caller ID twice before it sank in who it was. I still thought of her as Lisa Franklin, but she had become Lisa Tannahill.

I knew why she was calling, and I didn't want to talk about it, but I also knew she wouldn't quit until she reached me. The call was close to rolling on to voicemail before I answered. I tried to sound normal, even upbeat.

"Hey, Lise, how are you doing? What's going on?"

I tried to keep the conversation at a distance, spoke of general things, tried to throw her off the scent with hints about business and romance, but none of that worked. She insisted on having my version of the story. I kept it short and factual. Jefferson was not the man who murdered Elliott and raped me, according to the DNA test results on my clothes, which yes, they did still have.

She was incredulous. I could hear her sifting through the possibilities.

I repeated my mantra. "It was dark. I was terrified and confused. It was him at the Tavern that night, and he threatened us. I was not the only one who witnessed that part." I stopped. I didn't want to sound defensive.

"But he was black? You're sure he was black?"

"Lisa—"

"Do you have any idea who it might have been? I've been thinking back—"

"Stop it, Lisa. Please. Stop." I still thought of her the

way she was when we were in college, a flame-haired sylph. I had seen very little of her through the years since.

"There were guys we knew back then. Can you think of anyone it might have been? I'm trying to think..."

"If I had known someone else who it could have been, don't you think I would have said so at the time?" I was about to change the subject, then get off the phone, but I waited just a fraction of a second too long.

"Hey! What about this? Could he have been someone you knew in Africa? You know, black American, black African, in the dark, like you say, couldn't he have been from Africa? What about—"

"Lisa, will you shut up?"

Shocked silence.

"I'm sorry." My voice was still too loud and combative sounding. I took a deep, calming breath and closed my eyes. "I'm sorry. But you just have no idea what you're talking about. This is not a TV show."

I'm uncomfortable on phones, because I can't see people's faces. You can hear a smile. You can smile, and the smile will be communicated in your voice. But on the phone, sometimes I worry: What am I not seeing?

I tried to repair the damage. "I'm sorry. I'm under a lot of strain."

"I can imagine. I'm the one who should apologize. It was thoughtless of me."

I heard sympathy but also puzzlement. And did I hear suspicion, too? How could that be? That was the paranoia of the guilty poking up through my thoughts. I wished I could see her expression. On the other hand, if I could see her expression, she would see mine. "There's nothing I can do about it. My name is pretty much still out of it. The court proceedings don't have anything to do with me."

At last, she dropped it. She offered news of old friends, chided me for skipping all our class reunions, and urged me to come visit her. I got a lump in my throat and a momentary ache for her and for long-ago good times. I wanted to reach out to her, but I didn't have the heart for it. Eventually, reluctantly, she let me go.

The room had grown dark in the short time we'd been talking. I switched on the standing lamp by my desk and saw my face reflected in the window. The light was odd, directional, and my eyes looked hollow underneath my brows.

I argued with myself, tested for the millionth time the great what-if that dominated my life: What if I had told the truth back then?

There is a moment, on a knife edge, when you have to blurt out truth or tell a lie. And if you lie, that's the second wrong, and from then on, to tell the truth you have to own up to that. And the longer you wait the worse it gets. And after more than twenty years? I had only to taste the murky undercurrents of the Internet to know how bad it would be. Oh, I didn't even have to do that. All these years, it has seemed as if I withdrew into myself in the aftermath of a violent crime, but the fact is that we were isolated to begin with. We might have stayed that way, and my life might have been very different, if it hadn't been for Lisa. She wasn't just my best friend. She was my first friend, and I sometimes think my last.

When we first arrived in Virginia, Pop didn't care if I attended school or not. He was happy to tend the house and plant a garden, saw that as the rest of his life, just living there. Well, he was on his way to fifty. I was young, and I wanted to go to college. I consulted a counselor at the local high school. It made me shudder to go into that place, a little brick building full of children. Incredible: Some of them were my age! And yet, I'd already lived a lifetime more, seen so much more of the world and done things they couldn't dream of. The counselor thought I'd go to high school for a year, but I scotched that plan out of hand. There would be no transcript, but I was better schooled as a child than one might imagine. So the plan was, I took a high school equivalency test, which I passed with ease. I scored high on scholastic aptitude exams, too. By then, I had set my sights on Sweet Briar, a small, secluded and exclusive women's college only three miles from our house.

Pop and I howled over my college entrance application essay. I did play the missionary card, but I also made Pop out to be some kind of disenfranchised colonial land baron who had fled political unrest. The story of our escape from Africa, as I styled it, actually left me gaping. It was a bit of a thriller, but in broad outline, it was true. I was faintly nagged by the feeling that I was an imposter, but I wasn't. I was certainly Kate Cranbrook. I was unique. I was amazing. I was accepted to the freshman class of '87.

I signed up for ballet and fencing and horseback riding, history, philosophy, English and world literature, and math. When classes started, the other girls were almost a surprise to me. Honestly, I had never given them a thought. I had looked forward to being in America, to having a house like the one we now lived in, and to going to college. The idea of meeting girls my own age and making friends among them hadn't even crossed my mind. They talked easily about subjects that left me dumb: TV shows, pop music, movies. I had never seen or heard of the shows, bands, and movie and TV stars they liked to talk about. I felt a different kind of person altogether, alien to their shared life experience.

And of course, I lived at home. I hadn't realized that most of the other students would be living in a dormitory at the school. In my fantasy, which came true, I lived in a big house with Pop while I was in college. I began to understand that a gulf separated me from the girls who lived on campus. I saw them only when I went to class, and then I sat center front and paid attention to the person teaching. The other girls knew each other intimately, shared a world of common interests, spent hours, days and nights together, and seemed to have no secrets from each other.

Only one other local girl came to campus every day for class the way I did, but she was a scholarship student, a lonely outsider in a school for well-to-do girls. She was pale and freckled, with ginger hair. I could see she wanted to be like the other girls, longed to be accepted by them. Some of the girls were nice enough to her, others less so. Three good-looking chums always sat in the back of English class together. The poor local girl tried to be friendly with them, and afterward I would hear them snicker. I heard them refer to her as a 'townie'—a new word to me. From the way they said it, I could tell it was not a good thing to be. But she was not like me. I lived apart by choice.

One day, I heard the back-row clique chattering before class about how legwarmers were on sale in Lynchburg.

Foolishly, the townie volunteered, "I found this at DresSmart for ten dollars." She was wearing an impossibly ruffled, over-long cotton dress. The other girls murmured, looked the townie up and down, and said nothing.

When she was gone, a cute little strawberry-blonde with a ponytail chirped, "Well, honey, as long as you understand that you look like you got dressed for ten dollars, that's great." And they all burst out laughing while the ponytail preened.

Her eyes met mine. I wasn't laughing, and she flushed. She always made a point of snubbing me after that.

When the townie figured out that I lived off campus, too, she ran up behind me one day as I left my last class and suggested we carpool. She was a mousy little puss with a strong, peculiar accent and frumpy clothes. Her teeth were so dirty they backed me up a foot. She drove an old truck, I a new convertible.

I said, "I don't think so." Her eyes were stricken, so I added, "I don't always go directly home." She still seemed hurt, so I threw in, "I have to shop on my way home." Still crestfallen. I gave it one last try. I smiled and touched her shoulder. "Some other time, okay?"

I was aloof from everyone in those days. I looked and sounded strange and different, more grown-up and foreign. I knew they talked about me. Since I didn't have any friends, I concentrated on my lessons. I was an excellent equestrienne, the best. I excelled in ballet, too, and I made the dean's list that first semester and every semester I was there. I was beautiful and confident about my appearance, and a lot of them resented that, too. No one had ever taught me false modesty.

If my isolation was nearly complete, Pop's was absolute. I amused him no end, making fun of my classmates, mimicking their accents, telling him about their giddy, girlish ways. Pop had no contact with the school. He met some of the other parents at the beginning and end of the year, and at a Christmas party in December. Afterward, he denounced them as idiots. He was ferocious in his scorn for the locals. He didn't have to work, so he had no contacts of that kind. He managed his money and read, mostly newspapers, history books, news magazines, and economic journals. He hired gardeners and began planting the grounds of our house.

The summer after my freshman year, we went to Europe. We spent a month in Paris, where we wandered days at a time in the Louvre, until Pop couldn't stand it anymore. Then we lingered days more just sitting in cafés and stolling through the Tuileries. We dawdled on the Riviera in July, walked the Promenade des Anglais in Nice, and listened to the strange sound the waves made on the rocky beach. We wandered down to Rome by way of Florence and Orvieto, flew to the Algarve long enough to sample fresh fried sardines with white porto, and finished up in Madeira where we watched the sun set on Funchal Bay. It was a happy time for both of us, I would have to say now the happiest we ever knew.

When I started my second year, I noticed a new girl in my riding class. She was tall and thin like a model, with thick red hair and high cheekbones. She smiled and introduced herself. Her name was Lisa Franklin, and she had transferred in as a sophomore. She talked to everybody, and I envied her easy charm. She had more friends after one week than I had after an entire year. The next day, she saw me in French lit and sat next to me. While we waited for class to start, she volunteered that her father was a colonel in the Army. She had lived in Germany, spoke German, and spoke English without a regional accent. Her mother's family was from Virginia, very old money, so old that it was gone.

"That's why I'm here." She rolled her eyes. "All the girls in my mother's family go to Sweet Briar."

"But you went somewhere else last year."

"Florida. I had a boyfriend there. That blew up in a major way." She made a little face and shook her slender shoulders. "It's a long story. I'll tell you all about it someday." She was like that: confiding. She made me feel as though she was choosing me to be her new best friend. "Anyway," she concluded, "I ended up at the old Alma Mater." She looked around, leaned in, and said under her breath, "I'm not sure about this place. It seems awfully... out of the way?"

And we both laughed.

After class we walked out together, and she asked me where I was from.

"Kenya."

"Where is that, exactly?"

I was so used to people knowing so little about that part of the world that I said, "It's in Africa."

"I know that." Big smile with a little eye roll. "Where in Africa? East coast, isn't it? Next to what? Ethiopia?" She stopped, fished a pen out of her pocket, and flipped to a back page of her notebook. There she drew a creditable outline of the continent and marked an area about where Kenya is.

I felt like a space creature meeting someone who knew about my planet. "I'm impressed."

"I'm an Army brat. Why did you leave? So you could go to school here?"

"That. Plus my grandmother died and left my father money and a whole lot of other stuff. Heirlooms, you know. Furniture. Jewels." Her eyes traveled to the large square-cut amethyst ring I wore on my right hand. "Things had gotten pretty rough there. My father had a business, but it got so he had to pay off corrupt officials all the time." "Had a business"' sounded downright respectable. It flashed through my mind how poor and filthy our existence was back then. I didn't want to be that person anymore.

She was listening with interest. "Do you miss it? Do you ever go back?"

"Oh no." I laughed. "We won't be going back to Africa. No, I don't think so!"

She smiled as though to laugh along with me, but she looked a little puzzled at my vehemence.

I didn't want to tell her about my squalid, awful origins, or how I'd really gotten here, so instead I told her we'd slipped out during an attempted coup. "My father was a pretty outspoken critic of the President. The coup failed, and you didn't have to be a genius to see that there'd be a crackdown. My father could have been in a heap of trouble."

All that was true, but I hadn't ever thought about it quite that way. Back then, I just wanted out, and the coup was my opportunity. I replayed in my mind the moment when we stopped at the checkpoint. An armed guard leaned in and looked past me at Pop, whose face was buried in his bunched-up bloody shirt. I paused and felt the cold shadow of the many outcomes that were possible that day.

Lisa asked, "What? Cat walk across your grave?"

I smiled. "Nothing."

Finally I had a friend. Lisa, confident and popular, began to pull me into campus life. She introduced me to her friends and told them I had come from Africa, which they already knew, but when Lisa told them, she made it sound less alien and more exotic. They, and especially Lisa, tried to draw me out about myself, which made me a little shy. I didn't want to tell the truth, and I didn't want to lie, so I glamorized and dramatized where I could, without absolutely making things up. My businessman father had dangerous connections. We'd fled under fire. We arrived with the clothes on our backs to claim a waiting fortune. I was still very different, still lived off campus, outside the mainstream of dorm life, in a private world with Pop. But I began to have a second life at school. I liked my new persona: Rich girl from African adventure story lives with mysterious father who fled political unrest. I liked the attention. And I liked Lisa.

On impulse, I invited her to come home with me for dinner one night.

She hesitated, but her eyes gleamed. I knew she was curious about the house and Pop. "Are you sure it's all right?"

I knew it wouldn't be all right with Pop, but I didn't care. "Oh there's always plenty of food. Anyway, Pop's a great cook. He can whip up something out of nothing. He does it all the time."

I brought her in through the back door and nearly swooned at the smells of butter, fresh minced garlic, and sautéed mushrooms. Pop looked up from chopping celery and carrots. The sleeves of his starched white shirt were rolled up to the elbows, and he wore a red chef's apron. He did a double take when he saw Lisa. The right eye zoomed onto me.

"Hi, this is Lisa. Is it all right if she stays for...?" My voice trailed off as we all contemplated the two thick filet mignon medallions on the cutting board.

Lisa had on a loose emerald green sweater that made her eyes look like jewels in the afternoon sun that poured through the kitchen windows. She pulled off a scarf she'd used to tie up her hair, shook the bright red waves out around her shoulders, and said, "Oh, I'll only stay a minute."

I held my breath while the moment hung in suspense.

"Nonsense." Pop pulled a sharp blade from the knife block and started cutting up the beef with a flourish. "We'll have steak tartare *aller-retour*. Been meaning to try it."

Having lived in Europe, Lisa didn't bat an eye when Pop served us both aperitifs, and she conversed easily with Pop about our travels and hers. Although I sensed she was impressed by the dining room and the silver, she maintained a well-bred disregard for our apparent wealth.

Just when I was starting to think the evening was a huge success, Lisa said, "So I understand you had a business and fled political enemies."

Pop's fork stopped halfway to his mouth. He let a beat go by before he answered her. "I had a business. We left during a time of minor political unrest."

"Was that the coup?" I started to correct her, and she amended, "Attempted coup."

"It wasn't even that." Pop flattened a dinner roll with his butter knife. "A disgruntled private in the Air Force got on the radio and announced that the government had changed. He was delusional. It was hardly more than a prank, very easily suppressed."

Lisa's eyes gleamed with mischief, and she wouldn't look at me. "But you had to shoot your way out." Her green eyes widened. "Didn't you?"

Pop gave me the evil right eye.

I was on my second glass of Bordeaux, so I rose to the bait. "That's how he got that scar. Good thing, too. His face was all bloody, or somebody might have recognized him on the way out."

Pop pushed his plate away and harrumphed to shut me down.

But I turned back to Lisa. "My father wouldn't leave Africa—he was far too stubborn. I was the one—"

Pop stood and raised his voice. "What are you saying, Kate, that I wouldn't leave Africa? I'm here, am I not?" He bowed to Lisa, offered her an after-dinner drink, and said to me, "You've had quite enough if you're going to drive your friend home. Or perhaps I had better do that?"

Lisa looked amused, and I felt my face get hot.

Throughout the rest of the evening, he was courtly, almost flirtatious. He bowed over her hand when she said goodnight. I almost thought he was going to kiss it.

As I passed him on the way out the door, I warned him under my breath. "Watch it, Pop."

In the car, Lisa said, "Your father is a handsome man."

"Yes, he is." It was true. Pop was not yet fifty. "Very charming," Lisa added.

In fact, he had played the role of the urbane, indulgent father to perfection. When I got home, Pop was as annoyed with me as I expected. "Lisa is trouble. You shouldn't drink. It loosens your tongue, and you say ridiculous things. Someday you'll say something you'll regret."

I brushed him off, but he caught my wrist. His fingers felt like iron.

"I mean it, Kate. You make a joke of it. What you did in that warehouse—"

"What I did!" I was speechless mad, but he was dead calm and sober.

He nodded almost imperceptibly. "Okay. What *we* did."

But I was still furious. "No. No, you're right. You are absolutely right. It's what *I* did. It was all me. I got us out. I was the one with the presence of mind to grab all the money when the first window broke. I was the one who understood what was at stake for us. I was the one—"

"We did find out what you were made of that day, Kate. I'll give you that."

Tears burned in my eyes. "I did what I had to do. And where would you be today if I hadn't?" I spun, flinging out my arms. "All this. That's what I did."

It was a cold moment. A rift as wide as the valley we came from opened up that night, then it closed. We made up. We let it lie for a while. I never doubted Pop loved me, but for the first time, I had the sense that he saw something in me that he didn't much like or approve of. It hurt and felt like an injustice. I was innocent, in my own unusual way. In circumstances more extreme than what most people ever face, I had acted on instinct with the comic-book bravado of a child with a toy gun.

Pop went to the kitchen and returned with two brandies. He handed one to me and sat down. He came right out and said I shouldn't get too close to any of the girls at school.

"What, not have any friends, are you crazy?"

"We have a good life here."

"And anyway, why, for God's sake? What happened is whatever we say it is. It's not as if anyone can ever find out what really went on back there."

"Don't be so sure."

I laughed. Not a real laugh. An angry laugh. "You're crazy. That place? Get the big picture, Pop. It was a riot."

"It was Kenya, Africa, but it's not as if they don't have police. What do you think Abasi Umbuyu was? We have no idea what they found when they went back to that warehouse. And it didn't burn down. They wrecked the front, that's all."

"How do you know that?"

"I sold the inventory, remember? It wasn't absolutely all you, my dear. I bought the airplane tickets. All I'm saying is, where we came from and how we got here is nobody's business but ours. You'd do well to keep your counsel, my darling daughter." He raised his glass.

"Easy for you to say. You're old."

His face darkened.

Tension drained out of me then, and I was able to smile for real. "You're an old man, Pop!"

That night, I dreamed, as I often did, that I was back in Africa. Sometimes I would see my mother hunched over her tattered Bible with a fierce expression, or I'd be in one of those big houses. Then I'd be in Nairobi, sometimes even in the warehouse, and I'd wake up with a sick feeling, wanting to be held. That night, I woke up and lay awake remembering what Pop had told me about the warehouse, that it hadn't burned down.

At the end of the year, Pop and I met Lisa's parents, and the five of us went out to dinner. They asked Pop what he did, and when he said he was retired, I could see them guessing at his age.

Colonel Franklin asked, "Retired from what?"

Pop was terse, almost to the point of rudeness. "Farming. Kenya."

"They had to leave when there was a coup." Lisa added with a wink that only I could see, "They barely got out alive."

"Why yes," Colonel Franklin said. "During Independence, was it? I believe we heard about that. The Mau Mau uprising. The Mau Maus are in Kenya, aren't they?"

His wife ventured, "Are they the very small people?"

Pop simply stared, and her husband laughed. He seemed unembarrassed, but Lisa rolled her eyes.

"Are you thinking of the Pygmies, dear? No, I think they're from the Congo." Colonel Franklin turned to Pop for confirmation.

"And elsewhere," Pop snapped. "Not Kenya, however."

"Anyway, the Mau Maus are not Pygmies," Colonel Franklin said cheerfully.

I cleared my throat. "Actually, Mau Mau is not a tribe. It was an uprising. A rebellious movement."

"Thirty years before the attempted coup," Pop added, "a decade before independence."

Pop was mostly silent for the rest of the evening, while Lisa and I told her parents all about school. Then Pop glowered twenty feet away while I lingered, telling them good-bye. Mrs. Franklin even gave me a little hug before they left. I wished I could go with them. I wished I were their daughter. I wished I could be what I seemed.

CHAPTER NINE

THE FIRST HALF OF THE next week dragged. Teaching weighed me down at the best of times, and the community college campus—small, new, of cheap construction and pretty much in the middle of nowhere—depressed me. I took to rushing off immediately after class so none of my students could detain me. They were local residents, not all college aged, some my age or older, and they made me nervous, paranoid. What did they know about me? Were they looking at me? Talking about me? I skipped out on office hours, too. I couldn't wait to get back to Richmond. Back to my new life and anonymity.

I said to Pop on Wednesday night, "You could come if you wanted. I'll be spending a lot of time with Anita. We have to meet about the budget, and we might go out to dinner. She mentioned something about dinner last Friday, and I put her off."

That wasn't true, but I was determined to make use of Anita. If he wouldn't strike up an appropriate relationship with her, then I would use her to scare him away. In the end, he opted for the comfort of his own den and bed and let me go alone.

Thursday dawned clear and warm. Under blue skies and sunshine, I felt the exhilaration I always did when I broke free and hit the road in my car with the top down. I turned up the radio to the max and reveled in the feeling of the wind whipping through my hair as I sped away. I was on the verge of a new life, and everything I wanted seemed within reach.

I flung open the windows when I got to the house in Church Hill and played Merit Chenobo's latest message. His speech, bookish and faintly English sounding, was instantly familiar.

"Hello, Kate Cranbrook! Merit here. I received your e-mail. I am in Richmond. There is a symposium Thursday night. I could meet you any time Thursday afternoon. Could we have dinner? Maybe you would like to come to the symposium with me, get a little update on the old country. Been a long, long time. I look forward to seeing you. Talk to you soon."

I laughed with delight at the prospect of being with him again. I didn't know what was going to happen when I saw Tony, and I had ideas, but at the same time, I was dying to see Merit. I decided to hedge my bets.

When I called Merit, I said, "Hey, I'm here today and tomorrow. I have to meet with a client and the guy I work with. I'll see you for sure, if not for dinner, maybe for a drink or lunch tomorrow. Can I call you later when I know what's going on?"

So we left it that we'd talk again later in the day.

"I can't wait to see you," I added.

"It has been forever."

His voice again transported me to a warm, familiar place. I cradled the phone against my heart and closed my eyes. The idea that someone would show up who had known me in Africa was both thrilling and frightening. And Merit was probably the one person I truly wanted to see.

I pulled into the drive of Mary's Grove before ten o'clock. A mixed wood of oak, pine, and walnut trees framed the scene in deep shade. The river stretched a sparkling sheen into the distance, and the open space where the garden would be had been cleared and raked clean. With my mind's eye, I drew in the neat lines of boxwood hedge and sketched in azaleas. I was choosing colors—coral, white, a dull gold—when Anita came out to greet me. She was once again well turned out, and she was disappointed that I didn't have Pop with me.

She led me into the sunroom. "Where is your mother, Kate? Is she still living?"

"Honestly, I don't know. She left us when I was a teenager. The farm we lived on was her father's." That was one of my more romantic fictions about our life in Africa. Pop was well aware of that one, and although he didn't approve of it, I knew he wouldn't trip over it. "My father worked on one of those huge farms in the Rift Valley." True. "He married the landowner's daughter and bought out her father." Not true. "She was terrified of Kenya after independence, and eventually, she went home to England."

"She's English?"

"Her father was. Her mother was Dutch." Why not? Most of the colonial families we'd known were one or the other, English or Dutch.

"And you had no further contact with her?"

"No. This was a long time ago. Two years later, Pop and I came to the U.S."

"And he never remarried."

"No, he never did."

"Was he terribly heartbroken?"

"She was a very beautiful woman, some said the most beautiful they had ever seen." Fact.

"He's a handsome man. Seems a shame. If she left because she was afraid to stay in Kenya, then why couldn't she have come to the States after you moved here?"

"I guess that wasn't the only reason she left. She also left the marriage. She was, um, difficult."

"Oh dear." Anita was sympathetic, but I could see she was also pleased that my mother was out of the picture. "Difficult in what way?"

"Oh, I don't know. Contrary." In my upgraded version of the past, my English mother was not an angry, vicious shrew who called me names and slapped my face. I never could quite figure out why the frightened mother of my fantasy would have left me behind in Kenya.

I smiled and turned back to business, but her mind wandered almost immediately. She wanted to know about my love life: Did I have one? If not, why not, if so, was it secret?

I figured Pop had been pumping her about the subject in what little time he'd had with her. I only had to ask, "Why, what did he say?"

"He wants what's best for you, Kate, I'm sure. I said, 'She's such a beautiful girl. It's a wonder she's not married. She must have men swarming after her.' And he didn't know. I was going to ask him if there was anybody special you were seeing, and he asked me! He said, 'What do you think of Tony?' And I said, 'Tony? Why, I never even thought of him.' He said, 'Some women like that type.' He is good looking. Don't you think?"

"Is he? I never noticed. I don't suppose I think so."

I was guessing she sensed that I was what made Pop unavailable to her. Maybe she would have liked to drive us apart. Lord knows I would have no objection to that. In my plans, she and I were going to be allies.

She nodded toward the window behind me. "There's Tony now."

I felt my face flush. But when we went outside to meet his truck, I saw instantly that something had gone very wrong. Tony had a woman with him. She got out and smiled at us. She was pretty in an average way, with straight dark-blond hair halfway down her back. Her eyes were plain gray-blue, her skin not particularly smooth, and her coloring fair. She had good teeth though, and her smile was nicer than I liked. I had pictured her as sour-faced and frumpy. She wore blue jeans and a cheap, cute top. And a wedding ring with a miniscule diamond. A gold cross hung on a chain around her neck.

Tony said, "Mrs. Blore, Kate, this is my wife, Beryl."

His eyes met mine briefly, and we both quickly turned to Anita, who greeted Tony's wife with a welcoming smile and told her how wonderful she thought Tony was. I held onto my smile with effort, and my expression felt like a mask. From the corner of my eye, I saw Tony sneaking anxious looks at me.

Anita offered coffee and asked Beryl if she'd like to go inside and sit down.

Beryl shook her head. "No thanks." Her mother had the kids, she said. She called it Mom's Day Out. She would take the truck, pick up a girlfriend in Petersburg, and go shopping in Richmond. "You have a beautiful house," she added. Her eyes skimmed the garden site, which consisted of bare ground, a few scattered ancient shrubs, and remnants of stonework. I was used to seeing it with an active imagination, as it would be one day.

Anita seemed to follow Beryl's thoughts. "You should have seen it two weeks ago. Tony's done a wonderful job of clearing and cleaning up the trees and shaping all those old rhododendrons. I never knew anybody with a better hand for pruning. It's an art."

Beryl said, "Oh, I know. He's like that at home. Always out there snipping this and lopping that."

"I bet your garden is immaculate."

"The yard is really his thing," she added. "I love the flowers in the house. He's got all those roses, you know."

"Oh, I didn't know you had roses, Tony."

Beryl rolled her eyes. "He's got hundreds."

Tony said quickly, "That's counting year-old cuttings and everything. Roses that I keep in the garden, that's, well, not a hundred. Maybe eighty."

Anita seemed to be astonished. I had three times that number in established roses, but I didn't say so. I was more interested in what Beryl had to say, because she had jumped back in with that tone parents sometimes get about their children, where they complain but you can tell they're claiming pride of ownership as well.

"He spends more time with the roses than he does in the house. He names the roses after the kids." She sounded almost bitter.

Tony said, "They help me with the roses. They like to be in the garden, too."

Beryl granted that was true.

On cue, Anita asked about the kids, and Beryl was on solid ground: daughters, Tara, Kim and Isabelle, the youngest was a boy. She'd have talked a lot more about her kids if she'd connected with another parent. After a pause, Beryl asked me if I had any kids.

I smiled apologetically. "No, I'm afraid not. Roses, yes, kids, no."

Anita asked me, "Did you know Tony grew roses?"

"Tony's roses are spectacular." I moved my eyes straight from Tony back to Anita, as if Tony's wife weren't standing between them. "I'm not going to use them here because I want everything to be authentic for the time we're restoring to. But I'll be using them for other projects. Quite a lot." I smiled at him again.

Beryl laid a proprietary hand on Tony's arm. "That'll be great, won't it, honey? You've been saying you want to get them out on the market."

Tony's attempt at a smile looked more like a grimace.

As if scripted, in the pause that followed, my phone hummed in my pocket. Normally it would have been off; somehow it wasn't. I made a little show of being startled by it, held it up, and checked the Caller ID. Merit. Perfect. I said, "Do you mind if I take this?"

I didn't even walk away. I just turned aside to take the call. "Hey, I can't talk right now. I'm in a meeting, but tonight is great. I had to make sure I'd be free. Can I call you back? Great. Can't wait to see you."

He barely had time to say, "Sure, no problem," before I hung up.

I turned back. Everyone was looking here and there, pretending not to listen, thinking whatever they thought. I liked it. Was it my imagination, or was Beryl pleased? Anita was curious, of course. And Tony, was he not so happy? Within minutes, Beryl left, Tony went to work, and I went back inside with Anita.

She was laughing when we sat in the sunroom. "So much for you and Tony! I thought he had eyes for you. I know your father thought the same thing."

"My father often has ideas like that, and usually he's wrong." Then I couldn't stop myself from asking, "You thought Tony had eyes for me?"

"Well, he's married, so that's that! She seemed like a nice young woman, didn't you think?"

What could I say?

She asked about my plans for the evening, but I insisted I was going to see an old friend, just a friend. She walked me out, and on the way, I said goodbye to Tony. When our eyes met, I thought I saw meaning, but I couldn't figure out what it was. He was a man who could hide his feelings when he wanted. I had him pegged as a straight shooter faced with the temptation of a lifetime. I liked the idea of me as a temptress.

CHAPTER TEN

O N THE WAY BACK TO town late that afternoon, I called Merit again and arranged to meet him at a Mexican restaurant near VCU. I stopped by my apartment and changed into slinky black pants and a light silky top that picked up the pale gold of my hair.

We arrived at the same time, approaching from opposite directions on the sidewalk in front of the restaurant. We knew each other instantly, in the way old friends do even after decades of separation. Recognizing him was easy for me: he was unmistakably African to my eyes. It was something about his very upright carriage and the way he dressed, in a tailored suit with a skinny tie. He spotted me easily, too. He had seen my picture in the magazine and on my website, and I didn't think I'd changed so much, either. In fact, he said so.

"I saw your name, and I thought of you. Then I looked at the article, and there you were. You have not changed at all."

"Thank you, considering you haven't seen me since I was fourteen."

We sat at a table for two by a window. Students streamed by outside in T-shirts, with backpacks and iPods, but the restaurant was quiet, voices muted and the clink of glass and dishes blunted by thick tablecloths and carpet.

Merit said, "I had no idea where you had gone. When I went back to the Valley, when my grandfather died, they told me you and your father left. You and your father and the other American."

"My father had the idea he could do imports, like be a middleman or something. He went into business with the accountant from the farm, you know, the secretary. They had a warehouse."

When our drinks arrived, he said, "So you have been in Lynchburg, Virginia, all this time. How did you end up here? Did you have ties here? I do not remember anything about that."

His voice seemed loud to me, but in a nice way. He was big, open, and relaxed. I never liked other people overhearing me, so I kept my own voice low. "My mother's family was from North Carolina. Her mother went to Longwood. She talked about Sweet Briar once, and I liked the name. It sounded rich and privileged. And it was here, in the States."

He leaned forward on his elbows. "I did not know you wanted to come to the States."

"I didn't when I knew you. I loved the farm in the old days. I still think of it as paradise."

His eyes became momentarily opaque. "It was a paradise for some. For the ones who owned the land."

I was instantly ashamed, and my face must have shown it because Merit reached out and covered my wrist with a huge, warm hand. His eyes were soft again. "You were a child. And what you say is true. It was a paradise for them."

"And I wasn't one of them. They let me in, so I could see close up that it was a paradise, but I was outside, looking in, like all the rest of you." I was invited inside the big house, with its dark, polished floors, ceiling fans, and low beds draped in mosquito netting.

But Merit never was, even though he was my best friend. His grandfather was a servant in the house for forty years. I thought about my mother, who was also never asked to come inside. She accused me of putting on airs. It wasn't my fault people didn't like her. She was a humorless woman, bristling with righteous disapproval.

As if following my thoughts, Merit asked, "Did you ever hear again from your mother?"

I shook my head. "We had fun in those days." I meant after she left.

Merit was silent, but he understood. My mother took a dim and suspicious view of my friendship with Merit. He was older than I was, and of course, he was black. When she left, I was free to tag after him as much as I wanted.

I said, "She didn't understand that you looked after me."

He smiled broadly. "Somebody had to. You were a fearless creature. Too much so for your own good."

I sighed, thinking of the past.

He sat back in his chair. "I missed you when you left. We went there, too, when the farms were bought out. I hated Nairobi. I thought you might be there somewhere, but I had no idea how to contact you. Were you there? This would have been in 1981 or so."

"No, not then."

Dinner came. Mine was an herby risotto with eggplant, his chicken parmesan. Merit handled his fork tines down, like a European.

Between bites, he resumed his story. "I went to the capital because my uncle was a big man in the government. But you know how big men are. They make enemies, and after Jomo Kenyatta died, Uncle Charlie had to leave the country. I went with him to England and got my university degree at Sussex."

"And now you're a famous speaker on African politics. I always knew you were destined for greatness."

He made a face and waved his big hands. "No, no, not famous. And certainly not popular in Kenya."

"But you did go back?"

"I taught at Kenyatta University. But I have been teaching in California. I am better off here. It is not like America in Kenya. You cannot spout off about the ones in power with impunity." He wiggled his eyebrows. "And I have been known to spout off."

I was loving every minute of his company. I felt like a long lost me for the first time in forever. I sat back, scanned the room, and caught an older woman staring at me with a sour face. She glanced away at once, but not before her gaze bounced off Merit. My first reaction was the usual paranoia, but then I realized something different was going on. Interracial couples were an everyday reality in Richmond, but among a certain element, maybe not a welcome one. I thought about the names people called the unnamed witness on the Internet. Great. How ironic. Half the world could condemn me for being racist, and the other half could hate me for hanging out with a black man. I shuddered and reached for my wine glass.

Merit looked up, his plate nearly clean. "You still have not told me how you came to this country. Your father always said he would never go back."

"We were living like rats in Nairobi, and my father's mother died and left him a small fortune. So of course I wanted to come, but he wouldn't hear of it. I never have understood what his beef was with his family. There was certainly some very bad blood. But still. His mother was the only one left, and she was dead, and there was all this money and a house and jewels and everything. But o-o-o-h, no." I rolled my eyes hugely and groaned.

That got a booming laugh. He held up his hand. "Oh, you do not need to tell me." Merit knew my father and his drunken rants about his family. "But he came around in the end?"

"Well." I stopped to eat the last few bites of my dinner and think about what he would know. "There was a coup."

"Attempted. Yes. It was over very quickly, from what I understand."

"But while it lasted, it was pretty intense, if you were in the middle of it. You weren't there, were you?"

He shook his head. I had been embellishing the story of my escape from Africa for so long that I'd almost convinced myself that Pop was some kind of disenfranchised land-baron-turned-businessman, or a dissident who'd fled a crackdown. I couldn't spin a silly story like that for Merit.

The waitress reappeared.

After she had cleared our plates, offered us dessert and left, Merit said, "And now, Kate, you are getting famous in your field."

"Oh no. I barely have a toehold so far. Anyway, I don't want to be famous. Just rich. And free."

"Free? You white people." Loud voice, big laugh, unselfconscious.

I glanced around but no one seemed to notice us.

"Come to the symposium with me. Will you?"

And so I went.

A small but intense knot of students, mostly male and mostly black, filled the first three rows of a lecture hall that was otherwise sparsely seated with a mixed crowd. I tried to slip into a seat halfway back, but Merit, in the spirit of treating me like a special friend, led me to the front. Walking the length of the room, I was acutely conscious of being white and blond. How utterly out of place and interesting I must have looked with an African professor's guiding hand in the middle of my back.

Merit left me to join four other panelists, who seemed to be representing two different political factions. None of it meant anything to me. I had never heard of the parties or the leaders. But I could still sense the enmity between Merit and the other speakers. One was angry because Merit was critical of the sitting regime, another because Merit was not more active against them in Kenya.

The latter, a very gaunt and sickly Kikuyu, challenged Merit for being in America, for having left Kenya. "How do you say you care what happens when you criticize from the safety of the U.S.?"

"You're here, too," someone shouted from the crowd.

The gaunt man lowered his head and glared up through

bristling white eyebrows. "For six weeks only, to bring the truth to you here. Then I return. I have been there throughout, and I will remain there."

The argument became more heated during the question period, and at one point, the crowd surged forward. I looked around nervously, not understanding the forces at work. Flash bulbs blazed on cameras, and I heard a scuffle in front. Then I felt Merit's firm hand on my arm, guiding me free of the scrum. I clung to him.

Someone yelled, "Professor Chenobo!"

When we turned, a camera flashed. By the time we were clear, I was shaken.

We went back to Merit's place in a nearby two-story apartment building, which he said was mostly occupied by graduate students from Africa and Asia. We drew flickering glances in the parking lot, and inside, the hallways smelled of cardamom and curry. The distant past welled up in the form of a cowering Malay cook I couldn't even picture.

Merit's small studio was comfortable enough, and as much as I hate curtains, I was glad for the heavily covered windows. The carpet was ratty, and I hesitated when I saw the upholstery on the couch and chair.

He apologized without embarrassment. "It was furnished when I rented it. I had the steam cleaners come, but the dirt and the stains, there is nothing to be done about them. They are permanent. But you can sit without danger." He laughed. "I will pour you a glass of wine. Red, yes?"

"Please. I'm still shaking." I peeked out the window. I saw only lights in the parking lot and my own reflected face. I flopped on the couch.

Merit put a glass on the coffee table in front of me. "I have a wife. She is in Africa. I sent for her, and she came to California, but she did not care for it. She went back after a few weeks. She does not want to come back again."

I drank down my wine and held out my glass for more,

although I noticed Merit sipped at his. He seemed quite calm, and I said so.

He shrugged. "I am used to fighting with words. It means nothing. At least here in the States, it is only words."

"Your wife doesn't want to come back to America?"

"No. Believe it or not, not everyone does. Her family is there. Her mother."

"Couldn't she bring her mother?"

"Her mother will not leave home. Neither one will. They are happy there. Doing well. Besides, with what I make, they are rich there. Here, not so much."

"Do you miss her?"

"Yes, and my children. Seriously? I think I will go back some day. But I wrote a book that does not endear me to those currently in power. That was one reason I came here."

"You don't have to explain it to me."

"That fellow, he had a point. I criticize from the safety of the U.S. But I will not do any good if I am dead. Here, I am writing another book. In this one, I will treat, among other things, the coup that you ran away from."

"Attempted coup."

He smiled. "What about you? Tell me more about what you have been doing in your life."

I leaned back and looked at the ceiling. "I went to Sweet Briar College, then I studied landscape architecture, and that's what I do now."

"You never married?"

Not my favorite topic. "Marriage isn't such a big deal."

He raised his eyebrows. "Perhaps not. It just surprises me that you have lived quietly in one place all this time. You were always so adventurous."

He was on to something. Funny he should have caught the scent that quickly. He hadn't seen me for... what? Something like twenty-five years. I knew what puzzled him, of course. Though he knew me from childhood, he didn't know about the crime; that was after his time, during the long years we were apart. So I told him.

"It was shocking, huge. You can't imagine, in a small town like ours. Our entire county has something like three or four murders a year and nothing, ever, as sensational as this." I stopped short. I didn't want to get into how Jules Jefferson's arrest polarized the community.

"And what was it? A chance encounter? You were in the wrong place at the wrong time?" His reaction was sober and sympathetic, but different from what I usually got. He was not horrified. He had seen people shot.

I shook my head, uncomfortable with telling him the details. I shifted ahead in time and told him that after the crime, it was a year before I resumed my college education. "I withdrew from everything after that. Eventually, I went back to school. But I suppose you could say I was arrested." The wine was making me ridiculous. "My relationships with men have been brief and not part of my real life." I was almost in tears with self-pity. My thoughts turned to Tony. Had I finally found someone? But he was married. At that moment, I felt hopeless.

As if speaking straight into my heart, he asked, "There has been no one for you?"

I was in danger of bursting into tears, but I shook myself out of it. "There was a whole string of men for a while there." I fell silent, thinking about the way Pop had dogged my heels, suspicious and angry about those secret and inappropriate liaisons. My mind swerved back to Tony, and I reached for more wine.

While I was sinking into a lugubrious, alcohol-enhanced torpor, Merit's attention drifted back to his main preoccupation: his book. He spread newspapers, photos, and clippings on the coffee table and sorted through them. I sat up and began to look through them. Some of them covered the 1982 coup. Actual newspaper clippings. Merit would have been eighteen.

"After independence in 1963," he said, "many of us joined Jomo Kenyatta's government in Nairobi. Kenyatta was a great leader."

He rambled on, and I murmured,"Oh," "Ah ha," and "Mmm," to sound interested. I let myself sink back into memories of Africa, before Nairobi, and for the third time that day, the image of my mother cut into me. Did I miss her? No, never. What I felt was the pain of what she never was. What I remembered was her bitterly complaining late at night, bitching at my father, and sometimes, as if I couldn't hear, about me, how high and mighty and depraved I was. I was a child of ten! I looked just like her, if you could catch her, maybe when she slept, without that suspicious, twisted scowl.

With hindsight, I suppose I can see that she was sick, living out there friendless, far from home. She had gone to Africa with missionaries, several families. I don't think it was a big success, that mission. How she hooked up with my father, I have no idea. Neither of them ever spoke of it. She seemed to hate him. I remember lying still at night under netting, in complete darkness, night noises outside, mutterings between them, then louder accusations, her voice shrill, hysterical, his low and menacing. Sometimes a thump or thud, a cry or angry shout. Until she left. Oh, yes. I was glad when she did, and so was he, though without her restraining presence, he drank something awful in those days.

My glass was empty once again. I had bypassed Merit altogether and placed the bottle right in front of me. It was empty, and I wondered how much time had passed. Maybe not so much: Merit, bless his heart, was still expounding on the early years of independence.

"After Kenyatta's death, the ideals of the new Africa began to crumble. Tribal loyalties eroded national unity. Greed and corruption bred disillusionment." He tapped his finger on the table. "The coup in 1982 put the cards on the table. The opposition wanted nothing less than to depose the leaders of the new administration, and from that day, they were ruthless in defending their regime."

The history I didn't care about, but the coup was real enough to me. I began to look through the newspapers he discarded as he sorted through them. Nairobi. A clipping described the looting and police attempts to quash it. It estimated that one hundred forty-five people were killed, three of them white—an American, an Englishman, and a Belgian: C.J. Brewer, Roger Cage, and Andre Beligne.

I gasped when I read it, then quickly checked to see if Merit had noticed. He was absorbed in his own thoughts. I drew the clipping onto my lap, studied it, and couldn't resist a little puff. C.J. Brewer had been reported dead in the riots. When Merit wasn't looking, I slipped the clipping into my purse.

"What will your father think when he finds out I am here?"

I stretched and yawned. "He won't. Don't even think of it. You'll be my secret."

"Secret. You always were secretive, Kate. Why so secretive?"

"It's just the way I am."

"Tell me a deep dark secret. The deepest, darkest."

So I told him about Tony.

"That's it?" He roared and raised his arms in a big shrug. "You have your eye on a married man. That is not such a big deal, Kate. Maybe not the best idea, but not a big deal."

"If you want to know the truth..." An alarm bell went off in my head as I realized just how drunk I was, my guard way too far down. "I did get married once."

"Ah, you did! You said you never married."

"No, I said... what did I say?" I knew I had deflected his question without lying. "I said I had plenty of men in my life. That's true. But misleading. I'm sorry. Anyway, I did get married once. Jeez, I can hardly believe it, and I can't believe I'm telling you. It was a long time ago. It was a mistake. It was an impulse, a secret."

"And now you have told me. Was that so bad?" He spread his arms, and I smiled, but a lance of fear ran through me. He could have no idea of the depth and darkness of this secret. "So you got married once. Why is that a secret? And now you are divorced? Where is he now?"

"Who knows? There's no record of him anywhere. Hasn't been for years. Merit? I don't want to talk about it."

I couldn't. It was as far as I had ever gone. How could I tell him about that day? Drunk and giggling with champagne, I had gone down to the courthouse in Richmond with my birth certificate and taken out a marriage license. What had I been thinking? I didn't have to do that. What a fool I was! And then holing up at the Hilton for a long weekend before we were married by a bleary-eyed justice of the peace. How could I explain that life-altering blunder? "It was an act of rebellion, but at the same time, I was ashamed."

He shook his head, squinting as though he didn't understand. So I tried to explain, feeling my way from word to word. It wore me out, trying to be honest while protecting my boundaries. I'd told so many lies. I didn't want to lie to Merit.

"I was young, but in some ways, I was mature for my age. When we first got here, I traveled to Massachusetts on my own and claimed my father's inheritance from a lawyer. How many seventeen-year-old girls do things like that? You know I wasn't protected when I was young. I grew up much too early, too free. But at the same time, I was naïve. I lived at home while in college. I never dated, except the one time, and that... well..." I dropped my voice to a mutter. "That was a disaster."

"Your father doesn't know about this... escapade?"

"No one knows but the two of us. And now you."

"When was this?"

"A long, long time ago."

"You left him? You divorced him?"

I shook my head and blew out a huge breath. "That's the problem. That's what I'm telling you. I never did divorce him." I shrugged. "That's my deep, dark secret: I'm married."

"Why not divorce him now?"

"I can't."

"Why not?"

"He... there's no trace of him."

"You do not know where he is?"

"I don't think there is a trace of him beyond the record of our marriage."

"Have you tried to find him? Hire a detective. Get a PI to find him."

"No."

"Why not?"

"Just no."

"Okay, okay." He sounded sleepy, bored almost.

I had spoken more sharply than I intended. "I'm sorry. I don't want to go there."

I must have dozed off. When I woke up, it was way late, and it took me a minute before I even knew where I was. Merit was browsing among his papers, wide awake and absorbed once again in his work.

I jumped up off the couch. "My God, I have to go." I was already racking my brain to remember how much I had told him. Merit was going to have to be kept well apart from everyone I knew.

He drove me back to my place in my car and took a cab home.

CHAPTER ELEVEN

I SLEPT DREAMLESSLY BUT NOT LONG enough. Friday morning, my eyes were gritty, and the sunlight coming in the window made them water when I tried to read my watch. I was dying to turn over and go back to sleep, but I had a meeting scheduled for ten o'clock with Anita and the photographer from the newspaper. I briefly considered calling in sick or letting them start without me, but I couldn't. The publicity was too important for my business.

So I got out of bed, feeling headachy and slightly nauseated from all the wine. I made strong coffee and stood dozing with my eyes closed while I toasted half a cinnamon raisin bagel. I felt in the little fridge for cream cheese, swiped the bagel with it, and sank my teeth in. Heaven.

I showered, blew out my hair, and put on a light silk pants suit made of one of those amazing weaves that never wrinkle. It was a crisp ivory color just short of too white. I added some of my grandmother's jewelry: an eight-stranded rope of rose quartz and pearls. Too much? I didn't think so. I added pearl studs to my ears and studied my reflection in the mirror. I compared myself to Tony's wife and thought I looked pretty good. Better dressed, for sure.

I checked my messages: six! So much for my night of freedom.

At six fifteen, a message from Pop. "Kate, I suppose you're at dinner. Just checking to see how the meetings went. I know it's important." Ridiculous.

At seven thirty: Tony. Tony! My hopes rose. What would he say? He hemmed and hawed and then reported lamely what he'd done that afternoon. Then he seemed to want to say more, then he seemed to want to get off the call quickly. "You don't need to call me back," he added, as if I might. It was exciting and mysterious. I played the message twice more and saved it just so I could hear his voice.

At eight: Pop again. "Kate? Still at dinner? Just wondered how it went. Give me a call." Check in, in other words.

At nine: Tony again. "Kate?" Checking what time to be at Mary's Grove the next morning, and again he signed off abruptly. He was sneaking calls. I had to laugh. I wondered what he would have said if I had answered.

At nine thirty: Pop. "Kate? Just a little concerned. I don't like that neighborhood after dark. Just a little worried about you, sweetheart." Right. My safety. A wave of bitterness swept over me. My safety and security were my prison walls.

And at ten: click. No message. Pop's number.

"Oh, for God's sake." I erased all of Pop's messages, sped across town, and arrived at Mary's Grove. I got out of the car, went inside, and found Anita, Tony, and a woman about my age who looked vaguely familiar. Beryl was nowhere to be seen.

"Kate," Anita said. "This is the photographer."

I didn't catch the name. She had lusterless, gingery hair and the kind of coloring that had all the worst aspects of redheadedness without the red hair: mealy white skin and freckles so dense they almost ran together. I wondered what she could do: dye it red and use more white makeup and blush? Then I dismissed it. Not my problem.

My own hair color is natural, and I wear no makeup at all. I don't need it. Too many women cover up their natural beauty. Not me.

Tony said in a low voice, "I tried to call you."

I leaned in close and touched his arm with a fingertip. "Hey, we can talk later."

Anita stood up and beamed at all of us. "Let's go on outside."

On the way out, the photographer tapped me on the shoulder. "I loved the article about your garden."

I thanked her and led the way out onto the sweeping front lawn.

Anita had dressed for the camera in a long red tunic and slim black pants. Tony looked outstanding in an ice-blue golf shirt and chinos. It was a gorgeous day for a photo shoot, but the photographer had no concept of light. She tried to photograph us with the morning sun behind us, with us standing in the deepest shade of the trees. Then she tried to put us in front of the water with the sun in our eyes. She put Anita close up in direct sun so she was squinting and sweating.

I took charge as tactfully as possible and set up a shot of the three of us in the middle of the slope. Our heights were good together, Anita and I both about five foot five and Tony five foot ten or eleven. I supervised several artful shots of the house and grounds with the river in the background. Then we went inside to photograph Anita in the flattering light of her own sunroom. I posed for what I was sure would be a dynamite shot of me with my design on an easel.

The girl wanted to know if I would email her the design of the garden. I let a long few moments go by before I answered that ridiculous question. Number one, she was talking about expensive, proprietary information in a format that a clueless newspaper reporter couldn't read, and number two, I wanted her to use that shot of me next to it, looking like a million bucks. But I didn't say any of this. Instead, I offered to give her images I already had.

"In fact," I said, "I can give you a picture, in case this doesn't turn out the way you want it, of Tony and me at the Longwood garden."

But no. Naively, she came right out and told us she was trying get her own photography published.

When all the pictures were done, Anita served a tray of coffee and little sandwiches in the sunroom on a low wicker table. We ate in silence. Then Tony asked who was writing the article.

"I am," the photographer said.

Anita cocked her head. "Oh, are you a writer, too? I thought you were the photographer."

I was glad she and Tony asked about who would write the article, because I was supposed to know.

The reporter looked right at me. "I do plan to do a full-length feature, but I thought it would be a great chance to use my background in photography, if I could get some good shots today."

I played that back, fishing. "So you're trying to move more into photography."

"You know I've always loved that side of it. That was my real passion when I was in school. I was a journalism major, but I took Professor Kliner's Art of the Camera course when I was a junior, and then the class did that show." She turned to Anita. "Kate and I went to Sweet Briar together."

My life passed before my eyes. I did a lightning mental replay of everything I'd said since she arrived and concluded that I hadn't given myself away. She thought I knew perfectly well who she was, and finally, I did. The townie! Of course. No wonder she looked so familiar. I should have guessed from the clothes.

Then she said, "I was thinking, Kate, we could do another magazine article."

"I'm not planning any more magazine articles at the moment."

Anita asked, "Aren't you going to write a book?"

"I'm writing one, yes. I have a contract." Sort of.

"I could help," the townie said. "And I could promote it in the article about the party."

"That would be premature." I gave her what I hoped

was a firm and repressive look before turning back to Anita with a smile. "The focus of this article should be Mrs. Blore's garden. What she's doing here is amazing. It's a privilege for Tony and me to work on this."

There were murmurs all around. Anita demurred: No, she was lucky we were doing this for her. Tony seconded my appreciation for the job, and the townie sounded somewhat miffed.

"So," I said to mollify her, "what's your main beat? Gardens, society? The *Living* section?"

"All that, and events of general interest." She was zeroing in on me in a way that made me even more apprehensive. "Like, I saw you last night. I tried to flag you down, but you didn't see me."

I blinked.

Then Tony asked, "What was the event, Sabrina?"

So that was her name. Sabrina. Then I remembered: Sabrina Cole. I interrupted. "Your last name is still Cole, right, Sabrina? That's your byline, isn't it? I think I've seen it." A lie.

Sabrina glanced back and forth between Tony and me. "Yes," she said to me. Then she turned back to Tony. "The symposium at VCU about Kenya."

My memory of the night before was alarmingly incomplete, but I knew I didn't want to announce where I had been, or with whom. I tried deflection. "You know I was born in Kenya."

Of course, Sabrina knew that, as did Tony and Anita. Sabrina went straight back to her point. "I was there last night, too. I saw you, but you didn't see me. You were with that speaker."

I played it down. "I saw something, a flier, I forget where, and I was interested. I don't keep up with what's going on there politically, but I thought I'd see."

"And you knew that one speaker," Sabrina persisted. "What's his name?" I didn't supply it, so she grabbed her notebook, flipped through, and found it. "Chenobo. Merit Chenobo."

I had a flashback to the night before, of Merit working his way back to me, answering questions from students and bystanders, including evidently, Ms. Cole.

Anita was all ears. "You knew the speaker from when you lived in Africa?"

Sabrina said, "He told me you were an old friend from Africa."

"I knew him from when we were kids, and I haven't seen him since."

Anita seemed to be delighted with that information. "How interesting! Do you have many friends in Africa?"

"No, none." My voice sounded overly emphatic, so I added, smoothing my hair back and trying to sound casual, "I didn't know what had become of Merit until a few weeks ago."

Sabrina had been fiddling with her laptop. She spun it around and showed us the screen. "I took one picture with you in it. It's a great picture. Don't you think?"

We all looked, and I felt myself flush, which was the last thing I wanted.

I hate that I blush so easily. I can manage my expression, but I can't do anything about the color of my face.

In the photo, Merit exuded physical power and power of personality as well. He might have seemed sexually powerful to them as well. To make it worse, I clung to his arm with both hands. I knew I had been rattled and felt threatened at that moment, but I didn't look it. I just looked delicate and graceful hanging there. It was a great picture of me—I have always been photogenic—but I had meant to keep Merit and my friendship with him off the radar.

Anita leaned in to study every detail of the photo. "He's very handsome."

I said, "It was a fun, chance encounter, but an awful

crowd. Very rowdy. Frightening. I was glad to get away. So, Sabrina, do you have everything you need for the article about Anita's party? Are we about done here?"

We all stood, and Sabrina showed us her yellow teeth. "Sure, I guess so. But I did need to talk to you."

Anita showed us out. What I wanted was a little time with Tony, and he was lingering as if to wait for me, but I could feel Sabrina breathing down my neck. I caught Tony's eye and lifted one finger, then I led Sabrina to my car.

I tossed my things on the seat and jangled my keys at her. "Is there something I can help you with?"

"I just wondered when we could talk about that other thing."

"What other thing?" *What a pest.*

"I called your house."

The hackles rose on the back of my neck. "What? When?"

"When it first hit the news. About the Jefferson appeal."

I couldn't find breath to answer. She looked like someone enjoying the sight of a car wreck, eager and hungry. I licked my lips. She was a classmate, so of course she knew all about Elliott and me, about the trial, oh, everything. I checked: Tony was too far away to hear, though he glanced toward us once or twice. A sudden, fierce anger brought tears to my eyes.

She said, "I talked to your dad. I thought maybe he'd tell you I called."

"You told him you were a reporter—"

"I am."

I spoke through clenched teeth. "That means you leave the victim out of it."

"I just thought you might like to tell your side of it. Maybe you still think it was him, or maybe you have an idea who else it could have been."

She had the hide of a reporter all right. I couldn't help the wetness in my eyes. It was anger, not defenselessness or sorrow, and it made me angrier that she seemed to sense weakness.

She said with a show of sympathy that didn't fool me one bit, "Well, if you need a friend in the media at some point, you can work with me. We could do an exclusive interview. Lay it all out from your point of view."

I wanted to bite back, but something told me it would be stupid to antagonize her. I twitched up the corners of my mouth with an effort and said, "Excuse me." I got in my car, stalled around, and took out my phone.

I raised my eyebrows, and she slowly withdrew. I stared back. I was afraid to look at Tony, for fear she would follow my eyes and tackle him. I was sending him telepathic messages: *Don't leave. Wait for me.* Finally, reluctantly, Sabrina got in her own car and drove away. I heaved a huge sigh of relief and climbed back out, feeling positively shaky.

Tony had been rummaging around in his truck, but he stopped when I approached, and our eyes met. Relief poured through me as we both glanced at Sabrina's disappearing car. I wanted to run and throw myself in his arms. Maybe I could have. Instead, I walked over to him slowly. It was after noon, and the sun was hot, the shade in the surrounding woods deep and dark. I took off my jacket, shook it out, and pulled my hair up off my neck. A cool breeze drifted up from the river. Tony leaned against his truck. His skin looked dark and smooth against the ice blue of his shirt.

Close up, I could see the gold of the sun reflected in his eyes. "Hey. You called?"

His lips curled up a little. "It was nothing. I was going to say I wouldn't be here early." He seemed to be pretty sure of me, and I didn't mind that.

"Did you drive all the way back to Virginia Beach last night?"

He nodded. His eyes traveled down. I'd worn a little

lacy shell under my jacket, hardly more than a camisole, with a next-to-nothing bra underneath. I hadn't thought I'd take the jacket off. The warm, dry air felt good on my bare skin.

He said, "Nice necklace."

I looked down at the rose quartz and pearls that lay in the curve between my breasts, and warmth spread through my body. "Do you always drive all the way back at night?" Breathless. *Do you ever stay in town alone? In a hotel?*

He pulled his eyes back up to mine. "Depends. Most often."

He looked at my hair as though he might want to touch it. So I swept it all around to one side and left the other shoulder bare except for the thread-like strap of the camisole.

I had to think for a moment what his answer meant. "It's a long way."

"It's about two hours."

I was pretty sure we understood each other. "Where do you stay when you don't go home?"

The little smirk broke into a good-natured smile. "Cheapest motel I can find." Then he added, "Sometimes I split a room with Mike."

Mike again. I must have made a face at that, because now Tony laughed.

I said, "What is he, your chaperone?" It came out exasperated, but I matched his broad grin, and our eyes were locked together. He was teasing me, but that was okay. *Go ahead, toy with me.* It felt gentle, almost tender. He was keeping me off-balance, but I loved it because I was pretty sure it was going my way. I felt like saying, "What about tonight?" But he started throwing things in the truck.

"You're leaving now?" I couldn't help but sound dismayed.

"Soccer game after school." He ducked his head, looking sheepish.

I turned away so he wouldn't see how it stung me, that unwanted glimpse of domesticity. I didn't even like to think about the children angle, which was an even worse complication than marriage. I put on my jacket.

I started asking him about the job, incoherent run-on questions just to keep the conversation going. I trailed after him as he checked around for stray tools and picked up bits of trash. I glanced toward the windows where I thought Anita might be watching. I wondered if she'd seen me with my jacket off. Tony asked me about the book, and I said I'd use the Longwood garden. I told him I had a great picture with him in it and mentioned that I'd like to start using his roses. Again, I suggested that we could work together.

He paused and narrowed his eyes. "I don't know."

"Work is all I mean." Our eyes met. "Why not? We'd be good together."

"That might be why not." He threw one last empty soda can in the bed of his truck.

"Would Beryl mind?"

He didn't say so, but I knew I had it right by the way his face lost all good humor. The sense of fun we'd had a few minutes earlier drained away.

"I thought maybe you brought her yesterday as an amulet." When his face went blank, I explained, "To ward off evil." He didn't return my smile, so I added, "Just kidding."

I was starting to feel like a fool. Was he just playing me? Had I imagined that he felt anything for me? But when I turned to go, he followed me. I opened my car door, he held it, and for a moment I thought he might reach for me. I could feel his body pulling at my center, but he was on his way home to her, so I tossed my hair and dropped into the driver's seat. I said, "See ya next week," and he pushed the car door shut.

As I pulled away, I saw him in the rearview mirror

looking after me. I was still pretty sure of him, but I felt a little dashed. I'd wanted more, and after coming so close again, I was in a fever.

Disappointment faded as I drove west, mulling over in my mind every little thing we'd talked about. I couldn't have been wrong about the way he looked at me, the things we said about staying overnight. I laughed out loud at the idea of the cheap motel. Oh, definitely, Tony in a cheap motel. But then my heart sank. The idea of a cheap motel got me tingling inside, but the idea that I might just be a cheap trick for him made me squirm. I wanted more. He really liked me, didn't he? It was more, wasn't it? Did he feel the same way I did? Because I was crazy over the whole thing.

Before I knew it, I was pulling into my driveway. The house, as always, was beautiful, with the soft green hills and blue mountains in the background. But as I shut off the car, I felt oppression settle in. I knew I'd be in for the third degree, and sure enough, when I walked in the door, Pop was all over me. Where had I been? Why hadn't I returned his calls? How would he know if something had happened to me?

He had another one of those everlasting gourmet dinners going. I smelled mushrooms and butter—I sometimes suspected he would like to make me fat—and red wine on his breath as I whisked by.

He followed me up the stairs to my room, where I would have slammed the door in his face except that he was hanging on it. I didn't want him in my room. He would hover while I unpacked, trying to see what I had in my briefcase, looking for clues.

"I turned off my phone," I said, pushing him back with the door. "Okay? Think about it: What did I do last Thursday night when you were there with me? Do you remember how late I worked? I get tired, Pop."

He began to grouse about how he worried when he didn't know if I had gotten in safe.

"I know, Pop, I know." I tried to ease the door shut, but then he mentioned Tony. "What about Tony?"

He said Tony hadn't known where I was either. The door was about four inches open. I couldn't see Pop.

A few ticks went by while I sorted it out. "How do you know what Tony thought?"

"He called."

"He called here?" I was momentarily disarmed, and Pop tried to push his way in again. I stopped the door with my foot.

"Yes. He was looking for you, too." Pop couldn't see my face, either, and just as well, because I couldn't help grinning at the news.

I made my voice dull. "My phone was off. I was tired." How many times had Tony tried to reach me? What would he have said?

I pushed Pop back and quietly but firmly shut my door. I figured it was useful, Pop knowing that I hadn't been with Tony. If things worked out the way I wanted, one night, I would be.

CHAPTER TWELVE

B ETWEEN SOPHOMORE AND JUNIOR YEAR, Pop and I made another trip to Europe. Pop was happiest when we were travelling in the summers, especially in Europe. Although he loved our house and gardens in Virginia, he remained aloof from the people in our community. He insisted they were rural, overly religious, conservative, uncultured, and uneducated. Benighted, he would call them. Under all the bluster and disdain, he wasn't happy with our life there.

"I thought you liked the role of country squire," I said.

But I knew what he meant. I loved my new fantasy-come-true life in the States as a rich girl living with her father and going to a swanky college, and I had no desire to relinquish it. He sometimes talked about moving to another part of the country, or even to Europe, and starting all over, in a place where we could "be ourselves and fit in better"—meaning where *he* could fit in. I always put him off. I insisted that I first needed to finish college. But he was relieved and happy when we went away in the summers.

I suggested Paris, so I could practice my French and we could meet up with Lisa and her parents, who would be there for two weeks. Pop was adamant: no way would he make a fifth wheel, as he called it, with her two parents and us two girlfriends. He wanted only me for his companion. For the first time I began to get the sense that he depended on me, and that I was all he had. I didn't mind the idea so much then.

We settled on Portugal, where we spent a month on the Algarve. There, we were peaceful and solitary, safely shut away from both our past in Africa and our present in Virginia. I found myself missing my newfound friend, though. I sent Lisa postcards and often thought of things I'd like to tell her.

We stayed at a beautiful hotel with a palm court that opened onto the rocky beach. We drove to Faro, where the shopping was fantastic. Pop shipped home an entire case of very old Porto, and I bought Lisa dangling crystal earrings and a silk scarf with a hand-painted pattern of little animals and flowers. But by the end of the summer, I couldn't wait to go home and start school.

When we got back, we settled into our familiar routines. Pop was all about haute cuisine, and he had stocked a wine cellar. He employed a housecleaner and had the shopping done from lists he made. In the evening, after I came home from class, he sent the housekeeper home, and we both dressed for dinner. Later, while Pop cleaned up, I sat at my desk in the attic, looking out over the darkening fields and mountains.

But a subtle shift had taken place. As I started my junior year of college, I was being drawn into the community of girls my own age. I signed up for a seminar that met in the evenings, and on those nights, I had dinner with Lisa on campus. I began receiving phone calls, mostly from Lisa, who would chat with Pop while she waited for me to come downstairs—we had only one telephone, on the first floor—but one or two other girls sometimes called, usually about a class or an assignment or sometimes to invite me to go somewhere. Most of the girls didn't have cars, so I was in demand for the occasional shopping foray into Charlottesville or even Richmond. They wouldn't have asked me to go with them if it hadn't been for the car, and I told Pop that when he complained, which he often did.

"We're going shopping. It's girl stuff. For heaven's sake, Pop, sometimes I just want to be with people my own age."

I thought it would help if he could see it firsthand, so I invited some girls from classes, some of my more studious friends, to study for midterms at our house. Pop made a pizza with a yeasty crust, fresh mozzarella, and pesto. None of them had ever tasted anything like it. He charmed them with his courtly manners. He was by then a vigorous man nearing fifty, but he seemed old to most of my friends, and I saw him through their eyes for the first time.

We took over the living room, sprawling on the floor between the stately wingback chairs and Victorian settees. We shouted over each other, making fun of European history. Pop made a show of putting coasters under all our glasses and retired to his study. But when he drifted by later in the evening they—not I, they—were talking about boys. *Men*, they called the boys.

Afterward, Pop wanted to know where the boys were from, since Sweet Briar was an all-girls school.

"The University of Virginia, mostly," I told him. "One's from Hampden-Sydney."

"Have you met any of them?" He feigned polite curiosity, but the right eye was keen.

"One or two. They're as stupid as can be. Young and stupid, all of them."

"No younger than you."

"Light-years younger in every way that counts."

But he persisted. "It didn't sound like you were so disinterested."

I had said nothing, but I didn't correct him. "Wouldn't it be odd if a group of girls never talked about boys?"

What did he expect? Of course they talked about boys sometimes. Boys were on their minds. But I wasn't interested. I went to class and came home.

But then, it dawned on me, another new idea: Pop was worried about boys. He needn't have been. Those girls swooned over impossibly puffed-up and pimply boys who came to parties on the weekends. I had no earthly interest in them. They seemed very young and inexperienced. And they were hopelessly intimidated by me. Oh, they sniffed around me like ill-mannered pups. I was no innocent, and no one knew it better than Pop, and that was why he was so suspicious. But he needn't have worried about those boys. They would look away when I faced them down. I was too grown-up for them and, not to sound immodest, too beautiful.

Oh, I know as well as the next person that you're not supposed to outright call yourself beautiful. But what if you are? Was I supposed to not notice? I've never understood why women are expected to deny it, even to themselves, if they're beautiful.

"Stay out of trouble," he would say.

"What trouble?" I asked, smart-alecky.

Sometimes my friends would want to go to a movie, and other times, they would want to meet up with boys, and I'd go along with them. I would drive, like a parent, and stay aloof from the boys. I would lie to Pop, but there was nothing to it, so in a sense it wasn't even a lie.

"It's no big deal," I told him once. "We went to a movie. How weird would I be if I never went anywhere with anybody?"

One afternoon, I called him from Lisa's dorm to say I wouldn't be home until at least nine. "I just want to see an old movie on campus with some girlfriends. *Singing in the Rain*." I knew Pop loathed that one. In fact, we were going to drive into Charlottesville to see *Amadeus*. He loved Mozart and would have wanted me to wait and see that with him. I added, "No, no boys."

After I hung up, Lisa asked, "Why do you have to tell him no boys? Wouldn't he let you go out with anybody?"

"He would, but I don't want to deal with all the questions."

She said, "I never understood girls who sneak around. This is why it's better to go away to college. Who needs their parents interfering?"

Pop and I went out sometimes. He liked to go to concerts: symphonies, opera singers, famous pianists, and virtuosos, that kind of thing. On those occasions, we would go to Richmond or even spend a weekend in Washington, DC. He liked to get away and go out for dinner at a good restaurant. I liked it, too, but I also liked the music my friends played, Michael Jackson and Madonna. And Prince. They liked to dance to loud, goofy local bands in Lynchburg and Charlottesville. Pop? He hated rock 'n' roll. And dance? He'd rather die.

I lied about where I was a lot to avoid dealing with the issue. I felt I was missing something if I didn't go out with my friends to listen to music and dance. I was a dancer. I wanted to dance. So I'd tell Pop I was going to study with my friends or go to the library.

"On Friday night?" The right eye drilled into me. "Don't lie to me, Kate."

"I'm not lying." I looked him in the eye and threw it back at him. "I'm going to the library on a Friday night, when other girls are going out on dates. I'm the prissy girl in the white tower." That was how I had come to see myself, dramatizing as usual.

Pop growled in disgust. "You believe your own fantasies."

I'll grant that I was difficult. For the first time, I envied the girls who lived away from home, on their own to try their wings whatever way they wanted. But at the same time, I liked the life I'd chosen. I was torn. I was only nineteen! I didn't know what I wanted.

I warned Lisa, who might chat with Pop when she called me, not to say anything about us going out dancing.

She rolled her eyes. "Why not?"

"He thinks I was at the library."

"Why do you put up with it? Tell him to butt out. Tell him you're having some fun with your friends."

"You don't know what you're talking about."

But I was using Pop as an excuse. I made him out to

be an old-fashioned, super-strict parent, which of course was the furthest thing from the truth. At that point, I didn't care about going out, mainly because I hadn't met anybody who could tempt me. Boys my own age? Never.

Lisa was my kindred spirit. She was still hung up on the older guy from Florida, the one she'd dropped out over as a freshman. He'd graduated and gotten a job in Washington, DC, and she was seeing him again. She was with him most weekends while I stayed home. But weeknights, she and I went out to drink and dance. I wanted to close my eyes and move to the rhythm of a dark, pulsing place, and I didn't want to answer to anyone about it. We got more daring, going into night clubs where they weren't so careful who they served liquor to.

Pop continued to object. He knew I was lying to him, even though I vehemently denied it. One time, when I told him I had to go to the library to study, he offered to drive me to school and pick me up. That made me furious. He tried to say it wasn't safe for me to be driving around late at night.

I scoffed. "Not safe? Look at this place. What's the crime rate? Where's the crime? I drive two miles home from school in a locked car."

But of course, I often wasn't driving home from school but from smoky places with live music. Then from local dives with jukeboxes or funky amateur groups that were no good. I still disdained college boys, but I liked to pick up local guys to dance with. Those guys meant nothing to me. I was testing my powers.

"Your father would have a cow," Lisa said after I had flirted and danced with a particularly disreputable-looking local redneck. It cracked her up.

Actually, the guy was quite sexy in a punk kind of way, and he amazed me with his uninhibited, creative dancing. He spun me fast enough to make my hair wrap around my face. I was dizzy and breathless when I sat back down.

Late in the spring of my junior year, I went to the Tavern for the first time with Lisa. She was the one who knew about the Tavern, a grubby local joint behind a gas station on Highway 29. The inside was smoky and dark, with neon beer signs. The place was creepy, as a matter of fact, which was why I liked it. I was slumming; I wanted a dive, something down and dirty. Maybe I was rebelling from my princess persona, which was starting to feel like a cage. We went to the Tavern more than once.

Boys might have been intimidated by me; men were not. I could attract male attention when I wanted to. So could Lisa, but not like me. We competed, and between us, we'd often have everybody in the place looking at us out of the corners of their eyes. Or flat-out staring. We'd huddle our heads together and laugh, half drunk, and say suggestive things to the waiter when we ordered drinks. Maybe take off a shirt or sweater and sit around in a little T-shirt without a bra. Lisa was a stunner, but her skin was chalky white, while mine was every square inch peaches and cream.

We would flirt with anybody, men at other tables, the bartender, men sitting at the bar. We didn't have to pay for many drinks. We'd dance with strangers to music that the bartender played on a tape deck behind the bar. It got positively scary when we led guys on and then blew them off, but I was reckless enough to think it was exciting.

In the parking lot one night, a couple of guys I vaguely recognized were waiting for us by my car. They wanted us to go drinking with them after hours at a place they knew.

"Yeah, right," I said. "Fuck off."

I had never used that word before, and I liked the way it felt: tough. One of them, short and pudgy, blew us off, disgusted, but the other one, a good-looking guy, but macho with a big chip on his shoulder, didn't move.

I said again, "Fuck off. Get off my fucking car."

Lisa ran back inside, but I stood there and stared down Macho Man. Or tried to. He wasn't giving ground.

The bartender, an easygoing black ex-football player, came out and intervened. When the other guys drove away, he asked, "Have I ever carded you two ladies?" When neither of us answered, he said, "I'm going to suggest you stop coming around here before you get yourself into more trouble than you can handle."

It was almost the end of the year anyway. We were already picking out our classes for senior year, and Lisa, a drama major, had Elliott Davis as her faculty advisor, and the way she talked about him caught my attention. She was cagey, almost as if she didn't want to share him, and she always got a dreamy look on her face when she said his name.

Then one day we ran into him crossing campus, going in the opposite direction, and I realized I had seen him around. It was the briefest of encounters. I could tell instantly that Lisa didn't have anything going on with him—he paid no attention to her—but she was crazy for him, and what's more, I could see why. He noticed me, for sure. An electric current went zap, and we were both goners. Lisa didn't see it. I had one elective open for the fall, and I had half-decided on astronomy. I changed my mind on the spot. I was going to take Theater 101.

One more summer, one more year, and I would be finished with school. Then what? Everything had been changing so fast since we'd come to Virginia from Nairobi. Everything but Pop. It was crystal clear that his life revolved around me, and for the first time, it was an unpleasant sensation. Once it had been us against the world, with him as my protector and provider, but by that time, he was a man looking toward the end of the day. He was still vigorous, still handsome; it was like a trick of light. The difference was that he was at a destination, whereas I felt poised at a starting point.

Now, when I look back on myself at nineteen, it occurs to me that the whole time, I was setting myself up. But there's no use thinking like that. What happened happened: murder, the trial, and most recently, the exoneration.

Suzanne, determined to "help" me by keeping me in touch with the AG's office, came back on Monday just as I got in from teaching class. We sat once again on the screened in porch, while Pop hovered nearby. She told me she'd found one of the investigating officers.

"Why?" I made no effort to hide my displeasure. "What did you do that for?"

Suzanne's face fell, and her grey-blue eyes widened. "I'm sorry. I wanted to understand the case better. I wanted to ask her whether you would have to testify." She bit her lip.

I knew she wanted me to reassure her that it was okay, but I couldn't. I felt only the deepest misgiving and dismay. "I don't want to stir this up. I want it over with."

"But that's just it. That's what I found out. I can assure you now: there is no point in asking you to testify again all these years later."

"Of course not," I said. "I can't even picture Jefferson's face now. I know I was pretty sure at the time of the trial that I had seen him at the Tavern on the night of the murder." I only remembered the incident with Jefferson at the Tavern because I had to tell it over and over, to the cops, to the DA, on the stand.

Suzanne started to explain the legal proceedings, but I interrupted to ask, "Who did you talk to?"

"Elsa Gabriel."

I blew out my breath and glanced at Pop. "She's horrible."

Suzanne's lips parted, but she said nothing, looking pained.

"She must be ancient now," I added. She was a hag at the time.

Suzanne flinched almost imperceptibly at the contempt in my tone. Then she recovered her composure. "She's retired."

As if I would care. "The very mention of her takes me right back to that night." The memory was so real that I felt it in the pit of my stomach. I saw Officer Gabriel's predatory eyes. The Hyena, I called her. That was what she reminded me of: short, square, with a chin that was directly connected to her chest, round ears and close-cut, stiff hair of graying beige. Her heavy body strained her dark blue uniform, and she walked with a slow, swaggering gait, wearing orthopedic shoes and every possible piece of hardware and weaponry, radio squawking. I had hated her on sight.

Suzanne leaned forward. "I know. The people—even the ones who are on your side and who have helped you—you don't want to see them after a point, or think of them, because they remind you."

Suzanne thought she understood, but she didn't. Elsa Gabriel did not help me.

"Anyway, according to Lieutenant Gabriel, your eyewitness testimony was the lynchpin in the prosecution case. There was no question Jules Jefferson got into an altercation with Elliott Davis and threatened him."

Pop cleared his throat. "Jefferson himself admitted that, and all his friends."

Suzanne turned to him almost as if she'd forgotten he was there. "We do know it was Jefferson earlier, at the Tavern." She looked back at me. It occurred to me that Suzanne didn't seem to like Pop much. She always ignored him as much as possible. "Elsa said they never found the gun." *Elsa! How chummy.* "She said they only had the eyewitness testimony."

Pop spoke up again. "It was enough."

Suzanne waited a moment, then continued. "According to Elsa, there was only your eyewitness testimony that it was Jefferson who assaulted you later that night. If DNA testing shows it was somebody else later..." She made a pleading little shrug.

"It was dark..." I gripped the arms of my chair to steady myself. "I..." I felt cold and couldn't go on.

"I understand." Suzanne leaned forward and touched my shoulder with a tremulous hand. "I know, Kate. I know. But the point is, the DNA profile takes away the testimony, so there's no point in your repeating it. Elsa said eyewitness testimony is wrong more often than not when the attacker is a stranger, when it's dark, or in traumatic circumstances. And it deteriorates over time. Juries like it, but it isn't very reliable. She said there would be no point in your trying to testify again. No point at all. She understands, Kate. She knew you wouldn't want to be questioned again."

She sat back and folded her hands in her lap. "That's why they sent me and not a prosecutor or detective. There's no reason for you to be involved. I am here to keep you informed. If you want to be."

I made myself sit back and unclench my hands. "I'm sorry, Suzanne. I do want to know what's going on, and I'm grateful for all you're doing. I really am. Thank you." I meant it. I needed her. Like it or not, I had to know what was going on with the case.

When she left, I warned Pop, "This is an open case again."

He waved me off with a hand signal, the one that meant contempt.

CHAPTER THIRTEEN

O N THURSDAY MORNING OF THE week of Anita's party, we were sitting in the dining room, sun pouring in through the lace curtains. Pop had made eggs Benedict, and we were drinking coffee from my grandmother's silver service.

I told him I was going to go into Richmond alone, just for the day. "Anita wants me to help out with the house. She's bought new furniture and lots of fresh flowers. We might even go shopping for some cushions and vases. Unless you want to go and help decorate? If you do, I'll stay here. She would love it."

Pop said nothing, so I breezed on. "It's not Anita's fault the house is so awful inside. It was her mother-in-law's doing. I try not to come right out and say the old lady had rotten taste, but she did. Anyway, this could take all day."

Silence.

"If I finish so late that I'd have to drive home in the dark, I'll spend the night, but I expect to come home. In any case, I'll be home in plenty of time for us to drive in together for the party tomorrow night. It's only a hundred miles." I was up and heading for the door. "If the party runs late, we can stay in Richmond tomorrow night." I was almost out the door, calling back over my shoulder to where he still sat at the table. "Also, I've got to find time to shop for a new dress. I don't have a thing to wear."

I ran from the house into the bright summer morning. I had no intention of coming home that night, and there wasn't really all that much to do on the house. Anita was perfectly capable of furnishing her own home. I had other plans. I wanted to see both Merit and Tony, and I had an idea for another little project of my own.

When I arrived in Richmond, I called Merit from my apartment and agreed to meet him for lunch. I called Anita to say I'd come by that afternoon. And I called Tony to make sure Beryl wasn't with him. She wasn't. So far, so good. Tony would be at Anita's house, and we would see what happened that night.

That left me free for the rest of the morning. I brewed a pot of coffee and opened the front windows. A light breeze rustled leaves in the sycamore. I had told Merit I wouldn't hire a detective, but the more I thought about it, the better I liked the idea. It was scary, but it was a positive action I could take. I opened the phone book.

I immediately shied away from the firms with multiple investigators and offices in multiple cities. I wanted perfect secrecy, a single person operating in obscurity, which was why I started with the phone book. As if it had been designed especially for me, a small ad caught my eye: Max Confidential Investigations. It offered a single name: Max Weigel.

Then I paused. Merit had said to hire an investigator, but I didn't need a detective. I needed a divorce. So I looked up divorce lawyers, and that was even worse. Big law firms. I shut the book, then opened it again and looked some more. Apart from the big full and half-page ads, in the listing of attorneys, I saw the name again: Max Weigel.

I tried the Internet, searching for divorce lawyers and investigators. I saw all the same agencies and firms listed in the Yellow Pages. I had to Google Weigel by his name to find him, and the only listing was his website, which made me laugh. It was positively seedy, three pages of ugly fonts and the kinds of colors a he-man would choose. It couldn't have looked more down-market, and that was what I wanted.

So I dressed up like a woman who would drop in on Sam Spade. I put on a killer suit I'd bought on sale, made of a shiny black fabric, with a pencil skirt and a fitted jacket with a tiny waist and a longish ruffle from the waist down to the flare of the hip. I wore my grandmother's jet-beaded necklace and earrings. I thought about a hat but figured that would be too much, and anyway, I didn't have one. Then I checked myself in the mirror. I loved the outfit. I'd only ever worn it once, out to dinner and the opera with Pop. He was knocked out by it, but of course, he didn't count.

I set out with a queasy feeling in the pit of my stomach. I found Weigel's office not far from the courthouse in a neighborhood that was half residential, half commercial. Houses people still lived in tended to be rundown. The ones used for small businesses were more likely to be freshly painted and neatly landscaped. Weigel seemed to be the sole occupant of a small white-frame cottage with a sign in front offering a free twenty-minute consultation. Apparently, he was a criminal defense attorney, too, and by the looks of it, not a very successful one.

I glanced up and down the street, feeling stupid about being so furtive, and forced myself to walk up to the front door. I was so nervous my knees felt as if they could buckle any minute. My heels sounded loud on the plank porch, so I tiptoed the last few steps, feeling even stupider. I heard a soft animal sound from inside the house. I was leaning forward, trying to figure out what had made it, when the door opened. I jumped and cried out.

A man stood just inside the door, looking at me curiously. He was tall and bulked up with the heavy arms and shoulders of a fighter. I jumped again when I saw a large German shepherd standing next to him, also looking at me curiously.

The man glanced at the dog. "It's okay. She won't hurt you." It wasn't clear which one of us he said it to.

I pulled myself together and asked him very tartly if he did investigations. I was hating every minute of the ordeal, though I liked what I was seeing. He was the kind of person I thought I needed.

He stuck out his hand. "Yeah, sure. Come on in." His grip was crushing. "Max Weigel."

I gave my name as Katherine Brewer. For a split second, I thought he was going to introduce me to the dog, but catching my look, he seemed to think better of it. He motioned me into a bare front room dominated by a big green wooden desk. It was probably once a teacher's desk sold off at auction and painted to cover all the scribbling and scuffs. I had a choice between a straight wooden chair and a squashy fake leather armchair with a busted-out seat. I sat on the edge of the former. The dog went to a blanket in the corner of the room and lay down.

Max Weigel's hair was grizzled reddish brown, his skin dark and somewhat pitted. He was good-looking in a rugged way, a look I'd never cared for.

He sat behind the desk and checked me out for a beat or two. "I'm a criminal defense attorney, but I also do divorce. I have an associate who's a licensed PI. Most investigations do involve divorce, cheating. Like that."

"This is the situation," I said. "I got married quite a few years ago, and... how shall I put this? There seems to be no record of the man anywhere. No one knows how to find him, and I want to divorce him. How can I do this?"

He thought about that for a minute. "You got married, and you've lost contact with your husband. And now you want to divorce him."

I tapped my foot. Was the man an idiot? "That's what I said, yes."

"Well, the best thing to do is to find him and ask him if he'll agree to a divorce. If it's no contest, and depending on the situation, it shouldn't be a problem."

I shook my head. "I didn't say I want to contact him. I

don't. You won't find him. My question is, if I'm married to a man who can't be found, can I divorce him?"

He considered again. I began to have doubts about him.

"Have you tried to find him?"

"You won't find him," I repeated. "Take it as a hypothetical, if that will help." Surely a lawyer must have a concept of the hypothetical. "Suppose I once married a man who now cannot be found. Can I divorce him?"

He cleared his throat and shifted in his chair. "Just generally speaking, it's a good idea to find a spouse before you enter into the divorce proceedings."

He held up his hand when I began to stand up. "Short answer: yes."

I sat back down.

"But like I said, it's a good idea to find him if you can." He rocked back in his chair and spread his arms. "If your spouse has a pension, a retirement account, insurance, or any other significant property, you want to know about that. If you don't address these issues in the divorce, you give them up forever."

"I don't care about any of that."

"Besides, if you can find him and talk to him, you can ask him how he feels about the divorce." Weigel shrugged. "If you haven't seen him in years, he probably won't care, will he? If not, it can be very easy. And if he does have a problem with it, it'll give you an idea how to proceed."

"I do not wish to contact him, but it won't be an issue."

"Suppose he wants your assets?"

Again, I considered leaving the office. The dog was alert, its head moving back and forth as if it were following our conversation with interest.

Weigel sensed my exasperation and got to the point. "To start the divorce process, you have to file a complaint in the circuit court where you or your spouse lives. In your case, this means in the circuit court where you live. That Richmond?"

I thought about that before I said yes. "I have a house in Lynchburg and an apartment here. Can I do it here?"

"If you change your permanent address, you'll have to wait six months to establish residency."

I waved him off. "Forget what court it is. Then what?"

"After you file your papers, your spouse has twenty-one days to respond. If he fails to respond, the court will proceed with the divorce so long as service of process has been completed correctly. That's going to be the catch. If you don't know where he is, you can't serve him."

I must have looked puzzled, because he explained, "Service means he has to be notified that you've filed a complaint with the court. You can't just divorce him without at least attempting to let him know so he can respond if he wants to. Maybe he won't want to contest it. Probably not, according to what you've told me. But he has to have the opportunity. And see, this is what I'm saying. If you don't contact him, you don't know how he's going to react. If you've got any assets—" His eyes flickered over my clothes and jewelry. "—he might want something. I don't know that he'd succeed in getting anything. But he could try. You want to be prepared for that."

"Suppose he can't be found. Then he can't be served. Can I still divorce him?" God, it was taking the man a long time to answer what I thought was a pretty simple question. "Yes or no."

He looked amused, which made me even more annoyed. "Short answer: yes. If you can't serve him, Virginia law does allow for posting the Subpoena and Complaint on the defendant's door if you can find an address. If you can't find an address, then you can serve him by publishing a notice in the newspaper."

I frowned, but he droned on. "Now, whether or not your spouse responds, you'll have to appear before a commissioner in Chancery." He launched into what was obviously a canned speech. He talked about things like testimony, evidence, and appearances in court. I didn't like everything he said, but I liked the way it ended: "The judge should sign it within a few days. And voila, you're done."

The dog was asleep.

"Could you investigate whether he can be found?"

"Sure, I can do that." He harrumphed. "You'll be claiming grounds of desertion, I assume. You have to wait a year after the event of desertion before you file for an absolute divorce. I take it more than a year has elapsed?"

"Many years."

"Like other states, Virginia requires what you call a diligent search to locate a spouse who cannot or will not be found. After you've done that, like I said, you can serve the defendant by publication." He rattled on about affidavits and orders and filing this and that.

I repeated the one word that was bothering me. "Publication."

He nodded. "In a newspaper where the missing spouse could see it."

I pursed my lips and chewed the inside of my cheek.

Weigel asked, "What was his last known address?"

"The Hilton."

He cocked his head. "What about the marriage license?"

I faltered. "I think he had it last."

"You're so sure I won't find him."

"You can try. But don't... promise me, don't let him know I'm looking for him. I want no contact. None. Do you understand me? No contact. None. You promise me." I couldn't control my voice.

He eyed me with lips pursed. I took a deep breath and sat back. I watched his eyes taking in the contours of my body. I was glad I'd worn the suit, not that I needed Max Weigel's admiration, but the look on his face was gratifying anyway.

"What will this cost me?"

He set down his pencil. "A thousand for the whole thing."

"What if we start with the missing person... what did you call it? A diligent search? Suppose you try just exactly as hard as the law requires, no harder, and then let me know if you've found him."

"Two fifty. Do you have his social security number?"

I shook my head.

"What's his full name?"

"Carl Brewer."

"Date of birth?"

"I don't know."

"Approximate year of birth?"

He was asking too many questions. "I told you, it was an ill-advised fling. I hardly knew him at the time."

He waggled his pencil.

I asked, "How do you go about finding a missing person?"

"It's a database search these days."

"What determines whether you'll find him?"

"The quality of the information I have to begin with. People with unusual names are generally easier to find than people with common names. Carl Brewer is what I'd call fairly common. Women tend to be harder to locate than men because of name changes due to marriage. Not an issue here. A missing person with a decent job and a normal lifestyle is generally easier to locate. But I don't suppose you know about any of that."

He paused with his eyebrows up, as if I might confirm that for him yet again. Silence stretched between us. The dog, awake again, rolled its eyes to me and back to its master, chin still on the floor.

He cleared his throat. "Right." He looked back at his notepad, which had nothing but the name Carl Brewer on it. "People who're in and out of jail and people who're being chased by creditors are usually very difficult to locate. A person who has no paper trail leading to a home or business is almost impossible to locate. With nothing but a common name?" He waggled the pencil again. "We probably won't find him. Or we'll find too many possibilities. We'd have to contact them all."

"Try," I said, standing. "But try only just as hard as the law will require for me to get a divorce. And remember: no contact."

"Want to give me your number?"

He sounded skeptical, and I smiled for the first time. I liked it that he didn't know what I was going to do. "I'll come back next week."

CHAPTER FOURTEEN

BACK AT THE APARTMENT, I had to laugh when I looked in the mirror and saw the Mysterious Client costume. What had I been thinking? I changed into blue jeans and a gabardine work shirt, grabbed my briefcase, and headed for Miguelito's, where I was supposed to meet Merit for lunch. I made it just in time, only to find when I checked messages on my cell, which had been turned off, that he was going to be thirty minutes late. I called him back, got voice mail, and left a message that I was fine, I had some work with me, and I'd see him when he got there.

I took a booth by the window where the light was good and spread out some papers. When the waitress came, I ordered a frozen margarita and settled down to think about what I'd done, hiring Max Weigel. Or tried to think about it. My mind was blank, but the first drink felt good, so I ordered another. I ate the whole basket of chips, too.

Then I noticed the waitress simpering around in my peripheral vision. "Yes?"

She explained that she was getting off soon—*at noon?*— and I took the hint. I waved a too-big bill at her and said, "Keep the change, but first, could you clean this up and bring fresh chips and salsa? And more water."

When Merit walked in ten minutes later, I sat innocently shuffling papers with an untouched basket of chips, a new bowl of salsa, and a half-empty glass of water. He sat down and apologized.

I smiled sweetly. "It's nothing. I needed to look through this stuff anyway."

He told me that the class he was teaching had run over time. "The students are contentious. They show up, and I don't want to say they heckle me, exactly, but let us say their questions are well planned and very challenging."

"I hate that, when people pretend to be asking questions, but they've already decided what the answers are."

I wanted to focus on what Merit was saying, but it was a struggle, and the alcohol didn't help. I did tune in, however, when he mentioned that he'd been threatened. "Seriously?"

He pushed the chips around abruptly, frowning at the basket. "Of course not."

"What? Tell me."

"It was hardly more than graffiti. Someone writing on the blackboard. Anonymously, of course."

"Writing what?"

He waved his hand. It wasn't the first time he'd been threatened, and I didn't follow what he was saying very well because I didn't understand all the movements, countermovements, and tribal factions he was always referring to. I tried to look interested, but my mind was wandering again.

"You're Kikuyu," I said. That was safe; I knew that much. "So what exactly did it say? I mean, today."

He paused for a second, and I wondered if I had missed something. "It is not important. There is no real violence meant here. I erased it before the first student arrived."

"Did you report it?"

"Of course. But my report will come to nothing."

I wanted to talk about my own problems, so I didn't try as hard as I should have to understand what was going on with him. To me it was simple: it was a struggle for power; someone would win, and someone would lose. I asked him if he had seen the article in the paper.

He asked, "What article?"

"About the symposium."

He shook his head, frowning. "No, I do not follow the press too closely. Not that kind, anyway. What did it say?"

His mind was running in a completely different direction. He was probably thinking about what it might have said about his politics and the conflict between him and the other side. I was talking about the picture of him and me together.

By that time, we had ordered enchilada plates with iced tea for him and a margarita for me. I told him about Sabrina Cole showing a picture of him and me to Anita Blore and Tony.

He looked at me as if I were speaking another language. "Why is that a problem?" He smiled, but his eyes remained serious, even impatient. "Being secretive again, Kate? Why?"

"We're going to a party there tomorrow night. I'm going, with Pop. He's coming with me."

"And?"

I sighed heavily. "This Blore woman, my client? She's got her eye on Pop, an idea which I admit I've promoted, and he keeps asking her about my love life. She tries to figure it out, and now she knows I spent last Thursday night with you."

He made a short, incredulous laughing sound. "Hardly."

"Well, I mean, that's what she might conclude."

"You are overreacting. Why not tell him about me? Tell him I am here and why. What is the harm?" The booming voice.

I stirred my food, put down my fork, and concentrated on my drink. I could see why he might think it was a nonissue, and I sighed again. No one, not even my oldest friend, could understand my situation.

Merit said, "He would not even know who I am."

"Pop? If he saw you?" I considered that. "No, Pop wouldn't know you if he saw you."

"It could be fifty years, and I would know your father if I met him."

"I think it's best if you and Pop don't meet."

"He could not possibly know me to see me. He hardly ever did see me."

I was thinking hard. The margaritas made it difficult. "But my father would know who you were if he heard your name."

"Would he really? I thought he might have forgotten. It has been almost thirty years."

"Merit, your grandfather and your father both worked on the same farm as him. He might not remember your first name. But he would know Chenobo. He would be able to figure out who you are."

He ran a finger around his jaw line. "True." He raised his hands and dropped loose fists onto the table. "And what if he did? What is wrong with seeing someone you knew in Africa?"

"He wouldn't want me anywhere near the politics you're mixed up in."

"My politics could not be dangerous to you. How?"

"Anyway, he's a terrible racist. White Africans of his generation? You know they are. They all are. No, Merit, you don't want him to even know you're here."

He shrugged, gave me a broad smile, and held up his hands in a placating gesture. "I am not going to see him. If he finds out about me from this woman, I cannot help that."

We both fell silent, eating our enchiladas, which really were quite good, made with lots of cumin, cheese, and thick red sauce. I ordered a fourth frozen margarita—my second as far as Merit was concerned. For someone who weighed only a hundred and twenty pounds, I could hold my liquor. I pushed aside my plate when the drink came and watched Merit clean up the last of his rice and beans. We played a few rounds of whatever-became-of-so-and-so. In most cases, Merit knew.

Africa seemed so impossibly far off. I had lived my whole life since then. In Merit, I was looking for myself as he had known me, before so much had so irrevocably changed me. But it struck me that he knew so little about me that it was hopeless.

I sucked noisily with the straw at the bottom of my empty margarita glass. I should have known my inhibitions were alarmingly relaxed. "I'm suffocating in Lynchburg, and I want to be free of Pop. I don't want him hovering over me, worrying about me, being possessive. What he considers protective is oppressive. Do you understand what I'm saying?"

His face became expressionless, the way it did when he was bored but too polite to say so. "Yes and no. I understand how you feel about wanting your own life. I do not understand why you do not have it. Why not move to Richmond or Charlottesville? Or somewhere even farther from him."

"He would follow me wherever I went, like he did when I went to graduate school."

"Just tell him. You want your own place. I do not see the problem, no."

"It's not that simple. Plus, there's the money. It's all his." My mood soured even further at the thought of Pop and his iron fist on the purse strings.

"Do you not earn your own money? Enough?"

I tried a different tack. "I have this huge feeling of failure about living at home, never having been out on my own. I'm in my forties, for God's sake. What am I doing living this way? It's like my life has passed me by."

"How passed you by? You are in demand for your gardens. And you tell me you have had relationships with men."

"No man has ever wanted to marry me."

He raised his eyebrows and poked a finger in my direction. "One man did. The other night, you told me that you once married."

I waved him off. "Other than that. That doesn't count. I mean the real thing, where you find your soul mate, fall in love, and he asks you to marry him. Like what you have."

"It is not like the fantasy."

"Come on, Merit, I'm not talking about a fantasy. There's paper—you can have a paper that says you're married, and that doesn't mean anything—and there's real marriage, and don't tell me it's a fantasy. There is such a thing as a real marriage."

He held up his hands. "It's never too late for that."

"I'm not so sure. There's no one left for me." I slumped on that familiar, self-pitying note.

The waitress came with the check, and I sent her back for another drink. Merit declined with a flick of his fingers and looked at his watch.

"Do you have to get back?"

"I am not in a hurry." He settled back into the booth, but I felt I was keeping him against his will.

My fresh drink arrived. That made five. "You think I'm foolish and self-centered." Even to my own ears I sounded petulant.

"No, no. I am trying to understand how you came to this place. It was the crime?"

"That was certainly a turning point."

He cocked his head. "But that time is over, long over, many years ago."

"No, it's coming back to haunt me."

He paused in the act of popping a chip into his mouth. "Why? Did something happen?"

I told him about the Justice Project, about how they were now saying that Jules Jefferson was innocent.

Merit closed his eyes and shook his head. "Oh no. Oh no."

I leaned forward, thinking that at last someone understood. "I feel like I'm being plunged back into the past, just when I thought I was going to move forward."

"That man has spent twenty-two years in prison, his whole life." He shook his head again. "This happens in Africa. It happens all the time. You know that the British locked up Jomo Kenyatta for eight years. They blamed him without cause for the Mau Mau rebellion. So it happens here, too, apparently. To black men. Imagine, Kate, your whole life in prison for nothing."

I was stricken. "It was dark. I thought it was him. Everyone agreed he threatened us at the Tavern."

"How often do people say things like that? How would he have found you later that night?"

I rapped my drink down on the table. "Whose side are you on?" I didn't like the sound of my own voice, and I saw a couple of curious glances my way. I leaned toward him. "You blame *me* for this?"

Merit remained calm. "I do not blame you. What do I know? But it seems to me there are two tragedies here. Blame you? No, Kate, you were an innocent victim, of that I am sure."

I hate that phrase, "innocent victim." The prosecutor used it, and the jury ate it up. But how was I innocent? And they were now announcing to the world that the man they had locked up for twenty-two years was the one who was innocent. And I, the pretty college girl defiled, was the imposter. Guilt descended on me. I tried to think of Suzanne and what she had said about innocence and guilt, but my mind was blank confusion. I barely heard Merit's words as he moved on to a less intense subject.

"So what will you do tonight?"

I answered dully. "I'm hoping I'll spend some time with Tony."

"See, you do have someone."

That brought my attention back around. "But Tony's married. I know he would want to be with me, but he isn't free, not any more than I am."

"But still you hope to see him. What do you want? If you could have anything."

I had the uncomfortable feeling that Merit was talking along with me, humoring me, patronizing me, even, and I could hardly blame him. But I kept right on going. "If I could have anything? He would divorce her. If he did, then I could think about how I could be free, too. And then? Who knows?"

"You want to marry him?"

"I do." I was whispering. I was drunk.

Merit sat back and looked out the window while I nursed my drink.

I felt myself slumping, almost hanging on the rim of my glass. "There's more than one way to miss out. Maybe you never get a chance at a real marriage, or maybe you get yourself locked into marriage too young."

"This is how you think it is for him. How do you know his marriage is not real?"

I was vaguely aware of an undercurrent of disapproval, and it made me defensive. "He told me he's stuck. He married very young. His wife doesn't share any of his interests or appreciate what he does professionally. All she thinks or talks about is kids."

"The realities of raising children and working for a living are not exciting or glamorous."

"I've seen them together. Sometimes people make mistakes when they're too young. Sometimes it's a second marriage that's the real thing."

Merit just looked at me.

"There are lots of good second marriages."

"Name one."

"Oh, you know there are. You hear about it all the time." I couldn't think of one, though.

"They're good for a while, like the first ones."

I turned it back on him. "Isn't that enough? What do you want, forever? Who's promoting a fantasy now?" I was almost in tears, as angry as I was drowning in self-pity. "I just want what everybody else has."

Merit shook his head, smiling, as if to say he didn't understand anything I was saying. He stretched and locked his hands behind his head. "I do not know, Kate. It is nice to be in love. But it passes. For everyone, it passes. Just like it passed for you and this man you married long ago. What was he like, anyway? Who was he?"

"He was a man who worked for my father back in Kenya."

Merit looked confused. "You married him in Kenya? Back then?"

"No, no. Here. Later."

"He came here?"

I shook my head, then nodded.

Merit smiled broadly. "He showed up here. Like me."

"We thought he was killed back in Kenya. He stole from my father. He stole everything." I was making things up, out of control.

"But your father is rich."

"I mean..." I faltered. "He stole from him in Africa. There wasn't much left at the end. He was embezzling."

"You're telling me you married this man?"

"He was handsome. Charming." I realized I was babbling, but I couldn't stop. "You didn't know my father. When he drank, he could be brutal. In those days. This guy loved me. He adored me, you could see it, and he would have done anything for me. But of course, it was all a horrible mistake."

I needed to stop. I slapped down my napkin and slid out of the booth. "Merit, I'm sorry. I have to go. I apologize for dumping all this on you. I'm a mess. I really am. Don't pay any attention to anything I say."

"It's okay, Kate." He reached out as if I might need help to stand, and I brushed past him in a huff. But it took all my concentration to navigate between the chairs and tables on the way out.

For a second time, he drove me home in my own car. He said little more.

I wish I had listened more that day. I wish I had drunk less and listened more. I was just so full of myself and my own problems.

Sometimes I hate myself.

CHAPTER FIFTEEN

I N THE CAR, ON THE way back to the apartment, I called Tony. I got voice mail, told him I was sick, and asked him please to tell Anita that I would try to get there later.

Merit stole a look at me. "I hope it is not often that you drink three frozen margaritas with your lunch."

I said I didn't finish the last one.

Merit followed me inside, handed me the car keys, and asked if he could use the phone to call a cab. I felt bad. I told him I was sorry, but I had to lie down. And I did. The phone rang, and Merit answered it. I couldn't hear, and I was so sleepy I didn't care, but I heard him say that I was in bed. He stuck his head in to say that it was Mrs. Blore and that he had told her I would call her later. I didn't hear him leave.

I could tell by the light when I woke up that it was well into the afternoon. I was still in my jeans and work shirt, but not feeling half as bad as I thought I would. I made a strong cup of coffee, called Anita, and promised I'd be right there.

On the way over, with the top down, the fresh air blew the fog out of my head, and excitement bubbled up in its place. I couldn't wait to pick up where I'd left off with Tony. I found him on site with a whole new crew, rock guys. They'd been laying down the hardscape all week. A quick check revealed no Beryl. Good. A double take revealed Mike. Ugh. But it looked as though they were nearly finished for the day anyway.

With a smile full of meaning only for him, I said, "Hey, Tony. Can you stick around for a while? I want to measure one more time, maybe pull up the markers, and talk about what we need to get done tomorrow." I added under my breath, "Maybe we could get a sandwich."

Mike was hanging out nearby, as if he thought he might be included. I kept my back to him.

Tony kicked at the dirt. "I don't know. I want to get home."

What? Was he playing with me *again*? My patience snapped. "Yeah, well, so do I." I was angry, sick of pursuing him, sick of being teased with his now-you-see-it-now-you-don't bullshit. I waved my arm at the worksite and hardened my voice. "It has to look good for tomorrow, Tony. All of it."

I pointed out half a dozen things that weren't right yet—muddy footprints on the new pathways, scraps of forms lying around—and told him quite sharply that he was not to leave until they were all fixed.

Tony threw a glance at Mike, who turned away with a smirk, as if to say, "So this is what you deal with."

I stalked off in a fury. I convinced myself in a matter of minutes that I had completely changed my mind about him. He was a sleazy, half-assed flirt, a jackass, a jerk, a troll.

When I entered the house, Anita took one look at my face and said, "What?"

"Sorry. It's Tony." I decided to smear him. "He's been giving me attitude and trying to take shortcuts."

Anita's face fell. "Oh dear. That doesn't sound like Tony."

"He was surly enough with me just now."

"That's funny because I really did think he had a crush on you."

"Well, you're wrong."

She stiffened at the curtness of my reply.

I apologized, but added, "He pissed me off out there. I

want this to look so good for tomorrow, and he acts like I'm bitchy and demanding."

She took my hand and patted it. "It always seemed to me like he thought the world of you."

"No, there's nothing there, Anita."

"Oh well, I'm glad. I was worried that there might be something going on between you two. I mean, I would hope you'd get along in business, but I wouldn't like to see you get mixed up with a man who's got a wife and little children. I always say, if you go with a cheater then either you lose, which is what usually happens, or if you win, the grand prize is a cheater."

I smiled and pretended to agree. "He's a loser." All my hopes were crashing down, and I knew I'd be miserable when I had a chance to think about it. I turned my attention to the house and forced myself to talk about throw pillows and fresh flowers.

At about five thirty, I took Anita with me to inspect the work site before I left, and everything looked good. Mike was gone. One kid remained, a teenager that I'd seen before who would clean up, rake, and throw leaves and branches, rocks and trash into the truck bed. Tony was scrupulously polite to both Anita and me, which made me even more annoyed because I thought he was trying to make me out to be a liar. When she said good night, she looked faintly puzzled.

I turned to go, and Tony stopped me with his hand on my arm. To the kid, he called out, "Take your time and finish up. We're going to get a sandwich."

The kid nodded and went on raking.

Tony called back to him, "I'll bring you something." Then he opened the passenger side door of his truck for me.

The first thing he said as we pulled away was, "Mike is Beryl's brother."

We drove into Sedgewick, to a sandwich shop Tony

liked to frequent. It was a small place run by a couple of women in an old white cottage on a street of shops. What would have been the living room and dining room of the house were set with red and blue wooden chairs and tables. We sat by a window away from the handful of other customers.

I was still miffed at first, but I soon unbent when I realized that, far from pulling back, he had come all the way over to my side. I hardly knew him. He was chomping away at corned beef on rye, whacking down chips, and gulping Dr. Pepper while I nibbled at a dainty wrap and marveled at a whole new Tony. Up close, he seemed coarser and a lot less cerebral than I had made him out to be in my mind. It was disconcerting, but exciting.

He began telling me that he had to go home every night because Beryl was so jealous. "She's pathologically suspicious."

I asked him if she had reason to be suspicious of him, and he said no.

"Is she jealous of me?"

"Oh, she's worried about you for sure."

The idea pleased me. I told him maybe Beryl should trust him. "Seems to me you play it pretty straight. I mean, I've been chasing you, Tony."

A look. A moment. We sat there, neither of us eating. I felt the pull in my gut.

"There's nobody like you, Kate."

That was exactly what I wanted him to say. He was as pent up and tied up by his life as I was. And he was telling me he had a feeling I was his big chance. "I don't meet a woman like you every day. Years go by, and I don't see one I want like I want you. It's like I'm watching a black and white film, and you come on, and it's in color."

I ate it up. I wondered what hold she had on him, other than the fact that he was married to her, and it soon became clear that Beryl's father was a builder who had put Tony on his feet in business.

"But you're on your own now," I said.

"Her dad has the note on the house."

"So what? That means she won't get evicted, right?"

"He co-signed for the truck, too." Nice new big truck all fitted out with toolbox and equipment, logo painted on the side.

"Again, so what? If you make the payments, it's yours."

He told me he'd been thinking about what I had suggested, about us being in business together. He talked about how good we'd be together.

Pop called in the middle of our conversation. I hesitated, then answered, thinking it would be easier if I went ahead and dealt with him. "I went shopping this morning," I told him while Tony listened. "Then I grabbed a bite of Mexican food, and it made me sick, so I spent the whole afternoon in bed at the apartment. I didn't get out to Mary's Grove until almost five."

I explained that I was staying in town and would have to go back out to Mary's Grove in the morning and wouldn't get home until about noon. We'd still have plenty of time to drive back in for the party. He complained and worried about how sick I was and said he thought I should come home. I was firm. "No, no, I'm fine now."

Tony paid the bill, ordering take-out for the kid.

Pop said, "Who's that?"

"Nobody. Oh, it's just Tony. I'm still at the house. I'm leaving now."

"Maybe you should come home. I made a soup." I heard concern warring with suspicion in his voice.

Tony had his back to me, counting out the tip. His T-shirt was old, sun-faded, and soft. I wanted to run my hand over the smooth, rippling muscles of his back.

"I'm going to go back to the apartment and go to bed early. I still don't feel quite right. I don't think I could eat anything."

"Are you all right or not?"

"I'm fine, but I was sick earlier, okay? I'll see you tomorrow." I hung up before he could drag it out any further.

Tony said, "This is what you were talking about. He checks up on you."

"I had to tell him I won't be going home tonight, or he'll go crazy thinking something's happened or I'm up to something."

"Are you? Up to something?"

Another moment. Our eyes met, and I felt a magnetic pull.

"You tell me." Breathless.

"I could get in as late as ten." All I could think about was his mouth.

The waitress showed up with the take-out and broke the spell.

I said, "Let's get back."

In the truck, I chafed him for the way he'd acted earlier in front of Mike, and he explained that he didn't want Mike giving Beryl ideas. I asked him what he was going to do.

"Do?"

"Are you going to stay married to her?"

"Do I want out? Sure. I mean, we got nothin'." He glanced my way, then scowled at the road. "I don't want to lose my kids, but I don't know. It's like being in prison back there. I gotta do something about it, sooner or later. I mean, what good does it do them if their parents are miserable all the time? What kind of message do they get from that? But I'd have to be able to see them. I don't know. I gotta think it through."

"Why put it off? Why not divorce her and get it over with?"

"I have to ease out of it." He pulled into the drive at Mary's Grove and shut off the car. "You don't know how she can come unglued. You wouldn't guess it from meeting her."

I followed him back out to the site, where Tony tossed a bag to the kid, and we walked out to the edge of the lawn by the river. He reached for the waistband of my jeans, playfully, and I pulled back to where we couldn't be seen from the house.

I looked for movement at the windows. "She could be watching us."

"So?" He was restless, pacing. "I don't have much time."

It was as simple as figuring out a place we could go for a while. All I had to do was say yes. Instead I stalled, indecisive.

The pacing stopped. "What?"

I didn't know what. It seemed too quick and easy. I didn't like having my cards called in that way. I was torn, desperately so. I wanted to throw myself into his arms. I knew we'd both go up in flames. But something inside me, the dreamer, wanted to save it for something bigger. We'd go somewhere and then what? It was going to be a quickie, and I wanted more. I hung back.

He traced the line of my waist with his fingertips. "Been a long time for you?"

"It's been a long time since it mattered."

"It's never been like this." He paused. "Is this about that thing that happened? You said something happened."

Okay, I'll be the tragic heroine again. "I fell in love just once before in my whole life, and it ended very, very badly."

"Nothing bad is going to come of this." He tried to nuzzle up under my hair, and I squirmed away. He was undeterred. "What happened anyway? Guy threw you over? Broke your heart?"

"It was a lot worse than that."

He was starting, just a little tiny bit, to get under my skin. I pulled away.

He quit reaching for me. "Who was he? What did he do?"

I started walking through the woods along the river's edge. "He was one of my professors."

"Oh man, this was a long time ago."

I whirled on him. "Not that long ago." How old did he think I was?

He did one of his short laughs, realizing what he'd said, and held up his hands. "No, okay, I get it. Older guy takes advantage." He tried to put on a serious and sympathetic face.

I snapped, "I was raped, okay?"

That stopped him in his tracks. "You... what?"

We resumed walking, and finally I said, "It seems I have a genius for inappropriate relationships. He was my drama teacher. He was married, except it was an open marriage. He and his wife agreed they could both see other people."

"You believed that?"

"It's what he told me. And yes, believe it or not, I did."

That little detail, Elliott's having told me he had an open marriage, hadn't ever come out. I'd never told anybody, and strange as it may seem, I never doubted it. It was only when I told Tony, and he assumed it was a lie, that I questioned it. And when I did, I knew instantly that he was right. Of course, Tony would know, cheating husband that he was himself, as it turned out. Knowing Elliott had lied to me that way made me suddenly very sad.

"What happened?"

"It was late. After midnight. We were in his car."

"You were parking." He had a funny look on his face. "And you're saying he raped you? I mean, he forced you or what?"

"No! He didn't rape me. He was shot. He was murdered right in front of me."

"Jesus."

We were at the end of the path, on a bluff that sent long shadows across the Appomattox.

His face went slack. "I don't get it."

"What's to get? Like I said, I was with him, and he got shot, and I got raped." I turned and started walking back toward the house. *How did I get myself into this conversation?*

Tony caught up with me and took my arm. "You can't leave it like that. Tell me what happened."

"It was a disaster. It was one big disaster, my entire senior year. I was in love. I think it might have been the only time in my life, for real." Had Elliott lied about his marriage? Was it just a fling for him? That new thought brought me up short.

"Who did this? Why? Did they ever get him?"

"Well..." I let a long minute go by. "There was a guy who threatened us earlier that evening." What could I say? I was determined not to lie. "He was convicted of the crime, but..." I felt as if I had sprung a trap on myself. "Turns out he didn't do it."

"He... didn't? I'm trying to understand this."

"There was an altercation. At a bar. Elliott was going to buy some pot, which for some reason he thought Jefferson would have for sale, but that turned out to be wrong. The prosecutor couldn't find any proof of it. Jefferson didn't have any drug charges against him. He denied he'd ever had or sold pot. He denied he had any that night at the bar, but Elliott insisted. Elliott wanted..." At that point, the whole thing struck me as ridiculous.

"What?" Tony started to laugh because I was laughing.

"He wanted," and I cracked up. I was laughing so hard I couldn't get it out, and Tony didn't know what was so funny, but he was laughing, too. I kept saying, "He wanted," and then I doubled over, breathless, until I was in tears. Finally, I pulled myself together and said, "Elliott wanted to use a credit card."

Tony gave a short huff and then looked puzzled. It really wasn't funny, not considering what happened later. Tony said, "That's pretty stupid. He thought the local pot guy would take plastic?"

"No, no, he wanted the bartender to give him cash back on a round of drinks. I knew him, the bartender." I sighed. "But he insisted he couldn't do it. Now that I think of it, I'm not sure Elliott had ever bought dope in his whole life. He was a drama professor, for Christ's sake. He was twenty-eight years old."

It occurred to me then that Elliott had been showing off. "I don't know what happened. There were different versions, and of course, Elliott didn't ever get to tell his side of it. Jefferson said one thing, and the bartender backed a good part of Jefferson's story, but he didn't hear all of it. I only heard part of it myself. Elliott probably really did say something snotty. It wasn't racial; Elliott wasn't a redneck. I mean, he was a college professor. But he was a snob about education, you know, class, and I think he put them all down when he couldn't look cool and buy the pot. But it got pretty intense. And anyway, at one point Jefferson said, 'Motherfucker, I'll kill you.' That was it. He said he'd kill Elliott, and he tried to weasel out of that at the trial, but the bartender heard it, and I heard it. And then later that night, Elliott was murdered."

It wasn't the whole truth, but it was the truth. It felt good to tell it. Apart from the investigation and the trial, that was the first time I had told anyone my story. It was such an overwhelming relief that I turned to Tony, clutched his shirt, and laid my forehead against his chest. He put his hands on my shoulders, then slid his arms around me and stroked my back. A strange, all-consuming happiness—no other word for it—spread through me, that I had been able to tell him, not everything, but even as much as I had, and it was still okay. Could there actually be a future in my life?

I sank into his arms, buried my face in his neck and whispered, "It feels so good to talk to you about it."

And then he asked the worst possible question. "So that guy. Was he the one that did it, or wasn't he?"

I pulled away from him again and started walking back toward Anita's house, my arms wrapped around myself, my heart sinking. I felt his hand on the back of my neck. I shook him off. "They found him guilty."

"Yeah, but you're saying he wasn't? I mean, if he raped you, wouldn't you know if it was him?"

I closed my eyes and said my thing. "It was dark. It was late. I was confused. I knew it was him at the Tavern."

"So the guy from the bar got nailed for the crime. Jeez, that was a long time ago. He wasn't in jail all this time, was he?"

I didn't answer.

"When did this happen?" When I still didn't answer, he persisted. "Like, what year?"

I sighed. "1986."

"And when did they figure out he didn't do it?"

"I don't know, a week or two ago."

"A week or two? Jesus, how long was that guy in jail?"

I didn't help him with the math, and he was a while concentrating, but he did work it out, and then he whistled and said, "Oh my God." And again, "Jesus." He looked stunned. "That's, like, his whole life. How old was he?"

"I don't know. Twenty-one. Twenty-two."

"He must be in his fifties now."

I stopped. "Okay, Tony, you've made your point." I drew myself up as if facing a firing squad. "I testified that he was guilty. I was the one that put him away." He was going to have to know that about me. That fact stood between me and everybody else in the world. "You have no idea what it's like."

To my immense relief, I saw comprehension fill his face. He took my hand.

I couldn't help that tears ran from the corners of my eyes. "I may be pretty evil, but I do feel the burden. I carry it around."

He put his arms around me again. "Not evil, Kate, what are you saying, baby? It happened. It wasn't your fault. Anybody could have made that mistake."

It was worse than that, but I took the comfort anyway. I buried my face in his chest again. My voice came out all muffled and teary. "It does help to talk about it. I never do. I can't."

"Okay, okay, you can talk to me about it. Jeez, all these years, keeping all that shit inside."

I took a big shaky breath. "He was my drama teacher, and he was directing a play, and I was in it, and a group of us went out for drinks after rehearsal every Wednesday night. This was right in the middle of my senior year. My friends all testified that I just rode with him and there wasn't anything going on. But it came out that everybody else left the bar a long time before Elliott and me. There was no reason for me to be in his car, because I had my own car, and I had left it on campus so I could ride with Elliott. Well. And the way they found him." I mumbled the last part, and Tony missed it. Elliott's pants were down around his ankles when he was shot. "Anyway, the defense attorney tried to make a big deal about how I was having an affair with my professor."

"What did that have to do with the crime, the murder?"

"Of course, that's what the prosecutor said. There's a law. You can't insinuate stuff about a rape victim."

"The guy who did it, he must've looked like the one at the bar."

I didn't respond.

"I don't guess there's any way they'll catch him now."

I didn't say anything to that either. We'd reached the lawn.

"What about your dad? Did he know about this professor having an affair with his daughter?"

I barely heard him. I was gripped by the creepy feeling that came over me whenever I thought too much about what happened back then, at that crossroads in my life. I shivered. I wanted the conversation to be over. "I went to rehearsal. Pop knew that. We went out afterward sometimes. But he couldn't have known about Elliott. He was always suspicious that I ran around and lied to him, but he didn't have any reason to think I was seeing Elliott."

"You were sneaking around."

He tried to kiss me, and I stepped back. "Don't. She could see us."

"You still sneak around, don't you? Why? You need to get over it. Shoot, you're no more available than me." He reached for me again.

I held up my hands. "Tony..."

"Let's go somewhere. I got a couple hours." His voice was soft, persuasive. His eyes covered every part of my body and came back to meet mine.

"I don't want to sneak around anymore."

"We won't. We'll be together, Kate, just like you want." He turned so he was between me and the house, hooked a finger in a belt loop on my jeans, and pulled me a little closer. "Kate, come on, sweetheart," he whispered. "Man, you're so beautiful. This is our chance. We got time. It's now, baby." He might have almost said now or never. His eyes were gleaming. The eyes with the gold in them.

"Tony, this can't just be the only chance. It can't be like that. If you're staying where you are, we need to break it off. If it's going to be more, let's act." I'd cooled off some, remembering the crime and Elliott and Jefferson, and with the cool came doubt. If he was going to lie to Beryl, maybe he would lie to me, too. Like Elliott. "Are you going to tell her how you feel? When? Ever?"

"Sure, yeah, I gotta do something." He was beginning to sound a little harried.

I softened, let my fingers trail down the front of his shirt. He pulled on the belt loop again. The heat between us was unmistakable.

I said, "Let's take it one step at a time. Let's just look for a little space. A little time together."

He grinned like an idiot. "A rendezvous." Another pull on the belt loop.

I pushed off. I wanted him to stop being stupid. I started walking to my car and took out the keys. "No. We both need to make a move. You need to let her know you need some space so you can figure out what you want." I stopped to face him again. "When are you going to tell her you have a problem?"

"I don't know. Not right away. I got to do it my own way, at the right time."

"Yeah, well, same here."

"I would think it would be a lot easier to tell your dad you were going to move out than it is for me to tell my wife I'm leaving her."

"He's not strong. He's old. It would be a blow. I've lived my life this way. He's spent his whole life taking care of me."

Tony looked unconvinced.

"There's the money to think of. A lot of money. It's all his, though. It'll be mine someday, when he's gone. I'll be rich, Tony."

The evening air was cool. I'd made up my mind that Tony was going to have to make a move to get free before I went any further. I didn't want a hook-up in a motel. I wanted something real. "One step at a time. Maybe you tell her you need some space to think, time to think about what you want to do with your life. Tell her things have changed. She must know that, right? I'll do the same with Pop. And maybe next week we can both stay in town." Our eyes met. "Deal? See how it goes."

CHAPTER SIXTEEN

W HEN I GOT HOME AT noon the next day, I breezed by Pop and went upstairs to get ready for the party. I had the most beautiful dress. It was short, well above the knee, and made of the loveliest washed silk in pale shell-pink, bias-cut to curve. It felt like rose petals against my bare skin, so cool, light, and soft. I wore it with just one piece of jewelry: my grandmother's diamond necklace. It lay cold and heavy on my throat. I rarely had a chance to wear it, but when I did, it was like putting on a magic cape. It had an aura of richness and bygone luxury. I studied myself in the mirror. Over-dressed? Maybe. Good.

Pop's eyes glittered when I came downstairs. "You look quite beautiful, Kate." His voice was husky, much too intense to suit me.

I brushed him off, saying, "You look nice, too."

In his tuxedo, he cut the fine figure of an elderly gentleman squire. He was the perfect escort for me, really. I wouldn't want to appear taken. What would be the point of that? And what better than to be seen with a rich father figure?

Mary's Grove glowed. Cars, mostly new, expensive, and immaculate, were parked everywhere, and people were arriving from all sides, bottlenecked at the front door, spilling across the wide front veranda and onto the velvety green lawn in the last light of day.

Just inside the front door, Anita greeted guests in a

stunning midnight-blue designer gown, with sapphires trickling down her throat. I delivered Pop and slipped away. When I glanced back from across the room, she had locked her arm around his. It looked as though the two of them were receiving guests together. That made me smile. He was already scanning the crowd for me, though; I was careful not to let him catch my eye.

Outside, I greeted several people I had met before and worked my way around the house to the site of the garden, keeping an eye out for Tony. The upper lawn near the house was cool and dusky, while the last sunlight lingered warm and golden on the treetops and the outer riverbanks. I spotted Tony down by the water—with Beryl—and decided against greeting the two of them. I couldn't imagine why he'd brought her. She had elected to wear some sort of ethnic costume—Cuban? Alpine?—with a boho-long multi-colored skirt and flared sleeves. She looked like a teenager with that straight dark blond hair. She was pretty enough and a good ten years younger than I was, but she couldn't possibly compete.

I went back into the lighted house, where I settled into chatting up prospective clients. My design for Anita's garden stood on an easel in the living room, and as I held court there, my spirits began to rise. What had I to be dissatisfied with? The scene was wonderful: my work displayed before a well-heeled and knowledgeable crowd that revolved around me, the men admiring and the women, too. I had arrived.

Anita moved up beside me, and I deferred to her, but it was my show, and everybody knew it. Pop watched proudly from the sidelines. At one point, I spotted Tony at the back of the room. I called him up and introduced him as the person who had the contract for the installation of the project. I mentioned that although we were doing a period restoration at Mary's Grove, Tony had developed a sensational line of new roses that I was going to be using in future designs. Tony ducked and bobbed modestly, but I could see that he was pleased. He answered a couple of questions. He made a good impression in a setting like that: polite, respectful, knowledgeable. The fool Sabrina Cole appeared on the edge of the crowd, pointing a huge flash in people's faces, shooting randomly from too close and too far.

Eventually, the most intense interest in the project waned, except for a knot of diehard hobby gardeners from whom I disengaged myself after a few minutes. I rejoined Pop and Anita. Sabrina pushed her oversized camera in my face and blinded me.

I said sharply, "Do you think you've taken enough pictures?"

My tone was lost on her. "Oh, tons!" She showed her unattractive teeth. "I take tons of pictures every time I come here. I'll show them to you next time we meet about the project. I could do the photographs for your book."

I think my eyes must have bulged.

Anita slipped her arm around my shoulders. "I must say, that was a lovely picture in the paper." She turned to Pop. "Did Kate show you that? Do you get the Richmond paper?"

A spark of interest flickered across his face. "Must have missed it. I read the news online."

"This was in *Living*. Beautiful picture of Kate."

"Thank you," Sabrina said. "I took it." She snuck around my other side and thrust herself into the middle of the conversation. Her clothes were stained, pilled, and ill fitting. What must Anita think of her?

But Anita couldn't think of anything but Pop. She gave him one of her sweet, shy smiles. "You still maintain ties with Africa?"

The connection between a picture in the paper and our maintaining ties with Africa was, of course, lost on Pop. He looked blank, then wary. "What for? Past is past."

"But what about that African professor? What's his name? Chenuba? Chebono?"

Pop's left eye showed mild curiosity, but the right was laser-focused on Sabrina. "You took this picture?"

I glanced at Anita. I didn't have the sense that she had ever noticed Pop's evil eye.

Incredibly, Sabrina rummaged in her camera bag and produced both the article and the picture. Pop glanced at the article, then studied the picture. "Quite a crowd. Excellent picture of Kate."

Sabrina flushed with pleasure. She seemed to think Pop was impressed with her skill as a photographer.

I said to Pop, "I had no idea I was being photographed. I stopped in out of curiosity and regretted it. It was very political and very unpleasant."

Sabrina prattled on. "His name is Chenobo. Merit Chenobo? He's lecturing at VCU, and he spoke at a symposium on contemporary Kenyan politics." She turned back to Pop. "I knew Kate in school."

He became unctuous. "Sweet Briar girl, eh? I don't believe we've ever met."

"No, sir. Though of course Kate and I knew each other, both being townies." She giggled.

Anita hesitated, puzzled. "Townies?"

Anita was asking me, but Sabrina explained. "We both lived at home when we were at school," She bared her awful teeth again. "We were the only ones that year. Not many local girls go to Sweet Briar." She was carrying on as if she were a guest at the party and we were socially acquainted. Would no one squash her?

Anita's eyes met mine briefly, but I couldn't find anything but good nature there. She was in some ways too nice. Not an inkling seemed to penetrate Sabrina Cole's armadillo-like hide, either. With a smile for Anita, I pulled away, disgusted.

Multicolored Japanese lanterns of red, yellow, and

blue glowed on the terrace next to the satiny silver of the Appomattox. Branches rustled in the darkness of the woods surrounding us. I heard a gust of laughter and found Tony chatting with a small group about their gardens, our project, Cuba, and whatever else. He was smooth in a social setting, no doubt about that. Beryl hung at his elbow. I joined them. Tony introduced me to a casually dressed couple who lived nearby and whose yard his crew maintained, and another woman in an expensive-looking green dress who said, "I love what you're doing here."

"You" meant Tony and me, and I picked that up on that. The man asked Tony a question about roses, and I met Beryl's eyes and smiled. She smiled back guardedly. I couldn't make out her expression, but I was guessing he hadn't told her anything yet. She wore the same gold cross she'd had on before. My eyes traveled back to hers, and I caught a glimpse of naked dislike. Or maybe enmity was the word. I smiled again because I knew she was jealous of me.

In business mode, Tony shifted, probably without even knowing what he did, so he stood beside me. I threw more "we" on the fire. The woman in green would be in touch. The man whose yard Tony maintained liked me. His wife looked observant, and I wondered, smiling as I turned away, what she made of our little drama.

I stopped by an outdoor bar by the steps to the river and had my first drink of the evening. Then I threw myself back into the party and made a point of circulating all the way around the house. People stood chatting or wandered in pairs everywhere I went. I made a game of intercepting every waiter carrying a tray and grabbing one glass of champagne after another. They were tiny little glasses. I tossed them back with ease, and I never for a moment lost my head. I forgot my annoyance with Sabrina Cole and the tug-of-war over Tony. I drifted out to the edge of the lights and voices, looked up, and waited while my eyes adapted to the dark. Stars glimmered, first a few bright ones, then more in between, then a shimmering silent blanket of them. I breathed in the fusty smell of clipped boxwood and humus, touched the diamond necklace, which had warmed on my body, and thought for once that my life was perfect.

When I went back inside, I found Pop and Anita deep in conversation; she was in deep with him, at least. I came up behind Pop and touched his shoulder. He turned to me as if relieved, tiresome as ever, and she took my hand. So sweet. Why couldn't he see that? She had evidently taken it to heart that she should get Pop talking about Africa. He was telling her, no doubt under questioning, about managing the farm in Kenya, and I realized I had arrived just in time.

I leapt in. "Remember, Anita? I told you he married the owner's daughter and bought the old man out. That was my mother."

Pop closed his eyes and shook his head faintly.

Anita rounded back on him. "Kate tells me that she went back to England. Her mother, that is, your wife." Her cheeks pinkened, and she touched her fingertips to her mouth as if afraid she'd said the wrong thing. Poor Anita. She was really stepping in it, and she knew it.

Pop stiffened. "My wife?" He looked at his wineglass and let a long moment go by. "My wife was a very headstrong young woman."

I said, "My mother was a religious nut. Unstable."

Anita tittered nervously, maybe slightly shocked. Then she dug herself in a little deeper. "When Kate speaks of Africa, it sounds lovely. Why ever did you leave?"

He treated her to one of his little signals, one which I knew meant he was dangerously irritated by her questions. "Things changed."

The champagne made me mischievous. I dusted off the story I used to tell my friends at school, an extreme version in which Pop blazed out our escape with a pistol. "It's how he got that scar." I pointed at his left eye, and she gasped.

I had him driving us hell bent for leather with one eye, my hero, rescuing his young daughter. I told it full-on dramatic and dead serious while he scowled. Anita fell all over him for more details while I slipped away and doubled over with glee just as soon as I was out of sight.

I was floating on the night breeze, riding on a cresting wave. Anita had Pop on a short, silken leash for the moment, whether he liked it or not, and Tony, well, I didn't figure I'd have a chance to be alone with him that night, not with Beryl hanging on him. But Tony seemed like mine for the having if I wanted him.

I paused to collect a few compliments on the artist's renditions, serenely owning that I'd done them all myself. A handsome man in a well-cut tuxedo turned on his heel to watch me drift on to the next group of people. I found myself laughing with delight at the success and possibilities that seemed to lie before me.

At last, in the cool of the night, the crowd thinned and began to roll away. I found Anita momentarily alone and thanked her, saying that the night could not have gone better for me.

She waved off my gratitude and spoke with genuine kindness. "We've been good for each other, Kate. It was good for me, too."

I asked, "Where's Pop?"

"Looking for you." She slipped an arm around my shoulder and gave me a little squeeze. "You won't see me running after your handsome father. I'll latch onto you and wait right here." She patted my shoulder.

"I'm on your side, believe me."

"You want your own life, and he should have his."

I couldn't have agreed more.

"Why don't you marry, Kate? You could have anyone you wanted."

I hate it when people say that. It isn't true. No matter how beautiful you are, how intelligent and talented, no matter how accomplished, even if you have money, it is never true that you can have anyone you want. And the worst problem is that sometimes there simply isn't anybody. In books and movies, there is always a likely man for the taking. In real life, there isn't always.

Anita brightened, and I was aware of Pop at my elbow. "I'm telling Kate she should marry."

The left eye was indulgent, the right impatient. He wanted to go.

I moved around Anita so the two of them were face to face and curled my lips at him over her shoulder. "Marry? Why? No, I'm content. I hear marriage is a trap."

Pop offered her a stiff little bow, and she gave him a kiss—just a quick little peck on the cheek—then fluttered back as if she'd surprised herself. I hugged her, and she beamed. Yes, for the most part, the evening had gone well.

CHAPTER SEVENTEEN

I N THE CAR ON THE way home, Pop complained I had left him alone most of the evening to fend for himself.

I said, "It looked to me like you were doing fine. You were with Anita Blore the whole time."

From the darkness, he growled, "Anita Blore."

"What? Standing next to her, you had a chance to meet and talk to everybody who came all night. There must have been a hundred people. How can you possibly say I left you alone?"

He was silent, radiating bitterness and anger.

Indignation swelled in me. "You could appreciate the fact that I didn't leave you alone at home. You want to be part of my life? This was a professional contact for me, Pop. She's a client. Half the people at that party were potential clients. Did you see what I was doing all night? I was circulating. I was working! Can't you see that? You're so fucking self-absorbed." I pounded the steering wheel once with the heel of my right hand.

At home I went straight to bed, slamming the door to my room and locking it.

All day Saturday and all day Sunday, I shut myself in my study except to take long walks. I avoided the gardens, climbing the hills, straying onto other people's property, picking my way through brambles and woods, and fuming over how I was trapped. I had to drag myself in to teach on Monday. I felt exposed every time I stood in front of class.

Suzanne came by Monday afternoon. It was getting to

be a routine, the weekly visitation from Suzanne, and I wasn't sure I liked it. She was nice and meant well, but she was so somber, and she wanted to talk about nothing but the murder, which I didn't want resuming such a major role in my life. I was keeping it at bay, resolutely pushing it out of my mind whenever I felt it creeping up on me. Still, when Suzanne called, I didn't feel I could refuse to see her.

It was high summer, hot and humming with bees, the sunlight brilliant and the shade deep. I waited for Suzanne on the screened-in porch, where I had set out a silver pitcher of lemonade and two cups. The pitcher frosted over, and droplets ran down the sides and pooled on the glass tabletop.

I heard her car on the gravel drive, then the doorbell rang. I waited while Pop let her in and led her out to the porch. I touched the arm of my chair as if to rise, and she raised thin fingers to say no need. I settled back and offered lemonade, which she accepted.

Straight and slim, she perched like a bird on the very edge of a wicker chair, touched the small cup to her mouth, and licked her lips. We tried small talk about the weather and what each of us had been up to lately. I mentioned the unveiling of a new garden plan for a plantation home near Richmond, and she feigned interest with soft ohs and ahs. When I said what about you, she went straight to courts and conferences for victim advocates. She seemed to live her whole life consumed with those grim matters. She had a pretty smile. She flashed it every now and then in spite of herself, but mostly she was sober, focused. I couldn't help feeling I would like her for a friend, but the constant outpouring of empathy was oppressive.

She had come to ask me if I wanted to attend any of the court proceedings in connection with Jules Jefferson's exoneration and release. I said no.

Gingerly, she asked, "Do you still believe he's the one who did it?"

"No."

"So you're okay with it if he's released?"

I changed position in my seat. "I didn't say that."

She leaned forward and her eyes widened. "The one who did do it, he got away with it. He could be out there somewhere. Does that frighten you?"

"He could be in prison somewhere for raping someone else, couldn't he?"

She shook her head. "No. There's a database now. They didn't find a match. He's not in the system. Elsa said it was unusual that he never showed up in the system."

"Elsa." The very name was sour to me.

"You're afraid of Jules Jefferson?"

I shook my head. "No, but I did put him away for twenty years."

"You think he'll blame you."

"Of course he will. His family already does. Now everybody will."

"You can't be blamed for being mistaken."

"I knew I didn't really recognize him. I mean, I knew I only recognized him as the one who was at the Tavern. They hounded me to say it was the same one later. I shouldn't have let them make me do it."

Pop cleared his throat. I hadn't noticed him hanging near the door.

Suzanne turned to look at him, then turned back to me. "What I can do is let you know when he'll be getting out. It may be quite soon."

"So it's definite. It's happening."

She nodded.

"Then, yes, I'd like to know when."

"Is there anything else I can do?"

"No." I stood. "I'll walk you out."

Pop held the door for us and watched as I followed her all the way to her car.

Before she got in, she turned and raised a quaking

hand to shield her eyes from the sun. "Elsa believes the investigation of the original crime should be reopened."

"I thought she was retired."

"She is. But she's the only one left from that time. The only investigating officer."

"She wasn't the lead investigator. Far from it. She played a minor part in the beginning, and I must say, she seemed to resent that." I made no effort to conceal my contempt.

"She did say that she felt the investigation was not handled well."

"The biggest thing she thought they did wrong was not letting her run the whole show. Her ambitions were being thwarted. That was the main thing. Just be aware that she has her own agenda. In her mind, this is all about her."

Suzanne looked down and fingered her car keys, squinting.

I said, "The sun is blinding you," and shifted to the other side of her.

I could see Pop fidgeting at the door. I leaned against the side of her car. Pop gave up and went inside, closing the door quietly behind him.

Suzanne returned to her point. "She thinks that you could go back to the people you knew at the time. I'm not sure what she has in mind. But she thought it was a classic case of racial injustice that they pinned it on Jules Jefferson." Suzanne smiled apologetically. "Those were her words. She thought they just arrested the first likely black male. After all, this is the rural South. And it was probably not easy being a female detective."

I had the sense that she was torn between Elsa Gabriel and me, sympathetic toward both of us and perplexed at my hostility. I wondered how Elsa Gabriel talked about me. The animosity between us had been mutual, to say the least.

Suzanne continued. "Anyway, if an investigation were

reopened, with your cooperation, maybe, who knows? Maybe with hindsight you could get some kind of closure. Justice."

"Without my cooperation, it's pretty unlikely."

"You would cooperate, wouldn't you?"

"I would not."

"You would..." She looked confused. "Not?"

"Suzanne, don't you think I have racked my brains? Don't you understand, actually I'm sure you do understand, I've lived and relived that hideous time of my life too many times to count. I will not reopen it, certainly not for the amusement and personal vindication of some bored retiree with no life of her own."

After a long moment of silence, Susanne reached out and touched my shoulder with a touch as soft as the brush of a bird's wing. "I'm sorry, Kate. I don't mean to upset you."

"I'm not upset. But I do not want to answer questions about the people I knew back then."

"Right. I don't think anyone can compel you to cooperate at this point."

I softened and pushed off from her car with a sigh. "I'm sorry, Suzanne. I don't mean to be prickly about it. But I do have to draw a line here. Elsa Gabriel was an observer, one who I thought was probably frustrated in her career, and now maybe she has too much time on her hands. For me, it's not an intellectual puzzle. It's a very real and horrible trauma in my life, and I am not going back there. My testimony was worse than useless back then. How could I possibly make things better now?" I smiled at her. "I'm ranting again. Thanks for coming. I appreciate what you're doing for me. And it's good to see you."

Impulsively, I hugged her, just a quick embrace of her shoulders, and touched my cheek to hers. She felt like a little soft sack of tiny bird bones, dry and lifeless, but she smiled with shy surprise and pleasure. I almost thought she teared up for a moment.

Then she slipped into her car, saying, "Bye," and drove off.

Pop's curiosity was palpable. We were still barely speaking, but at dinnertime that night, he made a big noise about the beautiful tomatoes he had harvested and marinated in olive oil and balsamic vinegar with basil. He expounded on the summer squash he was cooking up with sausage and orecchiette, and the fine Barolo wine he had breathing on the sideboard.

Then he casually began to talk about Suzanne, ignoring my grumpy silence. "Amazing she would think you'd want to listen to them arguing about whether they should let the beast out on the street."

I could not resist saying, "The point is he's not the beast."

"Bah." He made a sour face. "He's an animal. If he didn't do one crime, he would have done another."

"You make me sick." When he didn't respond, I said, "They want to reopen the investigation. Elsa Gabriel does."

"Bah." Another sour face. "Useless."

"No, she thinks if she goes back and looks at all my friends and asks me all about my life and drags up every bit of dirt she can find, she'll be able to figure something out. She wants to investigate the whole thing all over again, twenty-two years later."

He harrumphed, and we were silent for a while.

Then he said, "You won't cooperate with that. Don't have to. No reason for it."

"Suzanne says maybe I could get some kind of closure."

"Reminds me. You had a call. A reporter."

I brightened. "About the landscape project? Or the party?"

"Wants to know what you think about the Jeffersons. Apparently, they're saying you lied."

I laid down my fork very carefully.

Then he asked, "Would you really want to reopen the investigation?"

I left the table.

Upstairs, in my attic study, I did a search for my name. That had become an almost nightly ritual. I found nothing new, so I searched for the Jeffersons. They had come right out and accused me of lying, but they hadn't used my name. I gritted my teeth and fantasized about suing them for slander, but that would be stupid. They couldn't prove anything, anyway. No one could. How could they? The crime scene was long ago obliterated, except for my clothes and shoes and a bullet that didn't match any gun ever found.

The clothes had given up their one secret: that Jefferson was not the man who murdered Elliott and raped me. I was holding firm to my story: It was dark. I was terrified and confused. Jefferson was at the Tavern that night, and he *had* threatened us. He did. I was not the only one who witnessed that part. I thought about the shoes and Elsa Gabriel and bit a fingernail down to the quick. But what could she say? No one would dare blame the victim.

I spent an hour browsing other Justice Project cases. In none of them was a testifying witness dragged out and exposed for a liar. *Hey, I could make history here.* I burst out with a short laugh that sounded alien and hysterical to my own ears, and I clapped my hands over my mouth to stop it. Cold blood coursed through my veins.

By Wednesday night, Pop and I had resumed a chilly superficial normalcy.

As we finished dinner, I said, "I'll be leaving early in the morning. Don't wait for me at breakfast. I'll get coffee on the road."

He considered that, then nodded.

"I'll be back Friday. Probably. We'll see. Don't wait up."

He looked at me uncertainly, and I plunged on. "Things are going to change, Pop. I want to stop reporting my every move to you. All this, the way we live, it needs to change. I need my own life."

Maybe I expected an explosion or a fight. Or that he would be hurt. I was not prepared for uncertainty. It was so unlike him. It shook my determination, but I steeled myself. I'd been rehearsing.

"I have the right to live my own life. Why should I have to tell you my every move? You know this house is as much my home as it is yours, more. Why shouldn't I come and go as I please? I want some space. I'm going to be spending more time away."

At last, a small flare. "What haven't I done for you?"

"You don't own me! I am not a child who needs to be taken care of. And if it's time for me to move on, that's my decision."

He seemed to be in a sort of quiet panic. Even the right eye seemed paralyzed.

"Hey, it won't be that different, not yet, anyway. I want some time to myself. I need to make some decisions, think about what I want in life. I have a lot of years ahead of me." Unspoken was the thought that there would be many years without him. "It won't be so different, Pop."

He was crumpling, folding in upon himself.

"Come on, Pop. How do you like to spend your life? Managing your money. Tending your garden. I love this house and garden. I love the money! I'm not going away. Not entirely. Not yet, maybe not ever. I don't know what I'm going to do. Right now, I'll just be doing what I've been doing, spending a couple or three days a week in Richmond on my own. Is that asking too much? You've seen what I do there. I work! I love my work."

He looked old, and at that moment, I hated him.

Later that night, I lay awake remembering how I'd tried to break away when I reached my senior year in college. I kept thinking about all those years. All those lost years. I played my own words from that evening back in my head and figured that I'd kept my part of the bargain with Tony. I'd see him the next day. We'd spend the night together, I hoped. It was a funny feeling, knowing ahead of time that I was going to sleep with somebody for the first time. Brides must have felt that way in the old days. I'd never done it. Sex had always been spontaneous for me, if not reckless. Or forced. I fell asleep trying to imagine what it was going to be like with Tony, and my fantasies became dreams.

CHAPTER EIGHTEEN

I HAD NOT THOUGHT TO LOOK for the article about the party in the Richmond paper, but it was the first thing Anita wanted to talk about when I arrived at Mary's Grove Thursday morning. She was sitting in the sunroom wearing a beautiful blue and gold silk kimono and sipping an espresso. The little room, hardly more than an alcove, was warm and glowing with direct morning sunlight. Sweet-scented red roses left over from the weekend before were full blown, some hanging their heads and dropping petals on the glass-topped table.

Anita had a dozen copies of the Sunday newspaper piled up on the table in front of her. She offered me coffee, but when I accepted, she gave me a paper instead.

She pulled out the *Living* section and urged me to read it, then she kept talking so I couldn't. "That silly girl," she said.

I saw Sabrina Cole's byline and the group picture on the front page of the section. The picture was very flattering of both of us, and of Tony, too.

"Listen to this foolishness." She took the paper back out of my hands and started reading aloud. Sabrina had gushed about the "gracious" home, the "exclusive" guest list, the "blue blood," and the "internationally famous" designer. I thought it was borderline embarrassing, and I think Anita knew it was too much, but she couldn't help being pleased. She turned to an inside page where the article continued and showed me two more pictures.

"It's a pretty amazing spread," I had to admit after I'd scanned it and studied the photos. "I can't thank you enough, Anita. It's all your doing, and it's excellent free advertising for me."

"Oh, I think you'll find you impressed some very good contacts that night, Kate." She leaned back. "There's another party this weekend. Friday night, tomorrow, at the country club. You could come with me. There are people there you ought to see again. And some that you should meet. Come with your handsome father?" Her eyes had a conspiratorial twinkle.

"I'm not sure. I sort of had plans, myself." I was hoping for a breakthrough with Tony. I wondered if I could bring him along, but decided against asking her. "I'll see what I can do. It seemed like Pop had something going on this week. He said he couldn't make it into town. But I can try."

She leaned forward and touched my hand. "If you do find yourself free, you come ahead without him. I mean to invite you for yourself. But it would be marvelous to see him, too, of course." She bit her lip. "He doesn't have someone else he's seeing, does he?"

"Oh, no. It wouldn't be anything like that. It would be..." I cast about for a good excuse for him not to come. "A business contact coming through town." Through Lynchburg? It sounded wildly improbable to my own ears, but she seemed to accept it.

"Should I call him?" When I hesitated, she said, "He's the old-fashioned type, isn't he? I'd better not. You don't have to RSVP. Do you know where the club is? Come if you can, with or without Mr. Cranbrook."

"You really are being awfully nice to me." I looked beyond Anita's perfect ash-blond hair and saw Tony supervising bed preparation. My heart jumped.

She turned gracefully to follow my gaze. "He was here before I got up. He's in some kind of hurry."

"I'll go see what he's doing." But before I could rise, I heard the front doorbell.

Anita rose and answered the door. To my amazement, she reappeared with Sabrina Cole.

Sabrina spotted her article at once and beamed. "Great, huh?"

Anita said, "Very nice. I think it captured the event quite well."

I didn't answer. I was thinking what was great was the party, not the coverage of the party. I wanted to say, "What are you doing here?"

She treated us to another flash of dirty teeth. "I wondered what the next step was. In the project." To me, she said, "I thought you might be in here. And it looks like Tony's already hard at work. Can we talk?"

Anita stood up. "Well, you will excuse me." She gave me a warm smile and touched my shoulder as she left. The nod she gave to Sabrina was too cordial to suit me.

Sabrina sat down in Anita's chair. "I'm serious about photographing this project. I can promote your book, get you in the paper. You see what I did with the party." She pointed at the newspaper still open on the table.

I stood up without answering and simply left, heading out to the garden. Of course, she followed. Tony, who really did seem rushed and out of sorts, answered her questions as shortly as possible. He was shoveling enormous piles of rich soil and compost.

I went to my car, pulled out some files, sat down at a lawn table, and began to read. I was staring at invoices. Sixteen yards of this. Twelve yards of that. Sabrina tried to read over my shoulder, and I said something sharp about confidential financial matters between me and my client. I shut the folder and looked at her pointedly.

"I need to review my files right now," I told her.

I was beginning to think I'd have to be more blunt, when she finally hoisted her shabby shoulder bag. "I'll just take a few pictures, and then I have to get back to the office."

"Do you have Mrs. Blore's permission to take pictures today?"

Yellow teeth. "Oh, I assume so."

Fifteen minutes later, she waved and got in her car. Neither Tony nor I waved back. We looked at each other.

I said, "What a pest."

With Sabrina gone, at last, I turned to Tony with a huge smile. "I didn't think you'd be here this early. Do you want to go somewhere for lunch?"

He mumbled something about having too much to do.

That wasn't the right answer. "What's your hurry? Tony? Are we on for tonight? I thought—"

"I know, I know. Hey, Kate, I'm sorry. I gotta go back to Virginia Beach tonight."

"What?" I didn't think I had heard him right. "It's only Thursday. You have to be here tomorrow anyway. You're going home tonight?"

He hunched over the shovel and ducked his face like a guilty little boy. "I don't know, Kate. I think you're right. We have to take this slow."

I swore under my breath and walked in a tight circle before I answered him. "Did you talk to her at all?"

"Yeah, I tried. I didn't get very far before she got hysterical. Then she called in her whole family, and they're on me like a pack of dogs."

"Did you tell her about me?"

He wouldn't look at me. "No, I didn't get that far. I told her... I don't know... something like we said. You know, I got my business, all this back and forth, maybe I need a little more time to myself, or something like that, and I swear, she just ran with it. Screaming, crying, collapsing on the floor, clinging to my ankles."

He twisted at the memory, grabbing at the back of his neck. "Then she calls her mom and starts wailing, Tony this, Tony that, and her dad hears all the commotion, and they both come over, and there's this whole big scene, and

Kate, I admit—" He laughed shortly. "—I was backpedaling. I won't lie to you about that. I tried to say, this is between Beryl and me, and if there's some things in our marriage, we need to be able to talk about them without dragging in the whole extended family."

I stared at him.

"Anyway, I think I gotta go back there tonight, smooth things over."

"*Smooth them over?* Why?"

"Kate, trust me. I got to take it slow, okay? Give her a chance to get used to maybe I'm not there so much. Like you and your dad, you know? Take it slow, ease into it, look for the right time?"

I said coldly, "Sure, Tony, fine," and turned and walked briskly to my car.

"Kate, wait a minute."

I ignored him as he trotted beside me. Oh, he didn't want me mad at him either. So I didn't make it easy. When he grabbed my arm, I shook free and jumped into my car. I started it and threw gravel driving away.

So I basically went off the rails. It was only Thursday afternoon, less than a day into what I was telling myself would be my new life of freedom, and I was frantic because Tony wasn't playing into my hands the way I'd wanted. I couldn't think what else to do. What did I have, other than the Blore project and Tony? So I called Merit and asked if I could come over later. He wasn't exactly enthusiastic, but I wasn't in a state to pick up on subtleties. I stopped for take-out Vietnamese food on the way back to my apartment, where I stewed over noodles and drank an entire bottle of wine and part of another one, somehow losing the whole afternoon. I dimly remembered ignoring a call from Pop.

By the time I made it to Merit's apartment, I was drunk and testy. To explain my mood, I told him how my plans had fallen through with Tony. "I wish he would hurry up and divorce her."

My recollection of that night is unclear, but I know this. I tried to seduce Merit and failed. He held me at arm's length, gently, when he figured out where I was headed, then reassured me and let me down as easy as he could. I think we ate something. I think I helped myself to some beer in his fridge. I may have slept a while, and I know that he drove me home in my own car once again. I kept clinging to his arm and even cried some. I don't like to think about it. I was maudlin and ashamed. I have an unwelcome memory of his disapproval, which he could not entirely conceal. I don't even know how he got home. A cab again, I suppose. The whole thing is a blur, a night I'd just as soon forget but can't. I almost wanted Pop when it was all over.

I slept it off and woke up depressed. I had a Friday morning appointment with Max Weigel that I didn't even want to keep. I pulled on the same jeans and shirt I'd worn the day before—no Mysterious Client costume—and drove to his office, which looked seedier than ever to me in my sour mood.

The dog took one look at me and went straight for its bed. Max Weigel did the same thing. He turned without comment and went back to his desk. He sat back in his chair with an arrogant smirk, and when I was seated opposite him in the straight wooden chair, he said without preamble, "On what you've given me, which is not much, I found a slew of Carl Brewers. On the information you gave me, there's no reason to believe any of them is *your* Carl Brewer. Not much reason to believe any of them aren't."

I know I radiated my disgust with him. "Could you make a case that he's missing and that I've made a reasonably, what is it, 'diligent' attempt to locate him?"

"I could contact all the possible Carl Brewers in Virginia that are the right age and aren't obviously not him and ask them if they were ever married back then."

"Just find out if they were ever briefly married. If they deny it, then they won't contest the divorce, right?"

He looked at me for a long moment. "This might cost more."

I was getting hot, but I controlled my rising temper. I tried to make my voice cold. "How much do you want me to pay you to put together a case for a divorce on grounds of abandonment, without service, using the information I've given you?"

"Ms. Cranbrook—"

"How do you know my name?"

"I know who you are because you've been all over the newspapers for the last two weeks. Besides, it's part of the record of the marriage, which I found. It was quite a few years ago, wasn't it?"

"I told you that."

"You were very young."

"So you used the money I paid you to investigate *me*?"

"Chill, Mrs. Brewer. I'm not trying to make trouble for you. I'm trying to do my job in spite of you. With what I've learned, no thanks to you, I could make a case that there is no sign of Carl Brewer in any of the fifty states, practically since the day you married him. The man disappeared off the face of the earth, at least as far as the usual databases are concerned."

"Let me tell you something, Mr. Weigel—"

He held up a hand, and for some reason, that silenced me. The dog stood up, turned three times in its bed, and curled up facing the wall. Weigel took a placating tone, as if I were some kind of difficult customer. "Come on, Kate. I'm on your side. You've got to trust somebody. You can trust me. You have to."

"The man scares me to death. I don't know where he is, but if he finds out I am having him investigated, trying to find him, I don't know what he'll do. I don't know what he does that he doesn't want to be found, what alias he might use. You said yourself that people in prison, felons... what did you say?"

"People who are in and out of jail or people or who are hounded constantly by creditors are usually very difficult to locate is what I said. Maybe he's a child support scumbag, getting paid under the table, skipping around. He may be a deadbeat, but that doesn't mean he's dangerous. Unless you know something?" He watched me sharply.

"Well, he scares me. And I have my own reasons for not wanting it to get out that I have this disgraceful marriage in my background."

"Aw, come on, Kate. In this day and age? Don't be ridiculous. Lots of people have brief, ill-advised young marriages in their past. It means nothing, professionally. This isn't even the twentieth century anymore. You talk about it like it's the nineteenth century."

"It's not for you to tell me what I do or do not want known about my private life." I was short of breath with rage, and I could feel that my face was flaming hot. "You—" I pointed at him, jabbing. "—are supposed to respect my confidentiality, my privacy, I mean, this is all confidential." I stumbled for words in my spitting fury, and he made me even madder by starting to laugh.

"I'm not going to tell anybody anything about you, Kate. Not a word to a soul. I'm going to give evidence in court that a licensed and experienced PI determined that your husband is unlocatable. You'll be a free woman in a matter of a few weeks, and then you can take your secret to the grave."

I blinked, took a few shaky breaths and tried to calm down. "So what's the next step?"

"Filing, hearing, notice."

I stiffened. "What notice?"

"Publication."

"What?" I jerked forward in my seat and gripped the arms of the chair.

He shrugged. "It'll be pretty inconspicuous. Ever see one?"

I shook my head.

"See? Most people don't even see them, unless they're looking for something. Nobody's looking for this, according to you. And if he doesn't want to be found, even if he's around here somewhere and sees it, he's not going to do anything about it. Hell, why should he care? You might be doing him a favor."

"I'm not sure I want to go through with this."

He put on a bored, weary face. "Up to you. I keep the grand if you don't. You pay me another thousand dollars if you do." He shrugged. "Your choice."

So I did it. After what had transpired with Tony, I wasn't even sure why, but then I thought, *No. I am not doing this for Tony. I am doing this for me.* I said, "Do it," but not without deep misgivings. "I want him out of my life."

Weigel half-stood when I got up to go, but he didn't see me out. The dog didn't even lift its head.

Back at my apartment, I washed my hair and slipped into a tight little black dress.

"Oh, Tony." I sighed at my image in the mirror. "You are such a fool." Then I used my laptop to look up directions to Anita's country club.

On the way there, I relented and called Pop. His voice was weak, but I had hardened myself to him.

"Where have you been?" There was no demand, just need. He sounded desperate.

"Here. Working."

"You didn't answer the phone."

"No, I didn't."

"Will you be here for dinner?"

"No. I won't be home tonight at all. I'm on my way to a reception. Anita invited me. She thinks I might find some perspective clients. She invited you, too," I added, feeling malicious. "But I didn't think you'd want to be stuck with her all night while I worked the crowd."

He was silent.

"I'll be home tomorrow." And before he could argue, I hung up.

CHAPTER NINETEEN

THE COUNTRY CLUB ASPIRED TO an antebellum style with white Ionic columns two stories high, although the building was obviously less than sixty years old. I had taken a quick peek at the club's website and knew it had been chartered in the early fifties. It had been around long enough to cultivate an oak allée for the main approach. As I drove up, I saw women in long, full dresses on the lawn. The scene was like something out of *Gone with the Wind*. Pop would have liked it. I was going to look like a waitress with my short black dress.

The big house was warmly lit, sparkling and tinkling with glass and crystal chandeliers and murmuring with bright conversation. I was mentally prepared to explain myself and talk my way inside, but no one stopped me. And even though I was contrite about how much I had drunk the night before and still didn't feel great, I took a glass of champagne from a silver tray to brace myself. I didn't know anyone. The champagne hit my stomach just right: hair of the dog.

Not everyone was in a long skirt, but mine was conspicuously short. I felt a lot of eyes giving me the up-down, so I slowed and let them look. Someone in a uniform asked if he could help me. He was not challenging, just helpful, but at that same moment, I spotted Anita and waved. The uniform saw that she knew me and melted away.

Anita, perfectly turned out as usual, floated in the middle of a lively crowd, relaxed, accessible, and yet fully engaged. I was beginning to admire her. She immediately came to embrace me, and inexplicably, I teared up at her kindness.

I blinked and fussed to hide my reaction. "I told him about the party."

"I know. Thank you, dear." She hooked her arm through mine and drew me toward the back of the main ballroom, which faced through french windows to a back veranda and a lighted terrace surrounded by dark trees. "I have to confess, I called him."

"He isn't coming, though, is he?"

She sighed. "I wish I'd known you were. I thought you had something else going on."

"I thought I did. I'm sorry. I should have called you."

"No, dear, it's fine. I'm so glad you did come. It's just that when I told your father you weren't coming, he seemed to lose interest. If he'd known you'd be here, I think he would have come, too."

"Oh, Anita, I'm so sorry."

She waved it off and sighed again. "That's just the way it is, isn't it? You are the light of his life."

We both contemplated that fact ruefully. That, I thought, was why she cultivated me.

I didn't blame her, and I wished it could work. "Oh well. I didn't think he would come in any case. I spoke to him before you did and told him I'd be here. So he had it from me that I would be, and still he didn't come. I think he just wasn't in a mood for a big party. He's a homebody, you know. Almost a hermit. He wants to be holed up in his study on a Friday night. We live way out there in the sticks, and he likes it that way. Once in a while, he wants to come into the city, but usually just to go out for a good dinner and the symphony."

She brightened. "I love the symphony. I have season tickets for the Washington Symphony Orchestra."

"Perfect!" But I doubted he would go with her. It was maddening.

We stepped out onto the veranda, and she said, "There are some people I want you to meet."

She led me to a tent lit with red and orange lanterns. A waiter in a white suit offered me another glass of champagne, which I took. Those little shells didn't hold much. Anita introduced me to a couple whose names I didn't catch. I was distracted by the food. I hadn't eaten since breakfast. A table covered with white linen held a row of three-tiered silver trays stacked with canapés. My mouth actually watered. There were puff pastries stuffed with crab salad, little teriyaki shrimp kabobs, and a half-dozen other delectable-looking morsels.

No one else showed the slightest interest in the spread. I waited for the first moment when it was my turn to speak and directed the conversation, quite gracefully I thought, to the evening, which was lovely, warm, and dry with a gentle breeze. Then, I mentioned the terrace, which offered an enchanting view of the Appomattox River shimmering with moonlight and defined by a string of lights along the far shore. Finally, I brought up the sumptuous spread of appetizers and pretended to be just noticing them. The man helped himself to a little plate with a handful of appetizers, and I did the same. They were as good as they looked. I wanted to stand there and eat until I was full. Anita admired the food but didn't touch it, and the other woman ate a single cracker. I resolutely turned my back on the table, but I planned to lead them all away, ditch them, and circle back for more.

Anita took my arm again, kissed off the first couple, and introduced me to another half-dozen people. All of them had money, so I played up to them as best I could. We ended up promising to talk again, and Anita volunteered to make sure we got each other's numbers. Perfect.

And so it went for at least another hour. At one point, she introduced me to the person in charge of the country club grounds, which I'd been admiring. I did catch his name: Harvey Grant. Anita told me he had put in the vegetable gardens that supplied the club dining room in season. He was tall, lean, and tanned, and I wondered if he might be gay. He looked at me with something like awe, and I was reluctant when Anita dragged me away to meet some more of her rich friends.

At last, I broke away, pleading need of a bathroom, which was real after six of those tiny glasses of champagne and a glass of water, which I'd requested from a waiter mainly to get my hands on a bigger glass, although the cold water did taste good. I spotted a half-empty champagne bottle on my way to the bathroom. Cheap stuff. I checked around me quickly, saw no one, and swiped it. Two minutes later, I left the bathroom, giggling, with a big glass of what looked like Seven-Up.

Outside again, I found the table under the tent much depleted and almost deserted. I was systematically scarfing down the last pieces of one appetizer after another when Harvey Grant came up behind me.

"Whoa, not hungry, are you?"

I washed down a mouthful with a gulp of champagne and laughed. "You caught me! Yes, I'm starving. Didn't eat all day."

"Are you sure we haven't met?" He seemed utterly charmed, and it went straight to my head.

"I don't think so. When would that have been?"

And amazingly, he told me: a seminar on plant propagation. We hadn't actually met. He had seen me there and remembered me. I smiled and jumped into a discussion of roses, which had been the focus of much of the seminar. I finished the last bit of food in sight, drained my glass, and set it down.

When he asked me if I'd like a glass of champagne, I started giggling and couldn't stop. He laughed along with me, having no idea what was so funny. He flagged down a waiter, whose glance made me wonder if he'd been counting how many glasses I'd already had, but maybe that was paranoid. Harvey and I wandered off onto the dark lawns, where he began explaining what was planted where and what was planned for future beds and gardens. We found we both loved once-blooming old climbers and lamented the fact that so many people had little patience with them.

It's funny how these things can go. There I was, all my sheets to the wind, my focus out beyond myself in the beauty of the dark gardens, and he was trailing after me, to all appearances quite smitten, as long as he could gape at me unseen. Then I'm not sure what I did. Maybe I called a bluff of some kind. Maybe I slurred my words. Or maybe I swung around and came on too strong.

Anyway, I scared him off. Awkwardly, he made a point of mentioning a wife. Twice. I looked, and incredibly, he wore a wedding ring. It seemed blazingly clear to me that I had been right. He was gay. A married gay man.

"A wife." I wasn't sure what I meant or what my tone conveyed, and I couldn't read his expression. It was so dark.

We faced each other from a distance of not more than a few feet, but we were nothing more than dark silhouettes. Before he had a chance to move, I breezed by him on my way back to the house. I was furious—and embarrassed. For one brief moment, I'd thought I was going to seduce that man, lead him away and play a little game with him, have an adventure.

I stalked back into the lobby of the clubhouse and got mixed up in hallways twice before I found the exit. I saw Anita watching me curiously and fled to my car, cursing to myself.

Why, why, why? I drove out too fast and stopped abruptly in the parking lot to pull myself together. Shocking, I thought. I, of all people, was actually inept with men. At forty-two. Oh, I was hardly inexperienced, but something was wrong. I blamed my extreme isolation. I pounded the seat next to me. Why couldn't I have whatever man I wanted? It infuriated me. Wasn't it supposed to be easy if you were beautiful?

And excuse me, it's not as if I don't have as many doubts as the next woman, but damn it, I have been told many times that I am beautiful. I look in the mirror, objectively, and I see my flawless pink and white skin, wide, deep-set, dark blue eyes, naturally honey-blond hair, my cute little vampire teeth. My jaw line is clean, my neck long and round. My body. My intelligence. Am I intimidating? Am I too beautiful? How is it done? How am I not perfect? I should be able to have anyone I want—everybody says so. My jewelry, my clothes, my brains, my money, my success. What is it about me? How is it done?

I had reached the point where I was thinking that maybe I needed a supremely confident man when I thought of Merit, and my faced burned. I swore out loud again. For the second time in two days, I thought unwillingly of Pop. I actually missed him, he who knew me to the core and loved me as I was, poor thing. I ground my teeth until my jaw ached and my head hurt. I drove safely home and parked in front of my apartment without incident. I sat there with the engine off and tried to think, but nothing came.

"It was nothing." I said it out loud to no one.

I would explain it to Anita soon enough. I imagined telling her that Harvey Grant had come on to me. But what if he really was gay and she knew it? I would have to think about that. I could say he got weird with me. That would do it. I would refuse to elaborate, take the high road. I blew out a breath.

In fact, I never thought of Harvey Grant again, until now. Because that night, sitting in my car, roiling over the debacle at the country club, I finally noticed that I was gripping the steering wheel so tightly that my arms were getting sore. I peeled my fingers off and flexed them, blowing out a huge breath. I took another deep breath and another, slowly calming. Then I climbed out and stood staring. Merit's car was parked in front of mine. At least I thought it was his car. It was a white hybrid with a suit jacket hanging in the back and books stacked on the shelf in front of the rear window. Books about Africa.

Part of me was still miffed at him, but mostly I was glad he had come. I ran up the stairs, thinking that he must be waiting for me on the chair on the porch. I burst up to the landing and stopped when I could see he wasn't there. I climbed the last few steps slowly. The door to my apartment stood ajar. Had I left it unlocked? Never. Did he have a key? How could he?

I knocked on the door jam and called his name. No answer. I knocked again, called again, then pushed on the door and stepped across the threshold.

And there he lay.

He was face down, but I had no doubt who he was. For a moment, I froze in place, trying to process what my eyes were telling me. Merit sprawled on the floor of my apartment. A sickening, frightening smell repelled me.

I think I screamed but I'm not sure. I know I dropped to my knees and shook his shoulder, and I was shocked at how inert he was, and how cool. Not cool. But not warm. Not a living body, you see.

I kept calling him, "Merit! Merit!" Then I saw that I was kneeling in blood that had pooled out from under his body, and I knew he'd been shot in the chest.

I fumbled in my purse with shaking fingers. All I could think of was to get out of there, so I called Tony. Crazy, but I thought surely he would help me. He had to. I couldn't stay there. It rang and rang while I moaned and paced, and when he finally picked up I kept saying, "He's dead, he's dead."

Tony couldn't seem to get what I was saying, shushing me and saying, "Kate, what are you calling me here for?"

"My friend Merit is dead! Don't you hear me? Dead! Dead! He's been shot!"

He finally snapped to what I was trying to tell him. "Call 9-1-1, Kate."

I said, "No, get me out of here!"

"Kate, you have to call 9-1-1."

"No, Tony, I can't be involved in this. I can't. I can't stand it, not again, not again."

"Kate—"

"I'm leaving," and then I heard a siren. Somebody else must have heard me screaming and called it in. I got up, and I must have touched my face because I realized my hands were wet, so I rubbed them down my sides. I looked down. There was blood on the hem of my skirt where I had knelt, and there was blood on my sides where I'd wiped my hands. I started to scream again.

I don't know how much time went by.

Tony called again, but the cops wouldn't let me talk to him. They snatched my phone. A small crowd gathered. The cops kept me apart and asked me questions, always questions, questions, questions. I was hysterical, and I started babbling and saying it was my fault, all my fault.

"Oh my God," I said over and over. "It's my fault!"

It's all a little unclear in my mind now, but I remember one cop saying, "Did you kill him?"

And I moaned. "I brought him here. He's here because of me." I told them I was cursed, and I said some weird things about how it was all because of Africa, and I could never get away from Africa, and I could see the cop beginning to think I was crazy.

He asked me what had happened, and I screamed at him, "Are you blind? He's been shot, that's what happened. What do you think happened?" I mimicked him: "What happened?" And then I cried and wailed.

They thought I was so crazy they didn't even bother not to speak in front of me. One of them said, "He was facedown. How did she know he was shot in the chest?"

They searched my purse and car, looking for a gun or something to incriminate me. I kept saying he was my friend, just my friend. It went on and on, until they took me in, but they didn't arrest me.

They asked, "Did you shoot him?" And, "Why did you shoot him?"

I had no answers. I kept saying it was all my fault, and they kept asking if I shot him, which I denied.

In a rage of frustration, I tried to explain: "He's dead. I got him killed. He's been shot," and they looked at each other, and I said, "Oh God, I give up."

During an ominous lull, I scrambled to order my thoughts. My stomach grabbed at the echoes of own words, and I clapped my hand over my mouth, which had been running much too freely. I said, "Jesus," and one of the cops looked up.

Think, think, think. It could have been political. Merit had been threatened, and many people knew that. Why was that idea so familiar? I thought about the elderly Kikuyu's evil and embittered old mug. I gasped when I realized I could tell them quite truthfully that the old man hated Merit.

The cop who was watching me moved toward me. "Was he your lover?"

"No! He was my friend. My friend, my only friend." I knew I shouldn't be talking so much. I wrapped my hands around my jaws to stop them moving. *My lovers die, yes, but why my friend?* Unbelieving, I combed my memory for actions, movements, my exposures over recent weeks. The symposium. Lunch. The photograph.

"Ma'am, do you have a husband?"

"No, I do not!" But I did. Oh God. I did. A clarity too horrible to bear came down on me, and right behind it, white cold fear. A part of my brain registered the consternation on the cop's face. I thrashed. Hysteria. They expect it of a woman. It was an appropriate response to trauma.

Meanwhile, inside, the calculating me tried to weigh the situation. I squeezed my eyes shut, then opened them and tried to see. *Think, think, think.* I couldn't. I just saw my control dissipating. Too many people in my life, too many contacts, too much information out there.

They found my license in my purse and called Pop. Pop's attorney, Melson, showed up with a doctor I didn't know. Melson told me in so many lawyerly words to shut up, and then he threatened to sue the cops if they harassed me.

"It's obvious," Melson said, "that she came home and found his body. She didn't shoot him. With what? Why? Do you have any cause to believe it?"

I started in again about how he was dead because of me. I said I didn't shoot him. "Why would I do that?" I howled.

Melson got me alone, and then I realized Pop was there, hanging out of sight. I hissed at him, but Melson was in my face. "What happened?"

I looked at him, then at Pop and took a huge breath, my mind becoming clear at last.

He repeated the question. "Did you say you killed him?"

"He's dead because of me."

Melson asked, "Who was he?"

Pop said, "An African," as if that explained everything.

I put my head down in my arms. "Get him out of here." I told them I thought I might throw up.

The quack pulled out a needle and gave me a shot. I tried to yell at him. It was outrageous. Where were the cops? But I was running out of steam.

"He came here because of me." And then I explained. He'd seen me on the Web. He had an offer from VCU, but he was going to turn it down, but then he saw that I lived in the area, so he came. He wouldn't have if it hadn't been for me. I folded over and rested my aching head on the table.

Melson called in the cops and prompted me. "Tell them." And so I did.

And Melson said, "See? She blames herself because he wouldn't have come here if it hadn't been for her."

I kept saying, "He was just my friend. My only friend."

The cop asked, "What do you mean, he had an offer from VCU?"

Everything had gotten calmer on all sides. They had begun to see that, although I was hysterical, I wasn't actually crazy. They began to treat me sympathetically. They offered me water and allowed Pop, Melson, and the doctor to surround me.

My hands were folded in my lap, my voice zombie-like. "He teaches at Southern California. African History and Culture. VCU invited him to lecture here for a term. He was going to turn it down when he learned I was here and he emailed me, and I encouraged him to take the job. I wanted to see him again. We were friends when we were children."

I told them where I'd been all evening, and they said they'd have to check, but I could see they had little doubt they'd find out I was telling the truth. They took names.

Pop said, "She told me she'd be there."

"Then you went home to your apartment, and Chenobo was there. Why?"

Good question. "I don't know. I saw him last night. He... he made a pass at me. I turned him down. I think he must have wanted to apologize. Or try again." I felt awful telling lies about him, but how could it hurt him? He was dead. The terrible thing was, he might have been coming to apologize and give me a different answer. But none of that occurred to me until much later. At the time, I just knew I had to be careful, so I said the thing I thought would make them all stop asking questions. I felt Pop's hand on my shoulder, and I shook it off.

They asked me if he had any enemies, and I told them he might have political enemies. I told them about the symposium and about the threats on the blackboard, which he'd reported. I told them about the old Kikuyu.

I twisted in my chair and glared straight at Pop. "He was working for Kenya still. He was a great man. It's a tragedy that he's been lost."

Pop looked away, twitching his nose as if he didn't like what he smelled.

In the end, the cops didn't take me seriously as a suspect. They called Anita, who told them to the minute when I'd left the club.

The cop said, "We'll have to talk to all of them again, to confirm that you were there the whole time, but I'd say you're in the clear for now."

And that was how the awful night ended. The doctor gave me, or I should say he gave Pop, a prescription for a sedative, but I was already numb. Pop drove me home.

And for a while after that, everything is a blank.

CHAPTER TWENTY

I T WAS LIKE NIGHT COMING down on day, just as it had been like night coming down on day all those years ago. The sun was out and then it went dark. I had thought I could see my way ahead, and then all was darkness and confusion. Silence and oblivion descended on me.

I began to relive the crime. I hadn't been there in stark memory for so many years. I don't normally let myself think about what actually happened, hadn't allowed myself to for many, many years. But then, it came back to me unbidden with terrifying vividness. *I am dimly aware of shouting, and the car door flies open, my arm is pulled almost out of joint, I land on the ground, I feel sharp stones and hard pavement, there is a deafening report—POW—in my left ear.*

I couldn't hear right for days. I would say, "What? What?" And turn my right ear. However, it wasn't my ears but my brain that couldn't understand words.

Every question was a struggle. "Then what happened? Then what? Then what?" They wanted me to be so exact, and I couldn't talk about it. "What exactly did he do?"

Pop was always there. He wanted to answer for me, to shield me from their questions, but they wouldn't let him.

"Let her answer," they would say.

And he would say, "Can't you see she's traumatized? She was brutalized. She was witness to a murder. It's obvious what happened. Let her be."

Elliott had been shot dead with a single bullet, left

partially unclothed and sprawled across the front seat of his Volvo. He was alone when the cops found him in the early hours of the morning. It was ten o'clock the next day before they found me at home. Those are the facts.

They identified Elliott pretty quickly from the license plates of his car, and his wife, who had been making frantic calls all night, put them on to the rehearsals and the cast, who put them on to me as having been with Elliott when they last saw him. The cops found out I had a nine o'clock class that I had not shown up for and sent someone to the house.

Pop came upstairs to get me, but I fought him. I was crazy. I was wrapped up in a robe, lying on top of the still-made bed, and I still had on the blouse and skirt from the night before, but no underpants. My face felt hugely swollen, my lip split and throbbing, my eyes sore, and I couldn't open one of them. Pop went away, and a little while after that, a woman came in, not a cop, but some sort of emergency medical technician. After a while, I let her lead me downstairs.

I remember the Hyena, dog-faced and suspicious, first, because I had apparently left the scene of the crime and turned up at home, and second, because Pop had not called the police right away the night before. But everybody else was sympathetic.

The car was found a little more than a mile from the house, and Pop said I had come home late in an alarming state and refused to explain what had happened. He said I must have walked home. Yes, he had wondered, yes, he'd been worried, yes, he had asked me, but I wouldn't tell him anything. In the end, they had to accept the fact that I was half out of my mind.

They took me to the hospital in Lynchburg, where I was examined by a doctor who reported vaginal bruising and tearing in addition to the obvious contusions on my body, plus a black eye and the split lip. It felt like my nose was broken, too, but it wasn't. The cops took my clothes and shoes away with them.

I could never have imagined how long it would take to process an experience like that. The hospital, the questioning, the lineup, the whole story told again and again until it made a coherent narrative of that fateful night, all that took up every waking moment for days that stretched into weeks and then into months. Then there was the trial. At last there was a cold, dull peace of a kind as the storm passed.

In the aftermath of Merit's death, scenes from that long-ago ordeal engulfed me as vividly as they had in the weeks first following the crime, even though it had been more than two decades. Sounds like the slamming of a car door, the voices downstairs when the cops first came to the house, the seamy smell of my own soiled clothes, all those sensations flooded my brain.

Pop hovered over me, guarding me ferociously. So I passed the weekend and more, sequestered in my room, trapped once again in the nightmare. The doctor visited and gave me shots. Pop plied me with pills. In my drugged state, I could hardly tell the past from the present. It was the same room, the same trees showing through, the same grief and terror. Sometimes when I awoke, I would lie and puzzle over the summer sun leaking through the curtains: the first crime happened in the dead of winter.

I heard the phone ringing in the hall. Suzanne called, I later learned, and Pop told her I was ill. I dimly heard my cell and tried to get up, but Pop rummaged through my purse to find it, and I sank back in bed, unable to deal with it. Sometimes during brief, wakeful interludes, my hearing would be preternaturally acute. I heard Pop telling someone that the shooting had brought back unpleasant memories and I needed to rest. The doctor came again and gave me more pills.

I was drugged and cut off for days, maybe a week.

Then one night, I refused the pills and threw off Pop like overly hot covers. I locked my door and looked at garden magazines until I drifted off to sleep. Having been in bed sleeping a druggy sleep for so long, I awoke in the night and lay wide awake, sleepless. Images of Merit kept returning to me. I reviewed everything that had happened after the police came to my apartment and after I went to the station. Answering questions. Pop's appearance, the lawyer, the doctor, then the drugs that blotted out everything. I finally drifted into a light sleep.

In the darkest hour of the night, I sat bolt upright and bit my knuckles. I got up and paced. I grew cold, huddled with freezing, sweaty feet in bed, and got up again. Wrapped in a robe, I watched the dark mountains forming up as hulks in the amber dawn. At first sunlight, I went downstairs, slowly, unsure of my balance, and made coffee. I could see Pop outside, striding across the lawn in his tweed jacket. I searched and found my cell phone lying on his desk in the study. I grabbed it and retreated back to my room.

At seven thirty, I began ringing Max Weigel's office, hanging up every time I heard it roll to voicemail. He finally answered at eight, breathless.

I cursed under my breath as I heard Pop on the stairs. My voice on the phone was a harsh whisper. "Weigel? You have to cancel that notice."

"Whoa," he said in a loud voice. It was probably not really loud, just not lowered furtively like mine.

I winced and pressed my hand over the speaker.

"Ms. Cranbrook? Kate?"

"Don't publish that notice."

"Too late. I put in the order the day you told me to do it. It ran that same week. It's still in there."

I swore again and hissed, "Does it give his name?"

"Of course it does. You have to—"

"Cancel it! Immediately. Stop it. Now, no more."

"Cancel the notice," he repeated with exasperating calm.

"Cancel the filing, hearing, notice, everything."

After a beat he said, "It's your money. And I've done the work, fair and square, on your orders. I'm keeping the money."

"Keep it, whatever. Cancel everything. Now."

"Yes, ma'am. So—"

"As soon as I hang up." And I hung up.

I crawled back into bed and bit my cuticles until they bled. The day stretched out, endless. Pop knocked at the door, and I sent him away. I never dressed, never left my room, ate nothing. That night, I decided on one more night of pills, which I had found in my bathroom.

The next day I woke up thinking about my classes. I went down to the kitchen and found Pop there, wanting to know what he should make for breakfast.

I ignored him and fumbled with the calendar. "What day is this?"

"Sunday."

What Sunday? "What's the date?" I was incredulous and dismayed when I saw that I had lost a week. I turned my fury on Pop. "What happened to my classes?"

"I called. Told them you were too ill to teach. You've hardly ever missed. Anyone could miss a week."

I made some toast and took it back upstairs with strong coffee. Then I sat at my desk and tried to plan my next lecture. I would write on the page and then read and reread what I'd written, uncomprehending. Names of plants looked as though they were misspelled. "A-z-a-e-l-e-a?" Really? Finally, I laid my head down in my arms and waited while sleepiness reclaimed me. I moved back to the bed, pulled the covers up, and lost consciousness again.

Early that afternoon, I heard a car pull up, a door slam, and the doorbell ring. I listened as Pop opened the door, not much caring what he did. Then I roused a little as I heard voices, his and another one, female. I picked my head up and listened. My neck began to cramp. Then I heard the back door. I went to the window.

Of all things, Anita stood on my doorstep. She strolled across the grass with Pop, her head bent close to his.

After a while, still groggy but curious, I went downstairs with a gnawing uneasiness in the pit of my stomach. They were in the living room. She held a glass of sherry, and she was dressed for a day in the country, in a soft plaid calf-length cotton skirt and a light cotton pullover with the sleeves pushed up to her elbows. She looked natural and handsome.

She hugged me, smelling fresh and sweet with a warm floral scent. "Kate, I'm so sorry. I know how upset you must be. Tony told me about the crime, the one when you were in college. My dear, I had no idea. How awful for you."

Pop watched, expressionless. I could see her examining me with eyes full of concern. I nodded, unable to speak. Looking down, I saw my own clothes hanging on me.

"Why, you're wasting away," she cried. "After what happened to you before, and then to see something so awful, it must have been too much to bear. I didn't imagine what you were going through. I still can't. You try to carry too much around by yourself. You need to let the people who love you help. We can't make it go away, but you needn't always be so alone."

My eyes met Pop's.

"Oh, I know you have your father," she said. "And he does what he can. But it's lonely and difficult for him, too." She held my shoulders and beamed at me. "I feel almost as if you are my own daughter, the daughter I never had."

My throat ached at the very idea of mothering. I'd done without it all my life.

"You need to let us in, Kate," she said. "You need to keep the lines of communication open."

I met Pop's eyes again. He was looking faintly ironic, standing behind her where she couldn't see him. As usual, he read my mind. Anita didn't understand at all. She understood nothing, just nothing. And the right eye burned. In the end, I left them, saying that I needed more sleep.

When I awoke three hours later, her visit seemed like something I had dreamed, but I was at last feeling somewhat alert. I sat at my desk again, and slowly, my mind began to focus on the neutral and familiar material I taught.

That evening, I went downstairs and ate my first real meal. Pop had roasted game hens, and I dove into my food with a sudden craving need. I left the table as soon as I had finished, and stalked into the living room, where I found my cell phone. I had last seen it in my room the day I called Max Weigel.

I snatched it up and glared at Pop, who had followed me out of the dining room. "Don't you ever answer my phone again."

"You couldn't take calls," he said feebly. "You wouldn't have known what you were saying."

"You have no right! I am not your zoo animal to imprison. Let go of me! I swear to God, Pop." The name was an explosion. I was insane with fury. "Pop, God damn it!"

I went to the kitchen, needing to get away from him, and looked out the window at a fine summer evening. Pop might have been able to answer my phone, but he didn't have the password to check my messages. I ran through them: some student, worried about a grade; Anita, saying she had heard what happened and wondered how I was, unable to disguise the curiosity in her voice; and no less than six messages from Sabrina Cole, asking me to call her. And at that moment, it rang. I answered automatically.

"Kate?"

It enraged me that Sabrina spoke to me as if we were friends. I said coldly, "Yes, what is it?"

"How are you doing?"

I ignored the question. "What is it?"

Pop tentatively stuck his head in from the hall. I burst out the back door and walked quickly away from the house.

"I'm doing an article on Merit's death."

So she was on a first-name basis with Merit, whom she had never met, except as a nuisance asking questions from the press. "Dr. Chenobo," I corrected. "I have no comment."

"Apparently, you were there."

"Where did you get that idea?" My voice was freely raised as I crossed the lawn in the direction of the woods.

"I heard you found the body?"

"If you have questions about that night, you can call my attorney." I should have hung up, but I hesitated for some reason.

"It's an interesting angle, his friendship with a local businesswoman he knew from Africa."

"It's not an angle, period, interesting or otherwise. There's no connection whatsoever. It's a complete non sequitur. Random. The police found no connection."

"I heard you were there for some time answering questions about what might have happened or who might have murdered him."

"You were misinformed. They had questions, but I had no answers because I had nothing to do with it."

"Coincidental, though. It's your second time on the scene of a shooting, isn't it?"

I shut my mouth, speechless with rage. Finally, I said, "How dare you?" Was she threatening to expose me as the witness in the old crime?

"Hey, Kate, I'm your friend."

My friend? I was spinning on my heels in the grass, enraged.

"I wasn't saying that because I meant to write about it," she whined. "I understand. I want to work with you. I understand you're laid up on account of the shock. It's a great human interest story though. Touched by violent crime, not once, but twice. 'Touched by Tragedy,' I'm thinking. People would be interested. Sympathetic. The ties with Africa and all. It's not your everyday story, and I took that great picture of you and Merit."

It took me a minute to swallow my fury and reply. "You are talking about identifying a victim of rape. Without permission. Your editor will never allow it. I would sue you." I wondered if I could.

"I went by the site, by the way. It's coming along great, ready for plants. I talked to Tony. He said you guys didn't have a photographer for the book yet, and he agreed that you could at least look at my portfolio. I mean, why not?"

I tried to control my temper. "Sabrina, I have just had a terrible shock. I'm not thinking about writing a book right now."

"Of course, of course." Her voice was cloying. "I know. Bad time. Are you going to be in town next week? Because I could meet then." She gave me no chance to reply. "In the meantime, I'll see what I can do about keeping you out of the article about Merit. My editor will want every newsworthy angle, but I'll see what I can do." She hung up.

I was alone in middle of the field, so I held the phone in front of my face and roared at it like a lion, with a sound that came up from the soles of my feet.

I called Tony and yelled into the phone. "What the fuck?" Then I bit my knuckles. I didn't want to scream at Tony that way. I sounded like my mother. "Tony?" It came out like a squeal.

He spoke close into the phone. "Kate? Where are you? Hang on a minute." I heard noises, then a door shutting, and he came back on. "Are you okay? I heard about what happened."

"You let her think she could be the photographer for my book?" I was pleading, my voice probably unintelligible.

"Hey, hey, hey. Where are you? At home? Are you okay?"

I struggled with a sob. I wished he were with me.

"That was the black guy who was shot, right? The one in that picture?"

I hadn't called him to talk about Merit. "Sabrina. What did you tell her?"

The sun had gone down, and the woods were dark masses on the hills around the fields behind the house. I glanced back at the lighted windows and saw Pop moving in the kitchen, looking out, no doubt, trying to see me.

"I didn't tell her anything. She did all the talking. I just said yes and no. She knows about the book. She asked if you had a photographer, and I said I didn't think so."

"She's a terrible photographer."

"The pictures came out okay when you told her what to shoot and how."

Whose side is he on? My temper flared again. "Well, exactly, Tony. A trained monkey could do that. I want a photographer who brings something to the table. With a book like mine, the quality of the photography is practically everything. The pictures sell the book, and the book sells the business."

I choked up again, and my voice broke up. "She wants to write an article about me finding Merit, like it's all my fault. Oh my God, Tony—"

"How could she do that? That's crazy, right?"

"Of course it's crazy, but she's a *reporter*!" I gulped air. "She's saying..." Hard to catch my breath. "She wants to be my photographer or she's going to write about me finding Merit's body. She's trying to extort her way ahead in her sorry-ass career. Using me."

A pause. Then a short noise. "String her along, Kate. Why not? Just so she keeps you out of this other business. It's a quid pro quo, right?"

"I don't know why we're even talking about this. I'm okay, but I just can't talk right now." I sounded quarrelsome and accusing. I cursed myself.

He muttered, "Hey, you're the one who called me."

I cut him off. "Look, I'll be there in a couple of days. We can talk then." When he didn't say anything, I added, "We do need to talk."

I was still steaming over Sabrina's call when I hung up. It actually lifted me out of my funk; I had to give her that much. I got my bearings. It was Sunday evening. I would have to get back to teaching, but that wouldn't be a problem. For the first time in nearly ten days, I was fully grounded in the present, wide awake and full of energy. I had been knocked flat, but I was determined to fight back. I resolved to get back to Richmond as soon as possible.

But before I could, Suzanne called.

CHAPTER TWENTY-ONE

S UZANNE'S VOICE WAS WINDBLOWN AGAINST the background noise of a car on the road.

"Are you all right, Kate? Your father said you were ill."

"I'm fine. I got over-tired. I was asleep when you called before. He told me you called, but I was only half-awake, and I forgot. Sorry."

I wasn't sorry, really. I was tired of her intensity, and after all that had happened, I didn't want her sympathy dragging me down just when I was beginning to get back on my feet.

"You know he was released, don't you? Jefferson?"

I paused. "Last time I talked to you, you told me that he was going to be released. Was he? When? Just last week?" I was still unclear about how much time had passed.

"No, it's been a couple of weeks now. The judge expedited the order because of the amount of time he'd spent in jail. Do you want me to come by? I'm driving right now, on Highway 29. It's no trouble."

While I waited for her, I quickly looked up the news coverage, such as it was, on my laptop. I was running a video when she arrived.

I met her at the door and said, "You were there."

Her cotton jacket hung on her thin shoulders as if on a coat hanger. Her skirt fell to mid-calf as if empty. I led her back out to the screened-in porch.

She followed. "Yes." Her voice was soft and careful, as

always. "I called that morning to see if you wanted to come with me, but you had already left. I spoke to your father. He didn't mention it?"

"No, he didn't." I hesitated. I didn't want to tell her why I'd been ill, why he might have forgotten about her call or would not have told me about it. The murder had received only passing coverage in the news. She could easily have missed it, and she would have had no reason to connect it with me.

She said, "I'm so sorry I didn't give you more notice. I was following up on a shooting victim in Arlington, and I didn't get back to you as fast I should have."

"No, no, it's fine. I didn't call you either. I mean, I'm confused now." I backed up the video. "He was released Wednesday, two weeks ago."

"Right." She moved a chair closer to sit next to me and watch the clip. "There didn't seem to be any doubt in the judge's mind about his innocence. I don't know. How do you feel about it?"

I shrugged, annoyed by her anxious attention to me. I hated the way she worried about my feelings.

Pop must have seen or heard her car because he came in and greeted her tersely. He stood behind us. On the screen, reporters surged around Jefferson and his family.

I said, "Suzanne says she called to offer to take me to see Jefferson's release. Not that I would have gone." I glanced at Suzanne, to see if that offended her. In fact, I thought her curiosity was morbid, but to her face, I could never help feeling how vulnerable she was.

She was watching the screen, and I turned back to it. Jefferson's mother and sister and a handful of reporters were there. When the camera panned, Suzanne was visible among the bystanders, looking foolishly covert with her collar turned up and her eyes shielded by big sunglasses on a gray morning.

The camera closed in on Jefferson's face. It was totally

unfamiliar, as if I had never set eyes on him in my life, even though I knew I had seen him at the Tavern those many years ago. He was much older, of course, middle-aged and beaten-looking, though he smiled as he walked out to his freedom.

A reporter asked him how he felt about the victim who had fingered him, insinuating something about whether he wanted to get even. Suzanne shifted beside me.

Jefferson's mother, dressed in a red suit and Sunday hat, took umbrage, leaning toward the microphone and saying, "He was not a violent criminal then, and he is not a violent man now. If the victim is afraid, she is still unjustly accusing a man who did nothing to harm her."

Jefferson said, "That young man and I exchanged words. No fight. Words. He had words for me, too. If I had been white and him black, none of this would have happened. My family knows I'm not a killer or a rapist. And now the world knows."

His mother reached for the microphone again. "She saw another black man. If she says she's still afraid of him, then she is still accusing an innocent man."

Suzanne's cold, thin fingers touched my hand.

I asked, "What will he do now?"

She told me Jefferson was staying with his family. He would be moving to Atlanta. "His mother's church took up a collection, and somebody found him a job."

We had forgotten Pop, and both of us started when he spoke from behind us. "Why did they think that the victim is afraid?"

I twisted in my seat. "What?"

"They're all talking about the victim being afraid of him. How would they know that?"

Suzanne said, "Maybe they're just assuming she would be."

"Or maybe word travels." Pop's right eye drilled into Suzanne. "Maybe you talked to somebody in the prosecutor's office or the AG's office, and then they asked questions on the other side, and next thing you know, it gets back to Jefferson." He was flushed, breathing hard through his nose.

Suzanne looked stricken. I remembered her thinking I would be afraid, asking about it. We all were silent.

She said, "I will never forgive myself if something about you leaked out because of me."

Pop was relentless. "Don't see how else it could have happened."

Suzanne's face flamed. "I'll get to the bottom of it, Kate. If that's what happened, it's unacceptable. Really, unacceptable."

I suppressed a curse. "No, Suzanne, let it lie. Please don't do anything about it. It's no big deal. Like you said, they could have assumed I was afraid of him the way you assumed I would be. Anyway, I'm not afraid." There was no reason to fear Jules Jefferson; I felt sure of that. "Not of him," I amended.

Suzanne assured me she understood, but Pop cut her off and said through gritted teeth, "I think it's reason enough to be afraid when someone is gunned down on your doorstep."

I said sharply, "Pop!"

But it was too late. Suzanne turned to him wonderingly, then back to me.

I stood up and began to pace. "It's nothing."

She looked at Pop, then at me, still mystified.

I swiped a hand in Pop's direction. "There was a murder in Richmond last week. Near my apartment. It had nothing to do with me."

"It was your friend who was shot, in the doorway of your apartment," Pop snapped. "How is this not threatening to you?"

Suzanne gasped. "Your friend was murdered? At your apartment?"

"I knew him in Africa. He was here speaking at some politically charged meetings. He was threatened. I wasn't there when it happened. He was alone out on the street in Church Hill."

"Not on the street. In your doorway, and he was shot just days after Jefferson got out." Pop forged on over Suzanne's little shocked and saddened noises. "And now those people are saying you feel threatened. Well, why wouldn't you?"

It was too much. I yelled at both of them, "Shut up! Will you just shut up?"

Through hands pressed tight on my ears, I heard the muffled murmur of Suzanne's distressed apologies and Pop's blunted rebuttals. I didn't care what either one was saying, I wanted to be away from them. I ran upstairs, slammed the door to my room, and yelled, "Go away!" when Pop knocked on the door a few minutes later, and then again in an hour, and again later that night. And for yet another night, I swallowed pills, as many as I dared, to get to sleep.

As I lay on my bed, waiting for the pills to take effect, I felt a very fresh fear and a crushing confinement. Suzanne could not possibly understand. And Pop's latest insinuations to Suzanne made me wild. How could he imagine such a thing, pointing a finger at Jules Jefferson again? It was utterly depraved. And of course, next the bungling Suzanne would look into how Jefferson knew I was afraid of him. And I wasn't! But Suzanne thought I was. Pop was right about one thing: It could only have traveled to Jefferson that I was afraid by way of Suzanne.

I was losing control. Not only were people learning things I didn't want them to know, breaking down all those compartmental barriers I had so carefully maintained for so long—Pop told Suzanne about the murder!—but also, there were things others knew that I didn't know they knew. Pop had known Jefferson was out. I had just found out that day, two weeks later, that Jefferson was out. The whole thing was making me physically sick. I thought about Suzanne, and then it hit me she would go to Elsa Gabriel. I felt like throwing up. Or maybe that was the pills. Heaviness stole over me.

"Damn it," I whispered over and over. "Damn it, I will not stay here."

CHAPTER TWENTY-TWO

I COULDN'T MISS ANY MORE CLASSES, so I left the house with a packed bag early on Wednesday after hardly speaking to Pop in the morning, and drove to the community college. I couldn't wait to stop teaching there. I left for Richmond directly after my last class.

When I arrived at my apartment, I parked half a block down the street and sat in my car. I called Tony, got voicemail, and didn't leave a message. If he wasn't answering, that probably meant he was in Virginia Beach. I was disgusted with him, but I couldn't help wondering if anything had changed. I thought about his voice on the phone and wanted him to hold me the way he had the last time I'd seen him. I wasn't ready to give up on him.

The afternoon was humid and still sunny, even at six o'clock. Heat began to build in the car. I was still dressed for class, in a dark blue silk pants suit. I'd hung the jacket in the back seat, but the white silk shell I'd worn underneath was hot. I thought maybe I would go up to the apartment to shower and change, then go somewhere. The apartment had been cleaned and painted as soon as the cops released it. Pop had seen to that. My papers and designs would probably have been moved around and mixed up by the cleaners. I could spend the evening reorganizing.

I shifted in the seat, feeling the backs of my legs getting wet. My pants were lined, and the lining was hot, so basically, it was going to look as if I'd wet my pants on the drive. I got out of the car and felt the cool breeze behind me as I twisted around to assess the damage. Not so bad. It would dry quickly in the air. A bit wrinkled, but the jacket was fresh and long enough to cover most of the damage.

My stomach growled, and still the apartment held me off as if it radiated some sort of violent psychic energy or a horrid bloody odor. Who did I know in Richmond? A few people. Not anyone I could call up to say, "Hey, how about meeting me for dinner?" I thought about a woman who taught at VCU, but I didn't have her number. No, it would be too weird to call her. I could have called Merit. That thought brought a wave of sadness. I could call Anita. But what I needed was to get back into my apartment. I tried Tony again. Voicemail. I didn't leave a message.

I began to walk around the block. I passed the old church. Then, half a block later, I stopped in front of a house with a sign: For Lease.

With the porch light, I could see a dark paneled entryway, a couple of steps up to a hallway, and narrow stairs. The house was two-storied, narrow, and very old, probably a total of four rooms and a bathroom, maybe a dormered attic. I stepped back and looked up: Yes, that would be fine. A new place was the answer. I went back out on the street. The building was dark red brick with a narrow black iron balcony on the second floor. I got out my cell and called the number on the sign.

Someone answered on the second ring. The house was not too expensive. Fine. I could have it right away. Perfect. I could see it right then because the owner lived on the same block. The fates were with me.

I found the owner's house and met a tiny, light-skinned black woman with a heart-shaped face. I told her I wanted to take the place and offered her a check. The woman looked at me funny when I said I didn't even need to see the inside first, and it gave me a moment of panic. Could she somehow know who I was? But by seven o'clock, I had the key.

My spirits rose as I climbed the porch steps and glanced to the left. I could see the small woman standing on her porch three doors down. Did she think I was crazy? I didn't care.

I unlocked the door. Inside, it was perfect, just as I expected. The rooms were small and cozy, dark and old-fashioned. I could get some cute cheap little wicker chairs like the ones in Anita's sunroom, with Indian print cushions. I wasn't sure exactly what I was doing, but my instincts were in high gear, and I knew to trust my instincts. I was on autopilot. I went up to the front room of the second floor. I just needed something to sleep on.

With a burst of energy, I ran back out to the street, found my car, and moved it over to my new address. Inside again, I powered up my laptop and began calling furniture stores. By the time I got to the third store, I had a script: I would cut to the chase and ask them if they could deliver a bed that evening. On the fifth try, I found someone who could.

"Never mind why," I said, although he hadn't asked. I could hear him wondering.

Then I thought about sheets and hung up on him. Sleep on a bare mattress? Definitely, he would think I was crazy. I stood looking out the front window onto the street and drummed my fingers on the windowsill. Then I blew out a big breath. Enough for one day. I took a room at a hotel.

I hadn't thought to pack pills to help me sleep, so I called room service for a sandwich, which I hardly touched, and a bottle of wine, which brought me the oblivion I needed.

In the morning, I went directly to Mary's Grove. Tony was there with a crew installing an irrigation system. To my intense irritation, I saw Sabrina Cole standing at his elbow, her sagging butt sprawled in last year's jeans, drab hair pulled back in a ponytail. She greeted me like a long-lost friend.

I ignored the greeting and asked, "What are you doing?"

But I could see what she was doing. She was taking pictures of trenches, networks of PVC pipe, electrical conduits, and control boxes. Lovely. I could sell my book in hardware stores. Who would want to look at pictures of such things?

"I had an idea," she announced with a big yellow grin. "How about if the book has more of an emphasis on how-to, all the stages of garden installation, how to get from design to reality. I think a lot of people would like to know about that."

I glared at her.

"I kept you out of the article," she said.

Good. No more stringing along. "You are not going to be involved in this book. You can forget that."

"The way we picture it," she continued, unfazed, "there'd be a bigger role for Tony."

Tony asked, "What do you know about planting roses, Sabrina?"

She grinned. "You can tell me all about it." She was actually flirting with him. "I can write, too."

"Then how about you write your own book," I said. "Mine is not about how to plant roses. The content of my book is between me and my agent."

I was turning to go back inside when I heard her say, "And what's up with the divorce notice?"

I froze for a split second, then whirled and rasped, "What are you talking about?" *So much for surreptitious notice.* I wasn't sure if Tony had heard her. He gave me a curious look and then went back to what he was doing.

Sabrina's close-set eyes were stupid but calculating, and I kicked myself for betraying my agitation.

She said, "I don't know why you won't work with us, Kate. You don't write a book like that in a vacuum. You need Tony, and you need a photographer. And I am not only a photographer but a writer. We want our share of the credit."

I turned my back on her.

She asked, "Who's your agent, anyway?"

I walked away without answering. I was so angry I went inside without knocking. It startled me as much as it did Anita, but she recovered quickly and brushed off my apologies, taking my arm.

I said, "That fool, Sabrina Cole, thinks she's going to get herself in on my book." I pointed out the window of the sunroom, where Sabrina was still taking pictures of Tony while he worked.

Anita peered out at them, then turned back to me, bewildered. She was way too nice.

I told her Sabrina was a terrible photographer and clueless about my subject. And she thought she was going to be my photographer and help with the book and get her name on the cover with mine.

"But that's up to you, isn't it, Kate?" She squeezed my shoulders and patted me, soft and maternal. "You can tell her no. Come sit down."

But I wasn't going to be sidetracked. "Now I can tell her no. Now that she's finished blackmailing me. Look at her. She's taking pictures of Tony planting roses. She wants to photograph every phase of the installation. You didn't agree to that. You agreed to have pictures of the finished garden in the book. Pictures I authorized. You agreed she could cover the party, that's all."

"What on earth do you mean, blackmailing you?"

"She's a reporter. She wants to get her stories in the paper, and she thinks she can use me. She found out I was connected, I mean, not really connected, but I was there afterwards when Merit was shot. She knew I knew him and she called me, at home, and threatened to make out like I was involved in the shooting. She was going to put that in the paper. Unless I let her in on my book."

Anita looked shocked. She made little 'tsk tsk' noises and said, "You do need to be a bit more careful about who you associate with, Kate. None of it's your fault, but—"

"She had the gall to contemplate a story about me, the tragic victim of crime, touched by violence again, the famous landscape architect with the exotic African past. She wanted to use that picture! It's crazy. Who would publish such rot? And without my permission. I would have sued her. It isn't news. It's ridiculous!"

I was getting seriously worked up. She wasn't taking me seriously; she was just trying to comfort me and shush me up. "She's a terrible photographer. I don't want anything to do with her. She claims we're friends. We're not, not at all. We went to the same school. She was a sad sack then, and she's a sad sack now. She lucked into all of it, stumbled onto the picture of me with Merit. I only saw him once, briefly. She lucked into covering your party and tried to pretend she and I were old friends just to get on the inside with you. Now she'll do anything to be the photographer for my book. She even wants to write part of it. Christ!"

She took my hand and drew me to the wicker chairs. "Kate, you've been under a terrible strain..."

I forced my temper down. I said, more calmly, but still indignant, "She threatened to make a spectacle of me. That happened to me before. Do you blame me? You don't know what it was like!"

She patted my hand.

"So I strung her along, and she kept me out of the shooting. That's what I call blackmail."

"I looked at all the articles about the shooting. She didn't write any of them."

"She was probably bluffing. Shows what kind of person I'm dealing with, though. Anyway, it's time to get rid of her. Don't you know her editor?"

She cast her eyes aside. "Slightly, socially, I suppose so."

"You said she could come and take pictures for the article about the party. You didn't tell her she could come back and pester us throughout the installation."

"No, I suppose not."

"You should call them. The paper. Tell them to get her off your property."

She sat back. "Oh, I don't know, Kate."

"She can't come over here and take pictures of your property, on your property, without your permission. Her editor wouldn't like to know she's doing that."

"He probably wouldn't like to know she's using her position to try to... blackmail..." The word seemed uncomfortable to her, which I could well understand. It was outrageous, what the girl was doing.

"Yes, but that's a quarrel between her and me over my book. He might not be as likely to intervene in that, although of course it wouldn't make her look good. But if you were to complain that she's on your property taking photographs you didn't authorize, he'd call her off."

She didn't want to do it, but in the end, she called the editor to please me. I had to invoke Pop, how upset he'd be if he knew about Sabrina threatening me and then trying to horn in on my book. And I had to hang over her when she finally made the call, to make sure she was clear. She was much too nice about it, but she did get Sabrina Cole's editor to say he'd call her in. I straightened and breathed out my relief.

We went to the window and watched—I intensely, she with trepidation and concern—as Sabrina fumbled for her cell, then argued at length while I growled at her from inside the house. It took her long enough, but she ended the call, talked with Tony some more, took two more pictures while I muttered curses, and then slowly got into her dumpy little car and drove off.

I said, "Thank you."

"Of course, Kate. I'm glad you told me about it. I'm glad I could help. I didn't think she would be that kind of person."

"Because you're too nice." I went back outside to tell

Tony I wasn't amused by his collaboration with Sabrina. All thoughts of reconciliation had evaporated.

I didn't wait for him to gather his slow wits. "So now you're working with Sabrina? Is that how you see yourself getting ahead in this business, Tony?"

"What? No." Simple flat-footed denial, as if he hadn't done anything wrong.

"Are you writing a book with Sabrina, Tony? You can teach her how to plant roses, and she'll write a book and take pictures, and the two of you can try to publish it. If you'd rather be in business with her than me, that's fine. Your choice, absolutely."

"Kate—"

"I'm serious. If you're going to side with her, fine. Do whatever you like. It's nothing to me. Just don't conspire with her to blackmail me."

"You said we'd work together."

"You and me, not her."

"Forget her."

"She's no part of this, and you led her on."

All he could do was deny it. I could see that he was getting frustrated. He couldn't figure out how to argue with me. The word "stolid" came to mind. "Stupid" was not far behind it.

Meanwhile, he picked up the nearest weapon. "You didn't tell me you're married, Kate."

"What are you talking about?" No question about it, my carefully constructed shields were crumbling.

He held up a hand. "Hey."

"What are you talking about?" I was so furious I almost shouted.

"Sabrina said you're trying to find some guy you're married to. I didn't know you were married. You neglected to mention that."

"It's nothing. It was a mistake. It's none of your business."

"None of my business?" That little half-laugh.

It struck me how colossally inarticulate he was. He made little snorts and looked away when he couldn't figure out how to answer me. I was used to being smarter than everybody else, but it did get old. That was what I loved about Elliott: He was so smart. Even Pop was smart. Tony was not exactly stupid, but he was no intellectual.

I said, "That's right. It's none of your business. It was a long time ago. Nobody knows where he is. I had to claim abandonment. I hate to even think about it, let alone talk about it or answer questions. It was nothing, a lost weekend. It's embarrassing. It's a matter of correcting records."

But he planted his feet and shook his head. "It's a matter of honesty. You know I'm married. I told you that up front. You're like it's such a big deal and I have to fix it before you'll touch me with a ten-foot pole, yet meanwhile, you're married, too, and you don't even tell me. You're mixed up in a crime. You got a murder in your past. A few things you never thought to mention, I guess."

I realized I was holding my breath. I let it all out. "This is ridiculous. What are we fighting about? How could I tell you all these things? When are we together? When do we talk? We hardly know each other, and the reason is that you're married, as in living with a wife and children. I'm not. I've done some crazy things. It's made me crazy. This whole thing is hopeless."

I turned away and struck a pose, tossing my hair and hugging myself. I even tried on a suggestion of a few tears. I waited for the ground to shift, and after a few beats it did.

"What are you saying, hopeless? Are you talking about us? I don't know, Kate. I get it, that you had some hard knocks, but I can't keep up with this. One minute, you're trying to make me divorce my wife, next thing I know, you're yelling at me. I don't know about you."

I couldn't speak, didn't want to blubber out loud, so I concentrated on holding still. Everything, everything was ruined. Everything I touched went so horribly wrong. Anita, who had been so nice to me, probably felt like she was humoring a mad woman. Tony seemed to think I was radioactive. Maybe I was.

I took a deep, shaky breath and found my voice. "I know. I'm sorry, Tony. I'm losing it, I know I am. And I can see it's not going to work. Nothing is ever going to work for me." I sounded all wobbly and out of breath.

"Aw, come on, Kate. You're upset. Anybody would be. First, that thing that happened to you, then you find your friend shot. I'd be acting crazy, too."

It pissed me off a little that he came right out and said I was acting crazy. I worked the tight muscles of my face.

Tony shuffled around behind me. "You know, I did talk to her."

I half-turned toward him, then turned back, skeptical.

"No, I did."

"You told her about me?"

"Not exactly."

I slumped. "I thought not."

"No, wait. I mean I told her I needed some space. Some time alone. Like she was crowding me."

"You moved out?"

"No. Come on. Be reasonable. This isn't easy, but I told her I wasn't going to run home every minute I wasn't working. That long drive and all. Always under suspicion, Mike watching every move I make."

A little teary snort escaped me. "Your duenna."

"What? Look, I was going to tell you I'll be staying here in Richmond tonight." The words hung in the air. "Of course, that was before you chewed my ass. I get that you're upset, but I don't need my ass chewed any more than it already is."

When I turned, he had a sly grin on his face. "Staying where?"

"I don't know. I was waiting to see you."

That shut us both up for a moment.

"I don't know what this is going to be, Tony." Then I had to ask. "How'd she take it?"

"Not good, but hey, I need a break, you know? A little me-time, for once, that's all." We started walking toward my car. "So how is it not my business that you're married?"

"It was stupid, a long time ago. I want a clean slate, though right now, I'm not so sure what I need it for." I put on a little more sulk.

"She says you dropped it."

"What?"

"The notice."

Wrong subject. "I can't explain right now. That's my point. How can I explain all these things? There's been no time for any of that. The whole thing with Merit upset me. I'm not myself. And that whole marriage thing, I don't like to talk about it."

He softened. "Okay, okay." He shook his head. "So secretive, Kate. I never knew anyone so secretive. And I don't see the reason for it."

"I feel exposed. I can't help it. I spend my life hiding. My past keeps hunting me down like a predator." I thought about Pop telling Suzanne about Merit being shot.

"But you don't have to be a slave to secrets like that. That you saw somebody shot. That you were once a victim of a crime. That you were married once. That you want a divorce. These are not big secrets, Kate. You hide things from everybody, and none of it couldn't stand to be out in the daylight." He touched my arm, stroked it.

"That's not your decision. They're my secrets. I'll keep them if I want to. And you don't understand. You just don't." I was softening. A need for comfort was beginning to overwhelm everything else. I looked up and squinted. The sun was high and hot, glaring on the river.

He moved his hand up higher on my arm. "You know, I can't help what Sabrina said. That was all her idea. But you did say you were going to put me in the book. I didn't make that up. You said it."

Had I? I had pictured us working together. I was confused.

He moved behind me and put his hands on my shoulders, hesitantly at first. Then he squeezed and stroked my arms, leaned his head over my shoulder, and brushed the side of his face against mine. He slid an arm around my waist and let his hand stray down the side of my hip, across my stomach. He whispered warm breath in my ear. "So, tonight?"

I pressed back against him, turned around, and our mouths met.

I pulled away, one eye on the house. "Not now." But when he caught my hand I let him hold it.

"Tonight?"

I nodded. I wanted it, but vague new ideas were boiling up in my mind.

Tony said, "We can talk. It'll be different from here on. We'll have time together. I'll work it out. I got it all figured out."

That hit me wrong. He had it all figured out. I bet. Elliott came to mind. I let him kiss me again, but then I pulled away.

He looked surprised. "What's wrong?"

I put my hand on his chest, then backed away and started walking to my car.

Tony followed, hovering, bumping up against me. "Tonight? Kate?"

"Yeah. Tonight." I glanced at the house.

Tony nudged me with his shoulder. "You're being secretive again." I didn't like the way he said it, with a grin, as if humoring me. "How about I come to your apartment?"

My apartment. Merit came to mind. Dead on my doorstep. A faint itch of fear crept up the back of my neck. I was barely listening to Tony.

"You want a hotel? But why pay a hotel? You got a bed, right?"

I nodded. "Yeah, Tony, my apartment. I'll wait for you there."

There was something I could figure out if I could just be alone and think. Instinctively, I kept the new house secret. That would be my future hideaway. I still wasn't sure where I was going with it, but a plan was forming in the back of my mind. I didn't know if it had anything to do with Tony. I began to have misgivings. He was a bit of an oaf, and I wasn't so sure he didn't think he could play me. We'd see about that. Given time. The power in our relationship had shifted. I felt a lot less desperate about him. I had more urgent business to attend to anyway. As I drove away, I glanced in the rearview mirror, and he was looking after me, hands on hips.

I did think that if I had Tony with me, I could face my old apartment, but when it came down to it, I had cold feet. When I pulled up in front of my old building and got out of my car, the nosy old woman across the street stopped what she was doing and watched me climb the stairs. I would be glad to get away from her. When I fumbled with the keys, I felt her eyes on me. I felt eyes behind curtains up and down the street. Imagination, I thought, but when I pushed open the door, I was seized with fear of what I might see.

Breathing hard, I forced my eyes to the spot where Merit had fallen. There was no trace. Pop had sent crime scene cleanup specialists. The very thought curdled my blood. I whirled, dashed down the stairs, and ran to my car. I got in, slammed the door, and locked it. I squealed my tires driving away and lurched to the curb three blocks later, stalling my car.

I called Tony and told him there wasn't any way I could stay there that night. "Maybe not ever again."

"Okay where do you want to go?"

"I'm not sure I'm ready for this."

"Jeez, Kate!"

"I know, I know. I'm sorry, but you have to remember, my friend was just murdered. Give me a little more time, Tony." I tried to sound emotional and soft, but what I felt was a growing resolve. Enough. I was not going to be able to move on with my life until I set a few things straight, and I was going to have to do that all by myself. Then maybe I could figure out what to do with Tony.

He was calling me sweetheart and baby and naming nearby cheap motels. I told him that I was going home and hung up before he could argue.

I couldn't even think about my new place, which was still empty anyway. I drove in a panic that only subsided when I was well out of town. Panic was slowly replaced by gloom.

I didn't call home, and Pop looked up surprised when I came in. I slammed the front door after me and ran upstairs. Pills. I would take pills. In the morning, I would try again. I heard Pop on the stairs, then hesitating outside my door, and I willed him away. He left without knocking, and I slowly relaxed.

I made plans for Friday. A bed, a mattress. I would feather my new secret nest. I soothed myself by decorating it in my mind. I would keep the old apartment as a blind and a decoy and a stage set. An idea was definitely forming, still very vague, very unclear, but forming all the same.

Friday dawned bright and clear. I packed with the idea that I'd be staying in my new house and headed back to Richmond without exchanging so much as a word with Pop. At a furniture store, I found a simple pine bedstead and paid extra for a rush delivery. I bought new sheets, pillows and a comforter, a bedside table and a lamp. I was setting up my new retreat.

Plus, I had another bright idea. I was going to hire Max Weigel as my bodyguard.

CHAPTER TWENTY-THREE

I SPENT THE DAY ORDERING AND carting around the furnishings for my new safe house. I even bought dishes and a set of crystal wine glasses and snifters from an antique store. I picked up a bottle of Martel VSOP to go with the snifters. I got distracted on the way to lunch and bought new clothes instead, including some pretty sensational lingerie.

For a while, I even forgot to be afraid or upset. I received deliveries all afternoon, humming and dancing while I put things away, made the bed, and arranged all the little decorative details I'd bought. The last of the furniture arrived between four and five.

I locked up and headed for Weigel's office. He was in, luckily, and alone except for the dog, which was friendly and relaxed until it recognized me.

"You stopped the notice?" I said briskly, walking past him at the door. Again, I faced a choice between the slovenly overstuffed chair and the straight wooden one. I went to the window and stood looking out at my car parked on the street.

Weigel plunked down behind his desk. It sounded like he practically broke the chair. "Sure did. Right after you called."

I hesitated. I wasn't sure I wanted to go forward.

He said, "Now you want to restart it."

I whirled to face him. "How did you know?"

He snickered. "Just a guess."

"The thing is, I think he may be dangerous."

Weigel narrowed his eyes, trying to look shrewd. "Anything to do with that shooting you witnessed?"

"What? I didn't witness anything."

"Found the body then."

"How do you know about that?"

"It's my business to know what goes on in this town. I'm a criminal defense attorney, too, remember?"

I dragged my fingertips across the windowsill and looked at them. Black. Maybe Weigel knew something. I tried to sound offhand, but I was conscious of my heartbeat. "Do you know anything about the case? Have they found out who did it?"

"Nope. Doesn't seem like it. I mean, they don't tell me what they've got, but I'd say no, they're still a long way from it. Why, is there a connection?"

I kept my back to him, leaning left and right so I could see down the street. "No, there's no connection with that. It has nothing to do with me. But I'm scared. I admit that."

A silence stretched out.

"If I resume the notice, can you protect me?"

"We can do bodyguard services. Same hourly as investigations. Usually my PI does it. And really, you ought to consider telling the cops if you think this guy is dangerous."

I sighed. "I'm asking you." I tried to keep my voice sweet. "Will you see me home? All my stuff is in that apartment. I can't go in there alone. I at least need to get my business files out." I sat down and crossed my legs and arched my back as seductively as I could in the plain wooden chair.

To my extreme irritation, he looked faintly amused. But then he surprised me. "Want to get a drink first?"

"I haven't eaten all day. Can we make it a drink and a sandwich? Then if you'll follow me home, I'll grab my stuff while you're there. That's all I need right now." He hesitated, so I added, "I'll buy, how's that?"

"You got it." He turned and spoke to the dog like it was his secretary. "I'm going out for a couple of hours, Bridge. Want to go outside?" He unlocked the back door and let the dog out.

"Your dog's name is Bridge?"

"Bridget. Great dog. Best I ever had. Smart as a whip and perfectly trained. Not that I did it. She was two when I got her. She's five now." He dumped water from the dog's bowl into the sink in the bathroom and refilled it. There was a scratch at the back door, and he let the dog back in. He took a dog biscuit out of the bottom right drawer of his desk and balanced it on the dog's nose. The dog sat motionless until Weigel said, "Okay," then it flipped the biscuit up with its nose, caught it neatly, and chomped it down.

He looked at me expectantly, so I said, "Pretty good."

"Smarter than a lot of people." Weigel pounded on the dog's rump.

Bridget wagged her tail and banged up against his leg affectionately. Weigel opened the bottom drawer on the other side of his desk and took out a shoulder holster and a gun.

"What's that for?" I sounded more displeased than I was.

He acted surprised. "I thought you were scared."

"Don't they say that guns tend to cause more violence than they prevent?"

"That might be true in general, but I'm a pro." He grinned. *Silly man.* "If your friend had had a gun, he might be alive today."

That gave me pause. "You can't just go over to somebody's house and shoot somebody."

"Why not? If he tries to shoot you."

"Would he have been allowed to carry a gun when he went over there?"

"If he had a permit."

"How do you get a permit?"

"Submit paperwork, take a course. They do a background check."

"But wouldn't he have been charged with something if he had shot that guy, whoever shot him?"

"He'd have some explaining to do, but I'd rather be explaining myself to the cops than getting the old Y-incision in the morgue." Again the cheerful grin.

I felt sick. "You're a real sensitive guy, Mr. Weigel."

"Sorry, but it's true. Didn't your friend say he was threatened?"

I nodded, frowning, still trying on this new scenario. Merit alive. The one who shot him dead. Weigel flipped a switch on the gun.

I asked, "What's that?"

"Safety."

"On or off?"

"On. Where do you want to go?"

"I don't know. River Café? We go in two cars, I guess."

"Back in a while, Bridge," he said.

His car, parked in the back of the building, turned out to be a brand new Audi, white with tan leather seats.

We crossed town and both parked without difficulty. Street traffic was draining from the center of town, and dinner traffic hadn't picked up yet. Inside the café was dark, half-full, and noisy, all hard surfaces. Wooden chairs scraped on wood floors, and heavy china dishes clattered on Formica tabletops.

We ordered drinks, and I said, "Not the typical getaway car you drive."

"I got a wreck I use for surveillance. Or rather, my PI uses it. I don't do much of the PI work anymore, like I said."

"How did you get started in that?"

"I started out as a cop." We paused to order, and then he continued. "That was fun at first, but then it got old.

239

It's dangerous, and the hours are long, the pay isn't too hot, and you see a lot of nasty shit."

"So you became a PI."

"No, then I went to law school. I started out as a criminal defense attorney, public defender, but that wasn't much better. The hours are still long, the pay still isn't too hot, and you still see a lot of nasty shit. Hear about it, anyway."

"I thought defense attorneys could make a lot of money."

"Oh, they can. Around here, mostly you end up defending drug dealers. That's who can pay. I'm not saying that's the only way to make money, but that was the direction it was going, and I didn't like it. Who wants to make a living getting drug dealers off the hook? Not me."

"So you went into something classier. Divorce." I caught the waiter's eye and lifted my glass. I was drinking vodka tonic. I looked at Weigel. "Want another beer?"

He drained his glass. "Sure."

I signaled it in.

He said, "No, I got a PI license, which is not too hard if you're an ex-cop. But private investigation does tend to be about divorce." He pushed away his plate, having wolfed his sandwich and fries the instant they were delivered.

My sandwich was not even half-eaten. I pushed my plate out, too. "Want my fries?"

He started right in on them. The man had an appetite. I thought that was a good sign.

I toyed with my drink, thinking about Tony. I couldn't make up my mind where things stood with him. "So, what does a divorce usually involve?"

He gave me a sharp look. "Your case? We've been through all that."

"No, I meant more generally. Like when there are three or four children and the wife doesn't work and all that."

"You got somebody in mind?"

I toyed with the straw in my drink. "No one in particular."

"You want a consultation? Because you already had your free one."

I felt my face flush, but I kept my voice neutral. "Jeez, you like your paycheck, don't you, Mr. Weigel?"

"Of course I do, Mrs. Brewer. You want to come over to my house and design me a garden?"

"I'm amenable to some form of barter. And please don't call me that."

"Ms. Cranbrook."

"Kate."

"Max."

I gave him a frank look, which he returned. Actually, it was a "come hither" I was attempting. I felt foolish, and I had an idea he thought I was foolish, too. I squirmed in my chair and drained my second drink. I didn't care if I looked foolish. I wasn't sure where I was going with all this, but I had a general sense of purpose. I forged on. "Have you ever been married?"

He sat back and folded his arms. "Nope."

"Never?"

"Nope. Almost, but it didn't happen."

"Why not?"

He relaxed again, elbows on the table. "I wasn't into it. She was great. Cute, nice, smart, lots of fun. But she had this whole plan. She wanted me to go into a big law firm where I could work twice the hours and make twice the money so she could buy a big house and quit work and have a bunch of kids."

"Not such a good deal for you."

"I didn't think so."

"So what happened? You broke it off? Or you said no, and she broke it off?"

"Ha! No, she stopped taking her birth control pills."

"You're kidding. She told you?"

"Nope. She just did it."

"And what happened? She got pregnant? Or you found out?"

Again the grin. "Sweetheart, I'm a detective. She had

one of those round foil cards that you punch the pills out of. I noticed they stopped being punched out."

"So you confronted her."

"No, I started wearing a condom. So she accused me of cheating on her."

"Were you?"

He made a face and waved his hands. "No, hell no. Why would I do that? If I didn't want to be with her, I wouldn't be. So then I stopped seeing her. It was all over at that point. I mean, she didn't trust me, and I didn't trust her. What kind of relationship is that? She didn't trust me, even though I hadn't done anything, and I didn't trust her because I knew she tried to trick me. So that was that."

"Do you ever go out with your clients?"

"Not usually. They tend to be conflicted and needy. They're going through a divorce."

I nodded. "And are you seeing anybody now?"

"I'm seeing you right now."

I rolled my eyes. "I'm a client. But I'm not conflicted and needy, am I?"

"No, I wouldn't say that. What about you? I mean, I know about the marriage, and I assume it's the only one, since it would have been bigamy to marry anybody else."

"I've seen people. But my career has been my life. I'm an old maid."

He snorted. "Right."

"You sound skeptical. It's what I am."

"You are an unusual lady, Kate."

"How so?"

"I think you might be just about the most secretive person I've ever met."

I flushed at that. Before I thought, I said, "I am sick of hearing that."

"If you keep hearing it, it must be true."

"Maybe I am secretive, but it's not because I have secrets. It's just the way I am. I like to keep myself private.

I don't like feeling exposed. But that doesn't necessarily mean I have secrets. I mean, deep dark secrets. I keep myself to myself."

He grunted, still sounding unconvinced.

"I suppose maybe in your line of work you'd get a little cynical about marriage and relationships. I mean, you see them coming apart all the time."

"I suppose maybe I do. I'll tell you this, an uncontested divorce with no kids and both parties working, that's not so bad. But when you've got three or four kids and the stay-at-home mom, you can pretty much count on it that it will be very expensive for the man and financially devastating for the woman."

"Why so expensive? Is that necessarily true? Excuse me, you can send me a bill if you want. But I didn't think we had alimony in Virginia."

He waved his hand. "Spousal support? It's not illegal. It can be part of a divorce settlement. Kids are expensive, though. Do you know what the federal guidelines are for child support when you've got four kids?"

Tony had four kids.

"The guy will be paying sixty percent of his salary in child support."

I was shocked. "That's ridiculous. Is that really true?"

"Oh yeah. I'll tell you, sometimes I get guys who come in here, wife doesn't know, and they want to know, what's it going to cost them to get out. Of course, I can't answer that. It depends how it plays out. It's complicated. But I can run that number by them and sometimes they quietly go home and wait for the kids to grow up. Start cheating. Give the girlfriend excuses why they can't leave."

I blinked and had the feeling he saw through me.

"On the other hand," he said, "sometimes you get the wife who trusts her husband, lets the husband's lawyer handle everything, or gets a half-assed attorney like a friend or a law student who doesn't know divorce or, worse yet, she tries to represent herself, and she'll end up with next to nothing."

"But if you had a case like that, what would you do? I mean, if you're the man's lawyer."

"Represent my client. I'm the lawyer, not the judge. Hey, let's go."

I paid, and he followed me back to the apartment.

As we drove up, I began to have a creepy feeling of being watched. Or maybe that was overstating it. It was more like my instincts were up. I went back and forth in my mind about whether it was the neighbors who were chewing the back of my neck or something else. I felt hunted. Vulnerable. When I got out of the car, it was all I could do not to bolt. Max was looking at me funny, and like everything else he did, it made me mad. But I stifled my anger. Max was becoming very important to me. I wasn't sure how yet, or in what way, but I knew it was true.

I stopped at the foot of the stairs and stood aside. Weigel shifted into action-movie mode. He actually shrugged his jacket loose so he could get at his gun. I didn't know whether to feel reassured or to poke fun at him, but I let him lead the way upstairs.

At the door, I gave him the key. He unlocked the door and pushed it open. I came to his shoulder and looked inside. Nothing. It was perfectly clean, quiet, and empty. I felt curtains moving across the street and scurried inside. Weigel set out to walk through the rooms. I pulled the door shut.

He came back to me a minute later and said, "Seems okay to me. Where was the body?"

I gave him a look. "I'll just be a minute."

I went to my desk and started shuffling through papers while he scrutinized the floor, probably trying to find bloodstains. I had decided to leave the apartment looking perfectly normal, as if I still lived there, so I gathered the bare minimum of active files and left the rest messy. I led the way out, ran to my car, and prepared to leave.

Weigel followed me out onto the landing. "You're not staying here?"

"No," I said in a loud voice so anyone could hear, except that there wasn't anybody in sight.

Weigel glanced around, puzzled. He probably thought I was crazy.

"I'm going home," I announced for the benefit of whichever of my nosy neighbors might be listening. Thanks for your help. Let me know what I owe you."

He said slowly, "O-kay," humoring me, or maybe trying to figure me out.

I got in my car and sped for the road home. I drove as fast as I dared, eyes on the rearview mirror, until I reached a point beyond the city limits where I could see all around me and could see no cars behind me. I pulled off the road into a gas station parking lot and waited. Nothing happened. I didn't have an immediate sensation of danger, but I still felt furtive, like a clever little animal evading all hunters. After a quarter of an hour, I pulled back onto the road, heading back toward Richmond.

I parked a mile from my new apartment and called a cab. I had the driver stop at a hotdog stand for two hotdogs and fries and at a liquor store for a bottle of cold champagne, a rather expensive one, on a roundabout route back to Church Hill. I saw the driver watching me in the rearview mirror guardedly, but I didn't care; he was nobody.

I slipped from the cab a block on the far side of my new place, watched the cab drive away, then put on dark glasses and hurried up to my new house, avoiding the landlady's house. There was no sign of life on her porch. I ducked inside the house and locked the front door behind me.

I didn't know what I was running from. I hadn't seen anything suspicious all day. I had no real reason to be as frightened at that time as I was. I was doing what I needed to do to feel safe. It was almost exciting.

I went up to the attic, where I'd set up a new desk and a comfortable reading chair with a standing lamp. I bit into one of my hotdogs. It was still warm inside, and juicy, but the bun was stale. I threw the other hotdog away and ate my fries with ketchup, slowly mellowing into the evening.

Tony's cell was off. There was no one for me to talk to, no one to call, nothing to do. I wasn't there to do anything. I was there to be alone. And safe. Nobody in the world knew where I was; I was pretty sure of that. I opened the champagne and let the fizz clear my palate. Then I sat in the reading chair, thinking, until it grew dark. I still didn't have a plan. I tried to formulate one but couldn't bend my mind to the task. Besides, I was finally starting to feel good. It might have been the champagne.

I went down to my nice new bed on the second floor, all made up with clean new sheets, and put on my new nightgown, a pink silk slip of a thing. A shame no one was there to see me, and of all things, it was Max Weigel who came to mind. Not that I liked him, but I wanted him to see me in my new white silk dressing gown, light and soft as a summer breeze with—no kidding—feathers around the neck.

I wandered through the whole house, until all the champagne was gone and a few shots of cognac as well. Eventually, my mind felt dead, and I knew I could finally sleep.

CHAPTER TWENTY-FOUR

W
HEN I WOKE UP, I hardly knew where I was. I didn't remember going to bed. But I was delighted with my new house, my safe house. I was playing at some sort of fantasy life, and I was on the run.

I had never stayed over to Saturday morning in Richmond, so I was in uncharted territory. I didn't have many options, since I didn't have any friends or jobs other than Anita, Tony, and Mary's Grove. So after tidying up the house and reading the news on my laptop, wishing I had thought to buy a coffee machine and coffee, I set out to see what Tony had gotten done in my absence the day before. It was time for the plants to go in, and I wondered what he had or hadn't found available.

I called Anita on the way over since she wasn't expecting me, and although she sounded surprised to hear from me, she readily urged me to come to her house. She met me at the door with a hug. She wasn't dressed for Pop or anyone else, and yet looked terrific. She was not a woman who needed a two-hundred-dollar haircut or designer clothes. Without a trace of makeup, with her hair brushed back from her face, she wore her years gracefully. In fact, I remarked on how relaxed and happy she seemed to be.

She laughed. "Wait'll I tell you."

In the sunroom, we sat and drank delicious coffee with little crispy apple tarts. She nibbled at one; I apologized for wolfing down the rest. I'd had one hot dog the night before, too much to drink, and no breakfast. I told her about the hot dog and no breakfast; I left out the part about how much I had drunk.

"You're young enough to get away with that," she said in a good-natured warning tone as I pinched up the last flakes of crust. "Just make sure it doesn't catch up with you. Was it a late night?"

She was fishing. I brushed it off. "No, I was..." *What?* I put on a tragic face. "I was trying to get my mind back onto my work. I've been so completely useless these last two weeks."

She was instantly contrite. She leaned toward me and touched my arm. "Oh, Kate, I am so sorry. I know what you've been going through. I've been worried about you, I really have been. And so has your father. He told me you were hardly back on your feet when you drove yourself right back here to work. I was afraid he thought I was demanding it. You know I would have understood if you took more time off, away from here, where that awful thing happened."

I sat back and thought about that for a minute. "When did he say that?"

She almost giggled. "That's what I wanted to tell you, if you didn't already know. He actually called me. He asked me out to lunch." My face must have shown something because she said, mock-archly, "Now, don't look so amazed."

"No, I mean, that's great. I had no idea. I thought, well, I don't suppose he had a chance to mention it. I haven't spoken to him since Tuesday, and hardly then, and I've had my cell off most of the time." I glanced down at my purse, where my cell was. I hadn't checked messages, either. "When was this?"

"Just yesterday. Honestly, Kate, sometimes I think neither of you would know what the other was doing if it weren't for me. You don't seem to talk to each other."

"You had lunch with Pop yesterday?"

"He called me. I couldn't believe it. I had just about given up, and I thought about calling him, but I don't know if he likes being pursued. They say men do, but in my experience, some don't. Not that I have that much experience. But a man like Miles likes to make up his own mind, don't you think? Of course, you know him better than I do."

"He called you to ask you out to lunch? When? I mean, when did he call?"

"Yesterday. He called yesterday morning and took me out to lunch." She sat back and glowed. "He told me you drove all the way home Thursday night and back in Friday morning. He was worried because you never do that. You stay in town on Thursdays, as a rule, don't you? He wondered if you were all right. I told him you weren't here yet, but I was sure you would be soon, which turned out to be wrong. But anyway, we got to talking, and then he asked me if I'd like to go out for lunch."

I didn't know what to say. She was obviously flattered and pleased. Finally, I said, "So you went."

"We had a wonderful time. Forgive me, but I was delighted when you didn't show up. We drove all the way to Gloucester! Went shopping. Had lunch in a cute little place." She was positively tickled. She shrugged. "I think it did him a world of good. He needs to stop thinking about you all the time."

Oh, no kidding. "I couldn't agree more."

"He's devoted to you. And I know it's a hard time for you, but he needs to let go. I told him, he can't make your problems go away by obsessing about them himself. You're a strong young woman, and you want your own life. I told him I thought maybe this was a turning point for you in spite of what happened two weeks ago."

"Did you...?" But how could I possibly phrase it? "It sounds like you spent the whole day together."

"The whole afternoon. We had a perfectly lovely time.

He's such a charming man. I only wish he were a bit less of a gentleman." She laughed, then turned down the corners of her mouth prettily. She was buoyant, but rueful, too, which answered my question. "Anyway, he wanted to know all about how I thought you were doing, and I told him I was only too happy if I could play a role in helping you two keep the lines of communication a little more open between you. I know sometimes it's hard for a father to talk to his daughter about these things, or for a daughter to talk to her father, for that matter."

"What things?"

She laid a hand on mine. "I think he's worried about how much that man meant to you. The one that was killed. He doesn't like to pry…"

I said, "Of course not," under my breath.

She didn't seem to hear. If she did, she missed the sarcasm. "And he knows you like to keep these things private. But he was afraid it was even more of a blow than you were admitting. When you still weren't here when we got back, he was afraid you'd gone home, and he didn't want you to find the house empty. Silly man." She sighed. "You need to keep those channels of communication open."

"Anita—"

"Like about this marriage thing."

I stared at her. "What marriage thing?" For a moment, an insane hope. "You and Pop?"

She looked confused, and maybe she had a moment of insane hope, too.

I repeated, "What marriage thing?"

"I know you have an unfortunate marriage in your past."

"I… what?" I sat back, breathless.

"Kate." Her was hand on mine again. "I know you were once married. Are married, I guess. Honey, it's no big deal. If it's a mistake, we'll get you out of it."

"No, Anita." I was scrambling to figure out what she could know and decided on the fly that there was no use denying it. "Really, it's embarrassing. Please forget you ever heard about that. How did you find out, anyway?"

She brushed by the question. "But that's just it, it's time you stopped running. Running from that terrible crime. Oh, my dear, I know I can't imagine what that was like, but you can't live your whole life by it. And this marriage, it's a trifling thing. And your father, he can help."

"No, you don't want to upset Pop with this. Believe me." I was casting about for something to deflect her. "He's not as strong as he seems. He worries, he gets upset, his heart—"

"Now, Kate, honey, that's what I'm trying to tell you. He knows all about it. He's not upset."

I froze. "Knows all about what?"

"Knows about the marriage." She looked exasperated, in a maternal way. "Kate, are you okay? Yes, he knows you foolishly got mixed up in a bad marriage when you were much younger. He knows it. You don't really believe your father thinks you're a virgin at forty-two?"

I blinked. "No, I don't imagine he does." I leaned forward. "He told you I was married?" My voice sounded strange to my own ears, but she didn't seem to notice.

"No, I was the one that told him."

I said, louder than I meant to, "You what?"

"But he already knew! At first, I thought he was surprised, then I think he was surprised that I knew. Like I said, if it weren't for me, I don't think either of you would know anything the other had going on. And I think he was surprised you trusted me enough to talk to me about things. That is, I think you do. I hope so, Kate, because I do care." She laughed. "I know, you know, he knows. Everybody thinks they have these big secrets, and everybody knows everything! It's crazy, Kate!"

"Wait." I held up a hand until I had recovered somewhat. "Let me be sure I understand this. He didn't tell you? You told him? How did you find out?"

"Tony and that little witch, Sabrina. Oh, you were right about her, Kate. I called again, and this time I think I fixed her. That girl is poison. I know she's not your friend. At first, I thought her knowing you in school and all, you were friends. But when I realized she's been trying to extort her way onto the cover of your book. You know she came back yesterday. Well..." She waved a graceful hand.

"They told you I was married," I said weakly. "Sabrina and Tony. That's it?"

"According to her, you were trying to find some man so you could divorce him."

"You didn't tell Pop about that part, though, did you?"

"Kate, what I am trying to tell you, dear, is that everything is out in the open. He knows you better than you think." She waggled a finger at me.

"He knew about the divorce?"

"Well, no, there was a misunderstanding about that. He thought he'd already taken care of that. He thought you were already divorced. Honestly, your little family of two, you're like the Keystone Cops. He thought he already paid the man to divorce you and leave the country."

I stared at her, truly bewildered.

"Really, Kate, if you would only talk to him. He loves you. You know that much, don't you?"

"Oh yes," I whispered. "He loves me."

"If you weren't his daughter, I swear, I'd be jealous." She sat back and studied her perfect ivory-tipped nails.

"How is it going, between you and him?"

She sighed. "He's a very reserved man. He has lived to take care of you, Kate, his only child, his motherless daughter. I think he feels bad about his wife having left him and you growing up without a mother as a result. You two have been so close for so long that, frankly, it's hard to work my way in. But I'm on it. And I think he likes me. I flatter myself that he appreciates the fact that I have helped to break down some of the secrecy and hiding that has become so habitual between you two."

"So what did he say about the divorce exactly?"

"He said the man was a ne'er-do-well employee of his in Africa. He says the man may have seduced you, or tried to, when you were much too young. He said—and he said it very affectionately, Kate, he's blind to your faults—he said you were quite a rebellious young lady when you were that age."

I found myself unsure how to get my bearings.

"Then at some point the man came here? And you ran off and got married? You tell me! I don't know what happened. All I know is afterwards Miles thought he had paid this scoundrel to get an uncontested divorce. Now he's keeping secrets from you! I thought maybe the man was an African?" She looked at me as if for confirmation.

I was beyond speech.

"But he said no, white." She grew serious. "For a minute there, I wondered if it could be that Chenobo man, but he said not." She was still looking at me questioningly, still trying to nail the whole story down.

I remained silent.

"Anyway, Miles told me he was very handsome and charming, maybe a little roguish? Too rough for his taste, anyway. Tall and redheaded? With tattoos and scars like a soldier of fortune." She was still waiting for me to confirm.

I closed my eyes.

"Honestly, Kate, relax. He thought it was funny. First time I've seen him genuinely amused."

I frowned into my coffee, trying to reconstruct what he must have said to her, and she to him.

"Anyway, I told him about how that little bitch was blackmailing you. He doesn't like language like that, does he? I'm afraid I shocked him when I called her that. And I assured him that she would be fired from the newspaper before she knew what happened.

"So he was sick with worry that you had a relationship with Merit Chenobo, but I told him I was pretty sure not.

Women can tell these things. I think it's just as you say, he was a dear friend, but not a love interest. That was true, wasn't it? Tell me that much."

I looked up. "It's true."

I sat very still. What should I do next? I considered my options. I had already told Max Weigel to reissue the notice. Should I go through with the filing? I felt a fresh wave of fear. I had to talk to Max again. Max. Somehow, he had to be the answer. I stood up to leave.

But Anita reached for my hand and drew me gently back down to my seat. "Now, Kate, if you are trying to get a divorce, does that mean you really are serious about somebody?"

When I hesitated, she became playful, reaching out as if to peck my knee with her finger. "My woman's intuition tells me there's a man."

I started to deny it. Then I realized she was playing right into my hands. "Okay, you've got me. There is. But it's early days yet."

I had her rapt attention, and again I had the strong sense of a plan forming in the back of my mind. I was still piloted by instinct, but my every step was sure. I didn't tell her anything, but I set it all up that day. It gave me a sense of power, made me feel like Kate Cranbrook stretching back through time, me coming into myself. It felt like destiny.

I called Tony on the way out. I was surprised he answered on a Saturday, at home. He must not have checked caller ID.

I said, "Thanks for outing me." I waited a couple of beats. "Telling Anita I was married?"

"Oh jeez, Kate, that was blown all over the place anyway."

Yes, my house of cards was coming down.

He started to argue, then make excuses, and I hung up. I drove back to Church Hill and had trouble finding a parking space. There was some kind of event going on. I sat so long at one intersection that I got honked at. In the end, I headed for home. For Lynchburg.

I drove slowly and sat in the driveway for several minutes before I went into the house. As bright as the afternoon was outside, it was dark and still inside. Pop sat alone in the living room. I said nothing, but I stopped. I felt tired. Empty.

He spoke from the shadows. "Sometimes, I think you aren't going to come home again."

"Don't be silly. Where would I go?"

CHAPTER TWENTY-FIVE

THE TENSION IN THE HOUSE was palpable that Saturday afternoon. Pop wanted explanations. Where had I been all day Friday and Friday night? He was dying to ask, but he knew it would infuriate me. Nothing had changed. He was clinging, wanting to guard me, wanting to know everything I did, everyone I saw, everywhere I went.

I decided to fall in with the idea that everything was absolutely normal. It seemed to be up to me to set the tone, and that was how I decided to play it. I had a lot of thinking to do, and I figured I could do it best if nothing were happening around me. So I behaved as though nothing had changed in twenty years. I settled into my room, then browsed in the garden until the day faded into evening.

That night, Pop outdid himself in the kitchen, as he often did when he was currying favor with me. He made veal liver moutarde and pulled wines from the top of the rack. I didn't know what he expected of me, or what he feared, or if he was braced for a fight. He seemed surprised that I was acting as though nothing was amiss. He didn't know whether to be grateful, smug, or suspicious.

He couldn't help probing when we sat down at the table. How had the week been? I made a noncommittal noise. Very casually, had Tony been there? I nodded, focused on the food and wine. He had cooked green beans almondine with green, yellow, and baby lima beans from the garden.

He said, "Apartment all right? Properly cleaned?"

I said it was fine. I told him I had spent Friday night

at the apartment. He would have known that was a lie. "I worked late yesterday at Mary's Grove. You know I don't like to drive all the way back here after a long day."

He would know that was a lie, too. For a wild moment, I thought he would accuse me of something, and I was ready to flame back. But he said nothing. Maybe he thought I was up to something. I was. I had set a plan in motion with Anita. Would I go through with it? I had mulled it over all afternoon, right up to dinner.

He cleared his throat, beginning to sound exasperated. "I'm surprised. Takes a brave girl to jump right back in and pick up where she left off. As if nothing's happened. I think a lot of young women would think twice about going on about their way like that."

"I'm doing what I've always done. That's worked out so far, hasn't it?"

His face was ruddy at the cheekbones. "I know what you're about, Kate. Know you better than you think. Think you fool anybody?"

I set down my fork. "I'm not fooling anyone about anything. I'm going about my work. I have a career."

He actually sneered. Oh, it was subtle, but it was there.

I felt my back stiffen. "What? You think it's nothing, just because I don't make as much money as you? Where did you get your money, anyway? The Cranbrook inheritance." I heaped scorn into my voice. "You wouldn't even have had that if it weren't for me. The money you took out of Africa? Without me? You know where you'd be without me."

He put down his fork. "Kate, I have always given you anything you wanted."

I squeezed my eyes shut and shook my head. I was brushing at cobwebs. He refilled my glass.

After a moment, I got my bearings back. "As long as it doesn't mean taking off my leash."

"What?"

"You give me anything I want as long as I stay here, or you go with me, or..."

The right eye was dark, unreadable. I was on dangerous ground.

"You're mine to protect, Kate."

I gave a short laugh that was more like a hiccough. I was irritated by my own sloppiness, just when I was trying to be so haughty. "I'm a possession, in other words. Is that it?"

"I've given you the life you wanted. All this—" He gestured around without moving his right eye from mine. "—you made it all up. You wanted all this, and I gave it to you. I gave you what you wanted, whatever you may tell the rest of the world, and whatever the world may think. Everything you've gotten, you've asked for." He was red-faced and out of breath.

"Fine, you win. No problem."

He slammed a palm on the table. "It's God's truth."

I snorted. When did he get religious? Then I made myself act nonchalant. I drank my wine and sighed. "No, it's true. You're right, as usual. I wanted to live here, I wanted the gardens, I wanted to be a princess, I wanted to be a rich daddy's girl."

He resumed eating cautiously.

I picked up my fork. "No, it's fine, really. Who cares about the world out there? I think about being off on my own sometimes, but really, I like my life. I like my persona, the independent unattached twenty-first-century professional woman." It seemed like a momentary lull in the hostilities. "I want to get out a little sometimes. Can you blame me for that? You never leave the house unless it's to drag along on the back of my skirt. You don't exactly hold up your own end socially. Did you ever consider that?"

He looked off balance.

"Like, why can't you ever cultivate any friends that I could meet and socialize with?"

His face was blank, as if I were suggesting something utterly revolutionary. Then he turned gruff again. "There's nobody around here either one of us would want to spend time with."

I let myself sound just breezily cross. "Oh, how do you know? You've never tried. And you know as many people as I do in Richmond. Seriously, I think you've met every single one. But did you ever strike up an acquaintance that we could follow up on? All those artsy, garden clubby people at Anita's party, for example. You couldn't make a single purely social friend? It's all up to me to network and meet people. I need that, you know, for my business. I know you don't think my business amounts to much, but it's important to me." I put a pout into my voice at that point.

He stared at me.

I pressed on. "I take you along, and then when I try to meet people and develop contacts, you get jealous. Or you criticize them and find fault, like nobody's good enough for you. I leave you behind, and you moan that I'm deserting you. You're impossible, Pop."

He looked down at his plate with a scowl.

I stifled the impulse to grin at him and set the hook. "Anita said something about a dinner at her house next week. Oh, I know." I rolled my eyes. "Now you'll say I'm trying to foist you off on her. She wants to give a dinner. It probably won't be just for us. She likes to entertain. People do, you know." I let that sink in for a moment. "She'd like us to come for dinner next Thursday night."

Cautious optimism dawned on his face.

"Well? What about it? Should I say we'll be there?"

He mumbled something. He was too proud to come right out and say it, but it was a yes.

I said, "Let's think of it as a whole new approach. A new beginning, how's that? We could be quite a catch, you know: the garden lady and her mysterious and charming father. A must on every truly hot guest list."

As I folded my napkin and stood up, I thought we were

both leaving the table in a cautiously optimistic frame of mind, though for very different reasons. I left him to clean off the table. I pulled my cell out of my pocket and dialed Max Weigel, pausing in the kitchen to pour another glass of wine.

Weigel answered carelessly, as though he hadn't seen who it was. "Weigel." The man had no polish whatsoever.

I tried to sound sweet. "Max?"

Pop was looking at me sharply as I let myself out of the kitchen door.

"Hey, Kate!" Weigel's voice changed completely in response to my tone.

So I immediately stiffened up. "You resumed notice?"

"Yep, right after you said to. Now I suppose you want to cancel it."

"What? No, of course not. I want to go through with this. But I'm still scared."

"Do you have any reason to think he saw the notice before?"

"No, none. But I'm still worried. Can you meet me Thursday night?"

"What for?"

His impudence annoyed me. "I don't owe you explanations. I'll pay you."

"You can pay me for the other day, too."

"All you have to do is bill me."

"I will." The man was insufferable. "So, is this for legal services or protection?"

"Both. I need to go back to the apartment. I... I'm going to try to set up a meeting."

There was a long silence on the other end.

He said slowly, "With... who? Not Brewer."

I nodded, which of course he couldn't hear. I was still thinking.

"With who?" he repeated.

"Listen, Weigel... Max, I haven't been entirely straight with you. I mean, I haven't told you everything."

"No kidding."

"I think I can get in touch with him. I've had some contact over the years. He'll probably want money to give up the claim he has on me. I want to try and negotiate something once and for all. I want the man out of my life. Forever. But it could be dangerous."

"Like I said before, if you think this guy is dangerous, you ought to go to the police about him, especially in view of the fact that your apartment was a crime scene not three weeks ago."

"It has nothing to do with that."

"You say. They might think different. And if it's nothing to do with that, then why do you think he's dangerous? I think it's because of the shooting."

"Oh, for God's sake." I was getting impatient. The man was infuriating. So dense. "All right, I'll tell them. You, however, are to say nothing. Not anything to anyone."

"I don't know anything but what you've told me. But you talk to them. They'd want the lead, however unlikely."

"I said I'll tell them."

We both fell silent. He was waiting, and I had not quite finished.

I whispered, "I think he wants to kill me."

Weigel sighed. "You really should tell the cops."

"I *will*. They'll find the same thing you did: no sign of him. They'll be no help with this."

"I don't know how you can be so sure. They have more resources than I do, and anyway, you told me not to try too hard, remember? So how do you think you're going to set something up with him?"

"Leave that to me. I have an idea. But I'm going to need you there Thursday night. Can you be there?"

"Hate to say it, Mrs. Brewer, but I think you're nuts. Yeah, I can be there."

I hung up.

I kept my head down for the rest of the weekend, biding

my time until I could get back to Richmond. Tuesday afternoon, Suzanne came again. Pop met me at the front door when I got home from class to say she was waiting on the screened-in porch. I took a deep breath and agreed to see her. We sat in our usual spots, I in my wicker chair, Suzanne on the flowered couch.

"Kate, I'm so sorry about your friend."

I cursed to myself once again that Pop had even told her about the shooting. I studied my cuticles. They were ragged.

"No, listen, Kate. It's important. It could be."

I lifted my head. "What do you mean, important? Of course it's important."

Her pale face flushed, and her eyes moistened. As always, I felt a pang for having spoken to her sharply. She was too fragile. I hated that.

"They want to reopen the investigation."

"What are you talking about, Suzanne? They haven't closed it. I don't even want to know about it." I got up to pace.

"No, no, the investigation into the first murder. The murder of Elliott Davis."

"What? No. We talked about that. I don't want senseless digging into memories that are painful to me."

She stood, too, distressed. Pop came in, an inquiring look on his face.

Suzanne glanced at him, then turned back to me and took my hands. "Please, Kate. Don't be upset. The last thing I want to do is make it worse than it already is. Believe me."

We both sat back down.

She told Pop, "They want to reopen the investigation into the first murder."

Pop gave her a curt nod. "No sooner let that animal out than another man was dead. Shot the same way."

I lashed out at him. "Oh for God's sake, Pop, he had nothing to do with it. Leave the poor man alone."

Suzanne flinched at my sudden anger.

Pop looked at me, then at her. "Who wants to reopen it?"

"There's a cold case unit. They're very dedicated and very good. They are as unhappy as you to realize that this crime has gone unsolved for twenty years."

He waved her off. "It will never be solved."

I ignored him and spoke to Suzanne. "I don't want the investigation reopened."

"Imagine if you could have closure."

"No. And why do they think they can do anything now?"

"Because of the second murder," she said.

I saw a glint of triumph in Pop's eye. Stupid. He was being stupid. They both were.

I whirled on Suzanne. I no longer cared if I sounded harsh. "It makes no sense. Jefferson couldn't have done the first one. That's the whole point. And the truth is, I never did know he was the one who shot Elliott. I only recognized him from the Tavern. We've been through all this."

Suzanne had a gift for the well-timed silence. When she was sure I had finished and my anger had subsided, she continued. "Elsa said—"

I cut her off. "Elsa Gabriel again? What has she got to do with this?"

Suzanne flushed. "I asked her to find out about the other case. About your friend that was shot. I thought it might help if I could tell you about what they were doing. She knows people in the Richmond PD. She was the one who suggested we reopen this one. She wants to help any way she can. She has never forgotten this case."

"Because she's still smarting about being passed over to head up the investigation. It's a grudge between her and her department." I was impatient. Suzanne was being dense, as dense as Pop. "But it's a waste of time. Jefferson didn't do the first one, and there's no reason to believe he did the second. Not just because he was out of prison." I turned to Pop and said, "It's stupid."

Suzanne reached out to me. "No, no, Kate, of course. You're right." She was placating me, which only increased my annoyance. "Jefferson is not a suspect, but they did check. He was in Atlanta. Remember I said he was moving there."

Pop growled. "Easy enough to run up here from Atlanta."

"No," she said. "He's accounted for. They thought of it, too."

I asked, "Then what makes them think they can make anything out of the old case now?"

"Elsa said—"

I could not suppress a cry of exasperation.

"Elsa said," she ventured again, "that because there were now two murders, it only made sense to consider them together. They were both shootings. Both friends of yours." She shrugged. "It's not much of a connection, but it's something. Otherwise, neither case has anything going."

I sat down.

Encouraged, she added, "Richmond agreed. They didn't know about the first murder. Of course it's a reach, there being more than twenty years in between. But the Cold Case Unit agreed to work this end."

Pop made a rough gesture. "What about those Africans? The ones that threatened the one that was shot. I call that a lead. It was African on African." He made a disgusted noise.

Suzanne continued evenly, "Richmond PD is looking into that. It's their top priority. But the Cold Case Unit is going to take on the Davis murder. Elsa has offered to coordinate between the two investigations."

I gritted my teeth.

Suzanne turned to me eagerly. "In cases like this, where a traumatic memory has been lost, they sometimes use hypnosis."

I stood up. "Oh no. No, I am not going to do that. I relive it every day. I don't need any help with that." I walked over to the window.

Suzanne assured me, "No one can make you do it if you don't want to. I wouldn't even try. It's entirely up to you."

I caught Pop's right eye, walked back, and sat down again. "I appreciate that."

Suzanne said, "The thing about a traumatic memory is that it doesn't ever go away. I don't have to tell you that, and you know I understand. For me, it was important to deal with the memory because I couldn't get rid of it."

"Did hypnosis help you with that?"

"No, there was no need to hypnotize me. My memories were never lost. And there was no gap of twenty years. I mean, it has been almost that long now, but at the time I was dealing with it, when I was in therapy after I was raped, I remembered everything. I still do. But you've lost your memory of what he looked like, from what you say. Or maybe there are other details. You don't remember how you got home, for example. So all I'm saying is, you might be able to recover it and deal with it if you were hypnotized."

The very idea was so anxiety provoking that I almost doubled over. I closed my eyes and held my stomach. I heard Suzanne's exclamation of dismay and felt the gentle tremor of her hand at my elbow.

"Kate, I'm so sorry. I don't mean to upset you. I thought it might help, but I'm going to drop it. I won't bring it up again."

I hugged her quickly. "It's okay. No, I understand what you're saying. But I don't feel like it would help, and I simply can't do it. I know they've put you up to this, I understand, but you can tell them I will not cooperate. I told you that last week, and that's still the way it is, for all the reasons I gave you before."

"I wouldn't have brought it up if I hadn't thought it might help, but yes, of course, you're right. They thought you might remember something that would help with the investigation."

"Even if I remembered a face, it would be completely

different today, so long afterwards. In the video, Jefferson was completely changed. It was dark. I was screaming and my eyes were shut a lot, I think."

We fell silent, and after a moment, I said, "Yours was solved. There never was any mystery."

She nodded. "And there was that closure. Until they caught him, I was in terror. Even after they caught him, I was afraid, but it helped. That was why I thought you'd want them to investigate and try to find him. If you're afraid."

"More than afraid, I feel guilty."

"Guilty!"

"Over what I did to Jules Jefferson."

Pop looked up.

Suzanne shook her head vehemently. "You didn't do anything to him. It wasn't your fault."

"I don't want to wrongly accuse another man."

"That won't happen. There's DNA."

"No. Tell them no. There is no way I will do it. Discussion closed."

"You don't want them to try to solve it."

"I can't explain it, but it's what I feel. I don't want to remember. It's been so long, I don't see the point. I want to move forward. I need my life back."

Suzanne said, "You know how you feel. Your reaction is your own, and it's as valid as mine. And whatever it is, I want to support you. I shouldn't even have brought it up. Elsa told me you would feel this way. She said you wouldn't agree to be hypnotized. She said you would never want to go there."

CHAPTER TWENTY-SIX

I FELT A HUM OF GROWING excitement under my skin. But it was up and down. Sometimes I felt I was taking action, getting a grip on my life in spite of everything. At those times I felt very much in control; I could stop everything if I wanted to, or move forward, whatever I chose to do. It was a heady sensation of power, all the more as I carefully maintained a calm exterior.

Other times, I felt exhaustion and despair. At those times, it seemed anything that did happen was inevitable, as if I were on a course, impelled, come what may, and couldn't stop. Pop seemed puzzled by my mood swings. He stayed out of my way, and I was pretty sure he could read nothing. He didn't know half as much as he thought he did about me.

My immediate problem as I prepared to go back to Richmond was to block him from riding into town with me. I knew he would expect to do that. He thought we'd drive in Thursday morning and arrive at Anita's house together for dinner. He might think we'd go by the apartment first, and he might think he'd have to be entertained by her while I worked with Tony for a while. But he thought we'd go to town together, as we sometimes had in the past. Didn't he understand? Those days were over.

Once, on Tuesday, he even asked me about it, though he was careful to be casual and oblique. "So what's the plan? For this dinner."

I knew he wanted to know when we'd leave, and he

wanted reassurance, but he was afraid to be weak or to admit he depended on me.

I pretended not to understand. "Dinner. On Thursday." I smiled. It was hard. I pulled up the corners of my mouth and slipped away busily before he could try to get more.

I waited until early Wednesday morning, then I breezed through the kitchen dressed for class. "So why don't you plan to show up at her house six-ish Thursday afternoon. Tomorrow."

His face went slack. Hah. I had caught him completely unprepared.

I smiled. "I'm going in direct from class this afternoon." It was, after all, my most recent routine. "I'll be busy all day tomorrow. See you tomorrow night."

I gave him a don't-you-dare-argue look and dashed out of the house. I felt the right eye on my back.

I left my car in an out-of-the-way spot, where students parked. I was apprehensive all day, half-expecting that Pop would show up to spy on me. Then toward the end of the afternoon, I cancelled my last class and stalked my own car before I approached it. I pulled out of the wrong exit and followed a roundabout route until, once I was on the road to Richmond, my glee bubbled over. No Pop! I was off without him. "Now, on to more serious business."

I spent the night at the safe house, parking several blocks away and approaching only after careful surveillance. I felt eyes on all sides as I smuggled in provisions for the night: champagne, cognac, and a fat deli sandwich. I was jittery, manic, on a high.

I sat in my third floor office with the sloping ceilings and ate, drank, and surfed the Internet. I read about GSR—Gun Shot Residue.

The prosecution and defense had both bored the jury and the court for hours during Jules Jefferson's trial. He had been tested for GSR, but not until two days after the crime. No GSR on his hands or clothes, the defense had said. No problem, said the prosecution expert. By the time he was arrested, he had washed both his hands and his clothes.

A lot has changed since then. GSR means very little unless a suspect's hands are bagged on the spot, but even then, smearing and contamination can totally confuse the situation. And the stuff is easily removed. In cases where they get good, clear evidence that a suspect fired a gun, the suspect is a moron.

I went out for coffee the next morning with my laptop and loafed over the news. When the stores opened, I went shopping. I found a beautiful skimpy indigo denim dress with just the right amount of spandex. It fit like skin. I'd lost a few pounds in the aftermath of the shooting, and a lot of my clothes were loose. The dress was a size smaller than what I usually wore. I figured I'd grow back out of it after a while, but until then I looked like dynamite in it. I found a beautiful turquoise and silver pendant. It cost the earth but went perfectly with my skin and the denim dress. I bought a pair of sandals, too, and then a pair of leather pumps, classic, not too high.

I arrived at Mary's Grove about noon. I drove past the entrance, parked behind some trees on the next block, and walked back to the house.

I startled Tony when I came up behind him on foot. He glanced around but didn't ask about my car. I had planned to say I put it in the shade. I could see that most of the plants were in and the mulch was going down. I told him it looked good.

Tony asked, "What's up with you?"

It struck me that I was over him, and I said so. "You know what, Tony? I'm over you."

His eyes widened. He made a short, incredulous laughing noise and then frowned as if I had described something wildly improbable. He was as handsome as ever, all brown and sweaty, hair in his eyes. And I felt absolutely nothing. How liberating. I felt powerful and calm.

Anita greeted me with her eyes searching over my shoulder. "He didn't come?"

"Not yet. He will. Separately. I wanted us to be in two cars. Anita, I'm not going to join you tonight, okay? Won't it be better without me?"

"Not coming? Why?" She led me into the sunroom and gave me a knowing look as she sat down. "Do you have other plans?"

I returned the look. "I do." Then I decided I had better hedge my bets. "Actually, I'm not sure. I'm thinking it's better if I don't."

She sat and patted the chair next to her. "But I'm afraid he'll run off the minute he realizes you aren't here."

"Tell him I said he would run off and tell him I'm disgusted. Tell him I said we don't have any friends, thanks to him." She blinked at my vehemence, and I waved her off. "Don't tell him I'm not coming. Tell him I said I would be a little late. Tell him I had to go get something for the job."

Her face clouded. "Get what? He'll ask."

"I don't know. PVC pipe?"

"Tony would get that."

"A plant then. Say you don't know." I smiled. "It's true. You don't." I shrugged. "Neither do I."

"I don't like to lie to him."

"That wouldn't be a lie. You really don't know. Do you?" I lifted my hands, like, simple as that.

She didn't smile back. "I mean about you coming. I don't want to tell him you're coming if you're not."

"Then don't lie. Tell him I said to tell him I'd be late. I am saying that. Tell him I said to tell him I'd be here no later than eight." I lifted my hands again. *Voila!* "I *am* telling you that."

"But will you be here by eight?" She was getting confused.

"Yes, no, I'm not sure, but I'm definitely telling you to tell him that."

She gave me a queer look. "So that's the truth?"

"Of course it is."

"I don't know, Kate. I hate to get off on that foot with him. He'll realize I misled him when it's all over."

"Act like you were misled, too. Even that's true. Probably."

"I'll end up telling him everything. It's my nature to be truthful." Her voice held a small note of gentle reproach.

"Don't you want him to yourself for a while this evening? Do you really want it to be a threesome?"

She sighed. "Well..." She shrugged and smiled. "What can I say?"

"Say whatever you like when eight o'clock has come and gone. Tell him I'm a terrible liar. Tell him I put you up to lying, if you want, except it wasn't lying. It was the truth."

She looked concerned again. "You have a funny concept of the truth."

"It's a matter of how much you say. Nobody ever tells the whole truth. How could they?"

She shifted toward me and put on a serious face. "Kate, I'm worried about you."

"Talk to him about that. After I don't come."

She leaned the other way and smiled. "So what have you got going on?"

I thought about what to say. "A rendezvous. I'm not going to say any more than that for now. I don't want you to have to withhold information. And anyway, I'm not sure anything is going to come of it. That's why I don't want to say one way or another whether I'm going to get here. If I get stood up, I might come here. Leave me free, okay?"

She tried a new tack. "What's going on between you and Tony? He keeps asking me where you are and what you're doing. Used to be, you two kept in pretty close touch."

"Too close. It went to his head. I've had to put a little distance there. You were right. He did have a thing for me, but you know there's nothing going on between us. I'm keeping him at arm's length until he cools off."

In the end, Anita gave up trying to figure out my plans and turned her attention to making sure the dinner she had planned would meet Pop's approval. I was as helpful as I could be on that score, even offering to pick up a couple of bottles of the right wine, which she was only too happy for me to do.

Before I left on that errand, I went over the paths with Tony and talked about plants still to be found. He was punctilious and sullen throughout. He made a big point of sticking strictly to business, and I refused to comment on his manner. I made it very clear that he should not try to come over to the apartment that night, telling him I wouldn't even be there. He told me not to worry, pouring as much irony into the words as possible. Poor Tony. Never quite caught up.

I left a little after three; I was getting nervous that Pop might appear early. It was amazing how well I knew him. I wasn't wrong. My parking spot was out of sight of the house, and I was looking sharp when, lo and behold, in the nick of time, I saw his car. I practically dove into the bushes. I ran bent over and stooped behind my car. Then I glanced around to see whether anybody else had seen me acting so strangely. There was no one.

As Pop pulled into the circle drive, I peeked over the trunk of my car. He was scowling at Tony's truck. I thought I was well enough hidden, but I froze anyway when he looked in my direction. I didn't think he saw me. He turned in place, sweeping a full circle. He would have thought I wasn't there as soon as he drove up. I always parked right in front.

I watched as he went to the door. It opened, and he disappeared inside. I figured I could count on Anita to pull him in and hang onto him. I jumped in my car and pulled away as fast as I dared. As soon as I was clear, I pictured Anita telling Pop he'd just missed me, but that I would be right back with the wine. That made me laugh.

Then I wondered if she would give away the whole game by immediately confessing that I might not be there that night and that I wanted her to lead him on about it. That thought sobered me right up. Anita was a damned fool. But then I thought, no, she would be sure I would come back with the wine.

I sped into town, found the wine, and at four o'clock, called her to say I couldn't find a good enough wine at the nearest store and that I'd be a while longer, but I'd be right back. That would hold them both down for a while.

I called Max and left a message that I'd be at his office at six. At five, I went back to Mary's Grove, approaching by the side road, parked where I had before, snuck around behind the smokehouse, and patiently waited for Tony to come out to his truck.

Thirty minutes later, I caught him there and said, "Hey, Tony, do me a favor."

He was surprised to see me, and he glanced around for my car.

Before he could speak, I held out the wine bag. "Give this to Anita. Tell her I have to change, and I'll be on my way back." I smiled sweetly. "I'm coming back here for dinner." That should be confusing enough. I was thinking I should never have told her I wasn't coming.

Tony took the bag from me with a dirty look and muttered something that sounded like, "Fuckin' crazy."

I figured he would take his time giving her the bag. I waited until he had stalked off before hurrying back to my car. I hopped in and sped off with my eyes glued to the rearview mirror. I had escaped for the moment.

I drove back to the safe house, stopping for more provisions on the way and then making the usual elaborate precautions to approach. I showered and dressed with great care. I put on the denim dress and admired the way the skirt stretched sideways across my hips in front. I put on a trace of makeup and blow-dried my hair. I tried the leather sandals, but it wasn't the right look. I put on the pumps, touched a minute amount of Jungle Gardenia to my throat, and called Anita again.

"Kate, where are you?" She sounded exasperated.

"What have you told him?"

She paused a beat, then said, "That you went to get wine. Then Tony showed up with it and said you were getting dressed and you were coming back."

"And what have you told Pop?"

"Nothing so far, but—"

"Please, Anita, I've got this new guy, and I want to see him, but I don't know if it'll pan out or not for tonight. It's complicated, and I don't want to get Pop all excited if it turns out to be a complete bust."

I stopped myself. I needed to set it up just right. I switched the phone to my other ear and slowed down, made my voice sweet. "Anita, I'll know what I'm doing in another hour, promise. I'm dressed and ready. This guy's supposed to call me. If he does, if I can see him tonight, I'll call you for sure and let you know right away, so you can make up your mind whether to tell Pop I'm not coming." I cradled the phone in both hands. "Don't you want to have him to yourself for a while? He does like you! I know he does. He just gets distracted worrying about me, and we both know that's no good. But if you feel you have to be completely honest with him, I understand, I do. Anyway, I'll call and warn you if I'm not coming. If I don't call, it means I'm on my way. So I should be there by... what is it now? Anyway, like I said originally, by eight."

"Kate—"

"Don't tell him about Max. Make something up. Please, Anita. Just give me a little time. Do me this one little favor, and I'll make it up to both of you."

"Kate, this concealment and hiding from him, it has to stop somewhere. There's no need for it, dear."

"I know. I understand. I know you're right, and I'm

going to work on that. But let me do it my way just this once. Believe me, it'll upset him if you tell him about Max."

"Why? No, it won't. What will upset him is not knowing if you're coming or not, or where you are. He worries about you the way any parent would worry about a child. He can't turn it off just because you're grown, especially after all that's happened to you. But I don't want to lecture you. Promise me you'll call me and let me know you're coming, so he can be at ease."

I sighed audibly into the phone. "Okay. I'll call you if I'm not coming. Otherwise, I'll just come on out."

She wished me luck.

There. I thought maybe that was perfect. Anita Blore was the self-appointed world guardian of family communications. I was a fool to try to work with her. The silly woman was so irretrievably honest that she had automatically believed everything I said. I was pretty sure of that, and it took care of Phase One.

CHAPTER TWENTY-SEVEN

Max Weigel was prepared to be grumpy after the way I'd hung up on him, but I felt the shock wave when he saw me in the new dress. He caught me looking at him looking at me.

I smiled openly and struck a pose. "What, you like it? It's new." I did a pirouette. I tried a little head toss and almost lost my balance. That was the wine. I smiled and said, "Oops." And we laughed together.

I sidled up to him. "Are you having a hard time staying mad at me, Max?"

He got serious. "It's not a question of me getting mad at you, Kate."

I smoothed his lapels, dusted away some imaginary lint, then glanced at him and snatched back my hands as though I'd been caught at something. I walked over to his office window and stood there hugging myself. I wanted to look dramatic, but I was enjoying myself hugely. Max was trying to be impassive, but I'd gotten a glimpse of his face, and I'd say he was flustered.

He cleared his throat and flopped into his desk chair. "So. Let's see if I've got this straight. Carl Brewer. You married him during a wild fling twenty-some years ago and then you lost all track of him. You hired me to search for him, but not so hard that I might find him, because you were scared of him. Then you tell me to proceed with notice of your intention to divorce him. Somebody gets shot, and you tell me to cancel the notice. Then you tell me to start it up again."

I turned and faced him. "You know how to spoil a mood, don't you, Mr. Weigel?"

He made a poofing sound. "I'd say you know how to spoil a mood, too, Mrs. Brewer."

It crossed my mind that I had let him down pretty abruptly at my apartment the last time I had seen him. "You think I'm playing with you."

"I think you've been lying to me. Maybe you're trying to distract me from that fact." He linked his hands over his stomach. It wasn't exactly flat. But he wasn't fat, either. Beefy. I caught myself sizing up his body and looked back at his face.

He continued. "You have no idea where he is. But no, wait, you're going to set up a meeting. He won't care about the divorce, but he wants to kill you. It's a pack of lies, Kate."

Was he always so rude? "It's not a pack of lies. It's complicated."

"It's always complicated when somebody gets shot."

"It had nothing to do with that."

"Did you call the cops and tell them about him?"

I steadied my eyes. "Yes. They weren't too interested. They said they'd look into it."

"No, they were surprised to hear about it."

I snapped, "What are you talking about?"

"I called them. They didn't know anything about it. They want to talk to you about it."

"Damn it, Weigel! You're supposed to be working for me. You said everything I told you was in confidence." I really kind of flew off the handle. "Max Confidential." I heaped huge scorn on the name.

He laughed. "All right, all right. Keep your shirt on. I didn't tell them anything."

I stared, uncomprehending. I turned away and then back.

He spread his hands, palms up. "I didn't tell them

anything. I don't feel like I owe anything to the Richmond PD. I wondered if you had told them. And I figured you'd lie." He looked smug. Thought he was so smart. "I guess I was right."

"Asshole."

He laughed again. And then so did I. In fact, I couldn't stop. I was giddy.

When I got my breath back, I said, "Let's go get a drink somewhere. And a sandwich."

I had to wait while he dragged out the usual maudlin good-byes with the dog. Every time I started to think there was something to the man, he would do something stupid and break the spell. Seriousness flooded back over me. I was playing my part too well. And not well enough. I had to get back on track.

I said, a little sharply, "We can go out for a drink. It's early. But this is a job. I want protection. I'm not saying anything is going to happen. I don't know anything. But I hired you because I don't want to be alone. I need somebody I can trust. I want to feel safe."

He gave me a long look, then opened the drawer and pulled out the gun. He checked the safety before holstering it.

"On or off?" I asked.

"On."

Outside, he glanced around questioningly.

I said, "I took a cab here. I'm riding with you."

When we got into the Audi, he asked, "So what are you up to, Mrs. Brewer? Back to business is fine with me. You know how to get in touch with this guy, or don't you?" He turned his head at a red light to look at me. "Or are you trying to flush him out?"

I opened my mouth, and he cut me off. "And don't tell me to shut up and do what you're paying me to do. I think you'd better fill me in."

"Where are we going?"

A hamburger joint, as it turned out. The place was also a bar with a loud TV and a pool table.

"This is classy." I said it in a snotty way, but actually, I liked the place.

I had a martini and a handmade cheeseburger on a toasted sesame bun with sautéed onions, french fries, and ketchup. It was delicious. Weigel ate most of it, in addition to wolfing his own.

I said, "Knock yourself out. Just leave my martini alone."

I thought we were getting kind of intimate, sharing food like that, but he was not one to be distracted from his goals for long.

He ate every last french fry, swiped up the last bit of ketchup with his finger, and licked it. "What are you up to?"

"It's like this..." I started to tell him about growing up in Africa, and when he interrupted to tell me not to fool around I blazed back in a low, hissing voice, leaning way forward over the table. "You want to know what I'm up to? You want to understand? Okay, I'll tell you the whole story. Shut up and listen."

He sat back, looking wary.

I needed Max Weigel, and I wasn't sure how far he would go to help me or how much he would believe. So I went back to the very beginning. I told him I was wild when I was a girl and got in trouble with men.

"One of them was Merit, and Carl Brewer was another. They knew each other, but where Merit was political, Carl was an opportunist. He was mixed up with the opposition like Merit, but only for his own profit. So when my father moved to Nairobi, and when his business wasn't doing very well, and then on top of that, the riots broke out after the coup, he used me for bait to get Carl Brewer to get us out of the country. When we were stopped, my father double-crossed Carl. We got out because my father turned him in, and Carl was shot. We thought he was dead when we left. But he wasn't. Then he showed up here. I met up with him and got to drinking, and it ended up I ran off with him for a weekend. We got married, but I never told my father that." I fell silent. I didn't like the look on Weigel's face.

He said slowly, "I'll be honest with you—"

I cut him off. "Why do people say that?" I mimicked him, singsong: "'I'll be honest with you.' I read an article that said when people say that, they're about to lie. If you think about it, it sort of implies that usually you do lie to me. Like it's a novelty: You'll be honest with me."

I was mad, but he seemed to think it was funny, which made me angrier. I felt my face getting red.

He was unruffled. "Yeah, well, I think it means I'm going to say what maybe I might normally think and not say. I was going to say I'm not so sure I believe this Carl Brewer guy even exists."

I sighed, weary and exasperated. He was being so dense. I stood up. "Let's go."

I refused to speak all the way to the apartment. Weigel maintained his good nature, but he was treating me like a spoiled, pouting child who was in his charge. I began to panic. I was going to have to break that mold.

My car was parked right in front of the door. I had met the cab there on the way to Weigel's office. Weigel made a move to lead the way up the stairs. I didn't know whether he was trying to be protective or gentlemanly, but I slipped in front of him and let him watch the back of my short skirt ride up as I climbed.

On the second-floor landing, I turned and gave him a smile for the benefit of anyone who might be watching. Then I let us in. In the living room, I dropped my purse and offered him a drink.

He said, "No thanks. I'm working." Still the genial babysitter.

I took two glasses and a bottle of white wine from the

fridge. I plunked the bottle down in the middle of my work table and poured myself a glass.

While he prowled through the apartment, I sat down on the canvas loveseat, crossed my arms and legs, and said, "If Carl Brewer doesn't exist, why did I hire you?"

"That's a good question."

"It has a simple, straightforward answer. He does exist, and I hired you to get rid of him."

"Get rid of him?"

"Get me a divorce. What did you think I meant? Jesus, Weigel, you must watch a lot of TV." I took a big breath and blew it out. I shifted, uncrossed my arms and legs, and tried a less adversarial tone. "Hey, Max, I realize it sounds like a crazy story, but it's true. How can I convince you? Oh!"

I jumped up and grabbed my purse. I searched through it and found the clipping I had taken from Merit's apartment, the one that described the aftermath of the attempted coup and riots. "There," I said triumphantly. "Carl Brewer."

He took the clipping, read it quickly and gave me a funny look. Then he handed it back. "Yeah. It says he's dead."

"What? Oh." He was right. "Damn it. But he isn't. Look." I grabbed his arms and willed him to believe me. "This shows I wasn't lying about the coup and the name. It proves Carl Brewer was there. I even told you he got shot and we thought he was dead."

He pursed his lips.

I dropped my hands and turned away. "Oh, what's the use."

"Okay, let's say he exists." He looked at his watch. "It's eight o'clock. You said something about meeting him here. That on?"

"No. At least I don't think so since he's not here. But he might show up."

I got up and poured another glass of wine. I added over my shoulder, "Sure you don't want one?"

"Am I still working?"

"If I say no, are you going to leave me here alone?"

He took a long time to answer. Then he took off his jacket and said, "I guess not right away," but when I smiled, he added, "If..." I waited. "If you'll explain a few things."

I sighed, nodded, and poured wine for both of us.

He looked at his glass, but didn't take it. "Did you ever see him again?"

"Yes, I've seen him."

"I thought he disappeared."

"He reappears sometimes."

"Does anyone else ever see him on these occasions?"

I thought about that one for a second. "Other people see him sometimes."

With a perfectly straight face, Weigel said, "Is he bigger than a breadbox?" And both of us laughed. "You married him, and then he disappeared."

"I've heard from him a few times over the years, mainly when he needs money. I don't tell Pop. I spend a lot, and I do it in cash, out of the ATM. I can put my hands on a fair amount if I need to."

"Why isn't there any record of him?"

"He uses a phony name."

I held out his glass.

He folded his arms over his chest. "What is it? The phony name."

"I don't know." When I saw his expression, I said, "What, you want me to make one up?" Wine sloshed when I gestured.

We stood there looking at each other—I was still holding out the glass—and something passed between us. He took the wine.

I continued, "So I hired you to get rid of him. I wanted to undo that stupid marriage."

"Why all of a sudden?"

"I wanted to marry somebody else." He frowned, and I

quickly added, "But that's all over." I waved it off, sloshing more wine, and sat down on the couch. I tucked my legs up under me and held the drink in my lap. I was sorry I didn't have bigger, more comfortable furniture. "Anyway, I was hoping I could pull it off without him knowing about it."

"But you heard from him."

"Not exactly. Pop mentioned some hang-ups. That was how it happened before. He'd call the house, and if Pop answered, he'd hang up."

"That's it? Where'd you get the idea he'd be here tonight?"

"I emailed an old Hotmail account he used a few years ago. I gave him my cell and told him to be here tonight. But he never called. Maybe he never got it." I shrugged. Then I looked around at the bare windows. "I think he might be watching, though."

Max moved around the room, checking out the windows. "You ever hear of Venetian blinds?"

"I'm an artist. I like natural light. I didn't know any of this was going to happen."

"Any of what? What are you afraid of? Why do you think he's dangerous?"

"He might be mad about the divorce. If he saw the notice."

"But why? He never sees you. What's it to him?"

"It's the usual story. If he can't have me, no one can." I paused. "That and the money."

"What money?"

"Pop's. When he dies, I get it. He's got quite a lot. Carl Brewer could even be dangerous to Pop, as long as he's married to me."

"Kate—"

"I know, I know. Tell the cops about him. Okay, I will. But he's old now. Anyway, I guess he's not coming tonight. Stay a while, though. I'd feel better. It's not even nine o'clock."

He spun my desk chair around and sat, but he looked about ready to bolt. "A while. I've got to feed Bridget."

"Stay until ten. Send me the bill for whatever you want."

I got up, turned off most of the lights, and filled his half-empty glass of wine. Avoiding his eyes, I said, "Excuse me, but I have to get out of this tight dress. I've had it on all day."

"You dress like that to go to work?"

I ignored that, went into the bedroom, and took off all my clothes. I put on the white silk robe with the feathers, hesitated, then stepped back into the pumps.

Weigel was up again, peering out the window at the street. When I struck a pose in front of him, I didn't like the look I got. I tossed my hair and poured myself another glass of wine. Then I thought, *the way to this man's heart is through his dog.* So I plunked down on the loveseat and asked, "Is Bridget a good watchdog?"

He lit right up. "Oh hell yeah, the best. I mean, she's amazing. Thing is, she's quiet. Some dogs, they hear something, and they start barking. Not Bridge. She'll nudge me or make a low sound that only I can hear. So she makes sure I know, and she doesn't let them know. She's real smart about that."

I curled up and arranged the silk robe on my bare legs. "Maybe I should get a dog. I had one when we lived in Africa, but hyenas got hold of him one night and killed him. Broke my heart. I missed him so much I never wanted another dog." *Pure fiction.*

He looked deeply sympathetic. "What kind of dog was it?"

"A Rhodesian ridgeback."

He nodded solemnly. "They're good dogs. A dog and a gun is a good combination. Dog lets you know if anybody's there, and then you shoot 'em." But he still looked ready to bolt.

I stood up and said, "Wait. I think I hear somebody on the stairs."

He listened, then shook his head. "He's not coming, Kate."

How could I tip the scale? Max was into trust, and he didn't trust me. So how could I get him to trust me? I prowled the room until the answer came to me: *Extend trust. Share.*

I tried to sound sweet and vulnerable. "Max, you know, I don't mean to be secretive. I trust you. I don't know why, but I feel safe with you." *Sincerity. Think sincerity.* I caught his eyes. "Things have happened to me." I made my voice smaller, almost childlike.

He was listening. I thought I felt a little spark.

I moved closer to him, tentatively. "I was the victim of a crime. A long time ago. When I was in college. I was in a car and the man I was with was shot, and I was raped." I saw a look of concern on his face and plunged forward. "I don't know if you've ever known anybody who went through something like that, maybe you did, since you were a cop. But you feel guilty." I thought about something Suzanne had said. "Guilty and dirty and ashamed. And it's taken me most of my adult life to get past the feeling of vulnerability."

But I had misread the look of concern. "Wait. You're telling me there was another shooting? Before this?"

"Unrelated, this was a long time ago." He was supposed to be feeling sorry for me.

"Anything to do with Carl Brewer?"

I shook my head. "It had nothing to do with him. I can't tell you any more about it now." I resumed the pathetic tone and averted my eyes. "Intimacy is hard for me." That much was certainly true.

I reached out tentatively and touched his shoulder, looking for that little flame. I let my hand fall. "I do mean it. I feel safe with you. I don't usually share this." I let my voice falter, then raised my eyes to his.

I saw nothing but suspicion. Something snapped. "Goddammit, Weigel. Don't you find me at all attractive?"

"Yes and no. You look sexy as hell, if that's what you're asking."

"What, am I intimidating you?" My robe fell open.

He said nothing, and I sighed, disgusted. I stalked across the room and whirled back on him. "Don't tell me. Let me guess. You're seeing somebody."

He shook his head, dead serious.

I asked, as nastily as I could, "What do you do for sex?"

He shook his head again, very slowly.

"What?" I was getting aggressive, but I couldn't stop. I kicked off the pumps. "What? Do you jerk off a lot? Is that enough for you? Don't you sometimes want to do it with a real person? Feel another body just as hot as yours?" I was shouting, but I didn't care.

He glanced left and right.

I ripped off the white silk. "Don't you ever want to fuck?"

He held up a hand. "Did you hear something?"

I clenched my fists. "No! I did not."

Then I did.

Nightmare-like, heavy steps pounded up the stairs, laboriously, furiously. Then, a voice on a gramophone turning too slow: "Kate. Kate."

Max called, "Who's there?" At the same time I screamed, "Max!"

He pulled his gun from the holster and flipped off the safety. "Who's there?"

The door slammed open. *NOW!* Two shots, each different-sounding, blew in my ears at one time.

I opened my eyes. I thought maybe they had killed each other, but Max was still standing. Pop was grunting on the floor. I went to him, bent over, and took the Ruger from the floor where it had fallen from Pop's hand.

Max said, "Kate, what are you doing?" and I shot him in the chest.

I placed the gun on Pop's body, which lay still, and quickly went to the kitchenette to wash my hands with soap and water. I looked down at blood spattered on my naked body. The three shots had been unbelievably loud, and they reverberated in my ears as I went back out to where Max and Pop were dead and dying. I pulled on the white robe, handled Pop's gun, threw it aside, and picked up his head and shoulders, getting blood all over myself.

I turned Max over to make sure he was dead. I set aside his gun, took his hands, and rubbed them in mine. He groaned, and I panicked. He stirred, but blood was pouring out of him. I didn't think he'd live. No, pretty sure not. I got more blood all over me as I straightened him out on his back. I heard voices. I ran to Pop, knelt, and lifted his head onto my lap. I rearranged his arms so they were peacefully crossed on his chest.

There was a banging on the door, and I yelled, "Help! Help! Help!"

Someone ordered people back, and the door opened.

The young patrol officer who was first on the scene was nice. His close-set dark eyes were respectful in his narrow face.

"My father," I said. "My lawyer. Guns." I wept hysterically. It wasn't hard to do.

The homicide detectives who arrived shortly afterward were more difficult, not quite so credulous. One said, "Okay, they shot each other."

I thought they seemed to accept it. But of course, they took me in.

I didn't even try to hold myself together. I was crazy. I told them it was all my fault, that I had killed them both, that they were both dead, and it was all because of those guns. I indulged in unchecked hysterics. They questioned me over and over, putting it together that my apartment was the same place somebody had been shot three weeks before.

Then they realized I was the same woman who had found Merit's body. Actually, what tipped them off was that I got edgy at one point and called Melson. They were taken aback to find I already had an attorney on call. By the time he'd sprung me out of there, it was midmorning the next day.

Melson drove me home. He didn't like anything I said, which wasn't much, but he didn't think they had anything to go on. He explained that experts would look at it. They would try to figure out who got shot first, and if whoever shot second could have gotten off an answering round. They'd ask everyone who heard the shots how far apart they were. The shot that missed: How did that figure in? What were they doing there with guns?

On and on, he droned, until I said, "Will you just shut up about it?"

He tried to follow me into the house, but I put him right back out. I didn't even offer him coffee. I told him to go away. I locked the front door and went up to my room without turning on any lights. I showered, wrapped up in a robe, and went to bed. I'd been up some thirty-six hours. I thought about taking pills and decided I had better not.

I lay on my back on the bed all day and tried to assess my situation. Pop was gone.

Pop. That was what I had called him. It sounded stupid to me for sure. I'd ask myself, Why had I killed Max? Because Max had known too much, I reassured myself. But then, I had grave misgivings. Would everything Max knew come out anyway? I began to be afraid it would. Maybe I shouldn't have killed him. Of course I shouldn't have. But I was thinking it might have been a strategic error.

What I didn't want out was the name Carl Brewer. That was what Max knew. The cops would know about Max Weigel and Miles Cranbrook. I wanted Carl Brewer left out of it. I didn't think anybody else knew that name. Then I did a fast sit-up in bed, and cold liquid ran through my body: the notice.

But why would the cops see that? I dropped back flat on the bed. I was afraid I knew the answer. It was my own fault, my one slip. It had been obvious that Max and I had something going on.

I snapped right back at them when the detectives probed about that. "He was my divorce lawyer. How unusual is that? For a divorce lawyer to make a pass at a client?"

That was a mistake, and I writhed every time I thought about it. For one thing, I was too sharp all of a sudden. For another, they hadn't even known about the divorce. Nobody knew what I was doing with Max except Max. I'd told Anita he was a new man. Why hadn't I just told the cops he was a friend? Made something up?

But I said he was my divorce lawyer, and the next thing, the detective asked was, "What divorce?"

I lost it when they asked about that. I didn't have to feign hysterics. That was when I said I wanted Melson there, and after that, they didn't get much from me about anything.

My teeth chattered as I lay there into evening. The room darkened. I didn't think they could fail to connect the two shootings. I would have been out of my mind to expect that. I was out of my mind, for sure; I was insane. But I didn't really think they'd believe for a minute that Merit was shot by an unknown political enemy, and then Pop and Max shot each other for unrelated reasons in the same place. Anyway, thanks to me, they connected them quickly enough. Still. What they had was that Pop shot Merit, then Pop tried to shoot Max, but Max was armed, and they shot each other. I didn't think they had any reason to believe I was anything but a hysterical bystander and a motive in Pop's deranged mind.

I turned over on my side and put the law out of mind. What I wondered was whether my life would hold together. I would go on teaching while my contract lasted. I doubted it would be renewed. I wondered how long it would take to probate Pop's will.

I got up and thought about calling Tony, but then I remembered how pissed off he'd been the last time. I thought about calling Anita but rejected that idea, too.

I lay back down. Would they talk to her? Of course they would. Hadn't Pop been with her?

I imagined it. She told him I was with a new man. She probably even gave him the name he heard me scream when he was at the door: Max.

I said out loud, "Didn't I tell you he would be upset?"

My mind spun back to the questioning and my own position. I had found one body and witnessed two more murders in Richmond. They would compare them, and they would figure out that Pop shot Merit. They wanted to know whether I knew. Melson had shielded me, but I had told them I suspected. I didn't know. I saw nothing. I was like a trapped animal on a raft in a flood, a raft made of sticks, leaves, and sod, precariously holding together, but bit by bit, losing pieces, shrinking.

Questions. Why should Pop shoot Max? A crazy old jealous father with a gun. I didn't know what Anita Blore would say, but I could imagine. Had she ever really liked me? I doubted it. She would turn on me. Dysfunctional, she'd say. Secretive. A liar. Unhealthy relationship. Blore, blore, blore. It was not against the law to have an unwholesome life.

I sensed that I would not be doing business in Richmond anymore. I would leave. I had the offer to go to Portland. Melson would get permission for me to go. I would go. Away. I had an impulse to flee. I would move out to the west coast. Maybe Tony would leave his wife and come with me. I would start a whole new life.

I must have been dreaming.

CHAPTER TWENTY-EIGHT

THE DOORBELL RANG.

After a while, it rang again.

I went to open it.

Suzanne.

I left the door open and turned and walked away, listless, in a fog, but dimly aware that she was not alone. A tiny, buried spark in my brain came alert, but it didn't penetrate the lifeless weight that oppressed me. I wandered onto the screened-in porch and slumped in the wicker chair. And then I froze. Bile lurched in the back of my mouth. I swallowed and grimaced at the taste.

Suzanne, yes. But behind her. Snooping and slinking and lurking and prowling behind her was the Hyena. Older, a wreck, but unmistakable. The very sight of her was riveting.

Oblivious, Suzanne said, "Kate," and took my suddenly wet and icy hands in her own warm and tremulous fingers. She babbled on about how she had heard what happened, but underneath her gentle solace, I could hear the unwilling germ of doubt. I couldn't make out her words, because it was in the same room now, on the porch, almost within reach, the menacing Hyena, its head lifting and dropping to catch the scent of fear.

Suzanne turned to the Hyena. "What do you think they will do, Elsa?"

It growled. "I can tell you what they should do."

"What do you think they should do?" Dear, sweet

Suzanne simply did not know when to shut up and leave well enough alone.

"What I would have done twenty years ago," the wretched Hyena said, "if they had let me." Its eyes never left my face.

"And what is that?" the clueless Suzanne persisted. I itched to strangle her. "What would you have done?"

"I would have bought a nice new pair of leather shoes like the ones she was wearing that night," the Hyena said, referring to me as if I were not there. "I would have had someone walk in them from where the car was found to where she lives. And I would have compared those shoes with the ones she wore."

Dead silence.

The Hyena said, "You didn't walk home that night."

I felt Suzanne's eyes join the Hyena's.

I could hardly speak, and when I did, my voice shook. "Get out. Get out of here this minute."

The Hyena heaved her cumbrous body, eyes still holding mine.

Tears of fury sprang unwanted in my eyes, and I turned away so she wouldn't see them.

Suzanne, fool, said, "Kate," and reached out, but I spat at her, "You too, get out. Don't come back."

It was the Hyena who suggested they compare the bullets from Max's and Merit's murders with, yes, the one that killed Elliott. They gave her credit for suggesting that. I saw her picture in the news. The little round ears, the heavy shoulders and the short legs, the strong jaws. And I thought I could see in the grainy newsprint the light of triumph in her tiny marble eyes.

So it then appeared that Pop was guilty of all three shootings. For the first time, officials in both Richmond and Amherst County sat up and connected the recently reopened twenty-two-year-old case with the two new ones. That was the Hyena's vindication. Having torn off that limb, she left it for lesser predators to dive on the scraps of flesh.

The laying bare of my life has since progressed with frightening speed.

Reporters joined the hunt in full cry. They were torn between two equally arresting angles to the story. The first was that I had lied. I had not unwittingly mistaken Jules Jefferson's identity. It was argued—in fact, how could it not be argued—that I had known all along that I was putting away an innocent man for life. I had testified that Jules Jefferson had shot Elliott, and while it might be understandable for me to have mistaken Jules Jefferson for another, unknown stranger, I could not have mistaken him for Pop. I not only failed to finger the real shooter; I had lied every which way on the stand, under oath.

The more salacious angle was that I claimed to have been raped. There was semen, and no doubt I had been beaten.

You cannot imagine how vile it is to read in print a strange man's pontifications about whether the original examination sufficiently probed the fine difference between whether I had first had sex and then been beaten, or had been beaten and then raped.

There was a brief uproar of mixed feelings about whether I was myself a victim, considering my age at the time of the incident. At twenty, I had legally been an adult, but still, very young and living at home with, as it turned out, the murderer. I hate the role of victim, but I figured if that's what I needed to be, fine. One reporter complained that the evidence from 1986 had not been compared with Elliott's semen as it should have been. They all stopped short of drawing other, even more thrilling conclusions, such as that my father had raped me. Was I lying about being raped? Melson gave up asking me. Suzanne, despite my rejecting her, defended me. *If only Jefferson had stayed in jail...*

While the story broke and rolled over the beautiful hills

of Western Virginia, I stayed home, besieged by reporters calling on the phone and sneaking onto the grounds about the house. I couldn't even walk in my garden for fear of long-range camera lenses. With Melson defending my right to refuse to incriminate myself, the silence from the official side was ominous. They didn't even bother to call me in for questioning. I was admonished not to leave town. Melson promised nothing and had little information for me. His manner was pessimistic, but then, that seemed to be his personality, as far as I had ever known it.

With days on end to pass alone, I set out secretly to write this, the story of my life. At the time, I didn't even know why. I didn't know who I could ever show it to, but the only way to understand another human being is to know her entire life story, from her point of view, and this is what I am trying to tell. You never know the full truth about anyone, how guilty they really are in a whole lifetime. Could I ever let another human being all the way in? I dare not. But some frustrated wish to share my reality drives me to write it all down.

I started with the seeds of my current crisis and found myself going back and back, and then rushing forward through this last summer. I sit in my third-floor office, looking out over the mountains. They are so impossibly serene. And I type away by the hour, with a light shawl wrapped around my shoulders and one of Pop's fine French wines near to hand. I opened an anonymous web-based email account and store each day's increment as a password-protected attachment to an email to yet another secret, web-based email box. Just in case they ever search my belongings.

I never watch the news on TV, and I have cancelled Pop's newspapers. Ignoring news online is not so easy. I can resolutely turn a blind eye all day, up to the time I go to bed. It's like an alcoholic getting through one day at a time without a drink—not that I have ever tried to do such a thing. But then I wake up in the night and cannot help myself. If I sleep through one night, or manage to stay in bed, it gets me the next night. It's inevitable. So usually, I give in. In the small hours, I throw off the covers, sit up in bed, and read the news on my laptop, not all of it at once, but in sudden spurts of need, until with a rush, I catch up on it all. I salt my own wounds reading blogs and comments. Because of what I did to Jefferson, I am called pure evil.

There was a brief howl over my marriage. Sabrina Cole, unemployed reporter, has not given up. She has a website, Sabrina Cole Online. Now blogging daily, she crows. She offers a biography of me, based, she says, on long-time personal acquaintance and—get this— *professional collaboration.* She calls me "intensely private" and alludes to my tragic past, my scars, and the dark secrets surrounding the crime that has so dramatically exploded in recent weeks. She talks about finding the notice of divorce in the paper, of my desperate reaction in her presence, and then raises the question, Who is Carl Brewer?

The police apparently looked into it and found nothing of great interest in the idea of a missing fly-by-night husband, whom I was divorcing for abandonment, and were content to believe that there was no connection between the brief marriage I hired Max to get me out of and the murders committed by my deranged, jealous, and possibly incestuous father. And there it stood. I had this from Melson.

Reporters, other than Sabrina Cole, miraculously made little of the marriage angle, but alas, my nemesis, the Hyena, is not one for easy answers, and the notice of divorce piqued her curiosity. She carefully considered the marriage certificate and dates. Her sharp nose picked up the scent of the clipping with the name Carl Brewer in it. Her filthy jaws ground away at these scraps. And then she struck again. Thanks to her, they dug up fingerprints from a very old offense, prints of one Carl Brewer, the man killed in Nairobi, according to the clipping. She urged them to compare Carl's prints with ones from the most recent shootings. The Hyena made sure they got it: "Pop" was Carl Brewer.

She had torn off another limb, and now they feasted. Semen from the 1986 rape, check: a DNA match for the recently deceased Carl Brewer. Military records for Miles Cranbrook, check: a different set of fingerprints altogether. This was not the same man.

Pop my father? Not. Who was I? Oh, there could be no doubt about that. I was and am Kate Cranbrook. The next question was with whom had I come to America? For whom had I claimed Miles Cranbrook's inheritance? Who was the gentlemanly squire who lived with me as my father? On every count, again, the Hyena had the answer: Carl Brewer.

Reporting these developments, Melson was even more solemn than usual. He summed it up for me. "It appears," he began, and paused.

I blew out an exasperated breath and shifted in the wicker chair. He really is slow. I don't care if he's a lawyer, he's slow. He is costing me a lot of money.

Finally, he said, "We are looking at the possibility that the man you called Pop killed three people."

"And his third victim killed him in self-defense," I added, finishing it for him.

I had an idea I could face questioning at this point, explain it all, but Melson cut me off. He started mumbling about rope to hang myself, and I interrupted him to say, "No, listen. I have an idea." My idea, just forming, was to provide a complete written explanation, which he, Melson, could review.

And he cut me off to say why this was not a good idea. And I cut him off, and he cut me off, until we both were standing, like a batter and an umpire arguing a call, face to face, red-faced and breathing hard through our noses. He was so like a big old cow, stamping and snorting, that I started to laugh. He didn't laugh. I stopped laughing. We both sat down. He then told me that in his opinion, I was not likely to escape charges.

At first, inexplicably, word that Pop was not my father failed to reach the press, except for the bitch Sabrina Cole, who had formed a symbiotic bond with the apex predator Hyena. Being only semiofficially involved in the case, the Hyena did not feel the need to be discreet about leaking inside news from an active investigation. In an "exclusive interview," retired Police Lieutenant Elsa Gabriel, credited with breaking the notorious multiple murder case, explained that investigators had not yet the full measure of the lies and fabrications perpetrated over more than twenty years by the "couple posing as Miles Cranbrook and his daughter."

I shouted out loud at that. "I wasn't posing as Miles Cranbrook's daughter! I am Miles Cranbrook's daughter! It was Pop! He was the imposter!"

I stalked around the house in a rage, but when I calmed down, it was clear to me: The Hyena smelled that there was more. She found something I had not thought of in years: the parental consent form for the marriage of a girl over sixteen but younger than eighteen required for the marriage license, signed by Miles Cranbrook and notarized.

How we had laughed over that. That was when I first called him "Pop." It was a joke, but it stuck. It worked, and it was a stroke of genius. The busybody hag of a court clerk studied the dashing groom's birth certificate for a full minute with a look of unconscious disgust on her face, while her slow brain computed his age. She stared at the consent form and turned it over and over. She actually fingered the signature and tipped the form to the light, searching for signs of alteration. I wanted to complain to her supervisor but thought better of it. In the end, it was all in order, and she had to accept it.

When the consent form came to light, the story lit up all across the board. As a teenager, Kate Cranbrook married a shyster who collected her father's fortune and posed as her father, successfully, for two decades before meeting his end in the act of shooting a third rival for his wife's attentions. Sabrina Cole's blog was buried in the avalanche of mainstream variations on this latest theme. Suzanne gave brave interviews in which she declared that a seventeen-year-old girl could not consent to marriage, which was why the consent form was required. I was, she insisted, an innocent victim of statutory rape, marital rape, and domestic terror.

At last, the true nature of the 1986 crime was clear: The man I called Pop, my husband, caught me with Elliott, dragged me out of the car, and shot Elliott. He took me home, beat me up, and raped me. No question that my life was a nightmare in the aftermath of that crime. What could I have done? What could I say?

You have to understand: If I had said it was him, they would have known he was not my father. What happened in Africa was not long in the past back then. I did the only thing I could do. I pointed the finger, deflected the blame.

It's true that I was young. Looking back, I took care of myself from a very early age. I took the brunt of my father's drunken furies when my mother left, and I never flinched. The trouble was, my father wouldn't leave Africa. He got that letter telling him he had inherited a house and many fine goods and a fortune. Did he care? He threw it away. Irascible, he was, and crazy with the drink. When he had passed out, I plucked the letter from the floor, smoothed it out, and thought about it. I liked Carl Brewer. He was handsome, sober, and reserved. I knew his eyes never left me when I was in the room, and I teased him. Oh, it was all my idea. Carl was my father's height and build, you see.

I never could have conjured up the opportunity. There was luck and circumstance to thank for that. The attempted coup, the rioting. Carl and my father were defending the warehouse. I was in the back. Both men were armed, Carl with the now-infamous Ruger, my father with something equally deadly. Glass broke in the front. A shot was fired. My father fired back. I whispered to Carl, and Carl shot my father, hit him in the back, a mortal wound but slow. My father spun around with an oath.

I took the gun from Carl and, funny, my father said the same thing as Max: "Kate, what are you doing?" And I shot my father in the face.

Carl and I instantly abandoned the warehouse to the rioters. In the mad dash to the car, Carl gashed his eyebrow on broken glass in a shattered doorway. Blood streamed down his face. That was good luck, too, because it was true that Carl was persona non grata with the administration that was, by that time, already regaining control. I drove, and when we were stopped, I said my father was wounded and that Carl Brewer was back at the warehouse, dead. There was a dead man there. But he never was Carl Brewer.

I had my father's passport and other papers, but Carl flew out of the country under his own identity. Once we got here, though, he had to be Miles Cranbrook. How else could we have claimed the money? I did not come to the States to struggle as the seventeen-year-old wife of a man who would have had a hard time making money for the kind of life I wanted, let alone enough to send me to college. And without college, what could I ever be? And with my own father's money sitting right there, my birthright? I suppose I could have tried to claim it as his daughter, but it would have been risky. I would have had to explain my father's death, which was reported in Nairobi as Carl Brewer's. I would have to prove my identity, and of course, Miles Cranbrook would have died intestate. Why go there?

If I had done that and succeeded, it would have been my money all along. I would not have been stuck with Carl, but you have to understand, at the time, I didn't feel as though I was stuck with him. He was a handsome, virile man of forty-five, and I was an unusually mature young woman who liked older men. To say that I was seventeen, well, let me just say that I never was what most people think of as a seventeen-year-old girl. I was, I would even say, in love with him. Of course I was. I would have said so at the time, certainly. I freely married him.

It was only later, when the twenty-eight-year difference in our ages came home to me, that I began to want to be free. It was only then that I thought about the fact that the Cranbrook inheritance was mine, and he had no right to it, and but for the role I made for him, I could have let him go as soon as I had a mind to. But then I think, maybe not. There was the violence that never ceased to dog my steps, ever since Africa. Thanks to me, Carl was a man who had killed once for what he wanted. And the penalty for me was that I always knew that he could kill again.

To be fair, Pop wasn't happy either. We had arguments in the early years about whether we should move away and start over. What he wanted was for us to live openly as man and wife. He tasted it on trips to Europe when we stayed in hotels as Miles Cranbrook and his young wife. Another time, for fun—and he liked this even better—we were Carl and Kate Brewer. I preferred my real name, Cranbrook. Either way, at those times, he swelled with pride and well-being when other men looked at me and understood that he slept with me at night.

I thought the truth about what happened in Nairobi could not be discovered after all these years, but the implacable Hyena set out to penetrate even that mystery. She will go to any lengths to vilify me. She actually picked up the phone and called the Kenya police. Who can believe this woman? She called Nairobi provincial and asked about the reported death of Carl Brewer on August 2, 1982. She sniffed out retired ACP Abasi Umbuyu, a police inspector in Nairobi at the time. All this was duly reported in Sabrina Cole's blog.

I gather from between the lines that Umbuyu was cagey until he learned that Pop was dead. Well, he might be cagey: Umbuyu was the one who gave Pop money to get out of Kenya. The Hyena reports that Carl Brewer was attempting to bribe Umbuyu, who of course was far too upstanding to accept any such thing, as late as August third. Umbuyu claims to have reported the incident to higher-ups, but at the time, it was impossible to determine whether Miles Cranbrook had been impersonating Carl Brewer or vice versa. The body at the warehouse was buried before Umbuyu could identify it, if anyone had cared, which they didn't.

So it seems the Hyena now claims to be closing cold cases on two continents. Whatever. There is no way they bring that one home to me. Best guess, my father died, untimely, in possession of the letter that informed him of the fortune waiting for him in the States. His secretary, Carl Brewer, and I fled the country after the riots and claimed the money, posing as Miles and Kate Cranbrook. I told Melson yesterday that Carl Brewer bullied me, raped me, and terrorized me into marrying him. It isn't true, but it's what I said, and I don't see how anyone can dispute it.

But Melson waved it off. "What happened in Africa is not an issue."

"It was Pop, Pop all along. He was guilty of everything. The old man was a murderer, a rapist, and a fraud."

He said, "You need a criminal defense attorney. I can recommend one."

It took me a minute to absorb that. "Can I afford it?"

Melson still manages the money, if he hasn't stolen most of it.

He suggested, incredibly, that it could very well cost me the house. My house!

I asked, "Couldn't I borrow on it?"

He said I could mortgage it, but then he asked, "Realistically, how could you pay on a mortgage?"

"What do you think?"

Anita Blore, my only client, has long since retreated into shocked silence.

I don't know if I can go on living here anyway. The hatred over the Jefferson case, it's unbelievable. I half expect a mob to flay me alive one of these nights. I get it from both sides: those outraged about the false accusation and those who say I undermine the credibility of rape victims everywhere. I've thought about leaving town, but Melson made a point of telling me I would only find myself in jail if I tried to "flee." Actually in jail. He tells me there will be a civil lawsuit, too, against Pop's estate, and he thinks we should try for a settlement with Jefferson.

"Be generous and quick about it," Melson says. "Get them to sign it."

Truly, I am ruined.

I made my first bargain with the Devil. I was hoping for a bargain with the law. I thought I could offer a confession to escape a trial and hopefully secure a lenient penalty for whatever charges I might face. I didn't even know what they would be: accessory after the fact of murder, maybe, or perjury, or obstructing justice. Whatever, I had no idea. Numerous charges, anyway, to all of which I would plead guilty, as long as I would not be charged with murder. I stayed up all night doctoring my story for them. Most of it was God's own truth. There was only one murder, after all, and that was just a matter of finishing what the old man failed to do.

I regret killing Max Weigel. I do. It was a terrible mistake. I would have been better off not doing it.

The defense attorney is a woman, dark, stocky, humorless, just what I'd expect Melson to come up with. We met this morning, and we hadn't even sat down before she started talking murder.

I said, "What murder? Whose? I had nothing to do with Merit's death. God knows I never would have hurt him. Even the Hyena knows I didn't shoot him."

"No," she agreed. "It's clear that Brewer shot the African professor."

"I loved Elliott. I didn't shoot him either."

"No one thinks you did."

"Well, I didn't shoot Pop. Max did. I think that's obvious."

She opened up her briefcase and pulled out a stack of papers.

I said, "I will confess to lying in the first murder trial. There were extenuating circumstances. I was innocent of the second murder and had no evidence to offer, although it's true I had my suspicions. How could I not? I witnessed the third murder, and I have told you and everybody else, including the cops, everything I know about what happened. Max shot Pop, and Pop shot Max."

Silence. I forced myself to shut up, sit back and wait, while she finished looking at whatever she was looking at and finally took off her hideous tortoiseshell reading glasses.

She said, "Let's go over it again."

I snapped at her. "Fine."

She began by belaboring the fact that two men had been shot dead at the scene. I gritted my teeth and pretended to listen patiently while boiling inside. Yes, one man was killed by a bullet to the brain, the other by a bullet to the heart. Extraordinary. This woman must bore juries to tears.

"There were three bullets," she pointed out.

"One of them shot wild."

She nodded curtly . "Carl Brewer shot wild. The third bullet was from the Ruger. It was found imbedded in the wall behind Max Weigel."

I shrugged. "Okay. So Pop shot wild. Then he got off a second shot."

"Is that what happened? You were there."

"It all happened so fast. But yes, now that you say it, I think so. That sounds right."

"How long afterwards?"

"How long what?" I hate lawyers.

"How long after he shot and missed did Brewer shoot Max Weigel?"

"I don't know if the one that missed was before or after the one that hit Max. Look, I was there, but I didn't see the fucking bullets. Are you crazy? There were three shots, if you say so. But which was which and when, how could I possibly sort that out? They shot each other, and there was a third shot. If it was behind Max and it was from a Ruger, then it was Pop's. Whatever. Does it matter?" I stood up and paced, pulling at my own hair. "Oh God, I hate this. This was why I didn't want to go to trial. They dig up every detail, harp on every little thing. What does it matter? They're both dead. I'm telling you everything. I'll plead to perjury, obstruction, whatever, just don't make me go through a trial again."

She said, "It matters. Please sit down. We're not done."

I sighed hugely and sat back down.

"Who shot first?"

"I-I don't know. It was practically simultaneous. I mean, I heard two shots." I squeezed my eyes shut and remembered the sounds cracking in my ears. I shook my head. "There were two shots. They sounded different, but they went off at practically the same time."

"Did both men fall?"

"I'm not sure."

"How long was it before the second shot went off?"

I was pretty sure it was a trap, and I was getting angry. "I don't know. Have you ever been in a situation even remotely like this? It's confusing. It's all jumbled in my mind. You're supposed to be my lawyer, what do you think?" I jumped back to my feet and pointed at the papers she was muddling in. "If you have a problem, why don't you tell me what it is? You're supposed to be working for me. *For* me, not *against* me."

She answered calmly, "The problem is there's a witness."

"A what?" I doubled over, expelling all my air.

"Nobody saw anything, but one person heard it."

"Heard what?" I thought frantically. *Had one of us said something? Cried out? Max's voice: "Kate, what are you doing?"* The witness had to be that busybody woman who was always spying on me.

"The shots."

"What?"

"A witness heard the shots."

I was speechless. I shook my head, unsure what she was saying, what it meant.

"Three shots. Two almost together. One afterwards. Definitely afterwards."

I shook my head again. What was she saying? I wasn't hearing words right.

She explained it patiently, but I didn't like the look of her. Not at all. She said, "Carl Brewer took a bullet in the brain. It had to be one of the first two shots. Those shots were from different guns. They had to be. They were almost simultaneous. Weigel fired only one. It hit Brewer in the head. There's no way Brewer could have gotten off a second one."

It was dead quiet in the living room. Crickets outside. The AC came on.

I spoke quietly, thinking out loud. This was my own lawyer after all. We were protected by attorney-client privilege. "The first shot went wild, I suppose. Max must have missed."

She was already shaking her head. "Two shots from the Ruger. One from Wiegel's gun."

"Pop shot Max, Max shot Pop. Pop must have shot wild as he was going down?"

"The Ruger." She consulted the papers again. "It's a single-action revolver. Have you ever tried shooting it? It's not an automatic. Not a hair trigger. It doesn't just go off."

I sat back, then leaned forward. "It works this way: Pop shoots wild, then shoots Max in the heart. Max's gun goes off, hits Pop in the head."

She opened her mouth, and I cut her off, triumphantly. "Max's gun was an automatic, wasn't it? It was! He showed it to me. Pop shot wild, then he shot Max in the heart. Max set off his gun on the way down, hit Pop in the head." I banged the coffee table with my hand. "That's it. That's what happened."

No response.

"What?" I asked.

"The first two shots were almost simultaneous. That's what the witness says, and—" She kept shuffling those papers. "—it's what you've said as well. More than once."

Another interlude of silence. Birds were singing outside. My brain wasn't working.

She continued, "Two nearly simultaneous shots, certainly not two shots from a single-action revolver. It's the timing, too. Bullet in the brain. Then time elapses. Fifteen, twenty seconds. Then a second shot from the Ruger." She let a few long beats go by. "Bullet to the heart. It's the timing."

"The timing according to a witness."

"Yes. Well. As you know, sometimes one witness is enough."

I threw her out.

Ah, what was I thinking, how did I get into this mess? I must have been dreaming again. Dreaming as I had once dreamed that I could be a rich girl living in a big house. Was it so wrong to dream? To act, to do what I had to do? All I ever wanted was what everybody else has. Peace. Freedom. My own life to live.

I have arrived at the end. This document, now

complete, contains the whole truth, from me to me, for once scrupulously honest. It will never be found. It floats in cyberspace, a tree falling unheard in a forest. It is a relief to confess, even if it is to no one.

I've been alone for so long, and I am alone now. The blood thirst worries me. For what I did to Jefferson, I seem to be the most hated person on the planet Earth. But I am not going to back down. I'll get another lawyer, someone younger, more intelligent, a man. Someone who'll be on my side, hire experts to contradict their experts.

And about what happened, I am sticking to my guns: Max shot Pop, and Pop shot Max.

ACKNOWLEDGMENTS

Infinite thanks to my writer friends! Laurie Cosbey read an early draft of this book and offered many valuable suggestions. Kate Moretti helped more than I can say, not only with thoughtful critiques at every stage but also with her enthusiastic support and boundless positive energy. Brenda Vicars Hummel and Melissa Rupert cheerfully and tirelessly read through countless revisions, always offering constructive feedback and encouragement.

At Red Adept Publishing, Michelle Rever's expert content editing improved my best efforts by a quantum leap. And to Lynn McNamee, owner of RAP, I owe a huge debt of gratitude for giving me a chance to begin with, and then for guiding me every step of the way, from first-round edits to final polish and publication. My deepest gratitude to all of you!

ABOUT THE AUTHOR

Elizabeth Buhmann is originally from Virginia, where her first novel is set, and like her main character, she lived several years abroad while growing up. She graduated magna cum laude from Smith College in Northampton, Massachusetts, and has a PhD in Philosophy from the University of Pittsburgh. For twenty years, she worked for the Texas Attorney General as a researcher and writer on criminal justice and crime victim issues.

Elizabeth now lives in Austin, Texas, with her husband, dog, and two chickens. She is an avid gardener, loves murder mysteries, and has a black sash in Tai Chi.

CPSIA information can be obtained at www.ICGtesting.com
Printed in the USA
LVOW10s1646201015

459019LV00002B/519/P